Lifetimes Ago

A LOVE STORY INSPIRED
FROM PAST LIFE MEMORIES

Susie Schecter

iUniverse, Inc.
New York   Bloomington

Lifetimes Ago
A Love Story Inspired from Past Life Memories

Certain characters in this work were or are real people, and certain events portrayed relating to those people actually did take place and are documented at the end of this book. However, this is a work of fiction. All other events as well as places, relationships, romance, incidents, organizations, and dialogue in this novel are based on hypnosis sessions or are the product of the author's imagination and used fictitiously.

iUniverse books may be ordered through booksellers or by contacting:

iUniverse
1663 Liberty Drive
Bloomington, IN 47403
www.iuniverse.com
1-800-Authors (1-800-288-4677)

ISBN: 978-1-4401-9994-3 (pbk)
ISBN: 978-1-4401-9995-0 (cloth)
ISBN: 978-1-4401-9996-7 (ebook)

Printed in the United States of America

iUniverse rev. date: 3/11/10

Dedicated to my mother for all her support throughout the years.

Acknowledgments

I wish to thank the South Orange County Writers Network for the assistance that made *Lifetimes Ago* possible. This book took years to put together and I have to thank Mike Shriner for standing by me through all the dead ends and rewards of research into the lives of Elsie Wilkins and John McDonald.

Preface

Many people suppose that belief in an afterlife is primarily a matter of faith. For Mike, my boyfriend, it was a matter of actual proof.

One Saturday night, Mike made an observation about our three-week relationship. "This feels like it was meant to be," he said. There was a hint of humor in his eyes, but his tone was serious enough to give me an idea.

"Well, we … " I forced a swallow, "we could find out through hypnosis." I thought with my background in hypnotherapy, I could hypnotize my new boyfriend to find out if we were soul mates, or to discover if we ever met in another life.

"I don't think I can be hypnotized. One guy tried before, and I don't think I was under."

"That's okay." I smiled. "That's what everyone says."

And that's how our story began.

He agreed to try to go into a hypnotic state, and as he has said many times since, he just did not realize what he was getting himself into.

Mike and I had been introduced through an Internet dating service and clicked immediately. I felt an emotional connection and there seemed to be an inevitability surrounding our newly-formed alliance.

In the beginning, we experienced many meaningful coincidences in our relationship, and I wanted to find out for sure whether there was a past connection between us, or had our meeting occurred at random under everyday circumstances.

One Sunday evening, rather than go to the movies or out to dinner, we stayed home for a night of hypnosis. Before we began, I explained to Mike about the subconscious mind and how it is a storage bank of memories, including everything that has ever taken place in an individual's life. Every word anyone has ever said, every emotion, every experience, every relationship is held somewhere in the recesses of one's subconscious mind.

I hoped Mike would be able to recall past-life memories that were stored in his subconscious. Though he was not completely convinced about the idea of prior lives, he was curious enough to proceed with the hypnosis to find out if we might be soul mates, or at least if we were meant to meet.

The initial hypnosis meetings, and those that followed, were more successful than I could have ever imagined. For approximately three months I collected our data. His ability to recall memories came just as easily as opening a window to a specific time in his past. Memories, details, and emotions also flooded him upon waking from the hypnotic state, and sometimes even days later.

During the sessions, he spoke in a soft voice as if talking was a difficult chore. Mike was a wonderful subject; very visual and able to go back in time to pick up impressive amounts of clear details, including vivid accounts of his everyday surroundings in Rensselaer, Indiana.

The information in this book about John Arthur McDonald and Elsie Wilkins was gathered over the course of approximately eight of these regression sessions.

I wrote *Lifetimes Ago* because it is my first-hand account of dealing with the possibility of reincarnation. The details Mike recalled under hypnosis have, for the most part, uncovered many indisputable facts. These facts took me more than two years to verify and document. Because the revelations were so surprising, I became compelled to research the veracity of them. I was determined to find out if the visual images were real past life memories, memories from his past in this life, or simply his vivid imagination.

The regression experience with Mike was emotionally overwhelming, as I believed I had stumbled onto a universal truth: positive proof that reincarnation was an actual phenomenon. The investigation and exhaustive genealogical research involving these two people was even more overwhelming with the amount of work, time, and effort involved.

Drawing upon verifiable facts from my research, I have crafted the fictionalized story of John and Elsie's courtship, where the struggle against social mores falls away, and they are joined together in a bold experience of rare and striking passion. Their love affair in Rensselaer, Indiana, is brief, but their story gives flight to the heart: love *never* dies. It preservers even after death, its powerful ties reconnecting in a future life.

I begin the story where, after an extensive search, I was first able to verify the existence of Elsie Wilkins.

Chapter One

Phoebe Wilkins looked on as her daughter, Elsie, hugged her favorite doll and playfully rocked back and forth on deck of *The Campania*. She had earlier learned from the first mate that all was well by the captain, who had proclaimed their progress toward New York Harbor at twenty-two knots, impressively speedy and very satisfactory. The date: April 22, 1911. Not only was this the day that they would make landfall, but it was also one day before Elsie's sixth birthday. Phoebe hoped this move would bode well for her, though she herself was growing more and more nervous as the miles of sea slipped past, carrying them to a new beginning.

Earlier in the afternoon the rain had fallen heavily, swooping in sheets across the wooden planks of the deck, and all passengers had taken refuge in their quarters below. But now, the downpour had subsided, and many of the passengers were on deck for fresh air, and any early glimpses of American soil.

Elsie was shedding her wool coat and smoothing her clothes underneath. She hadn't been able to wait for her birthday to wear her new, beige lace dress with matching wide-brimmed hat. Phoebe smiled, watching her carefully rub the dirt from her fingers onto her handkerchief to avoid getting any brown smudges on her white pinafore. She was proud that Elsie seemed to be growing up very nicely, despite the fact that she had never known her father.

Traveling from Liverpool, England, to America was a very bold move for a twenty-seven-year-old widow with a five-year-old daughter in tow, and Phoebe would not have ventured so far without a secure future. She was making the five and one-half day voyage to America to be married: an image to which she was still trying to adjust.

Phoebe collected her daughter, and together they picked their way starboard through a group of well-dressed, first-class passengers. As they walked, a strong gust of ocean wind surprised them from behind and pushed their dress skirts about in frenzies of lace and petticoats.

"Mummy!" Elsie giggled, holding onto her mother's skirt. "I'm going overboard!"

Phoebe reached for her daughter's hand. "You'll do nothing of the sort, young lady. I won't let go. Come along, now."

Elsie slipped her hand out of her mother's grasp and clapped it to her hat, reattached her grasp of her mother's skirt with the other, and allowed herself to be towed toward a throng of people who were leaning over the rails, talking excitedly and pointing.

Phoebe sidled up to a woman holding a youngster on one hip and shading her brow with the other free hand. The woman was looking toward the horizon at some low, rolling hills shrouded in fog.

"What is it? Do you see New York?" Phoebe had to shout over the din of cheers and whoops.

The woman pointed. "It's New Jersey just there," she said, returning the shout. "Slightly right … that's New York City and Staten Island."

"Elsie, look!" Phoebe hoisted her up so that she could see over the railing. "Our new country."

"America!" Elsie squealed.

Leaning against the railing while Elsie played nearby, Phoebe gazed out into the choppy greenish-gray water, trying to sort out her new life.

The voyage had provided much time for introspection. There was something about being out in the middle of the ocean for nearly a week that cleared her mind, putting her thoughts into a cloudless perspective, though she still had mixed feelings about leaving England.

Her stomach knotted with pent-up emotions, as she was already missing her sister, Emma. Ever since her husband had died, she and Elsie had roomed with her in a small, two-bedroom flat on Union Street in Maidstone. Even though she was going to live with her other sister, Jane, in Akron, Ohio, she was also nervous about the idea of living so far from home. Until now, she rarely traveled outside the Maidstone city limits. How was she going to adapt to living in an unfamiliar country? How would Elsie adjust to having a father? *The Campania* steamed ever nearer to New York.

Why did she feel so melancholy?

In one week, she'd marry Frederick Obee, a man whom she had met back in Maidstone; it would not be such a bad life. Indeed, she had also spent the last few months happily planning for it.

Frederick had traveled to America one year ago to find suitable employment. He was highly motivated and willing to work as hard as necessary to gain a better life. Before he left Maidstone, he had presented Phoebe with an engagement ring, promising that he would send for her as soon as possible.

She had received Frederick's letter, finally, saying that he had landed a job working at the Goodyear Tire & Rubber factory in Akron, which also explained that after six months of hard work, he had been promoted to floor supervisor. He had decided it was the right time to make travel arrangements for Phoebe and Elsie to join him in America.

Second-class tickets were twenty dollars more than steerage class, but he felt they were worth the extra expense. He had experienced the horrors of traveling steerage, the area that comprised the decks below sea level where the steering mechanisms were located. He recalled to Phoebe the memory of his journey, saying it made him sweat just thinking about it.

Frederick's compartment was damp, with individual bunks stacked tightly in tiers. He could not breathe in his berth because there wasn't any circulation of air in steerage. There was no fresh water or satisfactory toilet accommodations. The food was limited and often infested with bugs. He said he wouldn't allow his girls to experience such inhumane conditions. He loved them too much for that. In second class they would have the luxury of a cabin, clean bed linens, and they would be able to eat appetizing meals that were served in a dining hall. And for entertainment, they could enjoy live music.

Elsie carefully walked on a row of slatted deck chairs as if she were balancing on a tight rope. She was happy just the way things had been with her mum and Auntie Emma. She was sad to leave home, but then a little excited too, though she didn't want her mummy to get married.

She lost her balance on the third chair, jumped down, and joined her mother who was sitting on a nearby ledge.

"Mummy, do you have to marry Mr. Obee?"

"Well, Elsie … your mum does love him."

Elsie pursed her lips, deep in thought. "Will I get married someday?"

"Of course you will, silly goose. Someday you'll fall in love, too. You'll find a handsome man who'll be crazy in love with you. You'll get married and have children of your own."

"Will I be rich and live in a castle?"

"I don't know about that. But I promise you'll be happy."

"Are you happy?"

"I am. I'm just a little nervous, trying to do everything right on this long trip."

"It's been so-o long," Elsie rolled her eyes. "I like Mr. Obee, but does he have to be my daddy?"

"Yes, luv. You need a father to take care of you."

"I don't want a father to take care of me. I can take care of myself." She stood and proclaimed adamantly before her mother, "I'm six."

"Yes, that's right, luv. In just a few hours, you won't be five anymore."

Elsie pranced about the deck with her hands on her hips. "I'm six, six, six years old!"

Phoebe wished her natural father could see the joy on his little girl's cherubim face, its confident pout of authority framed in golden blond curls. But Thomas Wilkins's accident, with his buckboard cargo and horse, had left him crushed with fatal internal injuries. He had passed on, two months before Elsie was born.

Phoebe's thoughts of tragedy were interrupted with the announcement that the medical examination of first- and second-class passengers was about to begin. Because the weather had improved, and the ship was close to its final destination, steerage passengers were allowed on the upper deck for fresh air and socializing. These people were not eligible for examinations onboard and it looked to Phoebe that many of them paced with worried frowns. These steerage passengers, who would be ferried to Ellis Island after reaching the dock, were sometimes rejected from entry for a variety of reasons: disease, poverty, criminal records; the list was long, and those detained could face deportation.

Before their examination began, Phoebe wanted to see the *Statue of Liberty* from their vantage point aboard the ship. She grabbed Elsie by the hand and picked her way through to the port side of the ship where a crowd was gathering. It seemed like everyone on board jammed the rails to get their first look at a better life.

Phoebe drew a sharp breath. There, standing tall at the entrance to New York Harbor was the great lady, the *Statue of Liberty*; the symbol of independence, justice, and opportunity. The crowd around Phoebe was a mix of the elderly, the young, single men and women, and entire families. The all seemed to represent many different European countries.

A young fellow wearing a tweed cap and beaming with a ruddy radiance was pushed up against Phoebe by the crowd. "Being here is a dream come true," the man said with a Scottish accent. "That lady symbolizes my hope for the future. Are you arriving for the first time, too?"

"Yes," Phoebe answered, noticing the mist of emotion in his eyes. "It's a golden opportunity for me, as well. Good luck to you."

Yelps of delight erupted from those who had passed inspection. Phoebe reasoned that all first- and second-class passengers had the money for proper attire and the luxury of medical care before leaving the continent, so that they would be allowed to disembark with no problem. She and Elsie would easily pass inspection, as Frederick had informed her of immigration procedures, and she was ready.

As the interrogations continued, *The Campania* slowly sailed through the Narrows into Upper New York Bay, turning slightly northeast toward the tall buildings of Manhattan, and finally, to the west side piers of the Hudson River.

Phoebe was right; they had no difficulty passing their cursory medical examinations. She let out a big sigh of relief and went to sit on a nearby bench.

Elsie stood on her tiptoes along the deck railing, waving both arms wildly to people below on the dock. Other children joined in, and soon, about twenty youngsters were greeting the onlookers. One of the Irish boys suggested they play "Statue," which Elsie thought a wonderful idea.

She skipped over to where her mother was sitting. "May I play 'Statue' with the other children?"

"No, Elsie. We're here now. It will be our turn to see the immigration officer any minute."

"Please? I'm quite bored. I've been so good," she pleaded. "I'll be over there. Home base is right here," she said, pointing to a life preserver hanging on a hook.

"Very well, but don't venture out of my sight. I don't want to have to call you. Here, let me hold your doll."

She handed her mother the doll and ran to play with the other children. Elsie was "it" and turned her back while the others ran about and found positions. After ten seconds, she turned back, carefully watching for any movement. One girl had picked up a goblet and thrust it skyward to capture the pose of the *Statue of Liberty*.

The hubbub of the children giggling and racing about the deck did not help Phoebe's last-minute jitters; her hands were trembling. On the bench next to her sat a woman with brown, mousy hair and a pinched expression who seemed to be all alone.

"Your first trip?" Phoebe asked her, and the woman nodded. "Mine, too," she continued. "My daughter and I are going to live in Ohio, but we're from Maidstone. Are you familiar with Britain?"

"Oh, yes. I'm from Liverpool. I've been to Maidstone several times. But I won't be going back, will you?"

"No," Phoebe replied. "My fiancée has finally been able to send for us. We'll probably never see Britain again. Frankly, it's making me a trifle sad."

"I'm going to be married, as well." The woman fidgeted with a handkerchief in her lap, and went on to explain that she was a "picture bride" who had been contacted by a marriage broker about a man interested in marrying a proper English lady. She had sent photographs of herself to the prospective groom and was accepted by him.

"My husband died," the woman said, "and I thought this would be the best thing for me, but now I'm not so sure. I'm having second thoughts about it. I'm afraid I'm not so brave. I don't know if I've done the right thing."

Phoebe tried to offer reassurances that her decision had been the right one. She found that she felt much better after comforting someone else, thankful in her heart that her own situation was more mutually acceptable. After all, she was in love with her fiancée. She never let on, but thought how dreadful it must be to marry someone you never laid eyes on.

Elsie abruptly appeared in front of her mother, sniffling, with tears running down her face. "Mummy, I hate boys. They're all so horrid."

"What happened? Don't cry now. You'll get your dress all dirty."

The picture bride smiled at Elsie. "There, there," she said with consolation. "I'll bet you're a pretty girl when you're not crying." She patted Elsie's hand and stood to take her leave. "Excuse me. I've just heard my name called."

"Good luck to you," Phoebe offered. "I know you'll be just fine."

The woman smiled her thanks and Phoebe turned to Elsie.

"Now, Elsie. Tell me what this is all about."

Elsie wiped her nose. "A boy said I was stupid, and said I couldn't see worth beans. I'm not stupid, am I?"

"No, dear. Of course not. Why would he be cross with you like that?"

"He cheated. He moved, but said he didn't move. I saw him with my own eyes. He moved his shoulder like this." Elsie rocked her shoulder back and forth.

"Okay. Don't get yourself upset. He's probably just angry that he's out of the game."

"I hate boys! I've never met a nice boy. Ever! They're all so mean."

"They're not all mean. You'll find a nice boy when you grow up."

"How do *you* know?" Elsie said, raising her voice.

"I know because you're so nice. You'll attract a nice, sweet boy."

"I only want to love a nice boy, and marry a nice boy. What's his name?"

Phoebe chuckled. "I'm not sure of his name, Elsie. You haven't met him yet."

"Will I meet him in Ohio?"

"I don't know, but you'll meet him somewhere in America."

"Okay, Mummy. Promise?"

"I promise."

"Come now. Our name should be called soon." Phoebe steered Elsie toward the officer's desk. "We've already passed the medical exam, now we'll be asked some questions," she explained.

Phoebe was grateful for the prepaid ticket, enabling them to travel as second-class passengers, and affording them the privilege of interrogation onboard, rather than being ferried to Ellis Island. Frederick had said the wait to leave the ship could be up to six hours for passengers traveling in steerage.

"Is it our turn, Mummy?"

"Yes, any moment now. You can't cry anymore," Phoebe said, handing Elsie her doll.

"Wilkins!" the inspector called.

"Yes, sir," Phoebe said, approaching the immigration desk and holding Elsie by the hand before the man.

Elsie forgot about the mean boy and showed the officer her doll. "This is Elizabeth," she said. "But it's *my* birthday tomorrow. I'll be six."

The officer smiled at her. "Will it, now? Well, happy birthday. And what is your name? It's Elizabeth, like your doll's name, is it?"

She curtsied and smiled broadly. "No, it's Elsie, Elsie Wilkins."

"Yes. Yes, here you are. I'll put a six right by your name." The officer turned to Phoebe with a stream of rapid-fire questions. "Name?"

"Phoebe Wilkins."

"Where were you born?"

"Maidstone, England."

"Occupation?"

"Mill-hand."

"Married or single?"

She paused and lowered her head. "Widowed." But she hurriedly added, "I've come to the United States to be married." She showed off her left hand with its engagement ring, moving it closer for scrutiny, and was rewarded with his smile.

"Congratulations. Will your fiancée be at the pier to meet you?"

She smiled. "Yes, he will."

"Final destination?"

"We'll be going to my brother-in-law's house." She reached into her dress pocket to retrieve the street number. "The address is four twenty-eight, Champlain Street, Akron, Ohio."

"How much money do you possess?"

"Forty—no, fifty dollars."

"Are you a polygamist?"

"No."

"Anarchist?"

She shook her head. "No."

Elsie had wandered a few paces and the officer motioned to Elsie to return to the desk.

Phoebe nervously called to her daughter. "Elsie!"

Elsie quickly turned from the windowpane she had been pressed up against and jumped down onto the deck. She dashed over and stood up straight for the man wearing the uniform.

He quickly scanned mother and daughter for any noticeable scars or distinguishing marks. He checked "none" on the manifest and asked several more perfunctory questions to make certain they matched up with Phoebe's immigrant tag.

"Elsie Wilkins?"

"Yes, sir!" Elsie saluted him very gravely.

The immigration officer laughed. "Young lady, get ready to see our beautiful country. He then turned to Phoebe. "You're free to go down the gangway where a customs officer will check your luggage. Welcome to the United States of America."

"Yippee!" Elsie pulled on her mother's hand.

A gray, mist-leaden fog hung over the docks on the Hudson River. Frederick Obee paced while he waited on the pier. He gazed toward the bay, anxiously awaiting his bride's arrival. The daisies he held between sweaty palms began to wilt as he nervously watched passengers step off the ship and congregate on the pier. He wasn't certain he looked dapper enough for his bride-to-be, wearing a green serge coat with white, flannel trousers, but it would have to do. It was the best attire he owned. A brown Bowler hat hid his straight blond hair. Under his arm he carried a brightly wrapped box. With every passing minute, the pier grew more congested as weary passengers with suitcases gathered to greet waiting friends and relatives.

After a nearly three-hour wait, Frederick was rewarded with a peek of the woman he would soon marry. Through the mass of people and piled-high parcels, Phoebe looked cheerful, carrying a tattered brown suitcase on one side, and two large bundles under the other arm, with her daughter's small suitcase hanging from her fingers. Elsie tagged along, holding onto her mother's skirts.

"Phoebe, Phoebe," he cried out, waving his arms. "Over here!"

Phoebe heard his voice but couldn't see him through the mob. Following his calls alone, she hurried in the direction of his voice. She wished that she hadn't laced the corset so tightly; the chemise, drawers, corset, and lace petticoat were bothersome, and she could feel their restriction, as if her underpinnings were trying to keep her away from the man she loved. It was difficult to catch her breath.

"Come on, Mummy! Come *on*." Elsie pulled at her mother's lagging skirts.

Phoebe jostled along with her daughter, through masses of people, unloaded satchels, trunks, valises, baskets, and wheeled pushcarts. All belongings from the ship were piling up on the pier. The air was full of the odor of fish, which hung moist and heavy in the air like the fog.

"Elsie, don't pull on me so. You won't be able to find him, going off like that ahead of me."

Abruptly appearing around a mountain of accumulated baggage, Frederick, the man who had changed her life, was walking toward her, smiling, and offering his assistance. The first glimpse of her man on American soil was overwhelming. Her heart pounded and her legs felt weak. She shouted, "Frederick!"

They rushed toward one another.

Phoebe prayed she wouldn't trip with her luggage and fall flat on her face. Then she sank into Frederick's arms and unleashed a long, deep sigh. Phoebe looked up into his eyes, dropped everything she and Elsie owned onto the dock, and kissed him in sweet reunion. It wasn't proper to show such signs of affection in public, but on this one occasion she discarded her principles. Anyway, everyone all over the pier was kissing and hugging someone.

Phoebe glanced down and noticed Elsie breathless and excited, fidgeting and looking around as though she were afraid someone might witness the two of them kissing.

As her mother's embrace with Frederick continued with such a prolonged display of affection, Elsie yanked on her skirts and made a face of disapproval.

"I don't like having a father already," Elsie mumbled.

At that moment, Frederick released Phoebe, handed her the daisies, and picked up Elsie.

"And how are you, Elsie?" He kissed her damp cheek. "I've missed you, luv." He then put her down, being mindful not to wrinkle her dress. "How was your trip?"

"I didn't get seasick," she said proudly.

"What a big girl you are. I have something special for you," he said, handing her the brightly wrapped box. "Happy birthday."

"Oh-h … thank you!" Elsie put down her doll and tore away at the paper, raised the lid of the box, and held up a plump, sad-looking teddy bear. "A stuffed bear! I love it." She giggled, giving the bear a big hug.

"Teddy bears are the latest craze in America," Frederick said. "I wanted you to have one of your very own."

"Thank you," Elsie said. "He's so cute. And I'm happy we're going on a train. Trains are more fun than boats."

The next thing Elsie knew, her mother and her father-to-be were walking briskly with suitcases and packages in hand toward the train station.

"Mummy, wait for me, Elizabeth, and Teddy!"

"Come along briskly now; we have a train to catch," her mother said breathlessly.

Chapter Two

Twenty-three years later....

It was a good day to leave Akron, Ohio, behind with its bleak, gray skies and unseasonably cool and drizzly June weather. Elsie Wilkins would not be homesick, especially since she was more than a little pleased with her new-found luck. She shivered against the afternoon wind, checking her watch for what seemed to be the tenth time. Packing and deciding to move to Indiana hadn't been as distressing as expected. She stood on the rear station platform overlooking the train tracks, enjoying the fading away of the morning, delighted with her decision to begin using her maiden name again. "All the bad circumstances are behind me," she whispered to herself with a sigh.

Finally, at one in the afternoon she carried her suitcase on board the train with great anticipation of the journey west. Running on the nervous energy produced by determination and strength of mind, she had turned what could have been a sad time in her life into a potentially happy one. If James were gone, so much the better. A husband who walked out on you after only fifteen months of marriage is no love lost.

Under her black wool coat she wore an ankle-length beige skirt with a black belt bearing a silver clasp, and a white-high neck blouse with butterfly sleeves. She was proud of the ensemble, which she accented with a borrowed crocodile-skin handbag. She zigzagged through a narrow aisle until she found a window seat. A tall gentleman wearing a long, loose overcoat with the collar turned up abruptly stopped behind her.

"You look like you could use some help with your luggage," he said with a smile.

She was only struggling a little but didn't refuse the help. "Thank you. That's kind of you. I appreciate it."

"My pleasure." He tipped his Trilby hat. "I'm always willing to help a pretty gal in distress." He boosted her suitcase, placing it on the overhead compartment. He grinned and winked. "I'm glad I lift dumbbells."

"Me, too." Elsie smiled back. "It should be a nice ride, don't you think?"

"I make the trip often enough. It *is* nice; you'll enjoy it."

She sat and adjusted herself comfortably, taking a deep breath. The train jerked forward, the whistle blew, and her journey as an independent woman began. She liked riding the train and felt grateful, glancing out the window now and then, mentally saying goodbye to her familiar surroundings. Smiling, she thought about how good the seat felt compared to the wooden benches she remembered sitting on as a child. Thankfully, this new streamlined passenger locomotive also had a steam generator to provide heat. And the train was a lot quieter than the old ones, except for the sound of her suitcase sliding around on the rack overhead. The next time the porter came by she would ask him to put her luggage in the baggage compartment. Not knowing what she might need for the trip, she had packed every article of clothing she owned, leaving the luggage bulging at the seams; she prayed the hinges would not fail her.

The wheels began to slap on the tracks beneath her sensible pumps. She glanced out her window and saw two boys and a girl running beside the train as it departed. After awhile the children looked tired and stopped abruptly with white handkerchiefs in hand, waving goodbyes to the passengers. The engineer blew the horn in response. The three children raced away laughing, with the wind blowing and long grass dancing at their feet.

After a few moments, she closed her eyes and felt the gentle rocking rhythm of the train's motion, which allowed her to drift and feel drowsy. Now that the worst was over, it was easier to think about those bad times. Her mind turned back to the pain and disappointment that she had lived through, like that hot muggy summer day when James strolled out the back door after telling her he was just going out to buy cigarettes. She was now confident that this relocation would be just what she needed, and in fact looked forward to the change. The best thing she could do was to keep moving ahead and not dwell on her husband's disappearance. She looked up and saw the conductor standing before her.

"May I check your ticket, miss?"

"Of course." She opened her pocketbook and handed the ticket to him with an apologetic smile. "Do you think you could put my suitcase in the luggage compartment? It's making a racket up there."

"Sure thing. I guess I missed it earlier." He struggled with the heavy suitcase and gave a slight grunt. "Boy what do you have in there? Bricks?" He laughed.

"I'm sorry. I think I packed everything except bricks."

"You're stronger than you look."

"When I first boarded, a gentleman helped me with the suitcase," she said demurely.

He glanced at her ticket. "Rensselaer, Indiana. Are you moving there Elsie?"

"I hope to."

"What do you plan to do there?"

"Get a job with the New Deal Program."

"The New Deal sure has put a lot of people to work. Good luck to you." He smiled, then punched the lower right hand corner of the ticket and gave it back. "Have a pleasant trip."

"Thank you." Elsie appreciated it when people she didn't know were friendly. She hadn't felt this lighthearted in years and strangers seemed happy to pause and chat. She thought of Robert's convincing advice. There was no use going into this Indiana trip thinking about the past or being uncomfortable. She had worked so hard.

In 1932, she attended Akron University to study education. Although she felt a great sense of accomplishment, finding employment proved difficult. The country was deep into the

Depression and nobody was hiring new young teachers. She wondered how many more people would suffer without any income. She read in the newspaper that five million people had been unemployed in 1930, and on top of that, the school districts expected teachers to accept lower salaries. What bum luck for her! Elsie had begun to think her timing was off.

Finally, she had earned enough credits in education, but now there weren't any teaching jobs available in Akron. She thought perhaps she'd chosen the wrong profession until the Roosevelt Administration's program came along. Now her luck had turned. She had an opportunity to do what she loved and she was going to enjoy every minute of it. Even though she would greatly miss her family in Akron, she now felt she had control over her life.

On September 7, 1934, she would be employed with the New Deal Program, teaching the children of mostly immigrant laborers who built and maintained the railroads. Under the Emergency Education Administration there was a teacher-training program that would begin in the late summer. All she had to do was pass an IQ test and several reading assessments. She would be guaranteed eighteen dollars a week for six weeks. Robert, her favorite cousin, wrote that he was happy to help her and suggested she stay at his house as long as she needed.

She glanced out the window. The vastness of the emerald countryside looked peaceful. Once the train was beyond the Akron city limits, you could see for miles without finding a house, building, or another soul. The Ohio landscape was flat, but far from monotonous. Willow trees swayed gracefully and breathed an aura of hope. Her thoughts then turned to James, souring her mood.

Certainly he would not approve of this move. She remembered that he didn't approve of anything she did. She couldn't help but make a mental list of his criticisms. He disapproved of her independent nature, her education, the way she dressed, and was annoyed that she wanted to work outside the home. He would constantly bring it up to her that he should have married someone more like his mother, Jean, whom he thought was a real lady. His mother dressed in a ladylike manner with laced corsets, high-button shoes, bonnets, floor-length dresses, and always put her family first. Elsie sighed, thinking she was nothing like his mother.

Elsie refused to be trapped by old-fashioned clothing or old-fashioned attitudes, and wasn't taking cues on how to dress from European royalty and other traditionally minded women. Instead, she watched what the Hollywood movie stars wore. She used shaded makeup and loved her red Fedora hat, inspired by Greta Garbo. Elsie felt she was fashionable, wore just the right amount of makeup to complement her dark blond hair, and knew how to apply colors skillfully to bring out the little green she had in her eyes. She was sure she would make a good impression on new friends and work mates.

After a couple of hours she stood to stretch her legs, and then strolled over to get a drink from the water cooler. She was pleased to discover that sanitary drinking cups were free of charge. She quickly drank two full, cool refreshing cups and went back to her seat.

She leaned against the window and listened to the laughter of a young couple sitting across from her. It had been that way with James until they married. But after marriage, their conversations were short, sober, and practical. She gave a wistful sigh and smiled at the woman who looked back a trifle embarrassed. From this day forward, she would concentrate on her own happiness and upon controlling the direction of her own life. She couldn't depend on a husband to do that for her.

As the train slowed to enter the yards of the next town, freeloaders began jumping from the flatcars. After the train pulled in, there was a great deal of pushing, backing, and blending as cars were detached and changed. The stop lasted about twenty minutes.

Now with a cloudy sky and a clear track, the train was back up to speed again, pouring through the late afternoon.

When her stomach growled, she checked her watch. It was almost suppertime. She rummaged through her pocketbook until she found a Zero candy bar her mother had given her. With one quick rip, she unwrapped it and tossed the paper in her pocketbook. She ate the candy quietly as not to disturb other passengers. This snack should satisfy her hunger until the train made a stop and she could eat a proper meal at the station dining hall.

At 5:30 PM, the train pulled into a small station outside Dayton, Ohio. Elsie gave the "butcher" boy a dime for a meat sandwich and an apple.

"For a nickel you can have something to read," he said with a grin.

"No, thank you. Just the sandwich and fruit will do."

In the filtered light of the afternoon's long shadows, two railroad police ran past, chasing two young boys who had suddenly jumped from a train that was standing idle. One policeman brushed Elsie's shoulder in his hurry to catch the hobos.

Elsie took her meal back into the station and sat at the end of one of the long benches. A young gal with Claudette Colbert bangs sat down beside her.

"My pumps match your handbag," she said with a smile.

Elsie turned to look at her crocodile shoes. "They do!" She nodded gleefully. "My name is Elsie. Nice to meet you."

"Beth." She indicated agreement and smiled. Beth opened her small wicker basket and pulled out a piece of fried chicken. "Where are you headed?"

"Rensselaer, Indiana," Elsie said, removing the brown paper covering her food. "I'm going to visit my cousin who runs a small automobile shop. We've been close since we were kids. It was sad for me when he left Ohio three years ago. He inherited a house from his grandmother, so he's been writing to me all this time, begging me to come. I'm finally taking him up on the offer." She tapped her foot nervously as she munched on her sandwich.

"Why now?" Beth asked.

"He has a job lined up for me with the New Deal Program for teachers."

Beth smiled widely. "Me, too! I'm getting an artist position with the Public Works of Art Project. I'll be drawing and painting murals for several portions of the Federal Building in Indianapolis, Indiana."

"That's swell. How exciting to be an artist! You must be very talented." Elsie took several more bites of her sandwich, hurrying to finish her light supper.

Beth lifted a brow as she continued to eat. "I guess I am." She gave Elsie a thoughtful glance. "I think everybody is creative in some way."

"I'm glad you sat down by me," Elsie said, looking around. "We seem to be the only lady passengers traveling alone."

Beth gave a quick laugh. "I know. Isn't that the truth?"

Suddenly, a warning cry of "all aboard" echoed throughout the station, informing all passengers to take their seats.

"I'll be a monkey's uncle. That was fast!" Beth said excitedly.

Both women hurried back onto the steam locomotive.

"Make room for the ladies!" the attendant shouted.

Elsie turned to face her new friend. "It was nice meeting you. Perhaps I'll see your artwork someday. When I least expect it, there it will be."

"Wouldn't that be keen? My full name is Beth Louise Adams just in case you do. Maybe I'll see you at the next stop. Oh, before I forget, I love your makeup," she said, giving her a wide smile.

"Thank you. That means a lot coming from an artist," Elsie said, prior to going back to her seat. She wiggled her way into a comfortable position, pulled out a clean handkerchief from her pocketbook and began to polish the dull apple. When she was satisfied, she took a big juicy bite, feeling thrilled someone she barely knew had complimented her makeup.

Within minutes the train pulled out slowly, and an hour later the tracks went straight past a gleaming lake, so close to the water that the train seemed to be gliding on the edge of the lake itself. It was a magnificent sight. You could see the pastel reflection of the train in the water. The yellow-orange sun soon dispersed, swallowed by the edge of the water. On the opposite side of the lake, rose and coral began to flush the sky in a sunset concert. Several miles and some minutes later, it became the color of a fiery maelstrom, finally calming into a restful violet and the gray of twilight.

The hours wore on. It was nearly 9:00 PM before Elsie finally arrived at the Rensselaer train depot. She looked around but couldn't find Robert, so she grabbed her heavy suitcase and walked outside into the cold night. Her anxiety level grew with each step. Finally she spotted a blue De Soto that she thought might be his. All she could see was a shiny blond head of Brylcream hair resting against the glass, and hoped it was her cousin. She gently tapped on the windowpane. Startled, the man turned to face her, his eyes instantly widening. He swung open the door and jumped out.

"Elsie! I'm sorry. I got tired of waiting inside so I came back to the car for a smoke." A big smile shot across his face. "You're tops!" he shrieked, giving her a big bear hug. "Let me get this," he said with a grunt as he lifted the suitcase into the trunk. "Say, how did you ever manage three hundred miles with this heavy load?"

"I'm getting used to taking care of myself. Listen don't be sorry. I should be sorry. I know I'm late. There was a long delay in Indianapolis. I had to change trains. I was so nervous, knowing I was over an hour behind schedule. Not too many trains coming this way." All of a sudden she felt relief and joy that she had finally made it to Rensselaer. "It's good to see you. Gosh, I've missed you. Three years is too long."

She gave Robert another hug. With his light hair and playful personality, he had always been like a best friend to her. She was astonished to see that he was wearing a single-breasted black jacket. "You're looking dapper," she commented with a nod.

"I wore it especially for you. I know how important being fashionable is to you."

He walked over and opened the car door for her. "Here, get in. You must be beat!"

"I'm excited about being here, although traveling has a certain amount of fatigue that goes along with it," she admitted.

"It was a *long* trip." He blew out a stream of smoke that dissipated into the darkness. "You won't get to see the house just now; it's pretty dark around there." He tossed his cigarette on the asphalt, stomped it out and shut her door.

She acknowledged this with a shrug.

He jumped in the driver's seat and turned his head to check the rearview mirror as he backed out. "Tomorrow you can see the house in the daylight."

"Tomorrow will be perfect."

* * *

Robert suggested she use the large upstairs bedroom that belonged to his grandmother. The room was picture perfect in soft pastels, with a canopy bed in the center; otherwise it was simply furnished with an oak chest of drawers on the right wall and an oval mirror above it. An ornate, black jewelry box sat on the dresser.

Elsie took a quick bath, put on her lace floor-length nightgown, and fell fast asleep.

She woke late the next morning, feeling renewed in spirit and ate a hearty breakfast of sweet rolls and porridge, and drank several cups of lemon tea. After breakfast, Robert insisted that he take her to the new Federal Building so she could find out as soon as possible about the New Deal programs. They drove along a one-lane road that wound up and down the green hills of the Indiana countryside. Soon they passed a field of gravel and clay soil, with grain and livestock farms reaching as far as the eye could see. They stopped on a small street opposite a Catholic church and looked east along Elm Street, with the Federal Building rising above them.

"This is it," Robert said.

"Geez Louise, look at the line!"

"Maybe it will go fast," Robert said encouragingly.

Elsie rolled her eyes. "Since when does the government ever do anything fast?"

"You have a point. Anyway, I'll wait with you."

"Didn't you say you wanted to go fishing with a friend today?" She turned to look over her shoulder at the fishing gear in the back seat. "There's the gear, and there's a canoe already on the roof. No sense in putting everything away now."

"Yeah. I was planning on going, but I can cancel. It looks like it might rain."

"No, go enjoy yourself. Who knows how long this will take. I can take the trolley home."

He smiled, relieved. "Okay, if you don't mind. I haven't been fishing for awhile, and I do have a boat with me."

"When did you get that boat, anyway?"

"A couple of months ago. A guy didn't have the money to repair his tin can, so he gave me his fishing canoe."

"You might as well use it."

"That's what I thought. Good luck today."

"Bye," she said, opening the car door and jumping out.

* * *

Robert liked the solitude of fishing, but this time he thought he would welcome some company. He was going to meet up with John McDonald. John was originally from Buffalo, New York, went to college in New Haven, Indiana, and relocated to Rensselaer for a job. Robert had met and befriended him while working on his 1932 Ford Model B. Robert thought a day of fishing would be a great way to get better acquainted.

Robert was untying the canoe from the top of the De Soto when John pulled up behind him.

John stepped out of his car smiling. "Here let me help you with that," he said, going around to the front of Robert's car to lift one end of the canoe.

"Thanks. Great day, hey? Glad you could make it."

"Great day if you like rain. But you can bet I wouldn't miss the chance to get away," John said, laughing.

"Too many drawings?"

"Something like that. You know how it is."

"Sure."

After Robert tossed the fishing gear into the boat, the two men carried it over to the edge of the water and set it down on the sand.

The morning haze had just burned off around the lake which bordered the edge of town, though in the western sky clouds began forming thickly, looking dark and heavy with rain waiting to fall.

"Looks like it may storm," Robert said, glancing up at the sky.

John looked up at the clouds, noting their approach. "I don't care about a little rain. I've always liked thunderstorms." He smiled. "Let's get started."

Robert opened the tackle box and checked it one last time to make sure he hadn't forgotten anything.

"By the way, what are we using for bait?" John asked.

"Oh, I just picked up some night crawlers real fast on the way over, see?" Robert indicated a bag that looked like it was full of dirt. "Put a few of these babies on the hook. The catfish love 'em."

"Well, we should catch *something*, anyway."

"Yep. Looks good. Let's go. Just help me push this thing out into the water a bit, and then jump in," Robert said, pointing to the end of the canoe that was already floating.

John climbed in and steadied the canoe with a paddle, side-to-side.

Robert shoved the boat a little further out and hopped in. "We'll head over to the other side. That's the best place to get catfish," Robert said, pointing to a place about half a mile away near the shelter of some trees.

Robert grabbed the other paddle and the two started out, digging in hard against the push of the wind.

The slap of water against the boat and the fresh outdoor air was just what John needed; a great change from hunching over a desk at work filled with drawings. Geese honked and many other birds chirped and twittered about the treetops along the shore as the canoe moved through the water. John loved it.

"This is the hard part. We'll have it easy going back," Robert yelled over his shoulder.

They reached the far bank minutes later and Robert maneuvered close enough for John to jump out. Then, with his short hair tousled by the wind, he got out and John helped him drag the canoe up the bank, away from the waterline.

The men found large, flat rocks on the shore and agreed that it might be as comfortable as any place to sit. They cast their lines into the water and fished companionably without conversation at first, soaking in the sounds and smells of nature.

Robert was first to break the silence. "So, do you miss New York? The pace is much slower here in Indiana."

John chuckled lightly. "I lived in Buffalo. It's an industrial city; not very exciting. I think New York City is hectic and exciting, although I haven't been there in a couple of years. I just spent time in New Haven, Indiana, getting my Bachelor of Science degree. I'm an apprentice architect now, living on my own, but at one time I lived with my brother in a shabby apartment above Gabby's, a mom and pop general store."

"You both went to college?"

"Naw, my brother worked in a factory on the assembly line. I worked there myself a couple of months but I hated it. I thought the work was monotonous and the schedule demanding, so I decided I'd better go to college and get an education."

"How'd you get the money for college? Working the line?"

"No, I couldn't save any money at all working at the factory. As it turned out, I didn't need any money for school, though. In exchange for tuition, I went over to the junk yard, turned in a few old Studebaker parts, gave them ten dollars, my high school report cards, and I was admitted."

Robert laughed. "The old barter system. That's how I got this boat. I have a lot of old Studebaker parts lying around. Maybe I can become 'Joe College.' What's your brother doing now?"

"He's still working in the factory. He doesn't mind all those unbearable sounds around him. Screeches, whines, and rumbles of machinery echoing all day long—and the days *are* long. I spent most of my time blocking out the noise by daydreaming."

"I know what you mean. When you work for someone else you're stuck. You have no choice about what goes on there. That's why I have my own business."

"That's real smooth. I admire you for that." John pulled up his line and replaced the bait that was no longer there, and then cast it back into the water. "There are some things I do miss about New York, and one is going to the games at Yankee Stadium."

"Isn't Yankee Stadium in the Bronx? Far cry from Buffalo."

"It is. My father would take us by train. My brother and I loved it."

"Big Yankees fan, are you?" Robert jumped up, thinking he felt a tug on his line. Nothing. Disappointed, he sat back down again, turning to face John. "They're a good team all right."

"They're a great team with great athletes. Remember? Lou Gehrig is the only ball player to hit four homers in a single game."

"I know. It would have been five but that center fielder caught his fly ball. The 'Iron Horse' is something else, but one of my favorite Yankees players is Myril Hoag."

"Number twenty-eight. Outfield," John said, looking up. A flock of geese appeared suddenly and turned as if a single unit, changing direction toward the trees. "He can smack 'em right out of the park. In my opinion, he's the second heavy siege gun. You can always count on a hit when he's up at bat."

"He hit six singles last week. That's got to be some kind of record."

"He's a little younger than most of the other players and kind of a small guy, but he sure can play ball."

Robert scratched his head, trying to recall ball players' salaries. "How much do you think those guys make a year?"

"At least twenty thousand. Babe Ruth makes a lot more. He toppled from $75,000 to $52,000 this year. Poor guy," John said sarcastically.

A shadow crossed Robert's brow at the mention of all that money. "Hard to believe most people are starving these days, and those guys playing baseball are rich!"

"Some people have all the luck."

Robert nodded in agreement.

"How's your business doing?" John asked.

"It's putting food on the table. I'm doing much better since I installed a hand crank fuel pump to supply petrol."

"The petrol sales are making you the money?"

Robert fiddled with his line. "Yeah, that and the auto repairs. It started out as a bicycle repair shop, then expanded. With hardly anyone able to buy a new automobile these days, someone has to keep fixing the old ones, right?"

"Yep. Good for you. My father has his own small radio business. He keeps busy fixing them or putting them together six days a week."

"When you have your own business you have to work extra hard."

"My father worked hard when we were growing up. It had some advantages. My brother and I both got an allowance of fifty cents a week. And we got to go to Yankee Stadium—that cost money. We also had the biggest radio in the neighborhood, assembled from an old phonograph player. The cabinet was over five feet tall, made from red mahogany, and sealed in varnish. We weren't rich but we weren't poor, either."

Robert was pleased with the way the day was working out, especially for John. The fish tally: John three, Robert one. They continued fishing, but soon the dark clouds increased, bringing with them light sprinkles, threatening heavier rains to follow.

"Storm came in faster than I thought it would," Robert said.

The rain accelerated to a downpour. "Let's get out of here before it gets any worse. A little rain is fine, but this is ridiculous." John stood, packing up his gear. "It's been a great day, though. I enjoyed the fishing. I did better than I thought I would."

"Better than me." Robert chuckled. "Beginners luck, I suppose."

While they wrapped the fish in newspaper and stacked them on the floor of the boat, the downpour continued. The rain came sideways out of the sky as it rode on westerly winds that whistled toward them through the trees in the near distance. They put the canoe back into the water and hopped in, each grabbing an oar and paddling together in sharp, quick unison.

"It's a squall," Robert yelled into the rain, which was now driven hard against them in the violent wind.

"Bring it on!" John yelled back. "It's better than desk work."

"How's your Ford running?" Robert sputtered, rain dripping from his face.

"Better," John yelled over the sound of thunder. "Its better, but I can still hear a squeaking noise."

"Why don't you come by Sunday afternoon and I'll take a look at it? You can stay for supper."

"What? I didn't hear you?"

"C'mon over for supper on Sunday. Bring your automobile. I'll take a look at it," Robert shouted.

The heavy downpour slackened a bit, but continued to fall in sudden spurts.

"Are you going to cook?" John asked, a note of surprise in his voice.

"Naw. I have family staying with me."

"I wouldn't be intruding would I?" John wondered, helping Robert paddle even faster.

"Not at all."

"Sure, I'll be there. Around three?"

"Sounds good."

Chapter Three

At the foot of the porch steps a metal sign that read "Robert's Automobile Repairs, Petrol" clattered as it swung in the cool breeze. Early June flowers bloomed in window boxes, and in large pots facing the covered entrance. The house was still painted yellow, though freshly repainted in Robert's favorite, Canary Gold, a darker shade, and trimmed with a coat of bright white. Elsie sat in a black rocker nearest the steps and propped her feet on the bottom of the porch railing. "I'm so glad to be here. Rensselaer is beautiful," she said.

Robert stood in the doorway, holding the screen door open with one hand. "It's nice, isn't it? You'll like it even better when you start earning some money."

"I'm sure I will." She chuckled. "Pull up a chair and talk to me."

Robert went over to one of the other rockers and pushed it upright. He had tipped them forward to prevent rain and debris from building up on the seats. In the summer morning light, the chairs resembled nuns bent in prayer, foreheads touching the pew rails, he thought; a reminder of his brief encounter with Catholicism. He sat down and looked over at Elsie. "I hope you'll settle down here. It sure would be swell to have family close by."

"I think I will. There's no reason to go anywhere else. Life is good. After a few weeks of training, I'll have a swell job. I can't thank you enough for recommending me. But I don't think I can qualify for relief room and board because I've resided in Ohio for the last five years."

"You can stay here. That's what family is all about. The New Deal education program should work out for you, but what are you going to do until September?"

"I'll find something for the summer. I'm looking forward to—" She caught him scrutinizing her. "What are you staring at?" she prompted.

"Isn't your sweater on backwards?"

"You sound like James." She leaned forward in the rocker, twisting her hand behind and fingering the buttons of the sweater to show him the fine details of her tasteful clothing. "That's the trend, silly. It's nineteen thirty-four, you know. All you men are so far behind the times. It's comfortable this way. Plus, it looks feminine."

"You're right. It does look feminine. Something you learned at the university?" His teasing smile widened.

"As a matter of fact, I did." Elsie stood. "Would you like some hot cider? It's getting a little chilly."

Robert nodded. "I'd love some. But first I'd like to show you some magic."

"Sure I love your magic. You know that. Is it a card trick?"

"No, you'll see. Wait there." He went back into the house and returned to the porch a minute later. "Put these handcuffs on me. Check them out first to make sure there isn't any funny business going on."

Elsie looked over the handcuffs, and then snapped the fetters on Robert's wrists. Next, she put the keys in her skirt pocket. "Okay, try and get out."

Again, she checked to make certain the keys were safely in her pocket. Robert turned his back to her. It took him less than one minute to free himself from the handcuffs. Confidently, he faced Elsie and handed her the restraints.

"Wow! I'm impressed. How did you do that?" she asked.

"Magicians never give away their secrets."

She smiled. "Yes, I've heard that. This place Rensselaer is magical, too. I'll get us some cider now." She turned to look at

Robert's car. "How do you keep your automobile so clean with all this rain and dust?"

"Not by magic," he said jokingly. "It's not only clean; it's impressive under the hood with a synchromesh transmission, four-wheel hydraulic brakes, and shatterproof glass."

"Girls aren't really interested in that, are they? But I know guys like you are."

"Hm-m. Before I forget, what made Valentino so sexy? I remember you were a big fan."

"That's a funny question. Why do you ask?"

"My friend Betty mentioned that he was so-o-o sexy."

"His intense dark penetrating eyes and his masculine physique, silly," she told him with a little toss of her head.

"I never noticed. He just looked real creepy to me." He rolled his eyes at Elsie. "Gals have weird taste."

"You won't say that when a male blond, male movie star hits the silver screen and everybody thinks you're sexy with *your* yellow hair."

* * *

On Sunday afternoon, Robert was reading the funny papers and drinking a beer on the front porch when a green Ford pulled up.

John McDonald paused before going up the steps toward the front door. The jazz sounds of Paul Whiteman spilled out onto the porch.

Robert greeted his friend and shook his hand. "Hi John, glad you could make it."

"Thanks for having me over. It's a nice warm day."

"I've got something to cool you off. Like a beer?"

"Love one."

Robert picked up the newspaper and went into the kitchen, returning with the beer. He handed it to John.

"Thanks. Wow, that's cold." He sat down in the rocker.

"Yeah, isn't it great? I just bought one of those electric refrigerators."

"A Grigsby and Granow?"

"I think so. How'd you know?"

"I worked on the sketches for their headquarters in Chicago."

Robert sat on the porch swing. "Are you getting used to this lazy country living?"

"It's a great change. Rensselaer seems like a real friendly place. This morning I was walking in Riverside Park by the Iroquois River and people said hello as I passed them. It's picturesque and peaceful there."

"I like that park, too." Robert downed the last of his beer. "Hey, baseball fans are going crazy. What did you think of what Hack Wilson did yesterday?"

"Playing hung over at the Baker Bowl in Philly?"

"Nobody else would've misjudged that fly ball in right field. The Phillies got two runs on it." Robert shook his head, chuckling.

"They're going to get rid of him. The Brooklyn Dodgers are too smart to have anybody like that on their team." He paused and looked around, approvingly. "Nice setup you have here."

"I like it. I live and have my business all in one place. Hey, I know what's wrong with your car. I think I just need to grease the steering and suspension joints. It should run smooth after that, without any squeaking."

"Wow, how'd you know that? Just by looking at it?"

"Even above the sounds of jazz, I heard the problem when you pulled up." Robert grinned, nodding his head.

"You sure you want to work on it? It's Sunday, a day of rest."

"Doesn't bother me. You know I work for myself so my time is my own. Have you had any overheating problems?"

"I have in the past. Yeah."

"Well, if it happens again let me take a look at it. Ford Motor Company will replace some parts free. You know your Model B is an updated version of the Model A four-cylinder?"

"Sure. If you buy a new Ford it's a B, better than the old As."

Slowly, the screen door creaked opened. The sun's rays shone on Elsie's face and neck. She looked fresh, sexy, and sweet as she stepped onto the front porch. "Oh, hello there," she said musically, appearing surprised to see another man sitting on the porch. "What is all this man talk out here?"

Robert and John both rose, smiling at her. "John, I want you to meet my cousin. Elsie, this is John McDonald."

"How do you do?" She eyed John closely. "I'm pleased to meet you. Robert didn't say anything about a friend coming over," she said, slightly self-conscious.

"John's car is running a little rough, so I told him to stop by."

"Oh, I hope I'm not intruding," John said, looking at Elsie.

"No, not at all. Please, don't be silly. Oh, handsome automobile," she said, glancing out over the porch rail into the driveway. *Hm-m ... handsome man, too.* He didn't look like any of the men she had known in Akron. He wore brown and white spats with a beige shirt and brown suspenders. She had a hard time taking her eyes off him, and could feel her face flush every time her eyes drifted back in his direction. The chemistry between them was so strong it made her a little nervous. She liked his smile. It was unusual, casual. She never remembered being so intrigued by someone's mouth. But he had such a nice, friendly smile, and his lips were so appealing. This man was different; he was the type who, with just a smile, could make you go limp in the knees.

John shook her hand warmly and looked into her eyes. "I'm delighted to meet you, Elsie," he said.

Something about him was familiar, as if there was a sense of recognition. She knew immediately the introduction to John McDonald was going to make a big impact on her life. She could feel energy forming in the summer air. The kind of energy that springs up when you meet someone extraordinary.

"We're going to have supper in a few minutes. Would you like to join us?" she asked, taking off her apron and running her hands through her hair. While fiddling with her hair a soft, warm wind ruffled her flowered dress.

"Of course he's joining us." Robert glanced at Elsie with an awkward grin. "I know how much you like surprises."

"Well, you're right about that. It seems that Rensselaer is an impromptu kind of place. I love it. So that's why you asked me to make plenty."

Robert winked at her. "I'm determined to have you meet all my friends, one way or another."

"If you're sure it's not too much trouble, I haven't had a home-cooked meal since—God, I can't even remember the last time."

"It's no trouble," she assured John. Her heart pounded against her chest. "What do you do for a living, Mr. McDonald?"

"Call me, John."

"He's an architect," Robert said, with a lopsided grin.

"I'm an *apprentice* architect. There's a big difference. I was offered an apprenticeship position in town with J. P. Crawford and Company."

"That's swell. I'm fascinated with architecture. I think Frank Lloyd Wright is extremely talented and so ahead of his time. Would you like another beer, John?" She raised a questioning eyebrow at him.

"No thanks." He shook his head and smiled. "I'm good for now."

"Well, let's eat. I'm hungry," Robert said.

"I hope you like pork chops?" Elsie asked John.

He smiled at her. "I do. I love pork chops."

She smiled back. "Good." He seemed genuinely happy to meet her, she could tell.

"Say John," Robert began as he held open the door to the house, "you know Elsie's going to be teaching for the New Deal Program, right here in Rensselaer."

John looked at her. "Oh really?"

"Come on," Elsie said. "I'll tell you all about it at supper."

John followed Elsie into the formal dining room with Robert trailing behind. John noticed everything about her. He noticed the way she moved in her simple blue-flowered dress. She looked lovely. The dress was belted at the waist, and fell about three inches below her knees with a slight flare, and beyond … a pair of shapely legs. He tried not to stare at her full bust line under the sheer and loosely fitted bodice of the dress. Her blond hair fell in waves down to her shoulders, like a movie-star. He thought she was the sexiest girl he'd ever met.

After supper, Elsie went back to the kitchen for coffee and dessert.

John whispered to Robert, "Elsie's a real dish. Why didn't you tell me you had such a good looking cousin?"

Robert smiled. "I wanted you to see for yourself."

"Is she dating anyone?"

"No, not that I know of. She's just been in town a few days."

"She's very intelligent," John noted.

After dessert, Robert excused himself and went out to his shop to work on John's car.

John helped himself to another beer and sat with Elsie outside on the porch swing. The night was warm. Stars twinkled against the blue-black sky of early evening, and crickets chirped in the distance. Robert's cocker spaniel, Clementine, curled up at their feet. Elsie sipped a glass of wine as they gently swayed on the swing.

"So, have you moved here for good?" John asked.

"I think so, yes." Elsie smiled. "If I pass the entry exams I'll be guaranteed six weeks of teaching."

"Six weeks isn't very long. Do you have the option of teaching longer?"

"Of course. That's my goal. I heard that about half of the teachers will be eligible for hiring on as emergency education instructors."

"Hopefully, you'll be in that fifty percent. Are you going to be staying here with Robert? The house looks big enough."

"For awhile."

"I've only been here a short time myself. I'm new to Rensselaer."

After a couple minutes of awkward silence she spoke up. "We have something in common, then," she said, feeling a need to keep simple conversation going.

"We do. We sure do." He looked at her and smiled. "I'm glad Robert invited me over."

He didn't need to say that, she thought. She was happy to hear those six words. "Me, too," she said shyly.

"I like your hair."

She noticed his hand was now across the back of the swing. "Oh, thank you. I'm letting it grow."

"Looks good. Most girls have such short hair. A bobbled haircut or something like that."

"I know. I'm out of style." She took another sip of wine.

He smiled and shook his head. "I don't think so. No, definitely not out of style. Very attractive, actually."

"Really? Why, thank you."

They chatted about American architecture and American politics. Elsie said she admired Roosevelt for what he was trying to do for the country. She had read his entire, latest speech in the newspaper, and also admired Eleanor Roosevelt and reminded John that the First Lady encouraged women to talk more about politics during a speech at the 'Good Citizenship' session of the Directors and Supervisors of Vocational Education.

"I decided right then and there to take Eleanor Roosevelt's advice," Elsie said.

John was impressed with how intelligently she was able to discuss Roosevelt's New Deal, and how well-informed she was on all the federal programs that were being initiated. "I must say, you're the first gal I've known so interested in politics."

"Oh," she said, nodding slowly. "I'm very interested in politics. Well, it is really give and take with me. I don't have many domestic interests like sewing, knitting, cooking, much to my family's dismay. It seems like there should be more to life." She sighed. "I'm really inspired by the large number of women entering the workforce."

"You're selling yourself short. The pork chops tasted good to me." John ran a finger along the back of the swing and looked at her thoughtfully. "Anyway, that's not like the thinking of most gals I know. Don't you want to get married someday?"

She felt a little nervous at the mention of marriage. She wasn't going to say anything to him about her brief experience and ruin the moment. "Sure, someday." She quickly changed the subject. "Did you always know you wanted to be an architect?"

He looked out at the street for a minute and then turned his gaze back to her. "I suppose so. Yes. I was the only fourth-grader who owned a protractor. It must have meant something. I loved measuring angles."

She chuckled, low in her throat. She was feeling giddy for the first time in her life.

"Don't laugh." He took a swallow of his beer. "I was crazy as a kid—always sketching things. My parents encouraged me. They supported my work. In fifth grade I did a pencil drawing of a twenty-two floor skyscraper, and they proudly hung it in the parlor."

Elsie spoke up enthusiastically. "My father hung a framed piece of needlework I made. It read, 'Women Must Vote,' stitched on pre-punched paper."

John raised his beer in salute "Oh, I thought you said you weren't domestic."

"Okay, I admit; I did make one piece of needlework, but remember it was a political statement."

"Did you fight for a woman's right to vote?"

"I did. In 1920, I marched with my Auntie Jane in the Official Suffrage Procession of Ohio."

"You were mighty brave, and just a kid. How did your family react to you marching so young?"

"They didn't approve. Mum is so traditional that she didn't think voting was feminine."

"I take it you're different from your mother?"

"Oh, most definitely." She took a final sip of wine and changed the subject, nervous he was going to ask about her age. "Were you a good student?"

"Most of the time I was." He laughed. "But, yeah, I acted up a little—had some fun. I used to get in trouble for chewing gum, and was hit with a switch constantly for bringing different things into school."

"Like what?" She was intrigued with his aversion to following convention.

He cocked an eyebrow and said, "Marbles, sticks, stones … Well, one day I brought a frog to class. Miss O'Brian, my old maid school teacher, who rode a broom in the play yard, heard it—the frog, I mean—and made me sit on a wooden stool with a dunce cap on my head."

She laughed. "Oh, I bet you looked as cute as a bug's ear." *This man is too good to be true. And charming, no less.*

"I don't know about that. Cute as a bug's ear is not how I remember it. I'll tell you one thing: I never had a teacher who looked like you, though."

"Thank you, I'm flattered," she said, demurely. At the notice of humor crinkling at the corners of his eyes, she blushed. "Oh—you don't mean—"

He laughed. "No. But let me look closer." He feigned inspection, looking her face up and down, turning her chin this way and that. "Nope. No hairy warts here. How about a broomstick? You got a witch's broomstick hiding back there?" He looked behind the swing.

Clementine started to bark.

"Clementine be quiet!" She tried to restrain the corners of her mouth in mock seriousness, but failed in a peal of laughter.

"Even if it didn't appear that way, I meant to compliment you." He poked her in the ribs.

She squealed.

"What's going on up there?" Robert yelled from the backyard.

"Oh, nothing much," John answered.

"Robert, you have a crazy friend," Elsie called.

More laughter.

"I can be serious, too." He changed the tone of his voice. "So, Elsie, you like Frank Lloyd Wright?" She leaned into him, her hair soft and her delicate scent, sweet and alluring.

"He's my favorite architect. I like his overhanging roofs and how he combines structure in harmony with nature."

"I think he's swell, too. A real genius." John nodded approvingly. "He's fairly well known here in the Midwest. You weren't born in Ohio, were you? You don't have a Midwest accent."

"No, but my sisters picked it up. They were born in Ohio. I was born in England, came over when I was a little girl. I don't have an English accent either. Too young. I don't remember that much about England, but there are a few images in Ohio that remind me of Maidstone, where I'm from. Mostly, I remember how different the sky looked. Ohio wintry afternoons were rose-colored; Maidstone's skies were gray, never rose. I liked rose better ... much better. How about you?"

"I was born is Somerville, Massachusetts. We lived in a small house in the poor section of town, though my dad worked hard, and over the years we had some money and went to interesting places, like New York City. I remember it was always dreary outside and I was always cold. I used to wake to the sound of frozen snow pelting the bedroom window, and I knew I had to go down to the basement and stoke the furnace. My father insisted that either my brother or I be responsible for maintaining heat in the house during the icy winter nights.

"That's terrible. You had to do all that?"

John sighed. "Yep. So I would reluctantly roll from under the coverlet, cup my hands to my mouth for warmth, and scramble down the stairs. I had to shovel coal from the coal room through the furnace door. I would always get in trouble with my mother the next morning, because pieces of black soot clung to my Dr. Denton's."

"You'd be cute in Dr. Denton's, all right." She laughed, looking him up and down. "What about your brother? Didn't you two take turns?"

"He was lazy. I did the work most of the time. Once I bribed him with three pennies but David, being a tattletale, squealed, so I got punished."

"I know what you mean about siblings. You can't trust them." She smiled. "My younger sisters were a real handful." In contrast, she thought of dear, sweet Ruth Helen, dead at age three, but didn't mention it. "What's your favorite building?"

"The Empire State Building, of course. Over a thousand feet high—the tallest building in the world."

"Isn't it the Eighth Wonder of the World?"

"It is." He smiled at her. "Wonders never cease … that's for sure."

Elsie thought the night was turning out splendidly, with light puffs of warm air wafting onto the porch, punctuated by the sound of crickets chirping, and warm inquisitive glances from the dreamiest man she had laid eyes on in a long, long time. She smiled at him, took his hand, and led him to the porch railing where they could take in the clear sky, full of stars. "Just look at that," she said, pointing overhead. "A perfect night sky, just like in a Hollywood movie."

"And just for a perfect evening."

Elsie studied him to see if he was mocking or serious. He held her gaze without smiling. With a nervous little smile she cleared her throat and quickly continued. "Did you know I went to the same college as Clark Gable?"

"No, I didn't know that. Is he from Akron?"

"No, he was born in some other city in Ohio. But he worked at the Miller Rubber Company on South High Street and attended Akron University."

"Studying theater?"

"No, I believe it was medicine. He wanted to be a doctor."

"Poor fellow. He never made it. Maybe he'll get a chance to play one on the big picture screen someday."

"Maybe he will," she agreed.

Robert had finished the repairs on John's automobile and went back into the house. He peeked out the screen door, eavesdropping just long enough to assure himself that all was going well with the newly acquainted couple. Once satisfied, he quietly stepped back into the parlor. Periodically, he heard roars of laughter coming from the porch. He had never heard Elsie laugh so cheerfully, or for that matter, ever seem to enjoy herself so much. He felt good, knowing his introduction was something special for his favorite cousin, and for his new friend.

Chapter Four

Determined to get that teaching position, Elsie rode a bicycle Robert had laying in the backyard over to the local grammar school. She felt slightly tense as she entered through the school's attendance office. Several people trailed behind her, all looking anxious. Inside, three people sat behind a metal desk on the far side of the room. Its surface was heaped with papers and test folders. She mustered up some confidence and approached.

"My name is Elsie Wilkins," she announced. "I'm here to take the required tests for teaching. I signed up last week."

The man sitting between the two older women spoke first. He was a thin, dark man with the look of a bull terrier. "I'll check the list." He glanced around nervously, his gaze bouncing from person to person, his fingers tracing down the names listed on a page of interested applicants. He leaned over and fiddled with some folders, spreading them out before him. "Yes, here you are. Elsie Wilkins." He handed her two packets. "You have three hours in which to complete the tests. One test is an IQ test. The other is an eight-page reading comprehension test. Here's a box of pencils and erasers. Please help yourself. An instructor in the class will tell you when to begin. Any questions?"

"No, not right now."

One of the older women smiled at Elsie. "Good luck to you."

"Thank you," Elsie said, picking up the materials and proceeding into an auditorium almost full, its rows of regulation gray metal chairs largely occupied. The sun burned through the windows like a Broadway spotlight, illuminating about forty filled seats. Five bare bulbs hung from various places in the ceiling, giving out bright, unfiltered light. A tall man with hollow cheeks and hair the color of copper sat with his chair tipped back, and his feet propped high on a desk with bony ankles exposed. He was casually watching the room of applicants fill up. Most people kept their eyes looking straight ahead, while others sat quietly organizing the material on their desks. All wore serious expressions. Elsie sat down in the last seat of the first row and began sorting the contents of the folder, untangling instructions and tests. She crossed one leg over the other, contemplating how many people in the room would become employed. She saw her teaching position flash before her eyes, realizing one more time just how valuable this job was. She assumed that to most everyone here work meant life, or misery without it.

A bell sounded at five minutes before 10:00 AM. The instructor stood before the class and spoke in a loud, even voice. "Thank you all for being here today. You will have until 1:00 PM in which to complete two exams. There will be a ten-minute lavatory break after an hour and a half. Toilets are outside the auditorium to the right. They are marked boys and girls. Only mark on the booklets. No writing on anything else will be permitted. You'll find two blank pages at the end of each booklet that you may use for scratch paper. You many open your exam books labeled 'IQ Test,' but do not pick up your pencils until I tell you to do so."

In unison, all the applicants turned to the first page in their IQ booklets.

The instructor gave a wry smile and bobbed his head. "You may pick up your pencils and begin."

Elsie began perspiring heavily and felt weak all over, knowing how important these two tests were to her future. She swallowed and took a deep breath. Even though her heart was pounding, she was able to concentrate and weave through the test questions with ease.

Three hours later, she walked out of the room confident about her performance, yet curious about how the others did on their tests. More importantly, she reminded herself, her old unstoppable, take charge self had returned.

On the bike ride home, she couldn't help smiling as she watched small twigs snap under her bicycle tires, reminding her in some odd way of defeat against the other applicants. With one hand she brushed the hair from her face, daydreaming about her very own classroom full of girls and boys, savoring a vision of writing out her lessons on a large chalkboard at the head of the room. Her happiness was so great she could barely keep it all inside. She felt free and exhilarated while her blue crocheted sweater swung to and fro in the cool June breeze. Before long, she realized she was getting hungry, so she peddled faster to pick up the pace toward home.

* * *

Robert was fiddling under the hood of an old Model A out in front of his garage work shop.

"Guess what?" Elsie made her face a blank so as to hide her delight.

"What?"

"I passed both the IQ test and the reading test. With high scores, I might add."

"What, already? It's only been three days. Well anyway, I knew you could do it; you're a smart cookie." His eyes twinkled with pride. "I'm through out here. Why don't we go celebrate with a vanilla rickie down at the soda shop?"

"Sounds yummy. I'd love one."

"Henry's is within walking distance. Let's go."

They headed out to the front and down the sidewalk, arm-in-arm in companionable conversation.

"So, what's your IQ, anyway?" Robert asked.

"They didn't tell me. I only know that I was in the top ten percent. For certain, after the two-week training, I'll have a teaching position."

"After the six weeks is up they'll probably offer you a full-time assignment, then."

"That's what I'm hoping for. All my dreams are coming true."

They joked back and forth, trading humorous comments, which came natural to the two of them. Friendship between a woman and a man could be complicated during the best of circumstances. But friendship was effortless with her cousin, Robert. Maybe it was because she had always been truthful with him. They talked a bit about the family, about his life in Rensselaer and about relationships between men and women. It was as if no time had lapsed between them. *I hope John is as easygoing as Robert.* They walked from one end of the town to the other, stopping only at Henry's for a soda.

The sky was getting dark, with rain beginning to fall in big drops, so Elsie and Robert nearly ran down the street toward home. In a moment, the sidewalks and streets were drenched, but she didn't care. All she could think of was how good it felt to be with Robert, despite the change in weather, and how good it felt to finally be out on her own with a promising future.

* * *

Elsie sat alone, listening to *Dom McNeil's Breakfast Club,* with the morning sun streaming through the picture window. Robert stepped out of the chaos of his makeshift office into the parlor. "What are you up to today?"

"I'm not sure. I haven't decided yet. It looks nice out, though."

"Let's sit down and have something to eat."

Robert and Elsie sat across from each other at a small table where she nibbled breakfast from a basket of rolls and muffins. Robert was finishing up his large breakfast of scrambled eggs and sausage, but she didn't have much of an appetite.

Licking her lips, Elsie fluffed her hair over her shoulders, still pondering how to broach the subject that was on her mind. She had doubts about staying at Robert's house indefinitely. "I appreciate you letting me stay here. You're the greatest cousin in the world."

She was eyeing him a bit apprehensively, Robert thought, and he was concerned about what was to come. "But ...," he prompted.

"But I think I should move into a boarding house. There's one next to the grammar school. It's centrally located and I can walk to wherever I need to go."

He sat straight up, both hands wrapped around his coffee cup. "It's up to you. It's such a big house. You're welcome to stay. You're not in the way at all."

"Oh, I know. I'm comfortable staying with you," she murmured. "That's not it. I love this house. It's so large with three bedrooms and all, and I like the spacious wrap-around porch. It's swell. But I think it would be better for me to be on my own."

"I understand." He raised an eyebrow. "You're so damn independent! I remember that about you, even as a kid. You always tried to be the first one to sled down the snow hill."

She rolled her eyes. "I loved the challenge, and I admit I was competitive. You all were so slow, dragging your feet. Especially Edna, she moved like a snail."

There was a small silence while Elsie dabbed the crumbs from her mouth with a napkin. "Thanks for understanding. Don't take it personally. I appreciate what you've done for me. I can never thank you enough."

"You're sure you want to do this?" he said quietly, shrugging his shoulders. "Boarding houses cost money, you know."

"Oh, I know. Mum gave me twenty dollars. It was so generous of her. I plan on looking for work shortly. Hopefully, I can find something for the summer before school starts."

He gave her a wry smile, wondering if she were hiding something. "Does this have anything to do with a certain apprentice architect?"

She gave him a thin smile in return. "Oh, Robert. Don't make me blush. I like your friend very much, but I am a bit stunned. Do you know I told him last night that I'm not yet divorced and he still wants to see me?"

"No, but I'm glad you told him the truth." Robert paused, shaking his head. "He's a good man."

"I made it sound like it was nothing much. Not much of a marriage, anyway. I told him that James has been gone for such a long time that I don't even think of myself as married. He agreed. He really is special." She had to admit, John was indeed open-minded, charming, even fascinating and, yes, special.

He nodded. "Well, listen, I support any decision you make about moving. But why don't you sleep on it tonight?" He sighed in resignation. "I'd better get to work. It's getting late." He rose and stood outside the kitchen door where he was framed in the sunlight. "I've got two Model Ts out in the garage calling my name."

After Robert left, Elsie cleaned up the kitchen, hoping he truly understood her position on housing. With all the dishes put away, she went over to the window; curious to see any children playing, but the streets were empty. A good walk to clear her head would be just the thing to do, she decided.

The soles of her new oxfords slapped the hard concrete, bouncing with each step. Daydreaming, she stepped off the sidewalk and stumbled into the street. A horn honked, and the squeal of brakes made her jump back onto the curb. Embarrassed, she lowered her gaze to avoid acknowledging the giggles and stares from the group of teens in the car. She had better pay attention to where she was going.

Walking briskly, she turned the corner to find a small, wrinkly woman with droopy, but friendly eyes staring at her. The old woman was pinning a white bed sheet on a clothesline. Elsie grinned at her. "Hello there."

The neighbor beamed. "Well, hello. I haven't seen you around. Did you just move into the neighborhood?"

"Sort of, yes. I'm staying with my cousin until I get settled. You know the big yellow house on Riverview?"

"Yes, that one is a lovely house indeed." The old woman snapped the last clothespin on the sheet and came closer. "Where are you from?"

"Akron, Ohio."

"Ohio. I've never been to Ohio myself. I've lived in Indiana my whole life. Do you miss Akron?"

"Um, not really." She smiled and then quickly clarified her response. "Well, maybe just a little."

The woman looked at her with new interest. "Rensselaer is such a fine place to live."

Elsie looked at her thoughtfully for a moment. "I agree. I like it here very much, but I have family in Akron."

"I understand. Your mother and father? When you get to be my age you'll realize that family is everything in life." The woman returned to her basket of wet laundry. "Do you work?"

"I will be shortly. I'll be teaching with the New Deal Program."

"How'd you get that?" She seemed delighted with Elsie's good fortune.

"My cousin helped, but you need to be unemployed, pass the entry exams, and have some experience."

"Roosevelt is doing a fine job. I'm proud to be a lifelong Democrat." Her eyes widened. "You're not a Republican are you?"

"Not a chance. No."

"That's good. We don't need another Herbert Hoover in the White House. The best of luck to you."

"Thank you." Elsie brightened. "It's a fine day for hanging laundry." She offered a hand in friendship. "Hope to see you again."

The woman took her hand. "Same here, my dear."

There was a new spring in Elsie's step. Being away from Akron gave her a sense of freedom. The people she'd met so far seemed friendlier than the folks in Ohio. How wonderful this move was turning out to be, stolen away from her dreary, disciplined life back home.

* * *

The boarding house in the middle of town on Susan Street became an arrangement that worked out well for John, as he stopped by just about every night after work. As their friendship deepened, they spent as much time as they could together when he wasn't working. He appreciated Elsie's honesty, her great looks, her vibrancy, her intellect, and her sense of self-determination.

"You've been here about two weeks now," John said, holding her hand as they sat on the sofa in the front parlor. "How's it working out?"

"Oh, it's working out swell. I feel so—"

"Free?"

"Well, I'd say independent. It's terrible being obligated to do what someone else is telling you to do."

"You'll do well. I'm proud of you." He gave her a peck on the cheek. "Wow, this June weather is just sweltering tonight. What do you say we go for a walk, get some air, and then get a bite to eat?"

Elsie jumped up, pulling his hand. "That sounds perfect."

The Italian restaurant in town offered not only a traditional menu, but a nice breeze with both the front and rear doors standing open. John made sure they were seated in a secluded, dimly lit corner.

Elsie felt a case of sexual yearning coming on from the dreamboat sitting across from her. The flickering candlelight between them reflected off the red wallpaper, producing a soft rosy glow, and making John's face appear soft and tender, as though in a magical dream. But it was his carefree, boyish smile that threw her off guard every time, leaving her blushing occasionally. It was as though she could almost hear him softly breathing in her ear, and it gave her goose pimples just thinking that she wanted him near enough to do that. She gave her hand to him over the table and he took it, caressing each finger. Elsie melted into her seat, leaving her feeling like a mere puddle. He was so tender and sexy.

Elsie drew his hand toward her and caressed it, whereupon he cupped her chin and smiled, which made her melt all the more. "I hope nobody can see us," Elsie managed to say.

"Well, we can order now," he said.

"Good idea."

"Wine? Maybe a big plate of spaghetti?" He saw that she was looking at him with smoky eyes as if to say, *'Are you dumb or what? It's you I'm interested in.'* Men knew these things, he was positive.

With a controlled smile tugging at her mouth, Elsie toyed with the manicotti on her plate in silence. *He sure has a witty sense of humor. How could I get any luckier?* Well, she knew one way to get oh-so-much luckier, but nice girls didn't think about such things. Not at least, outside of marriage. She noticed he wasn't eating anymore, either. And as if suddenly on cue, they looked at one another and they both knew supper was finished.

The walked hand-in-hand back to Elsie's place where they picked up John's car, and drove back to his house with all the windows rolled down.

"Now, this is refreshing," Elsie yelled into the wind, letting her hair dance about.

Once inside, he turned on a small fan on the end table to keep them cool, and invited her to sit with him on the sofa. "Oh wait. How about some music?" he asked.

"That'll be keen. What artists do you have there?" She went over to the stack of '78s, sorted through them and selected *Did You Ever See a Dream Walking,* by Eddie Duchin.

With a secret smile, he put the record on the Victrola's turntable, switched it on, and let the needle down. "Maybe something to drink?"

She nodded.

"Rum and coke?"

"Sounds swell."

John poured two glasses and said, "I'm so glad Prohibition's over."

"Me, too." She gazed at him, her heart almost bursting with happiness. "I don't really drink much. Mum was terrified of any alcoholic beverage and what it could do to a person. I guess many people couldn't control themselves and were drunk all the time."

"Or that's what the authorities wanted us to believe," John replied.

"Do you think it's possible they weren't being truthful about the need to prohibit the use of alcohol?"

"Maybe. Maybe they wanted us to believe it was worse than it really was."

"Why do you think they would do that?"

"I think they really wanted to get all those Kentucky moonshiners. They really had a racket going on."

They were silent for a moment, then he searched her lovely, serene expression. "I hope you're comfortable enough with me to tell me a little more about your marriage." He took her hand and gently explored the backs of her fingers with his thumbs. "What happened?"

She took a deep breath and shyly avoided his gaze by staring into her glass. "When a spouse walks out one day without saying a word and never comes back, you will never get anything straightened out, that's for sure. In my heart, it's over. It's been over for a long time. It was a mistake. I wouldn't be seeing you otherwise." She looked at him and searched his eyes, which were so intense yet so compassionate. "I would get a divorce if I could afford one, or if I knew where he went. I don't even know that."

"You don't have any idea where he is?"

"No." She laughed nervously then took another sip of her drink. "I did try to make the marriage work, though I think James and I are different people with different values. I don't think I was the right woman for him, and ... certainly not the right kind of wife. He wanted Mary Pickford. He read an article about her in *Life Magazine,* and obsessed about her continually. He said she was feminine. He said she was beautiful. He thought a woman should bear a man's children, be a gifted homemaker, and be devoted and obedient."

John answered as though fascinated, letting out a long, low whistle. "Gee, that's not what I want." He chuckled. "Maybe he's back in Akron right now. Is he somebody I should be worried about?"

"No," she shook her head, hoping it was the truth. "Not at all. I'll probably never see him again. I don't even know if he's still living. He abandoned me years ago. *No one* knows where he is. Not *even* his family. If they do know, they're not telling me. Maybe he went back to Scotland." She paused. "I doubt it, though."

"I can't imagine anyone abandoning someone like you. I'm sorry you had to go through something like that."

"Oh, I've been through worse." She circled the rim of her glass with her index finger.

"You have? Tell me about it. I want to know everything about you. The good and the bad. The happy times and the sad ones."

"Maybe some other time," she said timidly, sorry that she'd brought up negative thoughts.

"No time like the present. Shoot."

"Well, I had a baby brother and sister, who both died very young," she said hesitantly. "My brother was only eight months old. He had meningitis. That was devastating for my family. Then in 1926, which was the very worst year for my family, my sister who was three, died of pneumonia." She added quietly, "I do have two living sisters back in Akron. I told you about them earlier. Lena is fifteen and Evelyn is thirteen." She decided to keep her sad story short and succinct.

"Ah-h … I'm glad you have younger sisters. But that's too bad about your other siblings. You've been through so much tragedy," he said, taking both her hands in his warm grasp.

A shudder jolted her back to the present. "I guess I have." She shoved the sad recollections down and cleared her throat. "I don't want to talk about morbid things." This man was so easy to talk to, she thought. She had never met anyone so understanding.

"I really want to know more about James."

"Okay. Well, his rejection of me was hard to take, but honestly, I had already begun to think about divorcing him. We were not at all suited. After we married, we couldn't afford our apartment so we moved in with Mum and Dad. Married life wasn't much different for me than it was when I was single." A little irritation crept into her voice. "There I was, still bickering with my sisters. Being married meant that I had extra work in taking care of not only him but the rest of the family, as well. Washing, ironing, and picking up after him. I worked and James complained. And my father was a stickler for cleanliness. He expected the house to be run on a tight and rigid schedule."

"My mother did most of the chores at our house. What sort of work were you responsible for?"

"Monday was washday. Tuesday, iron the clothes. Wednesday, do the baking. Thursday, wind the clocks and beat the rugs. And Saturday was bath night, and as an adult, I was still third in line, just like it had been when I was a kid."

John laughed. "Third? You had it rough."

"I'm kidding about the adult part," she said smiling. She was happy the conversation had changed from James to housework. "As a kid if I ever complained about having to do so much work, my father explained that I should be grateful I was not working in a sweatshop or a factory. He said it with a grin, but I thought that behind the pleasant facade he just might be serious."

"You must have had some sort of fun."

"I did." She tossed her hair back. "What about your childhood? What else did you do besides getting soot on your Dr. Denton's?"

He laughed. "I liked earning money. I had a business arrangement with the local corner newspaper captain. If the kid who handled the Sears store didn't sell all his papers by quitting time, I took over. I could keep a penny for every paper I sold and if the patrons were generous, they would tip me an extra penny. Before heading home, I would go to the five & dime for a licorice stick, two wax elephants, and a pack of Zeno blood-orange chewing gum. The loot would cost me about six cents."

"Sounds like parts of your life were happy."

"Yes, but I have never wanted to end up like my parents. I could never figure out why they couldn't discuss their problems. They yelled all the time."

"Maybe it was a simple case of incompatibility. Maybe they just weren't suited to one another."

Their eyes met and they held each other's gaze for several beats, then John broke the silence, though he continued to admire the studious concentration in Elsie's eyes. She was a breathtaking tomato no matter what expression she wore. "Can't say as I'd disagree there. It was really rough on my brother and me."

"Well, you made it through in one piece." She gave his arm a little squeeze. "I'm sorry such a nice person like you had parents who fought most of the time. That's not good for kids, all right. You haven't been married, then?"

"No, never. I'm not sure about it, either. But I would like to have kids someday." He hesitated, and looked straight into her eyes. "My parents split up when I was about ten. That was hard." His voice became clipped. "My brother and I remained with my father in Buffalo. It worked out okay. After high school I took a part-time job, bagging groceries at the A & P. My mother lives in Northern California now. She's remarried."

Elsie thought if only things were less complicated, but they weren't. And now they were getting more complex because John knew the truth about James. "Were you ever serious with anyone? Do you have a steady girl?"

He pulled her close. "I would like to think I do ... now."

"Who is it?" she whispered, knowing the answer.

"Let me show you." He scooped her up onto his lap and kissed her deeply, his right hand resting on her thigh, his little finger touching the top of her garter. She didn't pull away, only kissed him back, soft passionate kisses. The warmth in her eyes made him feel bold, and the smell of fresh gardenias enveloped him when her hair brushed against his face. Encouraged, he eased her sideways on the sofa and moved his hand up under her dress. His breathing became more ragged. One hand found her breast and the other moved her sweetheart neckline down to reveal her nipple. In an instant, his mouth was on her breast as both hands pulled at the right side of her bodice.

For just a moment, Elsie was torn. *Nice girls don't have sex with men they've known for only fourteen days.* Yet, this man was special and so desirable that she wanted to cry out in her yearning for him; even good girls could only stand so much passion without submission. She felt safe with him, and she was most certainly aroused. The desire between her legs was driving her crazy.

June in January had finished playing on the phonograph, and the needle scratched back and forth on the record. Elsie jumped up with the one ounce of caution left in her, adjusted her dress, and walked over to put the arm of the needle back in place. Flustered, she blurted, "I should go. It's getting late and the owner of the boarding house doesn't like people coming in after ten."

John stood, put his arms around her, and drew her slowly to his chest. He embraced her, and felt her soft breasts against him. "Do you have to go?" He lightly kissed her neck. "Can't you break the rules this once?"

His voice was a low, sexy rumble of hot and breathy words, and his hands held her close, making it difficult to formulate an answer. The best she could come up with was, "No, I'm sorry, I have to go."

His face clouded with disappointment. "All right, then. Give me a minute," he said hurriedly, and went into the pantry to grab his house keys and to adjust the bulge in his slacks.

During the drive back to Susan Street, Elsie, feeling awkward, was silent.

John filled the silence with pleasant small talk. He slid his arm across her shoulder, pulled her close to him, and smiled. Elsie smiled back and sweetly kissed his cheek.

She wanted to make love to him, but for now, refrained. She had known him for such a short time. She mustn't forget that she was still technically married.

* * *

Elsie kissed and hugged her pillow, tossing, and turning, imagining John's body near hers, on top of her … inside her.

The next morning, having had so little sleep, she expected to feel tired. Instead, she was energized. For the first time that she could remember, she felt gloriously alive. John McDonald was the most fascinating man she had ever met, and charming, to boot. He'd helped set her on this path to a new life that she hoped would continue.

She crossed over to the bedroom window where the white cotton curtains swayed delicately in the summer breeze. She glanced out at the small pond in back of the boarding house, admiring the brilliant reflections on the water made by a hanging tree branch as it dipped in and out of the water. The white and red petunias seemed to dance like cupids in front of the vegetable garden.

She sang to herself as she quickly dressed. The misery in Ohio was over and she felt her life taking a turn for the better.

As she opened the door on her way to look for work, she noticed a yellow package with her name on it, tied up in a white bow. Curiously, she opened the box and found two pounds of dark chocolates. A heart shaped card inside read:

> *These chocolates aren't nearly as sweet as you are. You're my one and only.*
>
> *John*
>
> *P.S. I can't get you out of my mind … and I don't want to even try.*

Chapter Five

The lunch counter at Woolworth's was crowded with shoppers on their midmorning breaks. Elsie edged into a recently vacated seat and addressed the clerk at the cash register. "Excuse me, sir. Are you the manager?"

A tall, skinny young man, appearing about twenty years old looked up and smiled. "I am."

"Are you hiring?"

"Yes, I have an opening. Normally I wouldn't, but my best waitress suddenly quit on me last night, short notice. If you give me a couple of minutes, I'll be happy to talk with you."

"Oh, wonderful! Sure, I'll wait. Thank you," she said, placing her pocketbook on the counter. She reached into it to get out her lipstick so she could refresh her smile.

"I shouldn't be long," the young man called as he popped into the kitchen.

While she waited, she ordered a cup of hot tea from the waiter behind the counter. She mused about the future between sips. If she worked here, what would her duties be and what would she wear? If it were a uniform, she hoped it would be attractive. Elsie glanced adoringly at the new dresses hanging on racks in the ladies apparel department. Clothes shopping would have to wait. In anticipation, she nervously kept shifting and crossing one knee over the other.

Finally, the manager came out of the kitchen and smiled. "Let's go over there," he said, indicating an empty table in the back of the restaurant.

Elsie put a nickel down on the counter for the tea and swung her stool around. Her knees bumped a tiny, gray-haired woman in a white dress who glared at her with beady eyes.

"Sorry. I'm so sorry," Elsie said, apologetically.

The old woman barked, "Good luck, dearie. My daughter put in an application here a month ago and hasn't heard a word since. There's a depression on, you know."

Nodding, Elsie merely looked at her and smiled.

As Elsie approached the table, the manager wiped his hands on the large, white apron that hung around his neck. He pulled out a chair for her. Most of the breakfast crowd had left. "So, what's your name?" he asked.

"Elsie. Elsie Wilkins." She offered her hand to him. Pleased to meet you Mr.—?"

"Hansen. You can call be Patrick." He flashed a bright smile and shook her hand. "Have you ever worked a lunch counter?"

Oh, if only she had. She wanted to lie and tell him yes, but honesty prevented her from doing so. "No, I'm afraid I haven't. I did serve my two younger sisters breakfast, lunch, and supper, though," she said with poise. "I'm very friendly and pick up new skills quickly. I'm a hard worker and I never spilled a thing at home. I could be a natural at this."

After a moment, he grinned. "A natural … I like that. Well, we open at 9:00 AM, Monday through Saturday, and close at 5:00 PM. There's no supper business around here. No one stays downtown that late." He looked across the restaurant for a moment, as though he were checking to make sure all was well. Abruptly, he faced her again.

"This is more than a lunch counter; it's a restaurant," he said. "It serves as a social gathering place for local residents. We get a lot of high school students in here who visit with their friends over sundaes and ice cream sodas. Because we're busy during the summer months, I have a rule about waitresses socializing. If passersby are asking for directions, or for a toilet, don't waste time talking to them. If they're hanging around, tell me and I'll throw them out. I just want paying customers."

Elsie nodded. "I understand."

"How are you with numbers?"

"Very good actually," she replied confidently.

He handed her a menu. "If I ordered let's say … soup with oyster crackers, mashed potatoes, ham and cheese on rye, and a chocolate ice cream soda, what would I owe you?"

She quickly opened the menu and scanned it for a moment. "Ninety-five cents. That's without a tip."

"Very good. You passed," he said, looking pleased. "I didn't even have to put a 'waitress wanted' sign in the window. You're hired. Can you start tomorrow morning at nine? I'll pay you fifty cents an hour, plus tips and one full meal."

"That sounds swell, but I have to be honest and tell you that I'm only available during the summer months. I'll be teaching school in September."

"Oh, thanks for letting me know. I appreciate your honesty, but I can still use you for now. The summer is when we're really busy. What will you teach?"

"English and general education. It's a special program for the children of railroad workers."

"Sounds good. I'll be happy to have you work here for a couple months and maybe fill in after that whenever you can; that's if you work out, of course."

"Of course. Thank you. What should I wear, Patrick?"

He quickly pushed his chair back, stood, and went behind the counter, returning with a green apron and a green shirt with the name 'Woolworth's' embroidered on the pocket in white. "You'll wear this. I hope medium fits. See you at nine. Oh," he added, handing her an employment application, "fill this out and bring it with you in the morning." He put his arm around her shoulder and escorted her to the door, closing it behind her.

Elsie stood on the sidewalk, the apron and shirt in one hand, the application in the other. She was very excited. Without even trying very hard, she had a job with a cute young boss. She took a deep breath and knew that Rensselaer was going to be the right place for her. Everything was working out just swell.

The next morning, she was so excited that she left the boarding house early. At eight forty-five she rapped on the door frame of the restaurant. With a small paring knife in hand, Patrick opened the door. Elsie handed him the completed application.

"Good morning. Thank you. I'll take a look at this later. You can start by filling the napkin holders," he said. "They're behind the counter. Then you may familiarize yourself with the menu after you finish with the napkins. Customers should start arriving shortly. Also, please rub the water spots off the silverware. I'll be busy slicing lemons and chopping parsley."

"Okay, will do. Thanks again for hiring me," she said, tying on her apron.

It took Elsie only a week to memorize all the food items on the menu, and the price of each one. She felt extremely comfortable with her new job, and made some new friends.

Elsie found out that summer sales at Woolworth's were up substantially from the previous year, mostly because of the clothing products they offered. More customers in the store meant more sales in the restaurant and bigger tips in her pocket.

* * *

John sat at Woolworth's lunch counter, waiting—watching the flies on the wall, as he put it—and watching the overhead fan blades swoop around. He'd done plenty of waiting for Elsie on Friday afternoons while she finished with her customers and various chores. But she was worth it. He winked at her as she finally took off her apron and went to him, giving him a peck on the cheek.

"Sorry, it's been so busy. Big shopping day. Anyway, you're early, aren't you?"

John reached under the counter where a dozen pink roses lay across his knees. "These were in a hurry to get here and surprise you, that's all," he said, handing the flowers to her.

"Thank you! Oh, they're beautiful," she said, burying her nose in their fragrance. "What's the occasion?"

"There's not any occasion. I just felt like bringing you flowers."

"That's so sweet," she said with a puzzled look. "You shouldn't have. I'm sure they cost a lot of money."

"It's okay. They're for your birthday."

She pursed her lips, catching him in an apparent lapse of memory. "Tsk, tsk, you know my birthday is in April, silly goose."

"Happy belated birthday, then." He grinned, grabbing her free hand and gently squeezing it.

"I'll put these flowers in water at home, and then I'll change my clothes," she said, walking out the door with him.

"But your Woolworth's shirt is so sexy," he teased, his lips curving into a come-hither sensuousness.

Elsie blushed.

"I can't help it. I've missed those perfect lips of yours. It's been more than eight hours," he said, pausing momentarily to assess the lovely face next to his. He watched her lips move, which aroused him instantly.

"It *does* seem like a long time." She circled an arm around his waist.

"Say, how about we take a ride over to Wolcott this evening," he said.

"Oh?"

"It has this great place I want you to see."

"Okay, you're full of surprises today!"

As they strolled along the street toward John's car, he moved closer and held her to him.

"Where are we going?" Elsie asked.

"You'll see."

"You're not going to keep me guessing about this place, are you?" she asked, whispering into his mouth and planting little kisses all around his lips.

"Sure, it will be fun to keep you guessing."

He avoided her gaze; it seemed, with the greatest indifference. She playfully punched him on the shoulder. "This had better be good."

"Everything's good, just for you," he replied.

Since they'd met, her feelings for him were becoming strong enough that she'd need courage to continue this relationship. She wished more and more that she was free of James. What was she to do about a divorce?

John drove through the streets of Rensselaer to the boarding house, where he parked out front. "I'll wait for you here," he said. "Take your time. Take care of the flowers. I'll be fine."

He seemed to sense when she needed him, and when to give her alone time. She kissed him lightly on the cheek, and stepped out of the car, carrying the roses. "I'll be back in a few minutes."

Several school teachers sat in wicker rocking chairs on the porch, watching a group of croquet players on the lawn who were swinging mallets and exchanging ribald remarks.

"Any bets?" one of the teachers asked Elsie as she climbed the stairs.

"On them?" She laughed, pointing a thumb over her shoulder into the front yard. "Not a chance. No gambling for me, I'm afraid." She was almost certain she wasn't gambling on John's intentions.

She returned twenty minutes later, wearing a green summer dress of rayon and Canton crepe, the skirt pleated and the bodice closed at the neck with a bow. Her hair was full, wavy and shiny. "I hope this is a suitable dress."

He surveyed her attire a moment, and then treated her to an apologetic smile. "Well, you look nice, but your skirt could be shorter."

A smile touched her mouth, but her mind raced in a dozen directions. "What do you mean my skirt could be shorter? Does this have anything to do with where we are going?"

"It might. We're going roller skating."

She took a careful look at his profile. "Oh, you finally spilled the beans! But I do like roller skating," she said, biting her lower lip. "Maybe I should have worn my tennis skirt. It would have been more appropriate, and of course, shorter."

"You look fine—very pretty." He saw that she seemed relieved. "Anyway, I thought you would enjoy it. Rhonda's Rink had its grand opening a couple days ago. It was originally a livery stable, then a storage company, and now it's changed over to a roller rink."

"Okay, let's go." John held her door open and she stepped into the car.

He swung through downtown, taking the back road that led to the highway. "There's a twelve-man band that plays at the rink. I hope I don't fall on my face. I haven't skated in years." He rolled the window down to let fresh air into the car and took a deep breath.

She did the same with her window and immediately the breeze was blowing around them, tossing her hair in compete abandon; a freedom that seemed to complement her new life. "So, you have skated?" she asked with a flirtatious tone.

"Once or twice," he told her. "Never to music though. The music can really throw you."

"Throw you on the ground? You're silly."

Half an hour later, they pulled into the parking lot of Rhonda's Skate Rink. She didn't even wait for him to open the door; she jumped out. The air was warm, the night still. She could hear the sounds of music as they approached the rink.

Without warning, John stepped forward and wrapped his arms around her shoulders, hugging her tightly. "I'm falling for you," he whispered, his breath soft and warm in her ear.

She just grinned, not knowing how to respond. But she already knew she'd never get him out of her heart, so why not relax and enjoy herself? Why didn't she say something like, "I'm falling for you, too? Or, "I'm glad." Oh well, next time I'll speak up, she thought.

The parking lot was crowded, and when they entered through the rink's back door, the place was hopping with people. It was a large building of about six thousand square feet with a huge plywood skating floor, a concession stand, and a stage set for the band. The sounds of instruments, skates, and laughter whirled around them. With a laugh, John shook his head. "Let's get something to drink before we attempt this."

John and Elsie walked over to the concession stand, bought their drinks, rented skates, and grabbed two open stools, where they talked and laughed over lime rickeys. A love for the drink made from lime juice, seltzer water, and sweet syrup was one of the many things they had in common.

John caught sight of a nearby sign that read 'Skate Smart.' "What does that mean, *skate smart*?"

"It means don't be stupid and fall on your face," Elsie said, chuckling.

"Or watch out for the skaters to the right and left of you."

John remembered hearing that young people came from all over the local area to skate here. Experienced couples skated around the rink in watchful balance, showing precision, power, and artistic ability. The band played bubbly tunes; the peppiest and most spirited music echoed throughout the rink.

Elsie watched one couple skate into a turn, their steps matching the music, then they spun around and skated backwards.

"Boy, look at those two. I don't think I can match that," John said, with a resigned smile.

"What? Giving up already?"

John stood, picking up his skates. "I guess we should give this a try. What do you think?" She stood leaning into him, her hair soft and her fragrance sweet and tempting.

With a laugh Elsie said, "That's why we're here. Remember, roller skating is the opposite of walking. When you walk, you put one leg out and then the other. In skating, each leg in turn moves back to push you forward."

"All right teacher," he said, leaning against the railing. "I don't want to concentrate that much. I just like the freedom and the speed."

Sitting on nearby steps, Elsie gingerly stepped into her roller skates. She laced them, stood, and pushed off with her back skate to move smoothly forward. Maintaining her balance, she made it as far as the low wall that blocked the skating floor from the viewing area. She turned and skated back to John.

He was still putting his skates on. Soon, he stood up, grasped the rail, and with his feet in a heel-tucked-into–arch position, he flexed his knees a couple of times, picking up first one skate and then the other to test his balance. Then he began to roll around a bit. Once he was comfortable with rolling, he turned to Elsie. "May I have this skate?"

He reached out and took her right hand. She felt a little awkward. The band played *Down Yonder*, and they sashayed forward. He put an arm around her waist, she moved into him and the awkwardness vanished. They skated at an even pace around the rink, keeping in rhythm with the music. "We're going so fast. You're a really good skater," she said, giggling. "This is so much fun!"

The strong rhythmic beat of the music inspired them to skate more gracefully and with less deliberate effort. They were now skating hand-in-hand when Elsie laughed lightly. "When we go around this corner, I'll have to remember to put my full weight on my inside skate. I felt a little off balance back there on that turn."

He shook his head and laughed again. "You're doing great. We're in sync." Energy and passion raced inside him.

Around the second corner he felt off balance and dropped Elsie's hand. He bent his knees, sank down a few inches and instantly improved his control. Then he came back up and took Elsie's hand again. "That was close. There's nothing like bouncing your keester off a hardwood floor."

"Or breaking a leg," Elsie said. As if on cue, a couple coming out of a turn did an abrupt jump together. Startled, Elsie stumbled, letting go of John's hand and rolling quickly to the railing. She turned to look around for him. He was right behind. "Geez Louise, they scared me," she said, shaking her head. "I almost fell on my face. I'm going to stay here for a moment and listen to the band."

"Sure, catch your breath. I'll be right back," John said. Skating alone around the rink, he built up speed. On his third time around, he went into the turn too fast and slid to a halt, bumping into Elsie, his hands coming to rest on her shoulders. "Wow, that was fun!"

"You're fast. Even skating backwards, no less." She couldn't stop her lips from curving. "You're really good at this."

As if pleased, he shrugged, then gestured toward the rink. "There're a lot of people out there better than me."

"You're being modest," she said.

When the song, *I'm on a Seesaw* ended, the drummer announced, "We will be taking a short break now, so you'd better rest up. When we return, we'll introduce the *Beer Barrel Polka*. You're in for a real treat." The crowd cheered and applauded the selection. Elsie excused herself and went to the ladies' room, deciding it would be a good time to freshen up.

John sat patiently waiting on a stool in front of the concession stand.

When Elsie returned, the band was back onstage and had just started to play the upbeat polka.

John pulled at both of Elsie's hands. "Come on, we'll have to skate to this. I like polkas."

She nodded in agreement and they both glided forward. John's knees were bent slightly and his arms thrust out like airplane wings. He looked like a big, adorable kid, and she giggled as they went around the rink. "Hey," she said, tapping him on the shoulder and falling in line behind him to imitate his wings.

They skated separately but maintained harmony, mirroring each other as they went along, accompanied by other skaters moving to the beat of the music. The music filled them with so much energy they didn't realize how fast they were going. Periodically, they would come together, he would make a half turn, and holding her hands he would skate backwards. It was at these intervals they skated like dance partners, and once, they even skated backwards together.

Elsie heart beat rapidly, thumping against her ribs as she inhaled a deep steadying breath. She wasn't used to all this physical activity. As the polka ended she stopped in the middle of the floor, taking deep breaths to calm down. The band announced that the next song would be the new romantic ballad, *Blue Moon.*

How wonderful! This was one of her favorite songs, and thankfully, it had a much slower tempo. She searched for John amongst the other skaters and spied him leaning against the wall, waiting for her to catch up.

When she approached, he gave her a sideways half-smile. "There you are. Care to join me?" he said affectionately.

Together they skated around the rink several more times at a leisurely speed and then simply rolled forward to an eventual stop. "Whew, I'm surprised I haven't fallen," he said, surveying her face. "Well, let me take that back, I have fallen ... I've fallen for *you.*"

His soft smile met her gaze. "I'm so glad it was me you fell for and not the floor," she said, filled with delight.

Her body tingled with the thought of his admiration. She was so happy he felt that way. This was the second time he'd said that tonight. But this time she responded, her heart racing with overwhelming joy. This was good. This was right. She had never met anyone with his combination of looks, charm, and intelligence, and couldn't help but be taken by him. His interest in her made him all the more alluring.

Chapter Six

Elsie hurried to finish her side work at the corner table in the back of the restaurant where she was filling the salt, pepper, and sugar containers from all the tables. John waited for her at the counter, sipping a cup of coffee. She twisted on the last container top and went to him, one arm stretched behind her back.

"What are you hiding?"

"See?" she said, producing a sheet of paper. "It's a danceathon. We could win two thousand dollars!"

"So it says." John pointed at the flyer, his eyes narrowed to slits. "At the Oddfellow Building? What kind of idiots would do such a thing?"

"It's all the rage. These contests are popular everywhere and people are winning cash! Please? We could both use the extra money, and have some fun, too."

"Don't we go dancing most Saturday nights? Don't we go to the picture show on Sundays? Don't you enjoy a box of fried chicken, a bottle of wine, and me, down in the park by the river?"

"Oh, I do enjoy our time together, John. I do. It seems like every day spent with you is just as swell as the day before. Honest," she said, holding up her right hand as though pledging an oath.

"And my time spent with you is the best, too," he said. "We don't have to go to these extremes in order to spend time together, do we? And besides, you seemed really tired just roller skating. Do you really want to dance nonstop for days on end?"

"But this is different. We're used to dancing; we love it, right?" John nodded. "Sure, but—"

"But it's not about the quality of our time together. It's about the money."

"Well, if it's money you need," he said, going into his back pocket for his wallet.

"No, stop. That's very sweet of you, but I don't want *your* money. I want us to earn it, you see? Anyway, you have a lot of pep and," she said, pointing to his feet, "those *dogs* are the toughest around. I think we'd make a swell team."

"I heard those marathons are absolute madness," he groaned. "People have fainted on the spot and even dropped dead. And the promoters must have chosen Rensselaer because a marathon has never been staged here. I'll bet they hoped that most people in Rensselaer had not heard about the negative aspects of dance marathons."

"I know it's a virgin city, but that doesn't matter. We could win. I know we could," she persisted.

"It's suicide to stand on your feet for over seventy-two hours, like some of those dancers. Those contests are fads to test human endurance. Plus, I think they're rigged. I heard they have professional marathon dancers. They win and the organizers just rake in the spectator fees."

"Please?"

He frowned in thought. "It *is* an awful lot of money, though, and we both have so much energy. I suppose I could get Monday off from work." After a bit he smiled. "Okay, okay … I'm game if you are, but I'm only doing this for you. Remember what I said when you're thoroughly exhausted out on that dance floor. I'll do it, but I'm still apprehensive about this whole thing. If you want my opinion, I think these callus carnivals are thoroughly sleazy."

"Sleazy?" She lifted her chin in challenge. "The Veterans of Foreign Wars and the American Legion are sponsoring the event, so it must be somewhat respectable. Have you ever heard of Vernon and Irene Castle?"

John shook his head no.

"They are a respectable married team of professional social dancers. Very honorable people." Elsie gave John a big hug. "Anyway, you're the best!"

John smiled. "I know you're competitive and you *do* love a challenge. That should help us out. And I do like the Romanesque style of the Oddfellow Building, if that's any consolation."

Elsie gazed at him, the lure of financial relief filling her with promise. "It will. And loving the venue should help, too. Come with me," she said, pulling him by the hand. "Let's go to the Oddfellow Building right now and sign up."

"When is it?"

"It starts Friday, July thirteenth."

"That figures. They're trying to warn us ahead of time. Bad luck for all."

She playfully pushed at his shoulder. "Oh, John, it will be fun, you'll see."

* * *

The object of the dance marathon was to see which couple could outdance all the others by staying on their feet the longest. But Robert said the object was to see which couple could *outlive* all the others.

"You shouldn't be doing this, Elsie," Robert told her as they sat on his front porch swing. The night was hot and humid, without a breath of air stirring. "I don't want your parents to have to come and pick up your body. July is not exactly the coolest time of the year for nonstop dancing. People drop dead—"

"Oh, Robert, don't. Let's not argue, okay? I'm going to do this. And don't tell Mum and Dad. You know they think this kind of dancing is sinful; my family might disown me." She remembered her father saying that the dance marathons were the first and easiest steps towards hell. She shook her head in disbelief. "I should be going now. Do you have time to drive me home?"

"Sure, anything for you. But I'm still not happy about this."

Elsie reminded herself that she could still back out, but didn't mention it to Robert. She spent two fretful days at work, pondering the pros and cons of entering the contest. Eventually, the pros won out. The lure of all that money was too much for her. Despite their controversial status, she thought the events were sufficiently respectable and decided, after much thought and consideration, to take her chances and participate as planned. Her life would certainly change if she could get her hands on a thousand dollars. To her, it was a fortune.

On the first day of the contest, the second floor of the Oddfellow Building was packed wall-to-wall with contestants and spectators alike. Elsie had read that dance marathons offered an inexpensive chance for audiences to be entertained. They also offered viewing audiences the novelty of feeling superior, and feeling pity for someone else. It may be a form of dark entertainment, she thought, but it *was* a way to make fast money. Lots of it.

Elsie held John's hand as they waited on the dance floor. Her only friend in the bleachers was Robert, who sat with his girlfriend, Betty. Elsie found them in the crowd and waved.

Robert stood and ran down the bleacher seats and out onto the contest floor. "Look, you two," he said to John and Elsie. "I feel compelled to be here and to support you, but I still don't like it. Be careful, will you?" He studied John's face with solemn interest. "I promised Elsie's parents to watch out for her. Don't let me down, okay?"

"Don't worry. I'll be careful with my beautiful doll here." John gave Elsie's shoulder a quick squeeze and smiled down at her.

Robert searched both of their faces, first one and then the other. "If you get the least bit tired and want to quit, I'll consider you the smartest couple on this floor. I'm reluctant to watch this torture, but I've paid our fifty-cent admissions, so we'll watch the insanity for awhile. Only for you."

Elsie was always able to count on Robert's encouragement even if he disagreed with what she was about to do.

"No spectators allowed on the dance floor!" the emcee's voice boomed through a megaphone. "Please clear the floor of anyone not participating in the danceathon."

"That's my signal," Robert said. "Be good, and don't take any wooden nickels." He then turned and dashed back up the bleacher seats to Betty.

A VFW volunteer was meanwhile checking lists and pinning numbers to all the contestants' blouses or shirts. A number twenty-two was pinned to the back of Elsie's silk blouse and she was a bit concerned that the pin might damage the delicate material. However, she was reluctant to say a word to the promoters about it. Because she had entered a contest that measured one's ability to withstand abuse, she certainly was not going to complain about a little snag in her blouse. She gazed down at her new, navy blue two-inch heels—probably a dumb mistake, she thought, but she couldn't help it. The shoes matched her ensemble beautifully.

The marathon opened with great fanfare. A group of out-of-work vaudeville performers burst onto the stage, singing and dancing. Then, after a few brief words about dancing in America, an American Legion member fired an air pistol to launch the event.

Contestants were required to remain in motion for forty-five minutes each hour around the clock. Music was to be performed by a live band at night, with a phonograph used during the day, or when the live band took breaks. But the only break the dance couples were allowed was a fifteen-minute recess every hour.

During the second set, the marathon emcee posed a question to the audience: "Ladies and gentlemen, how long can they last?"

Elsie wiped the perspiration from her brow. "I wish he would stop saying that," she said to John. "It only drains my energy and makes me think about being tired." When he wasn't barking it out, Elsie noted, you could read the same question printed on white placards pasted on the walls surrounding the dance floor. You couldn't get away from the words, and she was sure they were meant to wear down the dancers, besides creating drama for the audience.

"Now I know what a monkey feels like in a zoo," John said. "This is only about putting on a show for paying spectators."

Elsie was aware that some of the contestants participated in the dance marathon hoping to win the cash that would provide food or a roof over their heads. In any event, all the contestants hung their hopes on the prize money promised at the end of the contest's final grind. These reminders heightened her resolve to be the best.

After awhile, she began to feel tired, but refused to complain. "John, please hold me tight." He tightened his grip. She perked up with his support and was able to move freely enough to glance around the hall. She had earlier noted that Robert and Betty had disappeared from the bleachers, but now they had returned and were sitting below on the sidelines, holding hands. She desperately wished she were enjoying the spectacle with them, instead of nursing several growing blisters. Next to them sat a couple of John's friends from work who waved and smiled.

After the first twenty-four hours, Elsie left her shoes off, as she couldn't get them back on. She limped over to a nurse who massaged her feet and checked her pulse. Then she walked back out to the dance area. She counted the minutes to the next break. When the air horn signaled another rest period, she rushed off the dance floor to a curtained area filled with cots, segregated by gender. Elsie dropped instantly into a deep sleep as soon as her body touched the cot.

"Elsie," John said, tugging at her hand. "The air horn sounded already. It's time to get back. It's been fifteen minutes. Are you sure you want to continue?"

"Uh-huh." She stood from the cot, and leaning into John, slowly filed back onto the dance floor with him to begin another forty-five minutes.

It seemed to John that 'dancing' was often loosely interpreted. Most of the female partners shuffled along, while her male counterpart shaved by looking into a mirror that hung from her neck. Other contestants wrote letters on a special folding desk hung around their own necks. Still others read the newspaper, or knitted, or even slept as one partner supported the other's weight. The carrier in such a couple often tied the lagging partner's neck to themselves for additional security. Many women carried their sleeping male partners, despite the disparity of height and weight. Nothing escaped John's notice.

Elsie called him her dreamboat. He thought that just maybe he was the best boyfriend in the entire world. Who else would put up with this torture? Every part of him hurt. He did have a job, and he should be back to it by Monday, he thought.

A sign above the dancers ticked off the hours and ticked down the number of remaining contestants. The local press kept a death watch as contestants dropped out. By the third day, there were only nine couples left standing, and Elsie didn't know whether she could continue. The rules during this portion of the marathon were that feet must keep moving up and down and the contestants' knees must never touch the floor. To encourage lagging couples to continue moving, the floor judge used a ruler to flick the legs of contestants who were not shuffling sufficiently.

"Stumbling, staggering … on they go! Who will be the next dancer carried off the floor?" the emcee shouted into the microphone.

Elsie's feet were swollen, and it was becoming painful to move them. Plus she couldn't keep her eyes open.

At the end of one of the rest periods John couldn't get Elsie to open her eyes, so he was obligated to ask an attendant to wake her with smelling salts. Sometimes it seemed she was dreaming or living some sort of nightmare, as he heard her babbling nonsense and crying out while they were shuffling around the dance floor.

"Mum? Mum, are you there? I hear you; I hear you. I can't find you."

She began crying hysterically and when she doubled over in pain, John knew this was the end. He took her by the shoulders and shook her. "Oh, my God, E-Elsie!"

She stumbled and collapsed to the floor. John frankly had quite enough of this. He lifted her to a standing position. "That's it. It's time to quit."

She shot him a disbelieving glance. "Uh-h …" She grabbed her stomach and looked at him in agony. When she tried to shuffle her feet she bent over again, thinking she was going to vomit.

"Let's get out of here." He nodded to one of the promoters, signaling for assistance. The two men helped Elsie off the dance floor, and John whispered in her ear, "Geez Louise, I'm sorry, but this agony is not worth any amount of money."

John turned in their numbers, and the two stumbled out to his car. Robert was long gone, and none of John's friends were there to render aid. They had long since left the spectacle. He gently laid Elsie down in the back seat and drove her to the boarding house, already grateful for the soft bed that awaited him at home.

* * *

Elsie woke, not knowing what day or night it was. How long had she slept? *Oh, yes.* One night she had soaked her feet while sitting on the edge of the tub, but had gone directly back to bed. *What a shame we had to give up the contest.* Although crestfallen, the disappointment was quickly overshadowed with a wave of anxiety. *Where is John? Is he all right?*

She turned to her new bedside radio and every song was either a syrupy romantic ballad or a "he's-done-you-wrong one." Just as she was thinking that in this case it would be all right for a girl to telephone a boy, a knock echoed from the other side of her bedroom door.

"Yes, who is it?" she called, turning off the radio. As she slipped on a robe over her nightdress, she put on her slippers and noticed her feet were back to normal. She gave a sigh of relief and opened the door a fraction. "Yes, who is it?"

It was Mrs. Waters, the owner of the boarding house. "There is a gentleman on the telephone who wants to speak with you."

"Thanks, Mrs. Waters," she said, opening the door all the way and breezing past her.

Mrs. Waters followed Elsie down the hall. "We've been worried about you, you know."

Elsie smiled back over her shoulder. "I'm sorry, but I'm all right now." Then down the stairs she sailed and picked up the receiver. She placed a hand over it, watching Mrs. Waters descend the stairs, who thankfully retired discreetly into the kitchen.

"Hello," Elsie said musically into the receiver.

"Hello, Elsie. Jeez, I've missed you," John whispered. "How are you? It's not too late to call is it?"

"No, no. I was up and listening to the radio. I'm fine. How are you?"

"I'm fine. I've recovered. Have you?"

"Yes, thanks. I slept off the worst of it, I think. What night is this?"

"Wednesday. It's been three days. I've been worried about you. I stopped by yesterday but Mrs. Waters couldn't wake you. She was about to send for a doctor."

"I'm sorry. I think I remember soaking my feet at some point, but I don't remember anything else. I barely remember sleeping. But when I woke I was worried if you were all right, too."

"Did you hear about the fellow who dropped dead at the marathon?"

"No! What happened?"

"He collapsed on the dance floor and died from heart failure."

"That's awful."

"He was the same age as me. Twenty-four. He was number eight. Do you remember him?"

"No. I don't remember much. I'm so sorry I made you go through all that. I should have never mentioned that stupid contest. It could have killed us both."

"Oh, I would have stopped us short of that."

"I think you may have done just that."

"Well, it's over now. I'm just relieved we're both okay. Listen," he said with renewed enthusiasm. "I have to work this weekend but I've taken Monday off and I was wondering if you'd like to go for a swim. Remember, I was telling you how great it is at Ideal Beach?"

"Oh, sure, that will be fun. I heard on the radio that the weather is supposed to be really hot for the next five days. As luck would have it, I'm not working Monday, so that works out swell."

"Pick you up at ten sharp, then?"

"Super. I'll pack us some sandwiches. See you Monday morning. Good night," she said, dreamily. She could hardly wait to be with him again. She wondered what he would look like in nothing but swimming trunks.

"Good night," he said, and gently put down the receiver.

Chapter Seven

John waited for Elsie to secure the beach bag in the rumble seat of the freshly washed coupe, then helped her into the front seat. He couldn't have been luckier with his day off from work; a scintillating woman next to him, and a warm sunny day ahead at Ideal Beach on the shores of Lake Shafer. "Boy, you sure had me worried when Mrs. Waters couldn't rouse you," he said. "I'm so glad you're feeling better."

"You're so sweet to worry about me, but I think I was more worried about you."

"How would you know if you worried more than me?"

"Maybe we should have a worry meter. Let's say on a scale of one to ten, my worry for you was at ten."

"I'll tell you what I'm worried about: superstition. I was never superstitious before. They weren't kidding by starting that thing on Friday the thirteenth."

"Oh, I was always superstitious. Now you know why."

John laughed. "I didn't want to say I told you so. But—"

"But you told me so."

"There, you said it." He gave her a light peck on the cheek. "It's all forgotten."

"Well, no permanent damage done, I hope." She raised her eyebrows at him.

"I think I'll be permanently superstitious."

Elsie laughed. "I won't ever make you dance again, if you don't want to."

They were driving past cornfield after cornfield; slightly rolling hills of green, the long, shiny leaves now more than knee-high in mid July, fluttering in the breeze as they passed by, punctuated only by an occasional farmhouse.

After riding an hour in the hot car John announced that they needed a filling station, so they found one in a small community next to the Grange No. 42 building, and pulled in.

"Look, John. They have everything here; groceries, a post office, gas, auto repairs, and see that sign?" Elsie said, pointing. In the window hung a separate sign in bright blue that read: *Poker Here, Every Wednesday Night.* "This place is a poker parlor!" she exclaimed.

"We're a little early for poker. But how convenient for people; they can fill up their gas tanks and empty their wallets all in one place." John laughed, opening Elsie's door. "But for now, we can sure get something cool to drink."

"That *is* a relief. My mouth is so dry."

John saw that the service attendant had come out to assist them, so he made a gesture toward the gas pump. "I'll take a dollar's worth."

"One dollar petrol coming up," the attendant said. "You can pay inside."

Behind the grocery counter, a middle-aged man with a baseball cap held open a newspaper. The headline read: *Slaying of John Dillinger Spurs Hunt for His Pals.*

"They killed Dillinger?" John asked in surprise. Outside, the attendant had lifted the coupe's hood and was checking the oil.

The man lowered his newspaper. "Sure did. He pulled out a gun and the FBI opened fire. The fatal shot passed through the back of his neck and exited just under his right eye."

"Where did they find him?" Elsie asked.

"Chicago's north side. He was coming out of a movie with some broad who ratted him out. She tipped off an agent. She wore a red dress to alert the FBI that the man she was with was Dillinger."

Elsie let out a low whistle. "I wonder what made her squeal?"

John laughed at her mock drama.

"Says here she wanted to collect the reward money and avoid deportation back to Romania."

"That would do it," John laughed. "Just curious, what movie did he see?"

The man scanned the paper, tracing the page with his finger. "*Manhattan Melodrama.*"

"I think I'll skip that one."

"Oh, John, I wanted to see that movie. Clark Gable is in it."

"Okay, fine. But don't wear a red dress. I'll get suspicious."

"You two gonna rob me?" the clerk asked with eyebrows raised.

"He's kidding. Relax." Elsie regarded John seriously. "John, let's pay for the gasoline, and would you like a Coca-Cola? I would."

"Make that two." John smiled at the clerk.

"That will be one dollar and ten cents," the man said.

John pulled out his wallet and gave the man a dollar bill, a dime, and a nickel. "Keep the change."

Back outside, the attendant had just finished washing the coup's windshield, so they hopped in and were off on the road again.

After another hour, they drove into the town of Lake Schafer. "I think the lake is this way," John said.

Two intersections later they saw the lake spreading out before them. John turned a corner and Elsie spotted a prime parking space directly in front of a small refreshment stand at the edge of the road. He pulled into it and shut off the engine, waiting a moment to stare at the lake before getting out of the car. He reached for Elsie's hand and she gave him a brilliant smile.

"Oh, John, you were right. This place is absolutely gorgeous." It was a beautiful Indiana day, the water glistening before them. Verdant hills gently rose up from the shore of the lake, with maple trees spreading out over their terraces.

Even at this early hour, John could hear sounds of the evening's orchestra rehearsing in the popular ballroom on the other side of the lake. For now, the summer day was in full swing; women strolled by in shorts, bathing suit robes, hats, and sunglasses. Towering over the lake stood a pair of toboggan slides that dropped guests nearly thirty feet, adding to the excitement of Ideal Beach. "It's nice here. Ready?"

Elsie nodded. "Sure. This place is swell."

"Let's get out," John said, hoping she wasn't apprehensive about lake swimming. He went around the Ford to help Elsie out of the passenger side and sweetly smiled at her. She collected her beach bag, they strolled past a few parked cars where the dock met the road, and continued on down to the end of it. There they found a set of wooden steps that led down to a smooth, white patch of sand. Elsie dropped her beach bag and shook out her towel, carefully digging the corners into the sand to hold it down against sudden breezes.

"Why don't we take a walk along the water?" John suggested. As he moved to give her a hand up from the sand his t-shirt lifted, showing a brief slice of rippled muscles.

"I'm going to take off my shoes. Aren't you?" Elsie picked up her beach bag and they walked together along the lake's edge. She tried to look at the water, but she couldn't keep her eyes off the man strolling next to her. He was handsome in the most classic sense; his face angular and chiseled with the kind of carefree smile that would stop any girl dead in her tracks. The sand was cool beneath her feet and she stopped to trace the name 'John' in the sand with her big toe.

"You have beautiful feet," he remarked. "That's unusual."

She stopped, wiggled them, and giggled. "Thank you. I'm flattered you noticed. Do you really think they're unusual?"

"Of course," he said, grabbing her around the waist, tossing her up, and then catching her again. "Women are the world's only hope for showing everyone how beautiful feet can be."

She laughed. "Hey, let me go." The lighthearted move startled her, but it secretly delighted her, too.

He swung her around and then gently put her down. "I can't help it if I love touching you. Anyway, your feet *are* beautiful. Hasn't anyone ever told you that before?"

"No. Oh, John, you make a girl blush," she said, hiding her smile in a pretend search through her bag. "I don't blame you," she said, finally. "I've never felt like this before."

"I can hardly work. You're always on my mind," he said, ca[ught] her gaze for one solid beat. He hadn't meant to say such [...] but he couldn't help it. He changed the subject by pointing [...] the water. "Those toboggan slides are something crazy. I [...] them, but there's nothing like seeing them in person. Le[t's...] and change into our swimming suits. Looks like we're [...] wet real soon and I can hardly wait." He winked. [...] enjoyed his company as much as he enjoyed hers. [...] something.

She threw back her head and laughed. "I love [...] be so much fun. I've never been on a water slide [...] up at the toboggan slides; the drop looked as en[d...] found freedom. "Those slides are big ... and scary."

"The ride must be pretty fast, judging by all those peop[le] screaming on the way down."

"Will you be screaming, too?" she teased. With that, she hiked her beach bag higher onto her shoulder and disappeared inside the ladies' bathhouse.

John went into the men's bathhouse, wondering what Elsie would look like in a bathing suit.

Minutes later, she emerged in a tightly knitted suit with black and white stripes around the bodice. She felt confident about how she looked in it and loved the way the shoulder straps could be lowered for tanning. Her white beach robe hung open over her suit, letting the ties dangle.

The water shimmered like slivers of shattered glass flowing to shore, gathering in circles around the dock pilings. She leaned against one of the pier columns near her towel on the sand, waiting for John, excited to be in this new relationship.

He finally came out of the men's bathhouse and caught up to her at the water's edge. "Sorry, I took so long. I had to rent this suit from the attendant inside. It was always too cold in Buffalo to bother with swim wear. He threw in this towel, too." John's eyed her suit with obvious pleasure in his manly gaze; he took her hands in his and stepped back from her at arms' length. "Wow! Look at you. I hear the cats calling all over the state of Indiana. Meow."

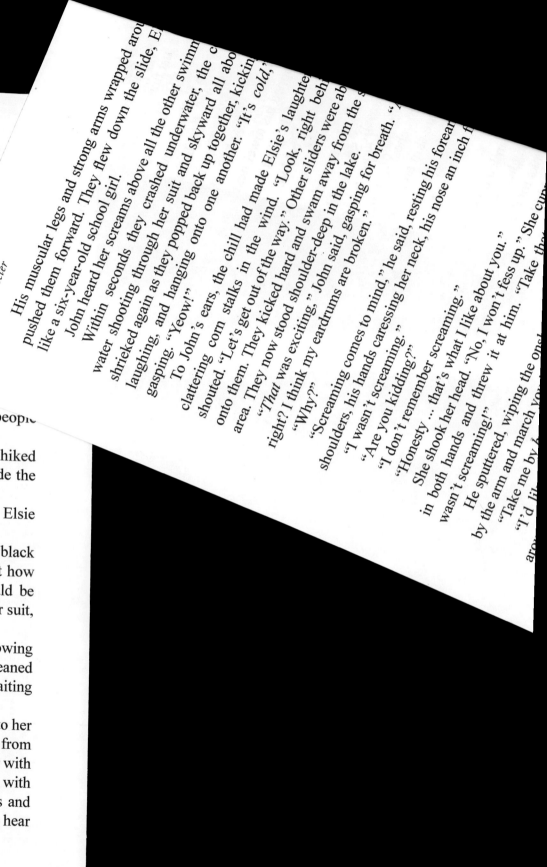

His muscular legs and strong arms wrapped arou[nd...] pushed them forward. They flew down the slide, E[lsie...] like a six-year-old school girl.

John heard her screams above all the other swimm[ers...]

Within seconds they crashed underwater, the c[...] water shooting through her suit and skyward all abo[ve...] shrieked again as they popped back up together, kickin[g...] laughing, and hanging onto one another. "It's cold," gasping. "Yeow!"

To John's ears, the chill in the wind. "Look, right beh[ind...] clattering corn stalks in the wind. "Look, right beh[ind...] shouted. "Let's get out of the way." Other sliders were ab[out...] onto them. They kicked hard and swam away from the s[...] area. They now stood shoulder-deep in the lake.

"That was exciting," John said, gasping for breath. "A[m I] right? I think my eardrums are broken."

"Why?"

"Screaming comes to mind," he said, resting his forear[m...] shoulders, his hands caressing her neck, his nose an inch f[rom...]

"I wasn't screaming."

"Are you kidding?"

"I don't remember screaming."

"Honesty ... that's what I like about you."

She shook her head. "No, I won't fess up." She cu[...] in both hands and threw it at him. "Take th[...]

He sputtered, wiping the ons[...] by the arm and march yo[...] "Take me by [...]

"I'd li[...]

thirty feet, adding to the excitement of Ideal Beach. "It's nice here. Ready?"

Elsie nodded. "Sure. This place is swell."

"Let's get out," John said, hoping she wasn't apprehensive about lake swimming. He went around the Ford to help Elsie out of the passenger side and sweetly smiled at her. She collected her beach bag, they strolled past a few parked cars where the dock met the road, and continued on down to the end of it. There they found a set of wooden steps that led down to a smooth, white patch of sand. Elsie dropped her beach bag and shook out her towel, carefully digging the corners into the sand to hold it down against sudden breezes.

"Why don't we take a walk along the water?" John suggested. As he moved to give her a hand up from the sand his t-shirt lifted, showing a brief slice of rippled muscles.

"I'm going to take off my shoes. Aren't you?" Elsie picked up her beach bag and they walked together along the lake's edge. She tried to look at the water, but she couldn't keep her eyes off the man strolling next to her. He was handsome in the most classic sense; his face angular and chiseled with the kind of carefree smile that would stop any girl dead in her tracks. The sand was cool beneath her feet and she stopped to trace the name 'John' in the sand with her big toe.

"You have beautiful feet," he remarked. "That's unusual."

She stopped, wiggled them, and giggled. "Thank you. I'm flattered you noticed. Do you really think they're unusual?"

"Of course," he said, grabbing her around the waist, tossing her up, and then catching her again. "Women are the world's only hope for showing everyone how beautiful feet can be."

She laughed. "Hey, let me go." The lighthearted move startled her, but it secretly delighted her, too.

He swung her around and then gently put her down. "I can't help it if I love touching you. Anyway, your feet *are* beautiful. Hasn't anyone ever told you that before?"

"No. Oh, John, you make a girl blush," she said, hiding her smile in a pretend search through her bag. "I don't blame you," she said, finally. "I've never felt like this before."

"I can hardly work. You're always on my mind," he said, catching her gaze for one solid beat. He hadn't meant to say such things, but he couldn't help it. He changed the subject by pointing out into the water. "Those toboggan slides are something crazy. I read about them, but there's nothing like seeing them in person. Let's go back and change into our swimming suits. Looks like we're going to get wet real soon and I can hardly wait." He winked. He hoped she enjoyed his company as much as he enjoyed hers. She was really something.

She threw back her head and laughed. "I love this! It's going to be so much fun. I've never been on a water slide before." She gazed up at the toboggan slides; the drop looked as endless as her newly found freedom. "Those slides are big ... and scary."

"The ride must be pretty fast, judging by all those people screaming on the way down."

"Will you be screaming, too?" she teased. With that, she hiked her beach bag higher onto her shoulder and disappeared inside the ladies' bathhouse.

John went into the men's bathhouse, wondering what Elsie would look like in a bathing suit.

Minutes later, she emerged in a tightly knitted suit with black and white stripes around the bodice. She felt confident about how she looked in it and loved the way the shoulder straps could be lowered for tanning. Her white beach robe hung open over her suit, letting the ties dangle.

The water shimmered like slivers of shattered glass flowing to shore, gathering in circles around the dock pilings. She leaned against one of the pier columns near her towel on the sand, waiting for John, excited to be in this new relationship.

He finally came out of the men's bathhouse and caught up to her at the water's edge. "Sorry, I took so long. I had to rent this suit from the attendant inside. It was always too cold in Buffalo to bother with swim wear. He threw in this towel, too." John's eyed her suit with obvious pleasure in his manly gaze; he took her hands in his and stepped back from her at arms' length. "Wow! Look at you. I hear the cats calling all over the state of Indiana. Meow."

She smiled coyly and pulled her beach robe closed. "Well, I could say the same thing to you. That may be a rental suit you have on, but it looks just fine on you." She gave him a kiss on the cheek.

This was pure Elsie, he thought. Bold and forthright. He loved it. No other woman he knew would say such a thing. "Then we must be perfect together," he said, letting her smile wash over him like the warm summer sunlight. The views were stupendous in this place, especially the one named Elsie Wilkins.

John dropped his towel next to hers and took her hand, leading her toward one of the giant water slides. He went first up the stairs, Elsie following close behind.

She could smell his scent as they climbed up. She identified it as sandalwood, she remembered, and she wondered where he had put it on himself. She would like to have done that for him, lightly touching his skin with it; a finger to the top of the bottle and then touching his chest with the perfumed liquid, smelling him, taking him in; bare skin and sandalwood. She thought of her bare breasts pressing against his scented chest.

He turned around and smiled at her, pleasantly interrupting her reverie.

She smiled back. "You're not chickening out, are you?"

He laughed. "Not on your life. Not me. Just don't look down!"

"Thanks for the warning. I'm right behind you all the way." She thought she'd like to stand behind him as his partner all the way through life. Silly girl, she thought....

He liked hearing those words, *'I'm right behind you.'* Elsie was different and this was one thing that he appreciated about her: she could maintain her unique identity and still encourage and support him, all at once.

When they reached the top, there was a small platform. John helped her to sit in front of him at the top of the slide, and pulled her close. They sat for a moment skin-to-skin, taking in the panoramic view, and the sensuous electricity between them.

"Ready?" he asked.

"As ready as ever," Elsie replied.

His muscular legs and strong arms wrapped around her and he pushed them forward. They flew down the slide, Elsie screaming like a six-year-old school girl.

John heard her screams above all the other swimmers.

Within seconds they crashed underwater, the cold shock of water shooting through her suit and skyward all about them. She shrieked again as they popped back up together, kicking, sputtering, laughing, and hanging onto one another. "It's *cold*," she yelled, gasping. "Yeow!"

To John's ears, the chill had made Elsie's laughter sound like clattering corn stalks in the wind. "Look, right behind us!" he shouted. "Let's get out of the way." Other sliders were about to crash onto them. They kicked hard and swam away from the splashdown area. They now stood shoulder-deep in the lake.

"*That* was exciting," John said, gasping for breath. "Are you all right? I think my eardrums are broken."

"Why?"

"Screaming comes to mind," he said, resting his forearms on her shoulders, his hands caressing her neck, his nose an inch from hers.

"I wasn't screaming."

"Are you kidding?"

"I don't remember screaming."

"Honesty ... that's what I like about you."

She shook her head. "No, I won't fess up." She cupped the water in both hands and threw it at him. "Take that, Mr. McDonald. I wasn't screaming!"

He sputtered, wiping the onslaught from his face. "I'll take you by the arm and march you into the principal's office."

"Take me by *both* arms?"

"I'd like nothing better, Miss Wilkins." He circled his arms around her, their lips met, legs and chests touching, water and skin and everything in between.

Elsie melted into him and was lost in his meaty tenderness; his mouth and fingertips roaming over her wet lips and face. She was sliding into a stupor, another world in his embrace. She was going to fall down right here at his feet and drown, she thought, if she didn't take control of herself. She reluctantly escaped his mouth and laid her head against his shoulder, her scattered wet hair matted around her flushed face. "Br-r-r, this water is cold. I thought I'd get used to it, but it seems like it's getting colder by the minute. It takes my breath away." She turned her face up and looked at him, her eyes searching his. But she was stumbling with the movement of the water, trying to stand on the sandy lake bottom, even though his arms were securely wrapped around her.

A dreamy look entered his eyes. "You take my breath away," he said softly. "You're beautiful." He held her up, making her stand before him, and took stock of her lovely features.

"Oh, now you're teasing me," Elsie said self-consciously. "I must look a sight with my hair sticking out every which way. I forgot my bathing cap." She lay back on the water to float briefly and wet her hair anew.

"You don't need one," he said, watching her float. "You're the bee's knees all wet." Her wet hair had turned a dark, honey color, and he saw the smooth shape of firm breasts, her nipples cresting with the cold. Slightly embarrassed, he looked away when she stood again, struggling to get the words out. "I have a great idea!" He circled her waist with his hands and lifted her up.

"Put me down—"she coughed, trying to suppress a laugh.

"Okay," he said, tossing her a few feet away.

When she surfaced, sputtering and laughing, she saw that John was admiring her predicament. "I'm going to get you for that," she said breathlessly, swimming in his direction. She jumped out of the water and onto his hips, trying to dunk his head one-handed.

He didn't budge—only laughed. "You're going to have to do better than that, little girl." She clung to him and he took power strides through the water, leaning this way and that, trying to throw her off. He loved teasing her.

She rode his back, hanging onto his neck like a rider without a saddle on a galloping horse. His scent, even after being in the water, permeated the air. She wanted more of it. But with a sigh, she released him and splashed back down, saying, "I give up. You're undunkable."

She dipped under the water and rose again, letting the cool, streaming rivulets flow from her face and play through her fingers.

"I'm having a great time. This lake is beautiful. Now I know why they call it Ideal Beach." She leaned into him, and despite the chilled water, felt the heat between them, felt his body, felt his arms lightly around her waist as she imagined more kisses, more of the taste of him.

"I knew you would like it here. Sometime we'll come back and have dinner at the ballroom, take in a bit of dancing?"

"Dancing?" Her eyebrows furrowed in stern gravity. "I'm not sure if my feet will join us."

John laughed. "We'll hold up on the dancing. I never met a gal like you who can be mature and still have a good sense of humor," he whispered. He wanted to nurture the relationship and get to know this girl.

She smiled at the compliment. "Thanks. It's funny. I feel like I've known you longer than two months." She knew, even as she watched him treading water, that soon they would be spending more time together, with more and more intimate, skin-to-skin moments, more kissing, more—she had to stop herself. What would she do when the time came to slide in between the sheets with him? She wanted to. But nice girls didn't allow themselves to go that far. Yet, she considered herself a liberated woman. Could she follow through? With a hand signal to point direction, she swam away from him with even strokes and a racing heart.

John waited a moment then swam to join her. They played in the water for nearly an hour, splashing about, then he started for the shore and she followed. The water was alluring, almost as much as the company. As he emerged from the lake he felt strong twinges of desire, and looking down at his swim trunks, realized the condition he was in. He wanted her and it was obvious. He shook the water from his head as they walked briskly toward their towels on the sand. Sitting down, he felt a little less self-conscious.

His hair was damp and tangled around his face, but to Elsie he was still gorgeous.

She stood in front of him shivering and laughing, and though she put her hand to her mouth, she couldn't stop the nervous laughter. Picking up her beach robe, she dragged it tightly across her shoulders. After a few moments she warmed up and sat down beside him.

Elsie turned to lie on her stomach to catch the afternoon rays of sunshine on her back. She rested her head on her hands facing John, took a deep relaxing breath, and smiled at him.

"The blue is gone. Your lips are pinkish again," he said simply, stretching out his long legs, leaning back on his elbows to watch. "Do you like the water? It seems to agree with you," he said with his usual skewed smile.

She wondered if he meant, '*Do you like being in the water with me?*' but said nothing about that. Instead, she slung her wet hair back over her shoulders and replied, "I love the water! I'm having a wonderful time."

"I love the water too, but as a kid I was scared of it. While swimming in the Mystic River with some friends, I almost drowned."

"What happened?"

"I dove under water and my eyes began to sting from the slime and dirt. I panicked a little and began swallowing water and choking. It was hard to breathe. One of my friends noticed my trepidation and irregular breathing, so he came over to help."

"That's a good friend."

John laughed. "He's the same friend who told me that spirits of dead Indians controlled the river. He said if the Indians were angry they would abruptly change the direction of the water and those caught in the conflicting flows would be lucky to make it out alive. I believed him. I was a gullible kid. Listen, enough about me. I want to get to know you better," he said, offering his hand to her.

She grasped it with a timid smile.

"Really, I want to know you," he persisted. "Tell me more about your family."

"Well, let's see," she started hesitantly. "I told you about my two younger sisters, Lena and Evelyn. Mum is really good at domestics. My dad—" She propped herself up on her elbows, resting her cheek in her hand. "He was killed, stomped by a horse before I was born. Mum said he worked well with horses, but on that day he was taken by surprise."

"I'm sorry to hear that. It must have been terrible for your mother."

"Yes, it was awful. She told me when I was old enough to understand that it was devastating for her." She turned over on her back and toyed with the edge of her towel. "I haven't told many people about it—I didn't mean to tell you," she said haltingly. "I've already told you so many terrible things that have happened."

"I'm glad you're opening up and being honest," he said emphatically. He took a deep breath before changing the subject. "Do you miss Akron?"

"I don't miss the city smell. Maybe I miss Mum and Dad and my sisters a little." She had to squint against the sun to see him. "But I still like Indiana much better. The people here are *very* friendly." She gave him a coy look, fluttering her eyelashes to make him laugh. "The boarding house is working out well, since it's close to both the restaurant and the school. I like the fact that it's such a short walk to work. I don't have to disturb Robert for a ride. I can just rely on myself. It's also not as dreary as it is in Ohio. Maybe it's just my perception, but everything seems brighter and more alive." She lay back listening to the buzz and hum of insects, and the laughter of children. "It's soothing to hear the sounds of nature around you. So peaceful," she mused. "Moments like this are meant to be savored."

She found it easy to talk to John, to confide in him. She now realized it was because he was so compassionate. She continued with a half-smile, returning to the subject of her father. "My step-father ... I'm very fond of him. He's just like a real father. Anyway, he's the only father I've ever known."

"You only need to know one," John said, running a finger over the curve of her shoulder. "Looks like you might be getting a burn."

"What should I do? What do you recommend?" she said, leaning toward him. "Am I getting too red?"

"Not for me," he said, putting his arm around her shoulder. "You have a healthy glow and you look radiant."

"You make me feel beautiful."

"You *are* beautiful."

An array of people surrounded them at the beach: young gals in airy summer dresses, women in fashionable swimwear, shirtless men, and children playing in the water. Elsie noticed people nearby occasionally glancing over at them. Maybe because they made such a fine looking pair, she thought. They sat there for an hour on the sand, chatting about Rensselaer, their upbringings, and politics.

When Elsie's hair dried it glistened in the sunlight, and he passionately wanted to kiss her perfectly shaped lips. It was still apparent that he wanted to make love to her and, he feared to everyone else as well. The more he tried not to think of it, the more intense was his desire. Maybe they could spend time alone again. Another idea came to mind. "I know," he said, snapping his fingers. "Why don't we go to the Chicago's World Fair next month? It's supposed to be really spectacular this year. Everyone is talking about it."

"The Chicago's World's Fair," she said, tilting her head to one side as she considered it. "I thought it ended already."

"No, they've extended it."

"Well, sure, I'd love to, but Chicago is quite a distance. It's much too far to drive, isn't it?"

"It's time for a geography lesson. Ideal Beach is farther from Rensselaer than Chicago is, but we could go by train. It'll be enjoyable," he said, his tone wistful. "We would have to spend the night, though. The fair is definitely a two-day trip," he said cautiously.

She looked at him with surprise, flushed with embarrassment. "Oh, I see. Well, I'm not sure—" she stammered, flooded with euphoria and trepidation, all at once. Had he been courting her in earnest, she questioned? He'd been gentlemanly enough, but if he wanted her for sex and nothing more, she wasn't interested. She sat there awhile, looking out at the glittering water. "I'll think about it." Her heart quickened a little at the thought of spending a night with him, the two of them all alone, but she told herself that was nothing but a gut reaction. She looked up and met his calm, questioning glance. He wouldn't possibly assume, would he, that they'd share a hotel bed just because they had shared a night of hot smooches and light petting on his sofa?

"Fair enough." He opened his arms. She leaned into his embrace and laid her head against his chest. "I don't want you to do anything that makes you feel uncomfortable," he said.

He looked and felt so appealing that it made her smile to herself. He made her feel so wonderful. His brown, tousled hair was damp, but that only made him more appealing.

"I wouldn't mind living by the water," he said. "Life would never be dull; it would be Ideal Beach. The air is refreshingly clean, the views breathtaking. And don't forget those slides. How about you?"

She raised her head, watching his expression contentedly. "I agree. It smells so fresh here. You don't know how wonderful it is not to smell rubber when you walk out the door."

He laughed. She looked lovely in her black and white swim suit. But he was sure that she'd look lovely wearing nothing at all. He suddenly stood, quickly wrapping his lower half with a towel in order to hide the evidence of his arousal. "I'm thirsty. Let's get something from the refreshment stand. I've got some change," he said, flipping two quarters in the air. "Decide what you want. The sky's the limit. Something to eat?"

"We can eat the ham sandwiches I brought, but I'd love a root beer float if they have those." She shrugged. "If not, any ice-cream soda will do." She jumped up, spring-kneed, driven by nerves. "I'll go with you."

She stole a glance at him as they walked toward the snack stand. She drew a sharp breath. He had a towel around himself. Here was a man so crazy about her that he couldn't control himself in public. That was something. The problem was that her Ohio circumstances with James and her parents had split her life down the middle. It was almost as though one half of her life was dark and dreary, and the other half bright and sunny. And morally wrong. But it was difficult to focus on morals when she'd enjoyed herself so thoroughly with John—far more than she ever had with James. She remembered that she had come to Indiana for a job, but was deciding that perhaps she'd found the love of her life instead. Could she really do this? Going away with John to the fair went against the grain of everything, every moral and every principle she had. Besides, she was still technically married. Was it right or wrong to look back on her marriage and allow what had happened with James to color her relationship with John? *And if it is wrong, how do I stop it,* she labored. A dark cloud hovered over her thoughts. Why did she even consider her husband in all this? He had left her years ago. She shrugged it off. She was so enjoying the day, and honestly couldn't remember the last time she'd been this happy. Finally, she gave up to the excitement of it all, and secretly decided then and there to go to the fair. She happily curled herself around John's arm as he ordered two root beer floats.

John smiled at her when she took her first sip.

"Could you hold this?" she said, handing the root beer back to him.

He managed to hold both floats with one hand. "Thanks. I'm really thirsty," he said, squinting at her.

"Hey, silly. You have to give mine back, you know." She gave him a warning look and went over to the other side of the stand to get napkins. "Do you like it?" she asked, returning to his side, watching him scoop up the vanilla ice cream with a spoon.

"It's the best root beer float I've ever had." He curled his mouth sideways in a half-smile. "Here you go," he said, handing back her float. "Do you want to try your luck on the slide again?"

She shook her head. "I'm a little busy here," she said, hoisting her float to emphasize her task at hand. "Anyway, it's getting late. Shouldn't we be heading back?" She glanced at John, regretting her words. She was having the time of her life. Why would she suggest leaving, she wondered?

"You're right. We'll finish our sodas, eat those sandwiches, and then get going," John said with a hint of disappointment in his voice. "It is a long drive."

After they ate and gathered their belongings, Elsie wanted to put on bright red lipstick, comb her hair, and fix herself up. "I'll be right back," she said, heading for the bathhouse. "I'll meet you at the car."

A few minutes later she had finished and was eager to get back to John.

He saw that her hair fell in cascades from a pretty white headband. She didn't look in disarray any longer; she looked lovely. He leaned out the driver's window and squinted to block out the sunshine. He let out a loud wolf whistle.

She laughed, feeling slightly embarrassed. How could it be, she wondered, that she held her future in her hands, with so many opportunities awaiting her, and saw only him? How could meeting him cause her to look deeper into her own destiny?

John backed out of the parking space and headed north on Spackman Road. He drove carefully through Lake Shafer's town center. Pedestrians walked in twos and threes along the side of the road, dressed in gay outfits as they headed for the Ideal Beach Ballroom for an evening of dinner, music, and dancing.

Elsie had more fun today than she'd ever had with James, even on their honeymoon. But she didn't want to compare them. It was too easy to do, and potentially dangerous. She wasn't in the right frame of mind to be fair, and anyway, next to James, John was a dreamboat.

It was a serene and mild twilight, the long summer day vanishing away when the Ford pulled up in front of the boarding house on West Susan Street. Clouds were slowly rolling in across the early evening sky.

John walked her to the door and placed his hand against her cheek. "You have some color."

"I know. I feel a little warm."

"I know what you mean," he said, a chuckle in his voice. "I've felt hot all day." He leaned forward and kissed her.

She felt her body warm to his touch, to his lips, warm and soft against hers. Oh, how she would love to spend the last few hours of the evening lying next to him, even if it were only snuggling in quiet contentment. But for now, she was happy feeling joyfully overwhelmed, just for a moment, by the feel of him against her. It was far beyond physical, though the attraction was a part of it. It was spiritual, not shallow in any way. As she unlocked the door she turned back to him, reached for his hand, and then softly said, "Thank you. I had a wonderful time."

He gazed at her, grinning, and she knew this was right. When he looked at her she felt good: a little breathless and almost dizzy.

He slowly released his hand from hers and whispered into her ear, "I'll see you soon. Love you." As he left her, he turned one last time and smiled, then climbed into his car, started it, and drove off into the night.

'Love you,' he had said!

Chapter Eight

John excitedly paid the fifty cents for himself and Elsie to gain access to the Chicago World's Fair—A Century of Progress Exposition—by way of the festive Twelfth Street entrance. The fellow manning the ticket booth was well-groomed, wearing a suit, tie, and a huge smile. "Good morning," he said. "I know you'll enjoy yourselves today. We have exhibits to appeal to everyone, from all walks of life."

The people in back of John and Elsie waiting to reach the ticket booth shuffled slowly behind them in long cues. Two long rows of American flags waved above them along the entrance walk.

Since the man seemed forthcoming with information, John decided to ask, "By the way, do you have a record of how many people have come through here already? The crowd is enormous."

"We won't have that record until the fair closes today, but when it opened on May twenty-sixth, we had two thousand nine hundred seventy-seven people come through here in the first hour."

John and Elsie looked at one another in astonishment.

The man who took John's entrance fee handed programs and maps to them both.

"Elsie," John said, moving through the turnstile behind her, "this is going to be an historic event. It's the first world's fair that celebrates color and lighting of grounds and buildings."

"This is perfect for an architect, then." Elsie smiled and opened up her map. "Look. Some of the fair has been built out over Lake

Michigan, with a walkway set up on what was the beach along Michigan Avenue. We're going to have a grand time. I'm so glad we came up here."

John's new Brownie camera hung around his neck and he toyed with it while Elsie browsed a kiosk, just inside the gate. "Let me get a shot of you," he called to her.

Elsie held up a tote that she had just purchased, and John snapped a picture.

"We can put all our souvenirs and treasures in here."

"Whatever you want, it's all yours," he said, smiling. "I'm glad we came early. The morning light is so inspiring; the buildings are all coming to life."

"The buildings are alive?"

"Definitely. If you notice, buildings always look and feel different with the changing angles of the sun."

"So they do, don't they? You're going to be a great architect, I just know it," she said, curling her arm though the crook of his. The sunlight shone on the grounds like a beam of happiness turned on in their lives. The vibrant colors of the art-deco style buildings glistened, making the atmosphere cheerful. Elsie felt like a new woman.

The brilliance spread out into the street, John noticed, illuminating the many modern exhibits and giving the ashen pavement a celebratory shimmer. People glided by, smiling, wearing their Sunday best, apparently unmindful of their troubles and the troubles of the country. They allowed themselves to forget for an hour or two that they were enduring a financial depression, that farmers in the plains states faced unending drought, and that food shortages also threatened the entire country. Faces of passersby seemed subtly altered by the splendor of the fair. The young appeared blissfully carefree, the adults less troubled and more relaxed. Children's faces glowed with excitement.

"Don't you think," Elsie said, "that this World's Fair marks a positive shift? It seems like all these people have hope for the future of America, just by being here; that the upbeat theme of the fair has inspired everyone's optimism. I feel it, don't you?"

"It *is* grand," John said. "And I'm happy we could be here together."

He marveled at the new midway built along the man-made island beside Lake Michigan. The architecture was still stunning, deliberate, and challenging under the August glow, even though the architects and designers had toned down the colors from the previous year. The raw reds were tempered to a purple red. The blues quieter and the greens less harsh. White was used more extensively, making a sensible modification to the color scheme while preserving the atmosphere of gayety and eliminating the glitz.

'Look!" he said, pointing to a rainbow of colored water spurting up into the sky. "That's really keen! I've never seen anything like it. Here, let's take another picture of you." He showed Elsie where to stand in front of the fountain, positioned his subject through the viewfinder of his Brownie, and pushed the shutter release.

Elsie checked the souvenir book to find out more information regarding the wondrous spectacle. "The text beside the map, says it's *A Century of Progress Fountain*. "It's the largest in the world; six hundred seventy feet high, and illuminated by multicolored floodlights. Wow, I've never seen such a thing, either."

As they continued to walk through the crowd, John noticed the peculiar architecture of the buildings. "Those jagged edges and bold colors look like they were inspired by the skyscrapers of New York," John explained to Elsie as he captured the structural designs on film. "I like what they've done. It's better than last year's version."

"I hope this is what we can expect on the other side of this depression," she said.

Beds of yellow roses and petunias were scattered across a manicured verdant lawn, bordered by clipped hedges. The sun warmed Elsie's shoulders as she strolled along. Every time she thought how much she loved the man beside her, she was unable to keep from smiling. Even the pressing of his fingers against hers was invigorating. And when he looked her way, self-confident and handsome with subtle amusement in his eyes, she could scarcely maintain her composure.

They turned a sharp corner past The Streets of Shanghai, and were awestruck by a sparkling, turquoise man-made lagoon.

Elsie beamed. "This is wonderful. It's so picturesque. I feel like everything was rolled out especially for us."

John smiled at her. "Maybe someday we can sail off to an exotic destination. Would you like that?"

"Boy, would I!" *This man is full of fun and surprises.*

A huge parade of civic and military organizations, with scores of bands playing patriotic tunes, marched down Michigan Avenue. Elsie leaned back against John's chest as the procession passed. She remembered that when she marched in the women's suffrage parade with Auntie Jane, the crowd of people did not cheer them on like the spectators were cheering these marchers.

After the parade passed, they wandered a little further to a fork in the walkway. Elsie spotted The Century of Progress Exposition. "Let's go in there. It sounds interesting."

"I'm with you, let's go," John said, his arm circling around her waist.

A handful of presentations recalled Chicago's frontier past, concluding with concepts for a remarkable future. John was impressed with the two dozen prototype homes, and a unique house of the future shaped like a wedding cake with glass walls. An experimental kitchen, full of laborsaving devices, promised easier times ahead for American homemakers. A novel new machine showcased how dishes could be cleaned after every meal.

John read the sign aloud. *"World's finest, most modern automatic dishwasher. Dishes actually dry in their own heat.* I need one of those," he joked. Then he opened a new Sears electric refrigerator and felt the cool air against his body. "This beauty comes with a three-year guarantee. Maybe with all these modern conveniences, you'll enjoy being a housewife," he teased.

Elsie glanced at him and they laughed. "I doubt it," they said in unison.

This woman, John was gradually coming to understand, was to be put in a class all by herself. She had a quality about her—an innate honesty, glossed with intelligence that he found intriguing enough to hold his interest. Even her clothing and the way she moved her body was impressive. The dress she wore today was very plain, but showed both style and taste in how it fit her.

Not wanting to miss a thing, John made sure they took their time browsing through an array of exhibits. The great New Automobile Presentation told the whole story of the construction, design, and materials of the modern automobile. They witnessed automobiles assembled before their eyes, driven away under their own power. John was particularly dazzled with the Ford exhibit. He looked over the exquisite details of the Ford Phaeton Deluxe V-8.

Elsie liked the Ford Club Coupe that would be available for purchase in 1937. "Maybe in three years I'll have enough money to buy one. If I ever learn how to drive, that is."

John regarded her thoughtfully. "I'll teach you. Don't worry. There's nothing to it. It will only take you a week or two to learn. I think these Fords are fine automobiles," he said, running a hand along the Phaeton's high fender. "But I'll probably buy a Packard next."

"Oh, you'd be a show off! The only people I know who drive Packards are doctors and lawyers." Smiling, she leaned into him and gave him a poke to the ribs. "Not young apprentice architects. Robert said Fords are affordable and they're the easiest cars to work on. You've had good luck with yours, haven't you?"

"I can't complain. Robert's probably right," he said, shaking his head. "The Packard was just a thought. Although, by the time I buy one I'll be an architect, not an apprentice architect, so then I *can* show off."

At about one in the afternoon, they headed in the direction of The Black Forest Village which offered a glimpse of winter life in the German timberland. Next to the village, Merrie England, a reproduction of English life and culture, held their interest.

Elsie happily posed for John's camera in front of a replica of Big Ben. The two wandered into the Old Curiosity Shop and marveled at a reproduction of Shakespeare's Globe Theatre. As Elsie exited the English structure, thoughts of Maidstone and her father whirled in her head.

John noticed her faraway look and hugged her, whispering, "I'm falling in love with you, Elsie. And if I forgot to tell you earlier, you look like the bee's knees this afternoon."

"Thanks, and you look very dapper, yourself." She circled his waist and gave him a sideways hug.

"Look," he said, as they walked along hand-in-hand. "It's the Hawaiian Village."

"Oh-h, let's go there. I'm ready to relax a bit. I've never been to Hawaii."

"Okay, and I'm starving. Are you?"

Elsie nodded and they headed for the restaurant. A waiter dressed in an orange- and yellow-flowered shirt sat them next to the band.

"For lunch today," the waiter said, "we're offering a special fish: grilled ahi in a mango garlic sauce, sprinkled with macadamia nuts. And that comes with a fresh pineapple shake."

Elsie laid a hand to her heart. "Ahi? I never heard of it. It sounds so exotic."

The waiter gave her a knowing smile. "Ahi is the Hawaiian name for tuna."

"Oh, I see," she said, smiling at John. "That sounds lovely. I'll order that."

"Make that two," John echoed. "Ahi, Ahi."

Palm trees swayed behind them while they waited for their lunch to arrive. On a stage in the center of the restaurant, a hula *halau* danced traditional hulas. In the far corner, a woman in a hibiscus-flowered swim suit was about to dive into a replica of the flaming volcano of Mt. Kilauea.

"I wonder what's in the bottom of that volcano," John mused aloud.

Elsie suddenly thought of a way to test how he really felt about her. "That whole scene over there is just to lure men into the restaurant. I think it's just an invitation for the bravest, most stalwart of Johnny Weismuller types." Elsie winked.

"What do you mean?"

"Maybe there really *is* lava in there. Maybe she needs rescuing? I read that Mr. Weismuller is supposed to be here. Maybe someone can beat him to it." The pineapple shakes arrived. Elsie took a sip and clasped her hands. "Delicious!"

"Say, about this Johnny Weismuller ... " Sometimes Elsie completely confused him which, he supposed, was entirely a girl's prerogative. It made her all the more enticing with her sly winks and little flutter of eyelashes. "Weismuller ... you mean that Tarzan of the picture show, the womanizer and crocodile wrestler?"

"That's the one."

"What's he got to do with volcanoes?"

"A volcano belongs in a jungle like Tarzan's, where he goes around rescuing helpless damsels in distress, don't you think?"

"You mean damsels like Jane?"

Elsie nodded. "Like Jane, of course. I'm sure there is at least one Johnny Weismuller type in this place who would rescue her." She stared at him without batting an eyelash. The woman in the bathing suit was poised at the edge of the volcano. "She might need help," Elsie finished.

It then dawned on him. "You don't mean—" John chuckled, then broke out in gales of laughter. "You don't mean ... me?" he sputtered. "That I go around rescuing helpless women?"

When he was able to look at Elsie again, she was regarding him without a smile. Uh-oh, he thought. Response required. "Elsie, you're the one woman who does not need rescuing. Believe me and neither does she," he said, pointing to the woman diver. "She's a professional. Look, there she goes now." John clapped enthusiastically after she flew from the edge of the volcano with her arms spread toward the sky. "She could probably rescue me if I were drowning."

Elsie clapped, too. "She's safe. You were right." She felt her face go slack and she smiled a slow, lazy smile. "You're so sweet. You mean so much to me."

"Likewise. But really, you need to get out more," he said, trying to hide a toothy smile.

More laughter.

After they finished eating, the hula dancers invited them to participate on stage. John stood with the men, hands on his hips and his arms akimbo, trying to follow the ancient footsteps. Elsie's arms fluttered along with those of the women dancers, but couldn't, for the life of her, get her hips to sway without moving her entire body. "This is difficult!" she called over to John.

He laughed. "Can't help you, sorry."

They remained in the Hawaiian Village for two hours. Elsie loved the atmosphere and didn't want to leave the small slice of paradise. She curled herself around John's arm as they reluctantly wandered out of the tropical village along the pathways crowded with fair visitors.

"I'd really like to see the opera stage and how they put it together," John said. It was built exquisitely proportioned with a spacious high dome, out over a body of water that was surrounded by four bridges. The Sixteenth Street Bridge connected the mainland with Northerly Island. The musicians assembled in the center of the magnificent stage, with a large balcony hovering over the water.

During the musical presentation of *My Blue Heaven*, Elsie watched John's every expression in a doe-eyed fog of longing. She could tell he was enjoying the number; he seemed lost in the emotion of the melody. A sensitive man was an unexpected gift in life, and she could already feel the tenderness in the evening ahead of them at the hotel. She could feel his fingertips on her bare skin, his warm lips pressed to her neck, her breast....

The bright sunlight was gone when they left the opera stage seating; the fair had dwindled to the small spaces around them in the waning twilight as they walked toward the exit gate.

"This has been an amazing day, John," Elsie said. "I've loved every minute of it."

"I agree, but I think my feet have had it. I'll be glad to take a break for a few hours." He circled his arm around her waist. "We can come back tomorrow, bright and early."

Once Elsie was safely seated inside the open-air fair bus with its motley canopy, she realized just how much her feet ached, too. "At the hotel, I wonder if they have two seats for us on the tub where we can both soak our feet?" Elsie took off her shoes to find two big water blisters, one on her heel, and the other on her big toe.

"Oh, I think we can do a bit better than that for relaxation."

She looked at him and smiled a little shyly. She was fairly certain about what he meant by that, but said nothing. Instead, she could already feel his touch and instantly melted at the thought of him lying naked next to her, on top of her, thighs and skin, his maleness heating up, warming her inside, their hearts beating one into the other.

* * *

John set their suitcases down, just inside the door of the hotel room, and switched on a small Tiffany lamp. Light streamed onto the carved bedposts, making the red wood of the dressing table glow. He kissed Elsie lightly on the neck in the subdued light and felt her hands reach up, her fingers traveling through his hair and mussing it. Her lips roamed down his neck and back to his face. He gently escaped, saying, "You've ravaged me, Miss Wilkins."

She smiled a fraction from his mouth. "Not yet."

"I imagine you'll need this?" John said, going for her suitcase and laying it on the bed.

Elsie took a few items from it and headed for the bathroom. She gave him a coy look. "I'm going to take a bath. I'll be out in a few minutes." She winked.

He grinned, lay down in bed, and placed his hands behind his head. "By all means, bathe. Enjoy yourself. I'll be here waiting."

About twenty-five minutes later, Elsie stepped out into the dimly lit room. John was sleeping soundly. He looked so innocent and sweet. He *was* sweet and lots of fun, she thought. She quietly picked up a brochure lying on the dresser and sat softly on the bed next to him.

After a moment, he felt her presence, and slowly opened his eyes. "Oh, hello there. You smell so good. Good enough to eat." He reached for her and slid a hand over her shoulder, his lips trailing every inch of his touch down her arm. He was hooked; he'd never let her go. He wanted every part of her and sat up to circle his arms around her, feel the warmth of her against him.

She saw under the sheet that he wore nothing at all, and just his nakedness excited her. His eyes smoldered with the steam of a man who was ready, except within this lust Elsie saw a tenderness that only meant love for her. He kissed her neck just below her ear and any thoughts she'd had disappeared. His kisses moved upwards and her lips parted to let her mouth taste the sweetness of his. She was breathing rapidly now as he gently pulled down the straps of her nightgown and cupped her bare breasts. She felt his wet lips and tongue on them, licking, pulling softly at her nipples.

He pulled her to his chest and felt her breasts against him. "Elsie, you're so sweet."

"I want you," she said with a quiet shudder.

"There is so much I want to say to you," John murmured as she pressed against him, letting his arms cradle her. "I want to tell you how much you mean to me. I want to tell you how beautiful you are. How much I need you. How much I love you."

"I love you, too. I'm so happy," she whispered. He pulled the two of them down into the bed and she felt his bare skin; the waiting hardness of him. When she could no longer lie in the sweet agony of his kisses and caresses alone, she whispered, "Now," and he gently slid between her legs, up into her. She was completely lost into him as they made love, and then again. This man was crazy in love with her; she had no doubt.

Elsie woke first to the sunlight streaming in through the window, her hair loose and hanging around her face. Her eyes were bright. She washed her face and hands in the fractured basin that sat on the washstand. She combed her hair and began making up her face.

John was now awake and watching her. Setting his paper aside, he lit a cigarette and continued to stare at her, knowing there was no quicker way to catch her eye. She turned and smiled at him. He could not help admire her alluring sensuality, her soft tan skin and beautiful sparkling eyes. Her natural fragrance engaged him. She looked radiant, even though he'd made sure she'd slept little the night before. He smiled, lost in the memory. Surely her thoughts now were preoccupied with him and their ardent lovemaking. He was quickly growing aroused again, just thinking of how her hot bare skin slipped against his as they moved together under the cool sheets. "You're not really getting ready for the fair, are you?"

"Sure, why not? That's the idea, isn't it?"

"What, and leave me in this condition?"

"What condition is that?" she asked, though she knew very well what that was.

"Why don't you come over here and see?" he said, placing his cigarette in the ashtray next to the bed and throwing aside the sheet that covered him.

They made love again, and Elsie couldn't imagine feeling all this passion at once, but she did. They took their time, exploring each other and listening to the quiet sounds of the day wafting in through the slowly fluttering curtains at their secluded window.

Elsie dressed in the bathroom and stepped out, wearing a dress with a floral print of tiny red flowers that were sprinkled against a white background. The bodice was trimmed with red rickrack, and the back fit low with three small, white buttons and a sash tied in a big bow.

John gave her an approving nod. "That's a lovely dress you're wearing."

"Thank you. My mother made it for me out of a couple chicken feed sacks."

"You're joking! That's interesting. I didn't know they put chicken seed in such feminine looking feed bags."

"You can find wonderful prints if you're lucky." Her eyes wandered as she reminisced about the past. "My mother is talented. She made us girls bathing suits, aprons, pillowcases ... you name it. Not all feed sacks were printed, though. When she got a plain one, she bleached it and made petticoats and bloomers. And all the leftovers went into the 'ragbag' for future quilts."

"Your mother must be very clever. I think you told me that you don't sew?"

"No, not if I can help it." She giggled. "My mother and both my sisters are great seamstresses. My mother is so skilled in sewing that she's able to copy the fashions in any women's magazine if she wants to. The sewing gene passed me by, I guess. You don't hold that against me, do you?"

"Let me see if I can hold this against you." He put his arms tightly around her. "I sure would like a chicken feed shirt."

"Maybe, someday. We'll see."

"When will I be able to meet your mom? And of course your dad, too."

"Well, there is the little issue of James. I'm afraid they're very conservative."

"Do you mean they think he'll come back?" The light in his eyes diminished a bit.

"I don't know, but in their minds, I'm still married."

"Even though you haven't seen him in almost four years? He abandoned you. Only a crazy man would do that. If he came back, you could have him committed."

"Yes, I know. I feel the same about it, but I am free now as far as I'm concerned." She smiled at John and placed her hands against his chest. "Anyway, I could try and make a feed sack shirt for you, but you probably wouldn't want to wear it out in public."

"Try me. I'm sure I would love it," he said, giving her a quick kiss. Abruptly, he took out his pocket watch. "We better get to the fair; it's after twelve. And I thought we could get an early start," he said with a laugh.

John walked arm-in-arm with Elsie along the fairground pathways, browsing through the remaining European villages. He was glad when she took interest in the leaning tower of the Italian village, and in the Irish village's background of Lake Killarney.

He was also curious about the midget city, so they headed in that direction. "In architecture," he told Elsie, "there are standard dimensions for doorway widths and heights, chairs, tables ... that kind of thing. I wonder how all that works in miniature?"

"Oh, I'd like to see that, too," she said as they approached. "Look at this plaque, John. It says that this next section of the fair houses the most amazing oddities known to man."

A colony of Lilliputians, living in miniature houses that were equipped with tiny furniture, appeared on the other side of a bridge. The smallest man and the smallest woman in the world welcomed them at the gates of Midget City. The couple, Margaret Ann Robinson and Captain Werner, smiled while standing snugly in a brown leather carrying case. They waved to the people gathered around the entrance. Apparently, they were the leading citizens of the village.

A new feature was unveiled—Robert Ripley's very first *Odditorium*. Among the most spectacular sights was that of the infant, Betty Lou Williams, who had a parasitic twin sister emerging from her abdomen.

Elsie grimaced. "This is awful. I feel so sorry for her. It's terrible all these people are gawking at her. Why, she's just a baby." Unbelievably, John had his hands on his camera. "Please, don't take a picture of her!"

He let the Brownie drop down onto his chest. "She's probably making more money than the senior architects I work with."

Elsie smirked at his remark, but John continued. "I applaud her for using what God gave her to earn a good living. Although in her condition, I don't know how long that will be."

"Her folks are probably collecting her money," Elsie said solemnly. "I hope that if she survives, her parents find a way to school her."

John searched his program. "I don't need a photograph, anyway. There's one of her here," he said, showing it to Elsie. A miniature clock tower caught his attention with the time. "Let's go see the living skeleton and the fat guy—then we'd better leave."

Elsie nodded. "Agreed."

The young, thin man, John Smith, was exhibited alongside his polar opposite—Fat Boy W. S. Burt. The last exhibit on their way out was Eli Bowen, the legless acrobat, his fat protruding directly from his pelvis.

"I've had enough. How about you? Let's get out of here, okay?" Elsie tugged at John's arm.

"Okay, let's beat it. We need to hurry over to the station."

On the train ride back to Rensselaer, John sat facing Elsie so that they could both enjoy a window seat view. The eye-to-eye encounter and the relaxing motion of the train prompted him to open up and talk about his early life in Massachusetts, the break up of his parents' marriage, his relationship with his brother, and even about a few of the women he had dated in the past.

Elsie noted that this was the first man who had ever spoken about his former relationships. Such bluntness, such honesty was refreshing to hear, but she wasn't prepared for it, so she didn't know exactly how to react. She remained quiet and mostly listened. She just thought to herself over and over that she was crazy about this man, and that she was having the time of her life.

"I don't know how to ask you this, so I'm going to just come right out and say it," John said tensely.

Elsie's heart thumped against her side and she gasped. Could marriage be on his mind? Whatever would she do about a divorce from James?

John gazed out the window, trying to muster up his confidence. "Elsie, do you want to come and live at my house with me?" He leaned over and gently held both her hands.

She tried not to look disappointed. "Oh—I don't know." She paused. "Would that be right?" She took a deep breath, realizing he didn't catch on to her thoughts about a marriage proposal.

"Why wouldn't it? We love each other, that's what matters." Not receiving any response from her, he continued. "I know it's a big decision. I don't want to persuade you. I just thought it would be a swell idea. I could use a feminine touch around the place. And I love spending time with you. Just think about it okay?"

She looked into his twinkling brown eyes. "Do you think we know each other well enough to live together? I mean, it is a big step. And what would people say? I could be ostracized from everyone I know. There are not many people who live together when they're not married."

"Are you going to live your life for other people? I know I haven't known you that long, but it feels like forever. I love you. And you love me, right?"

"Right." She looked down, feeling sad that he'd avoided the issue of marriage. "Then there's Robert and my parents. My family would not approve." She shook her head. "It could all blow up in my face. I'd like to, but I'd be a wreck the whole time."

"Don't get anxious. Elsie, you don't have to live with me. It's okay. We can still see each other everyday."

She nervously laid her hand to her cheek. "There's something I have to tell you. I mean, I should have told you by now. I wanted to, but I'm so embarrassed."

"What? What could possibly embarrass you? What is it?"

"I can't. The words won't come out."

"So, you have a big secret, then?"

"No. Not a secret. Well, sort of a secret. Yes."

"Is that why you're hesitating?" His voice grew louder. "What's the secret, for God's sake?"

"I'm having trouble saying it. Remember, the words won't come out." She picked up her pocketbook and said apprehensively, "Let me write it down."

"Okay, fine, write it down," he said, feeling exasperated.

Elsie rummaged through her pocketbook and found a program from the fair. She scribbled the few words on it, folded the paper twice, and handed it to John with a sigh. Then she stood and hustled down the corridor of the train.

With the folded paper in his hand he yelled down the hallway, "Elsie, you're being silly. What could be so bad?" The other passengers all stared at him. He looked down at the brochure in his hands and slowly opened it.

I was born in 1905. I'm sorry.

He sat for a moment in silence. She hadn't been truthful about her age. *She's older than I am. But so what? She looks like the cat's meow. What difference do a few years make? Although, she is really close to thirty.* He sighed. *But now I love her.* He stood to go look for her.

"Elsie! Come back to me," he called. She was slowing making her way back to her seat.

Self-consciously, she sat back down next to the window and forced a smile. "I feel like such a fool. I'm really an honest person. I never lie."

"I'm a little surprised, but it doesn't really matter. Robert did mention you could be older, but I forgot all about that." Elsie did not look relieved. "You look younger than I do," he added.

"Do you really think so?" she said hopefully. "Anyway, I think I'm more upset that I wasn't truthful with you. I just never imagined we'd get on so well, and you know … " Her eyes filled, forming luminescent pools.

John moved from his seat to sit next to her. He put his arm around her and gently picked up her right hand and kissed it. "You're the sexiest girl I ever met. Sexier than Jean Harlow. And your age means not a whit to me."

"You're just saying that to make me feel better."

"No, I mean it. You're much more attractive. Your nose is nicer. And I'm mad about you." He looked straight into her eyes. "You're my *blonde bombshell.* I've never felt like this about anyone. And I doubt I ever will."

Chapter Nine

John held Elsie's hand as they lay on their backs in Milroy Park, watching the clouds float by. The early September air was chilly in the late afternoon under the shade trees, so he had laid out their blanket on a sunny patch of grass. The scent of autumn in the air reminded him that football season was just a couple weeks away.

"That one looks like a giraffe," Elsie said, pointing to a long stretch of clouds with two bumps at the top. "See, it even has ears."

"I don't see ears. It looks like a bus," John replied.

Elsie turned to him, propped up on one elbow. "That can't be a bus. It doesn't have any wheels."

"It's been in an accident. Look, there's Robert coming to fix it," he said with a twinkle in his eyes, though he still continued to look up. "Look, there're two people making whoopee." He loved testing her sense of humor. He waited for her to dish it right back.

"I don't see them." She laid her head on his shoulder.

"They're gone. Either that or they shut the door."

Elsie laughed.

They had enjoyed a perfectly wonderful picnic lunch, consisting of chicken that Elsie had fried up at the boarding house, fresh pumpernickel bread right from the bakery, and for dessert, a slice of pumpkin pie. She had gone to great lengths to prepare food for the picnic basket, and John was appreciative.

"That was very sweet of you to go to all the trouble of putting together a lunch for us," John said, beginning to refill the basket with the picnic odds and ends.

Elsie laughed. "If I have any domestic genes at all, you must be bringing them out in me."

John raised his eyebrows at her. "Oh? Elsie. You know I don't want you to change for me one bit."

"I won't. Promise."

John had something else on his mind. "We still have some time before it gets dark. What do you say we take a drive?"

"Why not? September is such a lovely time of year with the leaves on the trees beginning to turn color."

John carried the picnic basket and helped Elsie into the car. "There you go, Milady."

They took a long drive through the woodsy area outside of town, along a dirt road that bordered a bank of tall trees. John abruptly pulled over and brought the car to a stop.

"Oh," Elsie said. "Is this a special place?" She looked around in search of eye catching scenery or vistas.

"No, not really. It's just special because we're together today."

"But ... ?"

"There's something I've wanted to tell you," he said, turning to face her surprised look, and reaching for her hand. "You know you're everything to me. I've never felt so deeply about anyone. I love you more than anything," he said, searching her eyes for any hint of reciprocation.

"I love you, too," she said, feeling a slight warm tingle when she looked at him.

"I've loved every minute we've spent together." His hand tightened on hers. "I need you." His free hand slipped into the breast pocket of his jacket and pulled out a small, blue velvet case. He gently opened it.

Elsie was looking at a ring, set with a glittering ruby.

John took a deep breath before continuing. "I would still like you to live with me. I want you to be the first person I see when I wake up every morning." He bent closer to her, his lips a fraction away from hers. "I know you have reservations about it, but I miss you so much when we're apart."

He kissed her with warmth that seemed to spring from his soul, and she felt his lips and his body down deep in her heart, a passion that wanted to consume every inch of him. She paused for a moment and escaped his lips to gaze at the sparkling ruby ring. "It's a beautiful ring, but I'm still not comfortable with that arrangement. Undoubtedly, people will think and say things about me. I could be shunned if my friends or co-workers find out."

"Let them say what they like. It's what *you* say that's important. I figure life is short and you have to do what makes you happy. Most fellas never find what I've found in you."

"I'd like to say yes, but I'm frightened." Her eyes shone. "A part of me wants to do it, but John I— " She threw her arms around him and buried her face into his neck. He wrapped his arms around her.

"It's true though, I won't have to miss you, either," she murmured. She felt deep down that she should grab this moment of happiness. For happiness, she was beginning to realize, didn't come around all that much. Her heart beat rapidly. She was confused and desperately afraid of losing him. He alone was the most wonderful experience of her life. And yet, this cloud that hung over her dimmed the full excitement of the moment. She was so tired of her life alone. This outward independence was more for show than what she truly had dreamed of for her life. After a long pause, she pulled away and looked at him. She could feel her pulse beating in her throat, and felt her face burn with a flush. She felt she just had to be a part of his life.

"Yes, I'll move in with you. Yes, I'll do it! I want to be with you as much as I can." Even though she thought she could be ridiculed, she was now willing to take the chance. Maybe they could pretend to be married, she thought.

His eyes filled with a special softness just for her. Then he released her and took her right hand and slipped the ruby ring onto her third finger. "Now you're my girl," he said, gathering up her hair in one hand as it if were the most sensual thing in the world. He touched the side of her face lightly, then her lips, and then her cheek.

"You won't regret it. I'll do all I can to make you happy. You're so beautiful." He leaned forward and kissed her again, softly, gently.

She responded in kind, wanting this moment to last forever. A gush of relief washed over her as she held him tight. Before John, she hadn't been called beautiful since she was a young girl, and hearing him speak those words over and over again made her feel gorgeous through and through.

On the way back to Rensselaer, Elsie looked at each dwelling they passed and began to daydream. When she married John would they have a brick house, or one like that Grand Victorian? Would their home have a driveway in front, lined with plush green landscaping and tall trees that arched above the roadway, or would the driveway be on the side of the house? She could only imagine. She hoped that someday they would marry. She had to free herself from James. Soon she must find a way to finalize a divorce. One thing she knew for sure: her life was on the road to being perfect. For once she was truly happy.

"What do you say we stop in at Robert's? He's having a Labor Day get together," Elsie said.

"Sure," John answered. "That's sounds like a swell way to celebrate two things at once."

As they pulled in front of Robert's, they could hear a party in full swing in the backyard. John went straight to the courtyard to join the others, but Elsie excused herself to go into the house to freshen up.

She went directly upstairs to the bedroom she had used the first few nights she was in town. Framed photographs of the family covered the bureau, the dressing table, and night stand. The furniture was painted white and the walls were covered in red- and-white-striped wallpaper. An eyelet bedspread matched the curtains on the windows, and shelves of books lined one wall.

She tossed her pocketbook across the bed, pulled off her yellow, polka-dot dress, and pitched it after the pocketbook. Then she fell onto the bed.

Leaning back on the pillow, she closed her eyes and had a sudden absurd desire to start singing. She wanted to savor the moment. She replayed the day in her mind ... everything John had said, everything she had said, everything they had done.

Stretched out on the bed, the darkness began to close in around her like a safe and scrumptiously romantic blanket. A surge of joy ran through her body. It would be so good to get out of the boarding house. On all accounts, it was a perfectly fine place to stay, but it always felt a little lonely and cold. She thought about her parents and wondered what they would think of her new living arrangement. No doubt they would not approve, especially her father. But she didn't need her parents' approval any longer. She was a grown woman of twenty-nine.

From outdoors, she heard Robert yell. "Hey Elsie … what are you doing up there?"

She stood and threw her dress back on, opened the window, and peeked out into the evening. The sunset was exquisite, with colors of deep orange and free flowing, deep smudges of purplish red. The sky enhanced the ruby on her finger and brought out its flame. Trees swayed in the wind. "I'll be down in a minute," she called. "I decided to change."

She turned and collapsed into a chair, twisting the promise ring off her finger. She gazed at it in awe for a moment before opening a drawer where she had kept a pair of overalls and a white blouse. She put them on, looking in the mirror, turning around side to side. Even though she was dressed in an informal way, the denim overalls fit her well and she still looked feminine. She looked down and saw that her hands were trembling. She chuckled.

It was odd; she wasn't usually this jumpy. But then again, she had never agreed to move in with a man who wasn't her husband. She was about to do something daring, something other women wouldn't have the nerve to do. She brushed her hair, washed her hands, put her ring back on, and finally glided down the stairs and out the back door to join the party.

That night the six of them all sat in the dark, drinking ginger ale, laughing, talking, and gazing up at the stars. It turned out to be a wonderful Labor Day party, Elsie thought. She proudly showed off her ruby promise ring to Robert and his friends. Her joy bubbled up like champagne as she told them the story behind it. However, she decided against revealing any upcoming plans to move in with John.

She hoped they could keep that a secret. She felt as she hadn't in a long time, as if all her dreams could still be realized.

* * *

On the day to celebrate Elsie's move from the boarding house, John gave her flowers and then took her to one of their favorite cities—Chicago. They spent two nights in the Windy City, taking in the sights. In the afternoon they took in a matinee—*Of Human Bondage*, starring Leslie Howard and Bette Davis. Later in the evening, they went out on the town and stopped at a night club. The hostess sat them at a small, intimate table where they watched a vaudeville show, featuring chorus girls, and listened to a thirteen-piece orchestra.

John was happy to see how much Elsie was enjoying the evening. "Shall we dance?" he asked, half in jest.

"My feet will keep up with yours, if you want to try it."

"We better not just yet. It hasn't been long enough since the danceathon."

"What about a slow one?" she said with a wink.

"Okay, real slow," he said, reaching for her hand.

The next day they climbed aboard the "L" to Westchester to check out a newly designed neighborhood. Westchester was Chicago's first perfectly planned community. John's project manager had asked him to evaluate the place with the intent of implementing a similar plan in Indiana.

John and Elsie walked hand-in-hand, touring the model homes. He wanted to show her the new Tudor suburb designed after an English town. The houses of stucco and hand-hewn timbers set Westchester apart from many other Chicago suburbs. Elsie was in awe with the neighborhood. Her hair cascaded around her shoulders as she twirled around in the middle of the sidewalk. "I would love to live here. It's so pleasant and pretty."

"Maybe someday," John said tenderly. "It sure is nice. I could be happy here."

Elsie thought about when she was first married and lived with James in a small apartment. When the stock market crashed they couldn't keep it any longer. Suddenly she blurted out what was on her mind. "It would be so wonderful if later on we could live in a neighborhood like this. It's an ideal place to raise a family."

"Ideal Westchester. Ideal Beach. I feel the casualness of Ideal Beach here, don't you? Who knows? Maybe I'll get transferred to Chicago."

"That would be swell. I'm so happy I don't have to live in Akron anymore, or with my parents. James didn't like living with my parents either, but he did want to stay close to Akron."

"I know a lot of people who had it rough. Many people who've had to live with their relatives still do—he wasn't much different," John said.

Elsie frowned. "James never complained about the smell of processed rubber. He—" She noticed John's annoyance at the mention of James, and was upset with herself for bringing him up again. She had already told him once before about James living with her parents when they were married.

John smirked. "He was lucky to have a roof over his head."

Quickly, Elsie changed the subject. "Everything seems so perfect here, just like in the movies."

"It does seem that way doesn't' it?" He took her hands in his. "I know perfection. I'm looking at her right now."

Elsie smiled and gave him a kiss on the cheek.

He glanced at his watch. "We'd better get to the station; we don't want to miss the last train home."

John bought an extra-edition newspaper before they climbed aboard the train. As he shared it with Elsie, he found the latest details involving the Lindbergh baby's kidnapping.

"They've finally arrested someone," he said excitedly. "A Bruno Hauptmann. He's a German immigrant with a criminal record in his homeland." He read aloud from the front page. "More than two years after the kidnapping, a gold certificate from the ransom money has been referred to New York police detective, James J. Finn, and FBI agent, Thomas Sisk. Finn and Sisk have been working the Lindbergh case for thirty months and have been able to track down many bills from the ransom hoard to places throughout New York City."

Elsie was familiar with the case and voiced her opinion. "When it was reported that the baby was being held on a boat called *The*

Nelly, I had a strong feeling it wasn't true, and that the baby was probably already dead."

John read silently to himself, then told her, "It's too bad. Such a shame. Hauptmann was arrested Wednesday after he passed a ten-dollar gold certificate."

"He should get the death penalty," Elsie said angrily.

"Yes, he should. They'll charge him with kidnapping and murder. Conviction on even one charge could earn him the death penalty," John said. "Let me finish the article, then you can read it."

She glanced at the photos of Hauptmann and the Lindberg baby on the front page. "He was so adorable with that deep dimple in the center of his chin."

"He was a beautiful child," John responded. "Only twenty months old. Mencken, the newspaper writer, said the Lindbergh kidnapping is the biggest story since the Resurrection."

"I know. Everybody is talking about it." Elsie yawned. "I'm going to try and take a nap. Wake me when we get there. I'll read the story later." She closed her eyes and rested her head against John's shoulder.

* * *

Elsie walked to the red brick building surrounded by a big gravel play yard. Once inside, she was immersed in the smell of freshly oiled wooden floors. Thirty-five desks, each with an inkwell, were nailed to the floor in a large, old-fashioned room that was so old, Elsie wondered if the building had been built during the time of Abraham Lincoln. Regardless, she'd only been teaching two weeks and loved it so far.

A large white partition separated two classrooms in the building. Each classroom housed two teachers, each with their own students. Elsie's desk was situated next to the bookshelves, with two long wooden benches running alongside. In back of her hung a map of the United States, rolled up like a window shade. Along one wall, above the bookshelves, three big windows allowed the sunlight to stream in.

The other teacher, Miss Williams, sat at her desk on the opposite end of the room in front of her blackboard. She appeared about twenty-five years old and attractive, with bright blue eyes and a friendly smile. She was kind to her students and, so far, Elsie hadn't heard her say a harsh word to anyone.

Elsie had carefully printed her rules for the class on a large piece of white paper that was displayed on an easel for the class to see as they entered the room. She had rules about talking, attendance, and when the children were allowed to use the toilet. After recess, she stood in front of the class as the children filed past her to take their seats.

When everyone was seated, she smiled. "Now class, this morning we're going to talk about personal hygiene. Does anyone know what personal hygiene is? Tommy Farmer."

Tommy stood by next to his desk and cleared his throat. "It's brushing your teeth so your breath doesn't stink."

The children all laughed.

"That's correct, Tommy. That's one important thing you can do. Thank you. You may sit down. Does anyone else know how to maintain good personal hygiene?"

No one raised their hand.

"Personnel hygiene would include … swatting flies, refraining from spitting, which means *no* spitting, and brushing your teeth and hair. Have your mother clean your clothing, and you must wash all of your body, not just the part that shows. In addition, eat well-balanced meals. All these things are important in maintaining good health and preventing any diseases such as that nasty tuberculosis we're all hearing so much about these days. We'll talk about all these things, and we'll review each one on the blackboard after lunch. But now it's time for our English lesson. Class, last week we learned how to spell some easy, everyday words. Today, we'll start with words that are a bit more difficult." She wrinkled her nose. "This morning, I swallowed a hearty spoonful of cough syrup."

The children giggled and made funny faces.

Elsie's eyes settled on Billy, who was looking around the room, trying to avoid her direct gaze. "Billy Hannigan, spell cough syrup."

Billy's body tensed. He looked down at his desk and opened his mouth. He mumbled, "C-o-u-g-h … "

"Please stand Billy. You know the rule about standing to answer," Elsie reminded him.

Billy gave out a slight moan, stood up, and to Elsie, it looked for all the world as though his knees would buckle and she'd have to pick him up off the floor. He gave a puzzled look. It seemed like he was trying to visualize the bottles of medicine at home. Nothing came out of his mouth. He made a face as she watched his concentration.

"S-i- ... " He paused. "R-r-u-p."

"That was close Billy. You spelled cough correctly. Syrup is a little tricky." She glanced around the classroom. "Does anyone know how to correctly spell syrup ... for ten extra spelling points?"

At the end of Billy's row, a pretty little girl with three first names raised her hand.

"Mary-Jean Lorraine," Elsie said, nodding in her direction.

She spelled the word correctly, with no hesitation.

"Very good. Excellent job, Mary-Jean Lorraine. You earned yourself ten bonus points."

Mary-Jean Lorraine seemed delighted, but most of the boys weren't delighted—they all made faces and groaned.

"Thank you, Miss Wilkins," Mary-Jean Lorraine said with a smug smile.

"Thank you Mary-Jean Lorraine for being an outstanding speller," Elsie said. She smiled, thinking how this young girl reminded her of herself when she was the same age.

Chapter Ten

E ven though it was a cold, blustery afternoon, with sprinkles of rain in the wind, Elsie decided to walk home the three miles from church. Her head sank into her linen collar as she let out a long, slow breath. She was living with a man in sin—that's what the women at church had accused her of. She was mistaken about the Episcopal Church members being kind and supportive, and wrong to believe the words emblazoned over the choir room entrance: *'Episcopalians—neighbors helping neighbors—sharing what good fortune comes their way.*

Her cheeks moist from tears and falling raindrops, she told herself she was beginning a new life. She must forget what they said, but it was difficult. It seemed so utterly extraordinary that four short months could have changed her life, given it a new sweet meaning, while harsh criticism now left her sad, weary. Dejected, she wiped away teardrops and lifted her shoulders in a shrug designed to cast off the heaviness of her thoughts.

Instantly, as if by God's grace, the rain stopped and she slowed her pace to reevaluate her living situation in a more positive light. She remembered what her mother had said; that life needs a little rain before you can see a rainbow. But today, there was not a rainbow in sight. She saw no break in the thick, solid clouds; the sky remained a dismal gray. In thinking about her own situation, she thought of her marriage to James as the rain, and meeting John … the rainbow.

Today, she took an alternate route home. Instead of walking through town, she decided to go west, away from the business district toward the more rural area of Rensselaer. She looked out over the rolling green fields as she walked along. Several boarded-up sheds stood among graceful old elm trees that swayed in the breeze. She thought about how blissful life was with John. How could her love and happiness be a sin? Walking along, she tried to concentrate on all the wonderful times they shared together. An afternoon breeze with a gentle scent from the fresh rain filled the air. She felt gloriously alive and it felt so right to be in Indiana, despite the criticism.

* * *

From the kitchen, John heard the sound of a car crunching along the gravel of the driveway outside the house. Through the back door window he recognized Robert's car and smiled broadly. He stuffed the rest of the English muffin into his mouth and went out to greet him with an eager wave. "Hey, buddy! How's it going?" he called.

Robert waved back, parked the car near the gate to the yard and climbed out, holding a brown and white puppy. "I brought you and Elsie a lively little present." Beaming, Robert held the puppy up in the air and gave its head a scratch. "Isn't she cute? Clementine had four more like this one." He put the pup on the wet grass; it wagged its tail and pranced over to where John stood next to the porch railing. "This is the one Elsie picked out a few weeks ago."

"A puppy … she sure is friendly," John said with a pat to its head. "How old is she now?"

"Twelve weeks. Old enough to be away from her mother, and to be in a home of her own."

John shook Robert's hand. "Well, thank you. Elsie's not home yet. I'm sure she will be surprised and thrilled to finally have a dog in the house," he said, glancing toward the back door.

"Where is she?"

"She's with the church choir members, practicing for Sunday's service."

"I can't wait around, although I'd love to. I have two jalopies waiting for me over at the shop. Can't get them started. You know those old Model T heaps … whenever it rains, they quit."

John grinned and nodded in agreement.

Robert picked up the puppy again and gave it a scratch behind the ear. "You be a good girl, now." To John he said, "Take care of the pup and let me know what you name her."

"Okay, I'm sure she'll keep us busy."

Robert put down the squirming pup and went to his car. "Say hello to Elsie for me," he said over his shoulder, "and tell her that she picked the best of the litter."

"Sure thing. And thanks again."

Robert was backing out when he stopped and stuck his head out the driver's window. "What do you say we get together Saturday night at Iroquois Park for a free picture show? They're featuring a new Fred Astaire and Ginger Rogers movie. I'm taking Brenda. Oh, I almost forgot. I have something for Elsie."

John went to the car window and waited while Robert fished in his pocket.

"Could you give this to her?" he asked, passing an envelope through the open window. "I picked it up yesterday."

John took the envelope and nodded. "I'll make sure she gets it as soon as she gets home. And Saturday sounds good; I don't think we have any plans."

"Okay, gotta make tracks. Bye."

As Robert left, the young dog scurried after his car. "Hey girl!" John yelled. "Come back! Here girl." He ran after it and scooped it up with one hand. Moments later, the sound of the engine died away as the car disappeared among the trees.

John wondered why Elsie hadn't called—it was nearly four o'clock and it was beginning to rain again. Underneath the yellow- and rust-colored leaves scattered around the lawn, John found a small stick to throw for the puppy. Initially, the dog went after it then stopped, her tail wagging as she sniffed a corn husk. For a few seconds, the puppy rolled around in the wet grass. After she relieved herself, John felt confident she could be allowed into the house.

Later, he sat comfortably at his drafting table with architectural drawings spread out before him. He was sketching ideas for construction of a federal post office in Hartford City. The puppy slept on a blanket in the next room. Another half hour passed before Elsie walked in. She looked disheveled.

John stood. "Hi honey. Why didn't you call me to pick you up? It's raining."

Elsie threw him a grateful glance. "It wasn't that bad. It was on and off. I'm used to walking in the rain."

The answer didn't satisfy him. She looked terrible. "What's wrong? You look upset."

She wrinkled her nose and shook her head. "Oh, I don't know. I guess I can't believe how narrow-minded some people are."

"People at the church?"

"Yes. Remember Joanne, the canary? The gal with the beautiful voice?"

John shook his head no.

Elsie made a face but tried not to say anything spiteful. "She usually solos on Sundays. You two met once."

"Sure, now I remember. What about her?"

"She thought we were honeymooners and said we made a handsome couple."

John smiled, agreeing.

Elsie bit her bottom lip. "Anyway, she asked about what happened at our *shivaree*. I told her we weren't married. I didn't mean to, but she caught me off guard. I didn't dare mention that I'm married to someone else and had a *shivaree* with him." She raised her eyebrows. "Although in Ohio, they called them *bellings*."

"I've heard about those crazy things. Never being married, I escaped that ritual. What's it all about, again?"

"When James and I returned from our honeymoon, some neighbors gathered in front of our apartment, banging washtubs, kitchen pans, and cowbells. They made a terrible racket. That racket is called a *shivaree*." She put her hands up to her forehead. Now, turning to the man who knew all about private struggles and inner strength, she confessed. "I could never tell anyone my husband ran out on me, and that now I'm living with another man."

"Why would you have to tell that to anyone, and who's this Joanne, anyway? You should have lied," John said, almost shouting. "Who cares what she thinks? It's not anyone's business what your marital status is, or *was*."

Elsie felt her stomach flip-flop and her limbs go weak. She had never heard John speak gruffly to her. She looked away, deciding how to answer him. *I might as well be out with it.* "The choir members glared at me with judgment in their eyes. They heard my whole conversation with Joanne."

"This happened in front of the *whole choir*?"

Elsie nodded with a woeful frown. "Emily said I was just trying to be popular. Her exact words were—"

"Popular? What a stupid thing to say."

She said, '*Some people think that serial promiscuity is a means to increase one's popularity.*' Can you believe that? And the choir director said as we left, '*Worship with friends whose faith far outdistances their troubles.*' " Elsie began to tear up. "Why can't they live their own lives and stay out of mine? They say there's a new sexual revolution. Well, where is it? It's theoretical. I don't see it accepted in my case."

John tried to make her laugh. "Probably approaching church members on their own grounds was not the best place to convince them of the real parameters of love and sex. But it was a good try."

Elsie knew he'd spoken in jest, but it only made her feel worse, like she'd done something else wrong. She opened her pocketbook to find a handkerchief and blew her nose. "Men and women who love each other have sex." Her bottom lip trembled. "We're not hurting anyone, or taking anything from—"

"Come here. Don't start crying," John said, opening his arms to embrace her affectionately. "They're jealous and they're intolerant. If I remember correctly, I know who Joanne's husband is. Isn't he unemployed and selling apples on Maple Street?"

Elsie nodded. "I think so."

"Then why is Joanne giving out advice? They don't have two nickels to rub together. She's just miserable seeing that you're happy. Church people can be very hypocritical, you know that. Don't you listen to anything she or anyone else says."

He sat her down on his lap in the chair near the fireplace and twirled his fingers around her hair. "Don't worry about it. They just don't know how sweet you are. This is perfect timing. I have a surprise for you," he said, standing up and letting Elsie sit by herself. "You're going to like it. Wait here."

Elsie leaned forward, waiting; her legs pressed tightly together, hands covering her knees. Her moist eyes searched John's for comfort as he came back into the room. He held the puppy like a newborn baby. The dog wiggled and pawed at him as he bent toward her, trying to graciously lay it in her lap.

"This bundle of joy should cheer you up."

"Oh-h, she's adorable," Elsie said, carefully examining the dog. "This is the one I picked out isn't it?"

John nodded. "It is. Robert said she's the best of the bunch, too."

Gently, Elsie drew the puppy closer and bent to kiss its head. A tiny smile curled the corners of her mouth as she realized that she wouldn't be glum for long around the puppy. "She's such a pretty color. And look at those long, reddish-brown ears. She's so precious. She's even cuter than I remember. What should we name her?"

"You decide. You're good at that sort of thing."

"I'll write down some suggestions, and we'll both agree on what name suits her best. How's that?" The pup wiggled in her arms, so she put it down on the floor where it rolled around, pawing the air.

"It's a deal. I'll finish my drawings, and then how about having supper in town? I want to take you to the Blossom Cafe. Will and I ate there the other day. Tomorrow we'll have to go to the store for pooch supplies. And we'll have to buy materials for a fence, too." John kissed her lightly on the lips. "I love you. Are you still upset with all that silly church gossip?"

His sudden display of affection lifted her spirits. "You made me feel so much better. And the puppy helped, too. You're just what the doctor ordered, Mr. John McDonald."

He thought for a moment. "Would you like a shot? Zoom!" He reached to grab her and she squealed, wriggling out of his grasp. She ran out the back screen door, the puppy scampering closely behind.

She yelled from the yard, "I changed my mind. I don't like doctors!"

"Hey!" John called. "Everyone's left me."

She slowly returned with hands clasped together, sauntering timidly to the door where he stood. "Never," she whispered through the screen. "I'd never leave you."

He slowly opened the door and pulled her inside, holding her in his gaze until his arms surrounded her. "If you don't hurry and get ready, I'm going to join you upstairs and we'll never get to town."

She swallowed hard, trying to dismiss the urgent desire to consume his body on the spot. "I've heard about the Blossom Cafe. I'd love to eat there," she managed to say with a smile. The puppy yelped outside, and John let it in. "Where is this Blossom Cafe?"

"Oh, it's across the street from the public square. It's a favorite among the mortuary people who work nearby."

"Gee, that sounds inviting." Her eyebrows furrowed.

"No, really. You'll like it just fine. It's a great place to eat. Oh, and by the way, Robert wants to meet at Iroquois Park Saturday night. The movie should be good. They're showing *The Gay Divorcee,* with Fred Astaire and Ginger Rogers. Miss Rogers is feeling good about being divorced. They made a movie about it. Oh, Robert is bringing a date. Bridgett or Beverly … something like that. And he said to say hello."

"I'm sorry I missed him. The gal's name is Brenda."

"What happened to Betty?"

"I'm not sure. Robert said something about her possessiveness, and he didn't think she had any sense of humor."

"Hm-m, interesting. Anyway what do you say; do you want to go?"

"Sure, it'll be fun. I hear it's a musical and I like them much better than those sticky-sweet, variety operettas like the one they showed last month, with Jeanette McDonald and Nelson Eddy."

"Did I ever tell you I was related to Jeanette McDonald?" John said, doing his best to keep a straight face. "She's my father's cousin. They live in California; Beverly Hills, I believe it is."

"No, you never mentioned it." She looked him in the eye. "Come on, you're pulling my leg, aren't you?"

John laughed. "Yeah, I am. There's no relation. I can't even relate to her movies. Come here, you," he said, placing his arm around her shoulders and giving her a quick squeeze. "You go get ready and the pup and I will have a chat."

They both laughed as Elsie headed up the stairs. The puppy yelped again, unable to follow her.

"She's cute, isn't she?" John called after her. "I'll teach her to climb up and down while we wait for you. I can tell this dog is smart."

"Is it all right to leave her in the house while we're gone?"

"Oh, sure. She'll be fine. I'll take her out back again for another bathroom session before we leave."

"What about chewing? Puppies like to gnaw."

"I'll give her an old rag to play with. She couldn't do much damage; she still has baby teeth."

"They're sharp, though," Elsie called down from the bedroom doorway. Clothing was strewn across the bed, and newspapers were spread out all over the floor. She picked up the clutter and sat on a low settee by the window. The dark clouds that lay heavily in the late afternoon sky were disappearing, carrying the rain with them.

Outside on the porch, robins pecked at the bread crumbs she'd thrown out earlier. She could see four funny-faced pumpkins she had carved lined up in front of the short hedges that sheltered a small rose garden. The scene was so peaceful that she stretched out on the bed, shook off thoughts of the past few hours, eased back against the white lace sham, and began thinking of names for the new puppy.

In need of writing paper, she reached to the nightstand and noticed an envelope bearing her mother's exquisite handwriting, which was something else she didn't inherit. She slit open the letter with a hairpin and drew out the sheet of paper. Lately, she was wondering a lot about what had happened to her husband, James, and how on earth would she manage a divorce. Would this letter shed light on his disappearance? An old tinge of resentment crept back into her memories of him. She began reading:

11 October, 1934

Dearest Elsie,
    I miss you so much. How are you doing? How have you and Robert been getting on? Do you fancy teaching the children?
    Your father, Lena, Evelyn, and your Auntie Jane send their love.

Your father is working hard at Goodyear. He said to tell you the insurance department needs help. How do you like it there? Your Auntie Jane says it's lovely. Favors England, I suppose.

Evelyn told me you have a new beau, John, I believe his name is. Why didn't you tell me about him? Are you two courting? Coincidentally, I haven't heard a word about James. Don't think anybody ever will. Evidently, he even left a week's pay at the plant over three years ago. Your father attempted to get it and send it to you, but the personnel office refused.

Lena has become so skilled at sewing, she's making her own patterns. She made her prom dress from part cheesecloth and hand-stitched crepe paper. The gown only cost $1.25 to make. We're so proud of her. We're proud of you too, luv.

I should be getting supper on the table. Your father is coming home early today. The family is all well. Thank God.

Please write back soon and let us know if you are coming home for the holidays. Your father agreed to pay for your train ticket. I hope to see your pretty face soon. I pray for you every day. Be well.

Love always,

Mum

Elsie sighed and leaned back, closing her eyes for a moment. A part of her felt relieved that James had departed without a trace, and another part of her felt somewhat disappointed that she couldn't talk to him about a divorce. What was not in question, at all, was the fact that she did not love him anymore.

Mentally, she went through the alphabet, writing all the appropriate female names she could think of for a dog. She reached 'P' when John walked in the room with the puppy following. John bounced on the bed, slowly climbed on top of her, and laid his head affectionately on her lap.

He looked up at her sweetly. "This dog is amazing. I showed her one time how to climb the stairs and she did it. I took her out to do her business so we can leave her indoors when we leave. Plus, I fed her. Boy was she hungry. And she's not the only one. I was about to fight her for the corn mush. Are you ready to go?"

"I'm ready. I think I have enough names here for a litter. Let's go, sweetie," she said, playing with John's hair. "Could you help me with this dress?" She went to the closet and pulled out the garment.

"Gladly."

Elsie noticed that he really did look hungry. But for what, she wasn't quite sure.

* * *

The Blossom Cafe was packed, bursting at the seams with dining patrons. John grabbed the only empty table, which seated two. His eyes scanned the menu. "Wine?" he asked.

"No thanks." She felt a slight niggling of dissatisfaction playing at the corners of her mind; she knew it wasn't right, but she couldn't help it. "Just lemonade for me."

"Are you sure?" he asked, his happiness fading a little as he noticed her drawn expression.

"Yes," Elsie said, simply. A couple of lovers across the room were smiling and laughing loudly. The woman wore a small diamond on her left hand, signifying their engagement. Since she'd moved into his house, John hadn't mentioned marriage. She tried to dismiss this line of thinking; she was sorry it seemed that John had noticed her change of mood. She gazed out the window. The rain had started up again, drumming relentlessly outside.

The waiter approached and John took the liberty of ordering for both of them. He wanted potted pork chops, a bowl of beef stew, and a glass of white wine. For Elsie, he ordered a steak well done and a mug of lemonade.

The waiter left and Elsie noticed he hadn't written anything down. "He must have a good memory," she remarked.

"We'll know that when we get our meals." John grinned. "Let's see your dog list."

Elsie pulled it out of her pocketbook and handed it across the table. "Here you go."

John glanced at it. "Daisy is cute."

"Is that your first choice?" She raised an eyebrow.

"Let's see now. This is an important decision." He traced a finger down the paper. "What about Millie?"

"Didn't you have a girlfriend name Millie?"

"Millie." He frowned. "No, you mean Nellie."

"That's right, nervous Nellie." Her gaze fell away from his.

John made a face as he tried to reassure her. "Don't tell me you're jealous of Nellie? She's back in Buffalo, and I … " he took her hands in his. "I'm with you now. You're the only woman in the world for me. I love you so much."

Those words washed over her like a wave of tenderness more powerful than all the adoring words that had come before. He had a knack for making her feel better. She decided not to worry about commitments or criticisms, at least for tonight.

"I might be going to Akron for Christmas. My mum wrote me a letter and said my dad will pay for a ticket."

"Do you want to go? Sounds like your folks want to see you."

"Part of me does. The other part wants me to spend Christmas with you."

"You don't have to make up your mind right now. Think about it."

She smiled at him and nodded.

After supper, they were laughing like teenagers when John pulled the car up in front of the house.

"Listen, it's the puppy. She sounds like she's dying," Elsie said, catching her breath.

"She's just happy that we're home," John replied.

"She could be hurt."

"No. She's just yapping loudly, that's all. She's a puppy. It's nothing."

John opened the front door to a chorus of piercing yelps, yaps, and claws furiously scrabbling across the hardwood floor.

"So much for your floor polish," Elsie said. "Oh my word," she added, as John swung the door wide open.

The floor was littered with scraps of shredded paper that flew up in a torrent of large snow as the puppy screeched to her feet in leaps of happiness and tail wagging.

"What on earth?" John said, scanning the parlor. "Where did all this mess come from?"

"Say, if I remember correctly, weren't you working on some drawings when I came home?"

"No. She couldn't get up on my drafting table." John went into his study to find that the drawing papers were missing.

"Look," Elsie said. "Here's a section of skyscraper windows." She handed him a scrap of paper.

"That's not windows from a skyscraper. But you really can't tell from any of these pieces. She really went crazy."

"You're right about that."

"Oh well, no harm done."

"You're joking."

"No, really. They were just a few ideas I was toying around with. I'm glad she was able to entertain herself while we were gone."

"I'll help you clean this up."

"Thank you. After all, she's your dog."

"My dog? I thought she was your dog; you took her from Robert."

"Nope, your dog. You picked her out originally."

"Nope, yours."

"Yours."

"Yours."

John ended the whole discussion by grabbing her collar and planting dog-style sloppy kisses about her face and neck, the real dog yapping furiously, and Elsie weak in the knees from his spontaneity. When he could no longer make her stand, he carried her and plopped her on the sofa where they began to undress each other.

Later, they listened to the music of the *Kraft Music Hall* and made love again. She felt that he played her body like a finely tuned instrument, and enclosed them both in waves of excitement. After lovemaking, they cleaned up and played with the dog, which they agreed to call "Millie."

Elsie's determination to move in with John, despite church members' criticism, and society's disapproval, had been more than rewarded because she was more than content; she was happily in love.

* * *

The brown, leafless remains of strawberry plants clung to the dirt at the far edge of the backyard where John was working. He hit the last nail into a wood rail as Elsie stepped out of the house, holding a frosty glass of iced tea. She handed it to him. "Here you go. I thought you might be thirsty for a cool drink."

"Thank you, sweetheart." He turned around to look over his work. "How does the fence look?"

She smiled. "It looks like it was constructed by a top-notch architect. Architects should be artists as well as engineers."

"I agree. I try to work in a wide variety of materials. I've gained an appreciation of all their separate qualities."

"I can vouch for that." She gave him a coy smile, a devilish gleam in her eyes. "This should keep Millie safe when we're gone."

John leaned against the fence next to her, his eyes appreciating the curves of her body from head to foot. "And us safe from her chewing up the house."

Elsie's heart beat a little more quickly when he was close, especially when he studied her.

"You look stunning this morning," he said, watching her movements.

"I feel good, even though I missed church."

"You're not going to let a few catty women keep you away, are you?"

"No, I'm not. I just didn't feel like going this morning."

Whistling softly, he stirred the thick paint with a piece of wood and dipped the paintbrush into the gleaming white liquid. "Since you're home, do you want to help paint? I have two brushes." He tempted her by holding one up for her perusal.

She took it and smiled at him. "Sure, I'd love to." As they painted the fence side-by-side, she thought about how sweet John was to her. She sensed his gentleness was genuine. Just because he wasn't pressuring her to divorce James, didn't mean he didn't want her to pursue divorce proceedings. She basked in his love, letting the emotions flow over her, reaching every part. She reveled in his admiration. How wonderful to live in the country, she thought, with a man she was crazy in love with. It sure beat being stuck living in Akron, working in a boring insurance office at Goodyear Tire.

Chapter Eleven

By the time John, Elsie, and Millie reached the Iroquois River, the park was already packed with people. A cordoned-off area displayed a sign that read, "Free Picture Show Tonight—*The Gay Divorcée*," and showcased photos of Fred Astaire and Ginger Rogers. Inside the roped area, straw covered the ground where people had spread blankets to sit on. Ahead, at the far end of the seating area, a large cotton sheet was stretched between two tall standards, upon which the picture would be shown. To one side of the sheet, a man dressed all in white stood on a platform with a bullhorn and a sheet of paper in hand. Straw bales and pumpkins lined the outer edges of the cordoned area, and many of the moviegoers sat on the bales, while children played with the pumpkins. The sharp tang of fall pervaded the evening chill, making the event seem like an autumn football game; people wore stadium coats and hats to keep warm.

John scanned the crowd and raised his hand in greeting when he spotted Robert and his date, Brenda. Robert returned the gesture and smiled broadly. They were holding down a prime location on a blanket under a large maple that was close to the moving picture projector.

It felt as though the three of them were walking toward Robert and Brenda on a colored canvas, under a canopy of orange, red, and purple leaves. The scene reminded Elsie of a Norman Rockwell painting; a good old American autumn, with lots of fallen leaves on the ground and children running and throwing them about. Amid the chatter, she heard a steady musical hum that took several moments to identify; the sound was coming from the flow of the river. She took a deep breath, inhaling its aroma.

Millie pranced over to Robert and Brenda, tail wagging. The dog nuzzled Robert's hands, so he hugged and petted her. "How you doing, Millie? Remember me? Good girl," he said, getting up and taking Brenda's hand to help her to her feet. Feeling a little awkward, he lit a cigarette. The scent of the tobacco stung the air. "Elsie, John, this is Brenda." Robert said cheerfully.

Brenda smiled warmly and shook John's hand.

She was the kind of woman, Elsie thought, that men probably looked at twice, and women, too, for that matter. She had good looks and seemed pleasant enough. Her dark fall of hair, thick and wavy, barely moved when she turned her head.

"I'm pleased to meet you both," she said, taking Elsie's hand in hers.

Elsie saw that her eyes were clear and pale blue like the sky. "Likewise. Good to meet you, too."

"Robert has told me so much about you," Brenda said, releasing Elsie's hand. "How long have you been a twosome?"

"Well, let's see ... just about five months now," John said thoughtfully.

"That's swell!" Brenda smiled. "You two make such a cute couple."

The picture should be great, don't you think?" Robert asked.

"I do. I'm looking forward to it," Elsie said. "Should be good. I enjoy musicals that aren't too syrupy, you know what I mean?"

"I sure do," John cut in. "No syrup here. This picture is going to be filled with legs. They say that new gal, Betty Grable, has a great pair."

"Well, *I've* never heard of her," Elsie retorted.

"You will. It's her debut picture. She's only eighteen, and they say she's talented, but a little too young for me," John quipped.

Elsie playfully poked his ribs.

John chuckled, went around behind her, and put his hands on her shoulders. "What?" he said into her ear. "I was just pulling your leg, you know. I only have eyes for you, er ... your legs, I mean."

Elsie gave him the gimlet eye. "You knew you'd better slide that one in."

"Well, sure. Your legs are nicer than Betty Grable's, any day."

Brenda beamed. "John, that's so sweet of you to say, isn't it Robert?"

Robert was caught off guard. "Oh, uh ... yeah, sure, if you say so. She's my cousin. I don't know about her legs."

"Robert!" Elsie said. "Thanks a lot. Don't mind him," she said to Brenda. "Most of the time he's my biggest fan."

"Robert told me you work with children," Brenda said. "I admire that. I respect anyone who has the patience to be around youngsters all day."

"It really doesn't take a lot of patience for me, "Elsie said, "but that's nice of you to say. What do you do?"

"I'm studying to be a nurse. I like it, though I'm afraid I find myself worrying more, with all the diseases a person could fall prey to."

"Nursing is a noble profession, though," Elsie said.

"Like teaching."

"Sure," Elsie agreed. "Although, I couldn't stand all that blood with nursing, not to mention all the death you have to deal with."

"The blood doesn't bother me anymore. I guess I'm getting use to it, if that's possible. Death is something I don't think I'll ever get used to."

Robert blew a stream of smoke. "Enough of this morbid small talk." He clapped his hands once in a commanding effort. "Let's all sit and get comfortable."

"It's not small talk," Elsie said, regarding Robert in a solemn gaze. "It's serious, right Brenda? You'll have to think about it one day."

"Killjoy," Robert said.

John sat down and made himself comfortable on the blanket. "We don't have to think about that now; not tonight."

"Right," Robert said.

Elsie and Brenda looked at one another. "Men," Brenda whispered.

"I know what you mean," Elsie whispered behind the back of her hand. She lay down on her back to snuggle with Millie, who stretched out beside her. She liked the soft feel of the cocker spaniel's hair. With one hand on the dog's neck, she looked up at John, who sat down beside her. "You're looking particularly dapper tonight, Mr. McDonald."

"Thanks. I didn't even have time to shave." Digging into his pocket, he came up with a packet of chewing gum. "Gum anyone?"

"Okay," Elsie said, popping a stick of it into her mouth. She crumbled the wrapper in a ball, sat up, and looked around the grounds. "Isn't this a lovely setting?" The river shimmered like an emerald necklace, peeking through the thickets of trees at the park's edge.

"It sure is," Brenda said, following Elsie's line of sight. "The water looks breathtaking, doesn't it? We'll have to come here for a picnic sometime."

"Yeah, it's real nice. Not as nice as the Chicago World's Fair grounds, but nice," John said.

"Hey, get this," Robert said. "Next Saturday afternoon we can get into the matinee in town if we bring an old tire with us." He laughed. "We just roll it up to the theater and present it to the ticket taker. Does everyone want to go? It's a good way to help me cut down on the junk lying around my backyard. I already checked … they're showing a Shirley Temple picture."

Brenda smiled at him. "Sounds swell, and I'd love to go as long as I don't have to supply my own tire."

Robert winked at her. "I'd supply more than an old tire for you."

"I'm up for a free show," John put in. "I guess Shirley Temple is all right, but I don't know what all the fuss is about. She's just a little girl with curly hair who eats lollipops."

Elsie was astonished. "You're joking! A little girl who can do *everything*. And do it well. She's extremely talented. I don't know how she can memorize all those lines at her age, and sing, too. She's a national icon. Everybody adores Shirley Temple."

John looked up at the sky and sighed. "Not everyone," he said, trying to hide a smile.

"My mother took my sister to the hair dresser to have her hair done up in fifty-six curls so she would resemble Shirley Temple," Brenda said.

"See this?" Elsie said, circling her arms around John and reaching up to play with his slowly curling lips.

John tried to keep a straight face. "Don't make me laugh."

"See?" Elsie looked at Brenda and Robert. "He's smiling; he likes her just fine. He's only fooling around. We'll be there. Robert has plenty of old tires lying around; enough for all of us to get into the picture show."

"That will be really keen." Brenda pulled a small picnic basket from the edge of the blanket to her side. "I brought some apples and popcorn. Please, help yourselves."

"I'll get some pop to go with the snacks." Robert stood, took Brenda's hands in his, and pulled her to her feet. He put his arm around her shoulders.

John dug into his pocket for change. "Here, get us all something," he said, handing Robert a quarter.

"Be back in a jiffy," Robert said as he and Brenda walked off. The American Legion had set up sawhorses and four, two-by-twelve planks, forming a refreshment table at the end of the parking lot.

John glanced at Elsie with calm confidence. "Alone at last." Millie's head shot up, and she looked at him. "Sorry girl. I didn't mean you, although you *are* cute."

He turned to kiss Elsie. "Do you still love me, even though I don't see what you do in Curly Top?"

Elsie gazed back at him, loving him. "You're such a tease."

He kissed her again and could feel her melting into him, her lips warm and moist from his. They lay on the blanket in silence, wrapped in each other arms.

She felt a shiver race up her spine. The rough brush of his five o'clock shadow was a sensual contrast to the softness of his lips.

Drawing back, he let his hands linger briefly on the curve of her cheek. "I don't know if I can make it through the main feature without wanting more of you." Leaving her with that, he turned and smiled as Robert and Brenda came back, carrying four Coke bottles.

"Thanks," John said, grabbing two.

"Thank *you*. Here's your change." Robert tossed John a nickel. "How's Millie doing anyway? She looks happy."

"Fine. She's a handful, though. The first night she cried for her mother. Elsie was up with her all night."

"And before she cried all night we came home to shredded drawings," Elsie added.

Robert laughed.

"Poor thing. She missed her mother," Brenda said.

"No, I'm only laughing," Robert replied, "because it's almost like having a baby, isn't it?"

John nodded. "It sure is ... without the foreplay."

"It's almost dark," Elsie said, nibbling an apple. "The show should start any minute now." She looked at John, studying him. The diminished light cast his face in shadows, and the ever-so-subtle rough skin that surrounded his mouth made him even more appealing.

A man on the platform banged two pieces of wood together and spoke into his bullhorn. "Ladies and Gentlemen. Please be seated. We're about to begin. RKO Pictures is pleased to present for your viewing enjoyment, *The Gay Divorcée,* starring Mr. Fred Astaire and Miss. Ginger Rogers. You will be among the first to see this picture before its world release later this month. First, we will present a cartoon, a newsreel, and a short subject: an *Our Gang* comedy. Thank you for your attention. Please enjoy the show."

"I wonder why the park is hosting it for free?" Brenda asked. "Usually they only run old films, don't they?"

"Unless it has something to do with those guys," John said, jerking a thumb over his shoulder at a group of men on the opposite edge of the park. They were setting up camera equipment and lights.

"Maybe RKO wants to film the crowd's approval so it'll better help them sell it to more theaters overseas," Robert suggested.

"Or just measure crowd approval without having to pass out questionnaires," Elsie said.

"Or maybe see if the movie is good enough to run in any theatre," John added.

Brenda piped up, gushing. "Oh, that would be fun to be interviewed, don't you think, Elsie?"

"I'll let you do that. I'd be embarrassed. Anyway, you look like the movie star."

John put his arm around Elsie and gave her a quick squeeze. "You do, too, sweetie."

Robert and Brenda nodded.

"I always thought it would be fun to be in pictures," Brenda said.

"It would be fun to live in Hollywood, and make the money the movie stars do, "Robert added. "I'd agree with that part."

Brenda took a sip of soda to moisten her lips. "Where do both of you live?" she asked Elsie.

John and Elsie's eyes met. They exchanged slightly startled glances, and then smiled knowingly at one another. "I'm living in the same place John is; at his house," Elsie said hesitantly.

Brenda smiled. "Oh, I think that's keen. I don't see why people have to be married to live together. You're independent thinkers. That's all the rage in Hollywood. There's, let's see … Paulette Goddard and Charlie Chaplin—they're not married."

Elsie sipped her soda, then gave a laugh. "Don't forget Orson Welles and his girlfriend, Virginia Nicholson. Also living in sin, or so they say."

"Elsie's always been ahead of her time," Robert said, grinning at her. "She likes to do what makes her happy, as long as she's not hurting anyone." He always felt something special with her. The feelings had always been there as children; a closeness. A bond that began in childhood had flowered into their relationship as adults.

"Thanks for the vote of confidence." Elsie winked at him.

"I say, if Hollywood is doing it, it must be all right for the rest of us," John added.

"Jolly good reasoning. I'll drink to that," Robert said, downing his Coke.

It was now dark, and the wheel turned on the projector. The unfamiliar noise seemed to spook Mille. She jumped up and began to bark.

"Sh-h, Millie," John said. "Lie down."

The puppy whined then put her head down next to Elsie. In the middle of the newsreel the projector broke down. Many people jumped to their feet, stomping, clapping, and shouting, "Put a nickel in it!" It seemed to Elsie that the moviegoers were convinced the shouting made the repairs go more quickly. A minute later, the big sheet came alive again amidst enthusiastic applause from the crowd.

Dragging a hand through her hair, Elsie whispered to John, "I'm having a good time. I rather fancy Brenda. She's open-minded."

"She is. I'm glad you like her. I do, too," John said, kissing her forehead. "That should make Robert happy." With a faint air of amusement lingering around his mouth, he lit up a cigarette. John settled back against the maple, toying with his soda pop, only vaguely listening to the *Our Gang* comedy. His mind remained focused on Elsie and his friends.

Elsie became aware of the dark; the new chill in the night air, and shivered. "Br-r, it's getting cold."

John hugged her. "Do you want to go to the car? We can still see the movie from there."

Elsie nodded and turned to Robert and Brenda. "What do you two think?"

"Sure, it will probably be more comfortable," Robert said.

Brenda nodded.

The two men picked up their belongings. Both couples strolled back to the parking lot, hand-in-hand. Millie trotted alongside.

Elsie smiled at John. A little quiver of happiness trickled through her. She'd experienced a lovely sense of contentment over the last few days. It was John's love and the great time she was having that filled her with such abundant joy. She finally knew that he was the only man she had ever loved. She saw how empty and loveless her marriage to James had been, and acknowledged that she was doing the right thing by remaining in Indiana. Besides, now she had a new friend.

She'd taken an instant liking to Brenda, even though the two women had entirely diverse styles, with the exception of their hair length, and entirely different tastes. Oddly enough, however, it seemed like a friendship had begun the moment they'd met. There was something so open and generous in Brenda's attitude. Elsie felt that meeting her was like walking into the sun after a long winter of intolerable cold, especially after the experience she'd had with the women at church.

Chapter Twelve

Elsie hurried to finish making a dozen ham sandwiches and pack them into a wicker basket. Four other choir members were also busy making food in the church kitchen. Gale, the newest member, a young mother in her early twenties, had just finished readying the soup urn.

Elsie noticed that she was drying her hands on the bottom of her apron and searching the faces of the other women. "What is it, Gale? Is everything all right?" Elsie asked.

"It's just that ... well; we *are* going to visit hobos. Do you think that's safe? We won't be attacked, will we?"

"Oh," Lila answered, arranging baked chicken on a tray. "We always do this a couple days before Thanksgiving. It's become an annual event for us. We've never had any problems. The men are usually quiet and grateful."

"Don't worry," Emily said. "We'll set up some of the food inside the train station building. They come from the camp down below, form a line, and walk through. It's safe inside."

Esther, a gray-haired, elderly woman with kind eyes and a robust waistline was wiping down the counters. "Looks like we're ready. We can get everything in my big Chevrolet, but two of us will need to walk. It isn't far."

"Only about five blocks," Elsie said, smiling. "I don't mind walking. My basket is light."

Emily picked up a red-checkered cloth and placed it smoothly over the snickerdoodle cookies in her basket. She gave Elsie a cold stare. "I'll join you, I suppose. Are you ready?"

Elsie was taken aback by her snippy mood, but remained undaunted in true holiday spirit. "Sure, let's go, I'm all set."

While the other women filed out of the kitchen toward the car, Elsie followed Emily down the church steps and out onto the sidewalk.

In the weeks following the bout with Joanne, it appeared that the pattern of Elsie's life was set, and that the residents of Rensselaer accepted her affair without starting a scandal. True, remnants of judgment still lingered in the attitudes of some church members. Especially Emily. Five blocks suddenly looked a lot farther than Elsie had remembered.

After the second block, the two women descended a bluff on a trail that led to the train station. Elsie thought it impolite of Emily to say good afternoon to a stranger passing by, when she hadn't spoken one word to her since they had left the church grounds.

Emily remained quiet as the two women continued to walk. Elsie knew she was being given the cold shoulder and tried to finally start a friendly conversation. "Where are you spending the Thanksgiving holiday, Emily?"

A long pause followed before Emily eventually responded. "My *husband* and I are having dinner at my sister Kate's house. She lives down in Wolcott."

Elsie ignored the husband jab, saying, "That's nice that you're spending Thanksgiving with family."

A long awkward silence followed while Elsie searched for something else to talk about. "Oh, I meant to tell you how much I enjoyed your sparkling rendition of *Love Me or Leave Me*. It's such a beautiful song, and you sang it so well. It gave me goose bumps." Elsie cringed when she heard herself placating Emily, but the hit song lyrics did stir up strong emotions. Elsie honestly thought she had done a wonderful job, and deserved some congratulations. *I'm trying so hard to be nice. Must they insist on hating me so?*

Emily smiled faintly. "It's a heavenly melody, and Ruth Etting is such an inspiration." She stopped suddenly on the trail and looked at Elsie long and hard. "I'm going to be honest with you," she said bluntly. "I don't believe in premarital sex. Why aren't you getting married?"

Elsie felt a sad frustration come over her. "I don't know. It's sort of complicated."

"Is he unable to marry due to lack of employment?"

"No, he has a job."

"Has he asked you, or even hinted at marriage?"

"Not formally, no," Elsie said with despair in her voice.

"My father always says, '*Why buy the cow when you can get the milk for free.*' I guess he's right. Anyway you look at it, you're wrong."

Elsie was speechless, thinking that Emily had been unnecessarily cruel with her remarks. She would never have been so mean-spirited. Now she had to hold back tears and pretend that the words didn't hurt. She wasn't going to give Emily the satisfaction of seeing her cry.

Silently, they crossed Main Street and headed in the direction of the gray billows of smoke that led them into the encampment. There, under the railroad bridge, several men were cooking food over an open fire, and others rested beneath chestnut trees. Baskets woven from tree branches and twigs were scattered on the ground. Off to the side of the campfire stood a floorless umbrella tent, along with Army blankets thrown across the dirt.

They were young men, whom Elsie suspected had recently graduated from high school or college, and should have been looking forward to a promising future, but now were searching for any job they could find. A few older men stood around who had probably worked all their lives, but now found themselves unemployed. It was a disturbing sight.

Instinctively, Emily hurried ahead to join the other churchwomen by the campfire.

Elsie cheerfully made her way through the bleak woods, looking for men who were hungry, and handing out sandwiches.

For the most part, the hobos were soft-spoken and polite. There wasn't much conversation; only murmurs of grateful appreciation for a simple meal. Elsie's heart went out to them. Their lives had been thrown into confusion and chaos through no fault of their own.

On her way back up the trail to the train station, she noticed one man alone down by a trickling stream that passed beneath a bridge. He knelt beside the water, holding a small piece of broken mirror in his left hand and a safety blade in his right. She made her way down the hill with her sandwich basket to greet him. "Excuse me sir, would you like a sandwich?"

He reached for a cloth on the ground, dipped it in the river, and wiped his face. His gaze followed the sound of her voice. "Who's there?" He seemed apprehensive, unsure whether to stay or flee. Then his mouth fell open. "Elsie! My God, is that you? It sure looks like you, but ... am I dreaming?" James rushed up the hill into a sunshine-filled clearing, wiping his hands on his pants.

He stood there, thinner than she'd remembered. The memory of James leaving that summer night flashed in her mind. His words played over again in her head. *'I'm going out to get cigarettes and maybe play some cards with the boys. A man's entitled to relax and have some fun after a hard day at work.'* He'd given her a reluctant kiss on the cheek and walked out the screen door, never to return.

Today he stood before her, wearing worn overalls and a short ragged coat, his bare feet clad in brown leather shoes. A black, weather-torn hat, anchored under a rock, lay by the stream down below. What looked like his bindle—a bedroll, consisting of a piece of canvas wrapped around blankets—lay against a tree near the river.

For a moment she just stared at him with her eyes wide and her mouth forming a small circle. "Oh, James, I can't believe it! I ... I don't know what to say. What are *you* doing here?"

She waited for a response, but James closed his eyes and sighed in discomfort. Then he opened them, their gray intensity seeming to beg her understanding.

But what else she saw deep within his eyes was a hurt so profound; she couldn't possibly know its source. Several awkward moments passed, then she finally blurted, "Oh, this is just plain wacky. You left me to become a hobo?" Her voice rose. "Where have you been all this time? You didn't take our marriage vows very seriously, James. And you didn't take me seriously, either. You were supposed to love me until death do us part. But you left after only fifteen months! That was almost four years ago!" She spoke quickly, with anger and determination.

His eyes filled with tears and his mouth twisted as he drew an uneven breath. "Wait a minute, Elsie. Calm down. Bloody hell. I don't blame you for hating me." He swallowed with seeming difficulty. "I thought what I did, I did for you. I *do* love you."

"Rubbish!" Elsie snapped. "You don't love me! If you loved me you wouldn't have left. Don't you realize abandonment is just as traumatic as divorce? More so sometimes, because it doesn't have the clarity of a mutual decision." She felt her stomach contract with distress. "This is a bloody nightmare! I'm going to pinch myself and hopefully I'll wake up." She proceeded to pinch her forearm in plain sight for him to see.

A female voice, high-pitched, interrupted. "Yoo-hoo! Elsie, is everything all right?" It was Lila.

"Oh yes, fine," Elsie answered in the direction of the voice. She glanced at James, then back toward the voice again, trying not to sound flustered. "Could you excuse us? An old chum is here. I haven't seen him in quite some time. We were just catching up."

"Sure, we understand. I just wanted to know if you were in any trouble. We heard loud voices."

"No, I'm okay." She forced a smile. "Thanks for your concern. I'm fine, really."

"She's just fine." James smiled broadly.

After the choir member left, James enclosed Elsie's wrist with his large, slightly damp hand. "Come with me. I know the perfect spot where we won't be seen."

She pulled away. "What makes you think I want to go anywhere secluded with you?"

His face was set with strain and unhappiness. "I deserved that. Don't you want to know why I had to leave? We can't talk here." He pointed up toward the train station. "All your church friends up there will have a run with this."

She nodded reluctantly.

"Wait here." He went back to the creek, picked up his belongings, and returned. He grabbed her arm. The ham sandwiches bouncing in her basket, he pulled her into the bushes away from the others. Roughly, they stumbled out of the shady woods into brilliant sunlight. The grassy area was spacious, level, and open. They followed a path to a towering tree, devoid of leaves in the November chill. Nearby, James found three large rocks that provided an excellent place for them to sit and discuss the past three and a half years.

For the first time, his face brightened as he gazed at her. "How did you find me?" he asked, breathless from the exertion.

Elsie attempted to hold back a smile. "It was a fluke, really. I thought to myself, where would James Hunter head off to? Back to Scotland? No. Back to live with his sister? No. I've got it! He's bloody roaming around the States, living as a hobo, presently bunking down in Rensselaer, Indiana. I'll try there."

"You were always perceptive, Elsie."

Her voice softened. "I saw a man alone who still had pride in his appearance and thought hard times hadn't taken that away from him. I figured I would ask him if he would like something to eat. Why were you shaving anyway?"

"I shave everyday. I'm not a tramp, for God's sake. In any event, that's not important. Listen luv, I left because I was going to lose my job. My name was plastered on the bulletin board outside the plant. I thought you'd be better off without me—one less mouth for your parents to feed. Your mum always gave me dirty looks at supper. But my leaving you didn't have anything to do with my feelings for you."

Elsie shook her head. Disbelief and sympathy merged. "You don't walk out on somebody you love. I'm sorry. I don't believe it. If you care for someone, you want them in your life. Why did you think becoming a hobo would change anything?"

He stared at her in silence, obviously thinking of the right words with which to answer her. "That's not true. I've talked with plenty of men who left the ones they love. I'm not the only one. I thought, like I said, you'd be better off with me out of the way, and I could travel cheaply riding boxcars, getting work where I could. I just have to watch my back when I'm carrying cash, that's all." He looked down at his shoes. "Maybe I was wrong to do what I did; leaving you alone without explanation. I felt bad about it. I spent many a lonely night thinking about you."

A flicker of anxiety crossed his face, and Elsie truly felt sympathetic. She marveled at her emotional turn around; now she felt sorry for the man who had abandoned her.

"I can tell you straightaway," James said, "that I thought you were disappointed in me, even if you won't admit it. I know I was never—"

"What makes you think I was ever disappointed in you?" she interrupted. "I never said I was disappointed, did I? I would have never married you if I felt that way."

He gave her an apologetic look. "I'm sorry. What can I say to make it easier for you? I was a lousy husband. Will you ever forgive me, or will you despise me for the rest of your life?"

She appeared flustered. "I don't hate you, James." The anger and resentment evaporated, and she started to blame herself. "You weren't the only one at fault. I wasn't the perfect wife, either. I wasn't what you were looking for. But if you had told me you were on the layoff list, I could have spoken with my father. He's been with Goodyear for more than twenty years now. I'm sure he could have found work for you." She laid a hand on his arm. "Oh, I almost forgot—you have some money there. I believe it's a week's pay. But it's been so long I don't know if you can collect it."

He hesitated before responding. "No. They paid me everything they owed me. I left after I received my check." He paused. "Unless it's money held back from when I started." James plucked up a stick and sketched in the soil. "I've been promised a job pouring concrete at a filling station that's being built in town. After that, I'll head back to Akron to pick up the money if it really is owed to me. I planned on visiting my sister over the holidays, anyway." He smiled. "That's jolly good news, though." Then he picked up his bindle and unrolled it to sit on. He extended his arm.

She had to take it; to refuse would be disrespectful.

Immediately, his strong arms encircled her, drawing her to him. "I've missed you so." He kissed her on the lips and she knew he was instantly aroused. "I'm as randy as a teenager," he said, running his hands up under her blouse. She wore no brassiere today, just a blue cardigan over a dainty yellow blouse. Her nipples rose to the touch of his fingers. He caressed her shoulders and her stomach, then tried to pull the blouse and sweater over her head.

Memories of ill feelings came flooding back to her. "For God's sake!" she said. "Get your hands off me!" She started to get up, but he pulled her back down. She turned to look at him straight in the eyes. "Are you trying to have a sex romp with me, here in the woods?"

"In my eyes we're still married, Elsie."

She composed herself, rolled away then stood, hands on hips, and looked down at him. "You are the only person in the world who thinks that! Our marriage should have been annulled by the church. It was a mistake and should have never happened." She picked up the wicker basket and brushed the hair out of her face.

James sat up on the bedroll with his arms wrapped around his knees. "We said our vows in front of God. You can never change that."

"Vows *you* didn't take seriously. How conveniently you invoke God when it suits your purposes." The afternoon turned cool and breezy and the sky darkened, making her feel anxious. She looked at him narrowly. "I'd better go. I have to compose myself before returning to the church group."

He made a move toward her.

"No, don't come near me."

"Don't be such a wet blanket," he said, standing and hugging her tightly. "Elsie, I'm sorry. I apologize for everything. It's just that a man doesn't usually see his wife wandering about the woods. I love you. I always will." He paused. "I never did ask you … what *are* you doing wandering around the woods of Indiana?"

Abruptly, she turned from him. With as much dignity as she could muster, she straightened her basket and headed out on a path in the direction of the train station, back to her choir friends. She had walked only a few yards, when James caught her by the arm and blocked her course.

"I'm not going to let you walk back alone."

She glared at him. "All right then, let's talk and walk." She pulled from his grip, looking at him doubtfully. "I'm afraid I've been here far too long already."

He picked up his belongings and walked alongside with his hand on her shoulder. "Tell me, what brings you to Rensselaer?"

"You remember Robert," she began. "Well, he arranged for me to teach the children of the railroad workers here. I couldn't pass up the opportunity. There wasn't anything left for me in Akron."

"What is Robert doing in Indiana?"

"He inherited a house here in town from his grandmother. It's a charming place."

"Plan on staying awhile?" James asked. He rummaged through her basket, pulled out a ham sandwich, and took a bite.

"I haven't decided yet. I'll see. I really enjoy teaching young children."

He abruptly pointed right, in the direction of the trees. Elsie saw nothing.

"I think your friends might have left you here in hobo heaven. I don't see the car that was parked there earlier. A black Chevrolet, right?"

She felt the panic rising in her chest as she nodded. "I do remember it was black; a five-passenger. Not all of us could ride in it because of all the food we had to bring. I walked with Emily." She could now see that the automobile had disappeared. The choir group had left without her. Maybe it was her innate optimism, but she had expected them to search for her and make sure that she returned safely with them. This was just another indication that they hated her.

"Don't worry, Elsie, I'm here. We'll go up to the station where you can call Robert. I don't want you roaming around these woods at dusk. The hobos start drinking whiskey when the sun goes down."

In that moment, she knew she had to get home. Home to safety, and to John.

James led her up a wandering trail and down a steep hill. They stumbled now and then over rocks and holes. The early evening air felt cold. She looked about her, hearing strange night sounds. She was frightened and stopped to stare at James. "Are you sure we're going the right way? The train depot didn't seem this far. It seems awfully dark and desolate out here."

James stood there, a mere outline of dark representing his head and clothing, a cryptic smile on his face. "Trust me. We're almost there. Straightaway, round this bend, you'll find the train depot." They picked up the pace and within minutes she saw a light coming from the train station.

"You should have more faith in me," James said. "But luv, listen, I do have a favor to ask of you. I want you to meet me on Saturday at three o'clock inside the depot. I want you to show up here and tell me everything you're feeling, everything you've been doing, and what you want to do about our marriage. Agreed?"

"I don't know. It's funny I don't even feel married." She looked up at the face of the man who had once been the husband at her side, the man she had lain with in their early days of passion. "Okay, agreed," she said reluctantly. As complicated as it had become, Elsie believed what he said and that his feelings for her were sincere. But she wasn't going to let him off the hook, even though she was in love with someone else. This was her opportunity to talk to him seriously about getting a divorce.

Once inside the depot, Elsie immediately telephoned Robert. After the brief call, she and James went outside to wait. They sat on a small wooden bench and, within minutes, they saw headlights approaching up the dirt road.

Elsie inched away from James while fiddling with the handles that secured the sandwich basket. *How am I going to explain this to anyone?* "Please, go now," she said to James. "I'm not in any mood to have to explain you to Robert or tell him a tall story."

James grabbed the five remaining sandwiches out of the basket and backed away. "I'm gone. I'll see you soon. Happy Thanksgiving." And then he vanished, disappearing into the dark woods.

Robert pulled up right next to the bench, reached over, and opened the passenger side of the car. He looked worried. "Are you okay? You sounded terrible. Was that somebody I saw with you?"

She jumped in, smiling faintly, trying not to let Robert see how shaken she was by her encounter. "I'm fine," she lied, instantly feeling guilty for not telling Robert the truth. She took a deep breath, let it out in a whoosh, and looked at Robert in the darkened car.

He caught her eye. "What?"

"Nothing." She propped her elbow against the window, put her chin in her hand, and looked out the window so that Robert wouldn't see the tears streaming down her face.

The house was unlit when they pulled into the driveway. She could hear Millie running back and forth in the house, barking with joy to finally have company.

Elsie paused on the door handle before stepping out of the automobile, gripped by Robert's unflinching stare, and the fact that she had never lied to him, or had even come close to it. "I ran into James today," she confessed.

"You did?"

She nodded. "The choir gals and I were passing out food at the hobo camp behind the train station. But please don't ask me to explain. I'm crazy in love with John. You know that, don't you?"

"I do, but ... you're going to tell John, right?"

"I'm confused. But for now, thanks for not asking any questions. I'll tell you, but not now, okay?"

"Okay."

"Thanks."

"Don't mention it." He hung out the window. "Have you been crying?" There was no one more sensitive that Robert, and she wasn't about to start talking and maybe mention things she didn't want to tell him. She needed time to sort out exactly what to say to him, and to John.

She looked away in the direction of the house, to hide her face. Millie was still barking.

"Forget I mentioned it," he said. Still puzzled, he waited to make sure she reached the front door safely, and backed out when he saw the front door open. He shook his head in the darkened space of the car.

Millie was dancing and jumping around with joy as she opened the door. The conflicting emotions of Millie's joy, and her own sadness, frustration, and helplessness were so great that Elsie began to cry all over again. She was relieved that John wasn't home yet, and felt a tiny flicker of hope that her meeting with James would not affect their night.

In the parlor, she walked over to the radio and turned the dial until she heard the *Grand Ole Opry* in progress. To relax, she sat with Millie on her lap, sipping a cup of hot tea and listening to her favorite music, while the events of the day tumbled incessantly inside her head.

To further calm her nerves, she went upstairs and ran a bath, scenting it with a heavy splash of jasmine. She climbed into the warm tub, eased into the water, and lay her head against the back of the cold porcelain, letting the emotions of the day drift away. She sighed with relief. The water felt wonderfully soothing against her skin. She lathered her body and her hair, sliding down under the water to rinse.

A knock echoed at the door, and John's voice called out. "Elsie? It's me. May I come in?"

"I'm having a bath."

"I know." Discreetly, the door opened and he whispered, "I thought you might want some company." He slipped off his undergarments and gently lowered himself into the water behind her. Then he put his arms around her, pulled her against his bare chest, and rained kisses on the top of her head. "I missed you today," he said affectionately.

His body touching hers felt good. She wanted to stay pressed up against his love forever. Whenever she was upset or worried, his presence always comforted her, always made her feel cherished.

"I missed you, too." Before long, she turned to face him and kissed him passionately. They made love in the tub, with slow country music playing in the background. The sex could have gone on all night. She was not prepared for how intense she felt being close to this man.

James entered her thoughts like an uninvited guest opening private doors. She wasn't going to ruin a perfectly wonderful evening by disclosing her unanticipated encounter. Not tonight. Not in this glorious moment of utter bliss.

Chapter Thirteen

Mrs. Armbruster gave Elsie a curt nod as they passed each other on the sidewalk. As the church's secretary, she would have normally stopped a moment to chat before continuing on. Elsie did not need to guess why she was rude. The problem was undoubtedly Emily; she must have been talking up a storm of lies all week about "that awful Elsie" necking with a hobo in the woods. Up ahead, she recognized two other church members coming her way, so she stopped with the intention of dishing out her own version of events—the truth.

"Mrs. Brown, Mr. Br—"

The couple stopped abruptly in front of Elsie, Mrs. Brown with her arm curled through her husband's. They looked at one another and Mrs. Brown looked away, her eyes averted from Elsie's gaze. Mr. Brown opened his mouth to speak, but his wife jostled his arm as a signal to keep walking. After they passed, Elsie overheard him say, "But it's not right, dear. Someone should say *something*. There are morals ... "

Filled with anxiety about her social future in Rensselaer, Elsie hurried on toward the train station. Even Anna Anderson, the parent of one of her students, never acknowledged her presence as the two passed on the sidewalk, one block from the depot. It had only been five days since her encounter with James, but gossip in Rensselaer seemed to travel as fast as the Spanish Influenza had sixteen years earlier.

Snow was falling in big, wet flakes. Elsie knew she could not spend too much time with James; as the snow piled up on the ground, soon it would be treacherous navigating the sidewalk, even for walking just across the street to the trolley line.

She kept her shoulders back and her pride intact as she opened the carved wooden entry door of the station, doing her best to ignore some of the townspeople who whispered as she passed inside. They would have a field day over her encounter with the hobo today in the train station.

James sat in the back of the building on the last wooden bench, taking refuge from the cold weather. He stared into the space in front of him, his face serene yet weathered. Steam rose from a cup he held in his hands. Beside him sat another cup. Her heart melted when she realized he must have spent his last nickel to buy her a cup of tea.

When he saw from the expression on her face that she was pleased to see him, he smiled. Maybe it wasn't longing he saw, but at least she wasn't upset with him anymore; she assuredly didn't detest him. "Sit down, luv. Have a cup of tea. I was bloody afraid you weren't going to show up because of this dreadful weather … among other things."

She smiled, carefully picking up her cup of tea. "You said three o'clock. It's only half-past."

He nodded with a grin.

They sat on the bench for more than an hour, drinking tea and chatting, speaking reluctantly at first, but later with liveliness and some pleasure. Maybe it was out of guilt or maybe out of obligation, but at the end of the conversation Elsie promised that when she returned to Akron for the Christmas holidays, she would speak to her father about James returning to his old job.

James did not agree to a divorce because he still thought and hoped he could patch things up between them. His unwillingness was partly her fault; she didn't tell him about John. She didn't want to hurt him and, more importantly, did not want her live-in affair with John to get back to her parents.

James reached out to touch her hair. "I'll keep my word to you from now on."

She doubted these words and looked away from his smile, down at the empty cup in her hands.

It was nearly five o'clock. Outside, dusk had shrouded the train depot in a blanket of near darkness. She had better hurry if she were to leave the station before full nightfall. They agreed that James would ride a boxcar to Ohio, and Elsie would buy her own ticket to ride the train officially. They said their goodbyes, and James went out into the cold hobo jungle again.

She opened her pocketbook and fished out a coin for the trolley. Snow was still falling when she stepped up into the car, where the air was cold, and the clanging of the bell especially loud. She sat in front, staring at a sign that read, "Spitting is Unlawful!" The overhead wires were already beginning to ice up, and the car moved slowly—about a hundred feet, then stopped. Each time this happened, the motorman stepped off the trolley to put it back on the wires. The trip took over an hour and it was almost six-thirty, well past dark, when she arrived home.

The snow crunched under her feet, and the stars twinkled overhead in the cold night sky like fireflies in a summer field. She opened the gate to the front yard and gulped at the sight of home, where the man she loved waited for her inside. Had she made a serious mistake? Thoughts clutched at her, making her insides churn. She knew all too well that tonight she should divulge her reunion with her husband. She would also have to tell him for certain that she was going to leave for Ohio over the Christmas holiday. Any man would not take well to the news of either issue, especially both at the same time.

John sat at the kitchen table, eating a hearty supper of pork, mashed potatoes, corn, and a steaming cup of hot cocoa to drink. Next to his plate, a book on architecture lay on the table with its pages open. When Elsie came in through the back door, he immediately stood and kissed her lightly on the lips.

"Evening, sweetie. I was so hungry I had to eat without you." He put his arms tightly around her. "Geez Louise, you're going to catch your death of cold. Better hurry and change out of those clammy clothes. I was beginning to worry about you. What were you doing out this late?"

"I volunteered at the church, and then I went shopping … couldn't find a thing." At that, she hugged him about the waist and held him tightly to her. "I'll be back down in a minute. I'm starving. Are there any leftovers? It's been an excruciatingly long day."

"Sure," he said. "I'll make a plate for you. Hurry back."

Safely inside their bedroom, she closed the door and leaned against it to catch her breath. Her heart beat rapidly and her face felt flushed. She slipped out of her damp clothes, and took several deep breaths as she slipped into a pair of blue trousers with a matching blue sweater that her mother had knitted as a gift to her the previous Christmas. Sighing with apprehension, she walked over to the dressing table and picked up a gold-backed brush. Staring at the angels and roses on the handle, she thought about how she was going to formulate what she must say to John. As she rehearsed the scene in her head, John protested her trip to Akron and said he couldn't be without her for the holidays. Secretly, she hoped for just such an outcome.

Somewhat composed, she went downstairs to the kitchen.

"I'm going to eat, then I'll come talk to you," Elsie called to John, who was now in the next room.

"Take your time," he replied.

The stove was still warm as she opened the oven door to find the plate of food John had prepared for her. She sat down at the kitchen table to eat. Two decorative oil lamps lit the room in a glow that permeating the kitchen with cozy warmth. Dreamily, she poked at her mashed potatoes, and stared up at the low ceiling with its dark brown beams. On the hob, the kettle began to whistle. She poured the hot water into a large, gray tea pot and fetched a jug of milk from the cool pantry near the back door. After only eating a couple bites, she pushed her plate aside. She wasn't as hungry as she thought. Slowly she stood, sipping from her cup of tea before stepping down into the adjoining parlor.

John watched Elsie walk toward him. She seemed immersed in her own thoughts. He sat on the edge of his over-stuffed chair, playfully throwing a ball to the dog to get her out of Elsie's path. But it was too late; Elsie accidentally stepped on Millie's paw. The dog let out a painful yelp.

"Oh, I'm sorry Millie," she said, petting the dog's head. The incident only added to her nervousness. She looked up at John from where she sat on the floor with the dog, her throat tightening with emotion. "John, I have something to talk to you about."

"Oh?" he said, eyebrows raised. "Relax, Elsie. I know what you're going to say."

She smiled, a nervous flutter rising in her stomach. "You do?" She slid over to sit on the floor in front of him, her hands resting on his knees.

"Yes, I do. Robert told me the church people are giving you a hard time—spreading rumors you were seen in the woods kissing a hobo." He bounced the ball next to her and caught it. "I'm not that naive; I don't believe those ridiculous stories. I know you have better taste than that." He rolled the ball to Millie, leaned over, and took her hands in his. "If I were you, I'd put a stop to Joanne trying to ruin your reputation."

"Joanne isn't the only one who's trying to ruin my reputation; there's another gal who has been just as vicious. Her name is Emily. I can't understand why they are both so hateful toward me." She raised her hands up in disbelief. "It's really hard for me to believe that these grown women at church really think I would kiss a hobo. What kind of a person do they think I am?" Frowning, she continued. "I wasn't kissing a hobo, for God's sake, but I did run into James near the train station."

"James? Your ah-h ... husband, James?"

"Yes, he's the bloody hobo the town is going on about. But I swear on my father's grave, I didn't kiss him." She blinked up at John. "There he was in the hobo camp, skinny as a pencil. Apparently, he's been wandering 'round the country, living in hobo jungles and working odd jobs. He said he was about to lose his job at Goodyear, so he took off running. Said he was doing me a favor."

"What a great guy. Why didn't you tell me this sooner?"

Guilt rushed in and replaced her anxiety. "I just couldn't bring myself to say anything, I'm sorry."

For a long moment John sat in silence, looking down at his hands clasped tightly around the ball. He gave her a one-sided grin. "I believe you didn't kiss him. Poor fellow; roaming around, riding the rods, trying to find work. The guy is over thirty isn't he? It's a new era since President Roosevelt took office last year, but even he hasn't been able to clean up all the economic problems yet."

Elsie's mind wandered and she began to lose the strength and resolve to stay positive. Deep inside, pain mingled with regret and sadness.

John sensed her brooding and handed her his handkerchief. It was large and white, with his initials, "JAM," embroidered in maroon on two corners. She wished these were the initials of her husband, her real love. She suddenly and painfully felt separate from him

She dabbed at her eyes as she looked up at him with uncertainty. "I felt kind of sorry for him," she said, her voice trembling. "Now more than ever, I want to find out what is needed to obtain a divorce." She was afraid she was seeing the end of something, as though she feared losing the man sitting in front of her.

John's face broke out into one of the biggest smiles she had ever seen on him. The contradiction to her foul mood completely confused her.

"That's exactly what I've been waiting for you to say: the magic word, *divorce*. If that's the case, I have some great news for us."

Elsie was so shocked by his positive reaction to her troubling news, that all she could say was, "Huh?"

"Today a college chum in Buffalo called to tell me that the firm he's working for is looking for another apprentice architect after the holidays. It would give me more responsibility with more pay. I'm going to telephone them Monday and see if I can get an appointment. What do you think? Have you ever thought of living in Buffalo?"

"Buffalo? You're going to Buffalo for an appointment? You want to live there?"

He put up his hands, signaling caution. "Whoa, I'm sorry. Let's slow down here. But the timing is perfect, don't you see? If you need to go to Akron, I could schedule an appointment for the first week of January in Buffalo and stay there with my father and brother over the holidays. Then come back here when I'm finished. Unless you want to come with me? We could stay somewhere else."

"I'd love to go with you. It's wonderful news. I'm so happy for you. Although I really need to clear up a few things in Akron." Elsie blew her nose and slipped the handkerchief into her pocket. "My sisters, as you know, have been writing to me every week. They really miss me, and I've told them to expect me."

"You do what you think is right," he said, getting up and pacing in front of her. "Maybe I'll get the position and we could start fresh in New York." He stopped and leaned against the parlor wall. "I can't tell you what to do, sweetie. If you want to go back and see your family, go right ahead. I'm not going to stop you."

Elsie continued to sit on the floor with her back against John's chair. "Now I feel dreadful all over again because I know Christmas is your favorite holiday, and I belong with you. Maybe something good will come from it."

"I'm sure something good will come from it. If I get the job in Buffalo we could live there and you'd be away from your silly church people. I'll even let you beat me down the sledding hill."

Elsie gave him a small smile. She appreciated his light regard of the situation, but she felt miserable and torn. There were several moments of silence, then she continued. "I'll visit my family until the first week of January, then I'll return. But I'll miss you so much." She watched his movements, trying to read his thoughts.

"It will all work out. Living in Buffalo, away from all this, would solve your problems wouldn't it?" He went to the liquor cabinet and paused, one hand on the doorknob. "Does James want a divorce?"

"He believes we still have a chance to be together again." Her voice became softer. "He has no idea I started a new life with you. Neither does my family. I'm supposed to set an example for my sisters. I fear my parents will be totally crushed if they knew I was living with you. Not that I need their consent—" She pressed one hand against her head in frustration, stood, went over to the sofa, and heaved herself onto it with a groan. "Why am I made to feel like the bad person here? He's the one who deserted me. Not the other way around. I shouldn't have been so nice to him."

John turned to face her then, a bottle of scotch in one hand, a glass tumbler in the other. "Maybe. But the main thing here is: I would like to know if there's any chance you could go back to him."

Elsie shook her head adamantly. "No, I'm not getting back together with him. Absolutely not. How can you ask me that?"

He unscrewed the cap on the bottle and began to pour. "Seemed like a reasonable question to me. Would you like one?" he said, holding up the bottle and reaching for another glass.

"Just a bit of brandy, thanks."

He took the brandy bottle from the cabinet, poured, and handed the drink to her.

She swirled the caramel-colored liquid around in the glass as she spoke. "I'm not getting back together with James. I'm going to try and put an end to a fifteen-month-old mistake. Although, there is the problem of money. James certainly can't pay for a divorce."

John carried his drink over to the mahogany table and sat down on the sofa next to her. "Don't be upset. Come here, you," he said, reaching out to collect her. "Let's talk about your other problem—Joanne. There's got to be a way to get her straightened out on your taste in men. I have a plan to help you get even with her."

"You do?"

"Monday, on my way to work, I'll knock over her husband's apple cart—by accident mind you," he laughed and took another swallow of his drink.

"Oh, John," she said, laughing. "What about Emily? Are you going after her husband, too?"

"I don't know Emily's husband. I don't know Emily, either. Let's concentrate on Joanne for tonight."

Elsie snuggled close, feeling his reassuring warmth. "Whatever you do, I don't want to upset the apple cart with those women at church, any more than it is already."

"I was just trying to help," he said with a grin.

"What would I do without you?" She slid onto his lap and put her arms about his neck, lifting her face for a kiss. "I'll always love you. You're so funny."

"You won't forget that when you're back in Ohio, and your family is sweet talking James to you, will you?" John asked, a hint of jealously in his eyes.

She stroked his head, her fingers toying with his hair. "I won't forget. I'll never forget."

"Well, back to your hobo husband, you say you're not looking for reconciliation, but it sounds like *he* is. Does he want to see you again? Did he suggest a meeting with you somewhere in town?"

"No, nothing like that. I won't see him again in Rensselaer. He'll take off before long."

"Remember, he's been living without you for over three years now. It's strange; all of a sudden the fellow wants to get back together, but he never made an attempt to see you or contact you in any way. It doesn't make any sense. In New York I believe there's a law that presumes death when a spouse hasn't been heard of for five years. James just about made it," John took the last sips of his drink and put the glass down on the coffee table. "Something is fishy here. I wouldn't trust him if I were you."

"Don't worry about him."

"You didn't tell him where you are living, did you? I don't want him showing up at the house. I might do something drastic. I do have a jealous streak."

"Of course not. No."

"He'd be trespassing, after all." John offered his hand. "Well, we can't do anything about it tonight. Let's get some sleep."

"It's not even nine o'clock."

"I know, but I'm tired. Can't do anything in this weather anyway."

Elsie nodded and swallowed the rest of her brandy, feeling it burn all the way down. She let out a deep sigh, feeling relieved they had not really quarreled over her problems. John had been surprisingly supportive. The only thing she regretted now was that she could not go with him to Buffalo, and that they would be apart for the holidays.

A chill sounding, rattling wind was blowing across the roof of the house. It howled furiously as they climbed the stairs to the bedroom. Millie followed. The liquor had relaxed them, and they both fell asleep quickly.

Hours later, Elsie woke to the sounds of banging. For a moment, she lay anxiously listening. Then realizing it was just the winter storm making the windows rattle, she sat up. She turned to look at John, who was sleeping peacefully. He looked so angelic lying there, so handsome that it almost brought tears to her eyes. She thought he was everything she wanted in a man: intelligent, cultured, and good mannered with a gentle nature. And what a great sense of humor he had. Another giant slap of wind overhead made her jump, and Millie sprang up onto the bed.

John opened his eyes with a groan. "It's only a storm," he whispered. "Go back to sleep." He felt the movement of the dog as she rummaged for a comfortable spot on the bed. "Millie! Get down." The dog hopped off the bed in a scramble of feet, and whined from the floor. "How can a puppy jump up so high?" He turned, fluffed his pillow and pulled Elsie to him.

"She's smart, remember?" Elsie snuggled up behind his ear and whispered, "What else will you do in Buffalo?"

"Hm-m, don't worry about that. Maybe I'll go look around New York City. Go to sleep," he murmured.

"I love you. I want to be with you. Do you love me?"

"Yes. I love you, too," he whispered.

And then, quite suddenly, his body felt heavy next to hers, and she knew he had fallen sound asleep. Long after, she still lay wakeful, staring into the darkness. She tossed and turned most of the night. Her last, rather hazy thoughts were spent wondering what life would be like as Mrs. John McDonald.

Chapter Fourteen

The children gathered their belongings and clambered out of the classroom faster than Elsie had ever seen; all arms, hands, and feet in coats, mittens, and snow boots, their little high pitched voices yelling, "Goodbye, Miss Wilkins. Merry Christmas! Happy New Year!"

"Careful, children, be careful on your way home! Merry Christmas to you and your families. See you next year."

However, Elsie wondered what the next year held for her. The memo in her hand simply said, *'Thank you for your participation in the New Deal Education Program. Please report to the Administration Office.'* It was an odd memo; she'd not received one like it before. Would she be transferred?

She pushed open the door to the office, where a pretty, dark-haired woman sat behind a cluttered desk.

"Hello, Mrs. May. I have a notice here, asking me to report to the office."

"Please wait a moment, Miss Wilkins." Mrs. May stood and went into an inner office, the one that said "Director" on the door.

She returned with Mr. Winslow, a tall, thin man with thick, wire-rimmed spectacles, who politely asked Elsie to follow him into his office.

He looked at her. "Please sit down, Miss Wilkins." Leaning against his desk, he folded his arms, and said hesitantly, "I'm sorry, but we've changed the curriculum for next year, and unfortunately, we had to eliminate your position."

A sudden chill shot through her and she stiffened, her heart pounding. She cleared her throat and gulped to steady her voice. "I'm sorry, too. I didn't realize the school was in financial distress."

"Our budget has been depleted," Mr. Winslow continued. "Those cost-conscious Republicans in Washington cut the funding for some of the New Deal programs, including some of the ones for education. I'm being pressured to cut teachers from our facility, and lower the remaining teachers' salaries." He looked guilty, his eyes averted. "I'm sorry to see you go. It has nothing to do with your work performance. We've never had a single complaint about you. Actually, there were a few complaints about your penmanship," he laughed. "We'll call you if there are any changes, or if something comes up," he said, quietly.

"This is so sudden. Is there any way we can work things out? Maybe a pay cut or something?"

"I'm afraid not. When your six-week contract was about to expire I went to bat for you in October to get it extended through June, but things have changed now. If there were any way to keep you I would have done it. I see you're from Ohio. I suggest you get in touch with the relief administrator in Akron and apply for a teaching position with the Emergency Education Administration for Ohio's New Deal Program. Those emergency instructor positions are higher paying."

"Thank you. I'll check into it, but the last time I was in Akron there wasn't anything available. Plus, I like it here better. Please let me know if anything becomes available in Rensselaer."

"We'll be sure to do that, and I'll write a letter of recommendation for you. I'm going to a meeting in a couple of weeks and I'll see if there are any programs that you are suited for." His eyes searched a vacant corner of the room. "I'm sure your students will be very disappointed, as we all are. It seems contradictory to wish you happy holidays now, Miss Wilkins, but I do wish you well. I'll have your letter ready when school starts again. If you have an address you'd like me to send it to?" He smiled faintly.

She nodded, swallowing her anxiety. "I'll give it to Mrs. May. And thank you for everything. I want you to know I appreciate the opportunity I was given here. And I've so much enjoyed teaching the children. Goodbye, sir." Elsie reached out to shake his hand.

He grasped it, saying, "Goodbye, Miss Wilkins."

Despondent, she left him smiling at her and walked to her classroom number four, *her* classroom, to put her personal belongings in the Christmas tote that one of her students had given her. In it, she arranged pencils, erasers, and ink pens neatly on top of the gifts of homemade cookies and dates wrapped in holiday paper. On her desk was a photograph that depicted happier times with her students. She sadly put it and the remaining memories of her classroom life into the bag, retrieved a few miscellaneous administrative papers from the desk drawer, glanced around the room, and walked out.

The trolley ride home was a blur. The events of the day crashed down on her, sapping what little strength she had.

Once inside the house and still feeling dazed, she bathed, scrubbing her body as though she could wash away the disappointing news. Afterward, she felt fatigued, but more than rest, she needed to talk to someone who loved her unconditionally. She picked up the telephone and dialed.

The voice on the other end was cheery. "Operator. May I assist you?"

"Yes. I'm calling Akron, Ohio, 4526."

"One moment, please." The operator paused, then said, "Connecting."

"Hello?"

"Mum, it's Elsie."

"Oh—hello, luv. It's so nice to hear your voice," her mother cooed. She sounded unusually upbeat. "You're still coming home on holiday, aren't you?"

"Yes, of course. I'll be arriving about eleven at night. Will Daddy be able to pick me up?"

"Yes. We'll both be there. Did you receive the money for your ticket?"

"I did. Thank you."

"When are you leaving Rensselaer?"

"On December seventeenth. Monday, late afternoon."

"It's going to take that long to get here?"

"Mum, it's more than three hundred miles. I'll be on train forty–five. It's scheduled to pull in at ten minutes after eleven. Hopefully, it'll be on time."

"We're all so excited to see you." Elsie heard the smile in her musical voice. "How was your Thanksgiving, dear?"

"Oh, we had a wonderful day, right into the evening. We ate at home with Robert's girlfriend Brenda, and my friend John. We had a good time, playing a new game Brenda picked up in Philadelphia. It's called Monopoly. It lets you pretend you're wealthy enough to buy and sell property."

"Hm-m, I've never heard of it."

"It's brand new. It'll probably be in all the stores shortly." She gasped. "Oh, I better go. This call will cost a fortune. See you soon."

"Bye, take care of yourself."

"Bye, Mum."

Elsie put down the receiver and sat at the telephone table for a long time, trying to come to grips with how her life had become so uncertain.

She went to the kitchen to make a cup of tea, where she noticed a note from John left on the counter.

Hi Beautiful,

I'm getting off work early and would like to do some Christmas shopping. Thought you might need some last minute gifts for your trip. I'll pick you up at 4:00 PM. Listen for my toot.

Love & Merriment,

John

It was 3:35 PM; she had just enough time to dress, fix her make up, and feed the dog. Suddenly she felt energetic. She ran up the stairs to the bedroom, looked in the mirror, and quickly smoothed rose rouge across her cheeks. Her reflection looked somewhat sad, but she was determined to remain optimistic about her future and the upcoming New Year.

Standing in front of the bedroom mirror in her bare feet, she slipped out of her proper teaching attire and put on a red, turtleneck sweater. Over that, she threw on a green jumper that made her look even more elegant and feminine than usual. The dress had a long, straight skirt and thick straps that tied at the shoulders. She fiddled with her hair, moving it to fall first over her left shoulder, then her right. Then she flipped it back, trying various styles. She combed it through with her fingers and adjusted the jumper. Just as she reached for a coat in the closet, she heard the toot of John's car. She slipped into her comfortable saddle shoes and ran downstairs. Stopping in the kitchen for an instant, she tossed corn mush into a dish for Millie, and dashed out the door.

When John and Elsie arrived in town, the air felt warm yet crisp, more like spring than winter. Hand-in-hand, they strolled down the decorated streets, looking in art and dress shop windows. In just a short time, John had melted her unhappiness like the sun on morning mist.

"You look ravishing and in the Christmas spirit, as well," John said, smiling at her.

She moved up against him, walking in rhythm with his steps. "You make me *feel* ravishing."

He gave her a quick kiss on the lips.

The sun disappeared below the horizon as they walked past a nativity scene in front of the Catholic Church. The town Christmas tree stood on the public square in the middle of Washington Street. It was lit in the brilliant colors of the rainbow, and children were assembled in front of it to sing Christmas carols. Elsie recognized one of her former students and rushed past with John, unwilling to share the day's unfortunate news.

They crossed Weston Street to Woolworth's, where a miniature synthetic Santa stood in the store window, ringing a bell. She looked beyond the Santa, inside the store where the cafeteria served customers just around the corner from the window. The idea of returning there to work full-time was not a pleasant one, yet she would if she had to. Of course, the whole issue would be moot if John found work in

Buffalo. He would be right in that case; moving would solve all her problems in Rensselaer. Surely John would support her in Buffalo until she found a job? This afternoon, things didn't look all that bad as she walked side-by-side with the man she loved, whom, she felt assured, loved her.

For now, and the next few days, she must deal with the issues at hand; one of them Joanne, who was walking toward them on her way to Woolworth's. It seemed as though she was looking in their direction.

"Hello," Elsie said with a nod.

Joanne looked puzzled, as if wondering, *'Who does she think she is speaking to ... me?'* She did concede a quick nod, however hurrying past without a further word, hugging her one large package to her chest.

"She's some piece of work," John said under his breath, and they both grinned. "Where's her Christmas spirit, anyway?"

"I think it was in that nod." Elsie grinned, her smile fading. "I didn't want to tell you earlier, but ... "

"But?"

"I won't be teaching after the holidays." Her eyebrows furrowed in frustration. "I was told it was a layoff, but I think Joanne may have had something to do with it."

"I warned you about her." John looked around, steering Elsie away from the storefront and back out onto the sidewalk with its holiday shoppers. "Sweetie, I'm sorry. I know how much you loved teaching. And damn. Now, it's too late to do anything about her, you've lost your job. Do you think it was her fault?"

"Hard to tell. Mr. Winslow, the school's director, said he'd write a letter of recommendation for me. That's a positive sign; it might be just a layoff."

"Sounds like if Joanne were involved, he didn't believe a word of her silly gossip. Though he might have needed to placate a few unreasonable parents by letting you go. I'm sure he hated to do that."

"Oh-h," Elsie groaned. "I hope not. I'm so embarrassed."

"Remember, your students seemed to love you."

"Yes, and I grew to love them, too. Oh well, I'll find something else. I'm not sure whether Joanne or Emily complained about me, or the school legitimately needed to cut my position." She tried to sound upbeat. "There's always the job at Goodyear. You know, the one my father can get for me in the insurance department," she said, wondering how he would respond to the idea of her moving back to Akron.

He nodded. "Sure, you could do that, though I wouldn't want you to leave. I guess it's something to fall back on, if that's what you want to do."

"I suppose." She drew a shaky breath, fighting disappointment. He had the perfect personality but didn't always react in a way that fostered security with him. The bookstore's cozy doorway beckoned on the left and she pointed. "Let's go in here."

John opened the door to Rensselaer Readers and they stepped inside, suddenly engulfed by a wonderful aroma.

"It smells like cinnamon in here," Elsie commented, looking over the paraphernalia cluttering the counter next to the cash register.

John sniffed the air. "Apple cider, I believe."

A plump woman, wearing a white apron and bonnet met them at the door. She carried a book with the picture of three reindeer on the cover. "Would you like some hot cider?" she asked, ushering them to a table where several mugs steamed with the source of the wonderful scent.

"Yes, thanks," John said, picking up two mugs and handing one to Elsie.

"Merry Christmas," Elsie replied, giving a courteous nod to the shopkeeper. She loved the spirit of the bookstore with its friendly, homey atmosphere.

"You'll have to excuse me; we're having a special story time for the holidays," the woman said, nodding toward the back of the store. Eight children and several parents sat on the floor, or in a big overstuffed chair, waiting for the woman to return, all eyes focused toward the front of the store where Elsie and John stood. Other adults, whom Elsie guessed were parents, browsed the book shelves.

"Look, John. She's reading a Christmas story to the children. Isn't that cute?" Elsie asked, feeling homesick for her classroom.

He nodded, putting his arm around her shoulder and giving her a quick hug.

"We'll be finished in a few minutes," the woman said. "In the meantime, feel free to browse around."

"Thanks," they said in unison.

They sipped their apple cider and browsed the bookshelves, looking for a book for Elsie's sister, Evelyn.

Elsie found ideal gifts in the "Big Little Books" section. She picked up *Little Women* and *Alice in Wonderland*, in hopes of expanding Evelyn's library, thus adding new elements of sophistication and adventure to her life. She took them to the cash register, while John browsed the adult sections, finally picking out, *The Last Days of Pompeii*.

"It's unbelievable how much incredible art was lost when Vesuvius erupted," John told Elsie.

"No doubt," she whispered behind the back of her hand as she listened to the last few lines of the children's story. "That's just a fictional story though, isn't it?"

"It is, but you want to hear something funny? They tried to make a play out of it once, and it was a flop. The volcano didn't explode, the ground never shook, and some of the actors fell off the stage."

"That must have been something. I wonder if the patrons were refunded their money," Elsie whispered.

"I'd pay just to see the chaos," John answered.

The children all clapped and giggled when the woman finished the story. She made her way back to the front where John paid for his book, thanked her again for the apple cider, and went back out onto the sidewalk with Elsie.

Next, they crossed the street to Sears, Roebuck and Company. The store bustled with holiday shoppers. To maximize their use of time, they decided to shop separately but promised to meet back at the entrance in an hour.

Elsie wandered around the millinery section. She found a floral kerchief for her mother and picked up a fashionable red cloche hat for her teenage sister, Lena. The line waiting to pay for purchases was growing longer with anxious holiday shoppers. By the time Elsie reached the cash register, the salesclerks looked aggravated.

One cashier stopped ringing up customers' purchases, and with a haughty, dismissive wave of the hand, went over to rearrange piles of hats and scarves that customers had tossed about.

Elsie stepped to the cosmetic counter when the cashier attending that register made a comment about how messy customers had been.

"Oh, would you like me to help you straighten up? I don't mind," Elsie said, looking at the lipsticks.

"No, thank you. It's my job. Thanks anyway. You might want to try the Fire Engine Red," she said, indicating one lipstick in the rack. "It's the most popular shade right now."

"I'll do that. Thanks for the tip."

"The boys all want to kiss it off," the clerk said with a giggle.

After trying on several new shades of lipstick, including Fire Engine Red, Elsie ended up at the front of the store, where a crowd of shoppers had gathered. They were huddled around the radio, listening to Christmas music. Elsie joined in, swaying to the rhythm of the new hit song, *Santa Claus is Coming to Town*.

A few minutes later John showed up, looking exhausted and carrying two large bags, filled with holiday presents.

"Let's go home. I'm tired of shopping," he said. "You know, they ran out of Monopoly." He shook his head. "The gal said they're getting more in a couple of weeks. I guess I'll be back. Is that a new lipstick you're wearing? It looks sexy."

"Do you want to kiss it off?"

"I do. How'd you guess?"

"The sales clerk told me."

"I'm not following you. I guess I'm tired from shopping."

"Forget it. It's an inside joke. Between women."

"I see," he said, giving her a quick hug.

On the way home, Elsie sat in the front seat with her coat on her lap, admiring the Christmas lights strung up on the neighborhood homes. The house next door to John's lit up the street with large, red and white lights in the azalea bushes. Green lights had been also fastened along the home's picket fence. In the picture window, a sparkling Christmas tree stood with a gold angel on top.

"Our house looks dark." She sighed deeply. "I wish we could decorate it and spend Christmas here. Just the two of us."

"That would be nice. Oh, listen … I hear Millie barking. She knows my automobile." He smiled, pulling into the driveway and shutting off the car. "You'll have a good time with your folks, but I'll miss you. You know," he said, turning to face her on the front seat, "I wish I could help you with the divorce proceedings. Don't let anyone make you feel it was your fault. He's got some nerve to disappear for almost four years and now you're stuck trying to make sense of it. It's just not right. I love you and would do anything for you. *He's your husband*, and what has he done for you?"

"I don't know. Nothing. I'm going over to his sister's house and talk to her about it. She lives near Akron. I was thinking … actually worrying, that strange things always seem to happen around the holidays."

"Like what? Like us both leaving Rensselaer?" Her cheeks grew crimson at that remark, especially since he was staring intently at her and waiting for an answer.

"No, not that." Elsie cleared her throat. "Well, let's see," she began. "People tend to drink too much since Prohibition ended; everybody celebrates the holidays. They can have a car accident— hit a tree or something, with all that drinking." She drew in a long breath and let it out. "Then, other folks get depressed and kill themselves. Still, other people become sentimental and run off and get married."

He grinned, sizing her up with a sideways look as he got out of the car. He went around to her side, opened the door, and offered his hand. "Sentimental after drinking a bottle of whiskey, I suppose. Funny what a bit of drink will do for a person. Try and look on the bright side. That's what you're always telling me. You're spending the holidays with family and that's what the season is all about."

He never picked up on the hint about marriage, Elsie thought. Or else he didn't want to. She needed to rid herself of James once and for all.

* * *

Monday morning was hectic. Elsie ran around packing, getting ready for her trip home. Millie seemed to know that something odd was going on; she followed Elsie from room to room, restless and whining.

"When should we take Millie over to Robert's?" Elsie called out to John, who was busy in his study.

"I'll take her when I head out of town."

Elsie popped her head around the doorframe of the study. "And when will that be?"

"Maybe I'll leave tomorrow, if you're leaving today. I have an interview January third."

"When will you come home?"

"That depends on whether I drive or take the train. But I should be back by January fifth. If we're lucky, I'll know if I have the job or not."

"You would know that soon?"

"My contact at the branch said they need someone as quickly as possible after the first of the year." John had spent most of the morning on the telephone, talking to his colleague from the East Coast branch, then coordinating with the secretary, who scheduled an interview for him.

He had then opened the desk drawer, taking out a drawing pad and one of the drafting pens he'd grown to prefer. He continued sketching out his concept of The International Building, a skyscraper for which city officials would soon break ground in New York City, catty-corner to the RCA Building in Rockefeller Center. He planned out his strategy as he drew, knowing that someday he would work on such weighty projects. For now, this and other sketches he could include in his portfolio to take with him to Buffalo for the job interview.

At about three in the afternoon, they drove to the train station. John checked the schedule and saw that Elsie's train would leave on time. He carried her luggage out to the platform next to the locomotive that would take her to Akron.

John pulled her into his arms and kissed her amorously; suddenly wishing they had another day, another night together. "I love you," he murmured against her lips, holding her tightly. "No matter what happens, don't forget that." He held her for a moment longer, then reluctantly released her. He reached into his pocket for a small box that he placed into her hand. "Merry Christmas, Happy New Year and should auld acquaintance be forgot," he said, kissing her sweetly on the cheek.

"Merry Christmas." She stared at him several long moments, searching his expression. The phrase didn't always mean something warm or homey. "What's going to happen with us, John?"

"Nothing. It's from *Auld Lang Syne*. It's just a figure of speech, Elsie. Don't worry so much."

"Okay, I'll try not to. Thank you for the gift." She looked at him and smiled. "Should I open it now?"

"If you like. Why not?"

"Um, you first." She reached into her large sack next to her on the walkway and pulled out a gold-wrapped gift with a silver bow on it. She handed it to him with a kiss. "Have a Merry Christmas, sweetheart."

John's face lit up. "You shouldn't have." He untied the ribbon and opened the box to find a silver tie clip and a light tan, short-sleeved shirt made from feed sack material. "Elsie!" He threw his head back and laughed. "Thanks so much. And here, all this time, I was mistaken about your domestic skills. It looks great! I'll wear it proudly."

"This isn't the first thing I've made, you know. Remember the pre-punched stitchery, '*Women Must Vote*' the political statement hanging in my parents' parlor?"

"Right. I'll just tell people that this shirt is a political statement."

"Since when is Springfield Mills political?" She pressed her cheek to his and held him tightly. "Oh John, I'm going to miss you so much. What would I do without you?"

"You'll be in my thoughts every day. And I'm as proud of this shirt as I'm sure your parents are of their daughter's political statement."

Elsie smiled. "Now, I'll open mine," she said, lifting the lid of a small box to find a teardrop-shaped pendant, a lovely sapphire surrounded by tiny diamonds, suspended from a thin gold chain. She held up the necklace. "Oh, it's beautiful. Thank you," she said, trying to hide her disappointment. They had been together six months and even now, there was no official engagement ring or talk of marriage. Still, she had the hope of a divorce from James, and a possible move with John to Buffalo.

Elsie hugged him tightly one last time. "Call me the minute you think I must be there," she whispered against his chest. "If I don't at least hear your voice, I'll go daft. Hopefully, when I come back I'll be a free woman. Good luck on your interview." She gently pushed herself away from him with great reluctance. "I'd better go; it's almost three–thirty."

Elsie climbed aboard with her luggage, but a friendly conductor stopped her, picked up her bags, and led the way down the corridor. "Merry Christmas," he said with a lightness to his voice.

She smiled and returned the greeting. "Merry Christmas." When he stopped, she handed him her ticket and quickly found a seat next to the window.

John remained on the platform next to the train, gazing up at her.

Suddenly feeling alone and already miles away from him, she became overwhelmed with emotion, looking away as tears formed in her eyes. She wiped them, put her face up against the windowpane, and forced a smile.

John smiled back at her, cheerfully mouthing, "Have a good time, and don't worry."

At that moment, she opened the train window and heard the words she yearned for.

"I love you," he said, blowing her a kiss goodbye.

She thrust her head out the window. "I love you, too," she said. "I'll be back soon. Bye."

Then the train slowly pulled away.

Chapter Fifteen

Elsie lay sprawled on the sofa in her parents' parlor, her mind occupied with thoughts of John. She had been in Akron five days, and each day she expected him to call, but he didn't. She didn't know how much longer she could stand not hearing his voice. She was ready to go to pieces.

Without much enthusiasm, she got up off the sofa and wandered over to the bay window to look out. The view revealed a wide sweep of brown fields, with patches of snow dotting the hillsides; small houses sat tucked amid brick streets. She closed her eyes, wondering what John was doing at that moment. Did he miss her? Was he thinking of her?

Her thoughts were interrupted by her father's voice. "I'm going out to the find a Christmas tree. Anybody want to join me?" His line of sight rested on Lena and Evelyn, who were perched around the coffee table, carefully cutting red and green strips of construction paper to make a chain, which they would later wrap around the Christmas tree branches.

Lena looked up and grinned. "I'd like to go."

"Me, too. Can I pick out the tree, Daddy? Lena chose last year," Evelyn pleaded.

"I did not! You did!" Lena shot back.

"No, I wanted the biggest one. Remember?" Evelyn glared at Lena. "Daddy said it was too tall for the house."

"It doesn't matter who picked it out last year. We'll all have a say this year," Frederick said, calmly turning to Elsie. "Want to go? You could be the tie-breaker."

"No, thanks. I think I'll hold down the fort; help Mum bake some cookies or decorate a few Mason jars."

"Suit yourself. We're going to cut down the most beautiful Christmas tree ever." He beamed. "Let's go, girls!"

Lena and Evelyn bolted toward the door and ran out onto the porch into the shimmering lights of Christmas, set against the gray, dreary sky. It wasn't close to dark yet, but already the neighbors had turned on their lights.

"Don't forget your scarves. It's chilly out there," Phoebe said, opening the screen door.

"Oh, Mommy, I have a warm jacket on," Evelyn said, as she reluctantly strutted back to the kitchen to get her winter scarf. Lena followed, grabbing the two red scarves from the coat rack and slipped one around her neck. She gave the other one to her sister. The girls cheerfully waved goodbye and danced out the back door with their father in tow.

Phoebe had been up since five o'clock to begin the baking for the family. After she finished the sweetbreads, she started the canning. She finished up the cranberries and mince-meat and later she'd start packing the Mason jars full of jams and jellies as Christmas gifts for the neighbors. Mason jars, lids, and sealing rings crowded the kitchen counters. Phoebe smiled and turned to Elsie. "Well, luv, how would you like to spend the day cooking with your mum? I'll pack the jams myself, but I'd like to teach you how to make an eggless, milkless, butterless cake."

"You're joking," Elsie said. "That sounds awful. How can you make a cake without the main ingredients?"

"That's what I'm going to show you. The cake is delicious. You'll see. It is the one cake that's good without frosting."

"Really? I would have never guessed. Where did you get the recipe?"

"*Reminisce.* You know … that magazine with all the great homemaking tips? I'm always reading it."

"You're so good at baking, Mum. It's very resourceful of you to make jams and jellies for gifts. I wish it were easy for me to be a homemaker. It's harder to go against what everyone else expects of a person."

Phoebe opened the pantry door to gather all the ingredients. Carefully, she combined the brown sugar, water, lard, and raisins in a saucepan and placed the pan on the stove. She then went to the table where Elsie sat, laid her hand on her shoulder, and in a soft tone said, "I'm happy we're here alone. I wanted to talk to you privately. Elsie, you don't look happy. I'm worried about you. Tell me what's going on."

"Oh, Mum. There's nothing to be concerned about. I'm having a few problems, that's all." Elsie paused, then shrugged. "I might as well be out with it," she said, giving her mum a guarded look. "You know my beau, John, well … "

"Is that the one you had Thanksgiving with?"

"Yes, and I just feel miserable that I won't be spending Christmas with him. I was so torn about leaving. When I'm away from him I feel sad. I love him and I'm … confused about James. I ran into him last month in back of the Rensselaer train station. There's a hobo camp—"

"You ran into *James* in Indiana and he's a *hobo*? For God's sake. Who would have ever guessed?"

"Yes, it's true. He's a hobo and he tried to get real lovey-dovey with me. After all this time, can you imagine? I thought he had a lot of nerve." Elsie's heart pounded, and she could hear the quiver in her own voice. "I couldn't believe my eyes. There he was, as skinny as a pencil. He's been out of work for quite some time, riding the rods around the country. He's down and desperate like so many other men. I see now how lucky we are that Daddy has a job."

"I know. I thank God everyday. Did James say why he left?"

"He said he was already humiliated about not being able to support me properly, and that he was about to be laid off from Goodyear. It was bad enough we were living with you but without a job he wouldn't have been able to contribute to the household. He just panicked when he saw his name on a list in front of the plant. I promised him I would ask Daddy if he can help get him a job."

There was a long silence, then Phoebe nodded. "I understand the position James was in. So many men did the same thing—you know that."

"That's true, but the spouses knew they were leaving. The men just didn't take off." Elsie threw her hands in the air in frustration.

Phoebe waited a long beat, inhaling the fragrance in the room. "Yes, Elsie men *did* take off without a word. James wasn't the only one. Are you terribly upset with him?"

Her daughter's eyes grew wide. "No, but at the hobo camp I thought I wanted to wring his neck; now I just feel sorry for him."

"It would be wonderful if your father could get him a job." Phoebe smiled and went to the pot on the stove to take the lid off. "Time to simmer. Come tell me all about Rensselaer."

When Elsie finished relating the highlights of her times with Robert and with teaching, she finally said, "Honestly Mum, I don't want to be with James. I need to find a way to end this, permanently. I want him to get on his feet, I guess, but I don't want to be with him. The only emotion I feel for him is pity."

Phoebe slowly turned and looked at her daughter in disbelief. "I understand you're hurt, but you have to get over your hard feelings. You married James until death do you part. The church would have agreed to an annulment because he deserted you, but now he's back and he wants to make amends.

"I was upset about him leaving you the way he did, but you must have compassion for his situation, and for his frame of mind. He felt dejected. It's so hard to make a living these days." She then shut off the stove to let the pot of raisin mixture cool. "Never mind making a living to pay all the expenses; it's hard enough to just put food on the table."

Elsie rubbed her chin and affected a big sigh for her mother's benefit. She went to the cupboard to find a large bowl, which she placed on the table. "I *do* have compassion for James. I respect my wedding vows, but life doesn't always work out the way you want it to. I love James as a person, but not as a husband. Do you realize that we were together only just a little over a year? We have been apart longer than we were married. I should have pursued getting an annulment."

Into the large bowl, Elsie sifted the flour, baking soda, salt, cinnamon and cloves that her mother had previously measured out. "How's this?"

"It's perfect." Phoebe gently took the sifter from her daughter, placed it on the counter, and held both of her hands. "I know, you have a point. You have every right to be angry with James. You can be right and, unfortunately, make the wrong decision in this case." She smiled. "You do love him, that's good. Hm-m, that's jolly good news. I know you don't want to hear this, but you must try and make it work."

Phoebe released her hands and continued. "There must have been a reason you ran into him. God works in mysterious ways. James was caring towards you. He didn't have to be. What did he say about your relationship?"

"He said it would be different this go around, and he would try and be a much better husband. But it's too late now. Timing is everything in life, and the time has long passed to mend this marriage. Mum, he walked out on me. I'm convinced I would have never seen him again if my church friends and I hadn't gone to the Rensselaer train depot, and handed out food to all the hobos living around there."

Elsie could tell her mother was now "getting down to brass tacks" as she so often called it. Her lips formed a thin, tight line and she spoke in small, tight sentences. "You need to give him another chance. He's mad about you. He said he was sorry, didn't he?"

Elsie nodded.

"He'll never put you through that again. So many men left their wives with no intention of returning. Elsie, luv, ask God to come into your heart. You'll see something wonderful happen."

Elsie drew a sharp breath and winced at the thought of her mother's preaching. "I was hoping you would understand. I didn't think Daddy would, or Evelyn, or even Lena, but you? I thought just maybe you would be sympathetic. I was wrong."

"You weren't wrong. I want what's best for you."

"I'm *not* in love with James," Elsie said, thrusting her hands to her hips. "I'm in love with John, and I'm proud of it. I just don't know if he found enough in me to keep him happy his whole life."

Phoebe made a grumbling noise and peered at her with a no-nonsense gleam in her eyes. "You don't sound confident about John. Why is that?"

"I don't know, exactly. I think it's because I care so much for him and I'm entangled in this situation with James."

"Has John ever been married?"

"No, he hasn't. Why do you ask?"

"It seems a little strange that a man nearly thirty has never been married."

Elsie rolled her eyes. "He's not nearly thirty. He's twenty-four. And his parents fought all the time. Why wouldn't he question marriage?"

"Twenty-four? That's five years younger than you. You can't be fooling around with a man five years younger."

Her mother seemed more interested in John's age than in domestic disturbances in the presence of children. "I'm not fooling around, Mum. You are so old fashioned! Five years isn't much difference. You can't even tell."

"That's what you think. Why would a young, good looking, working man get involved with a married woman who is pushing thirty? He could just be using you." Phoebe shook her head. "I don't want to be ornery, but I'm your mother and I don't want to see your heart broken. It's a good thing you're home now. Everything will work out for the best. You'll see."

"I don't feel like a married woman. Not at all. James has been absent from my life for so long—"

The telephone rang. Elsie ran into the parlor and fumbled for the receiver. "Hello," she gasped.

"Hello, Elsie? Merry Christmas."

"John … " she sighed. "I'm so glad you called. I've missed you so much." She smiled coyly at her mother, who trailed behind her, wiping her hands on her apron. Elsie sat down in the arm chair next to the telephone table, turning her face to the cushion behind her for privacy.

"I miss you, too," he said.

"I was wondering when I'd hear from you," she whispered.

Phoebe sighed and returned to the kitchen to finish the decorative labels for the jam and jelly jars.

"Sorry," he said. "The days have run away from me." There was a long silence. "I'm in Buffalo," he said excitedly.

"Buffalo," Elsie said, dreamily. "It must be nice to see your father and brother."

"It sure is. The house was so damn quiet when I came home from the train station. I decided to leave early for New York, figuring the trip would keep me busy without you."

After another long silence, he tried to sound upbeat. "It's snowing here. Guess we'll have a white Christmas. I'm wearing my feed sack shirt. It fits well. I like it. How are you getting along? How have you been?"

"Fine. Jolly good. Everyone in the family's doing well. My father and sisters are out right now looking for a Christmas tree." There was an awkward pause. "How was the drive?"

"It was a long drive—a long, cold one. My car was doing well until I got close to the New York state line. As I was heading toward Buffalo—whomp! A flat tire. I had to change a muddy flat in my new clothes. Luckily, I had a spare tire in the trunk."

"Oh, that was lucky," Elsie muttered.

"So, what are you doing with yourself?"

"I just helped Mum bake a cake. It's a thrift recipe. I've been just catching up with the family. I had supper last night with all my cousins. It was fun." She twirled her new pendant around her finger. "Will you be going to New York City? I wish I could be there."

"I'll spend Christmas and New Year's with my Dad and David, but I don't think I'll have time to go down to the city. The appointment is in Amherst on Thursday after all, so I won't be back to Indiana until probably the weekend. When are you planning on getting back?"

"I'm not sure. I guess the same time as you."

"I'll call to let you know for sure when I'll be home," John said.

"Okay. That will work out."

"Have you done anything about your marriage situation?" he asked at last.

"No, not yet," she said with a chuckle. "I only just arrived a few days ago, and I'm planning on talking to James's sister. She's my contact from here on out. If James does agree to a divorce, he'll sign the papers at her house. Maybe I should just go into town and consult an attorney? But I think they are very expensive." She paused. "How're your brother and father?"

"Fine. They're happy to see me. Surprised, too. My brother just got engaged about a week ago. I haven't met the lucky girl yet. Maybe tomorrow."

"He's younger than you, isn't he?"

"By a few years, yeah. He seems all excited about getting married. He wants to start a family. I'll tell you all about it when I see you. I almost forgot: I did some investigating and found out they gave your old job to a married man. Letting you go didn't have anything to do with a bad reputation."

She laughed. "Now I feel so much better. I thought the reason I was laid off was because of budget cuts. It means Mr. Winslow lied to me, anyway you look at it."

"I know, and it's not fair. I'm sorry Elsie; I better get going. Someone here wants to use the telephone."

"Are you on a pay telephone?"

"Not exactly. It's a telephone in the apartment hallway. All the tenants share it. Some old friends have invited me to a Christmas party tonight, and I have to get to the store. I hate shopping with all the crowds."

"I know what you mean," she said. "But a Christmas party with old chums sounds like a lot of fun." A sudden twinge of longing fluttered through her stomach. "Are you going to wear the shirt I made you?"

"I'm wearing it now, remember? I like it, and I love you; I miss you. Take care, sweetheart."

"I love you, too. And I miss you. Have a wonderful Christmas. Bye for now." There was a long drawl of sadness in her voice when she said, "Doesn't seem like Tuesday is Christmas, does it?"

"No, not really. It sure doesn't."

"Bye, John," she muttered, swallowing the lump in her throat, and thinking, dreading the idea that maybe he was slipping away;

going to parties without her, seeing friends he was perhaps more comfortable with.

"Bye, Elsie. Merry Christmas. And if I don't talk to you, have a Happy New Year."

"Same to you," she said quietly. What did he mean, *'If I don't talk to you ... '* The conversation had all been so ordinary, like she'd been speaking with someone she hardly knew, or an old family member she hadn't seen in years. She gently put the receiver down, walked past her mother and out the back door without putting on a coat, despite the bitter cold. Her heart felt as if it had been torn to shreds. Did he really have to hang up so soon?

Clouds had blown up suddenly, and the sky was overcast, almost as black as the mood that was descending upon her. How nice it would have been to go to a Christmas party with John. Meeting new people, sharing the holidays with someone you love. New Year's Eve would have been exciting, too. It was customary to spend the first day of a new year with someone special. Maybe next year, she thought.

She meandered around her mother's garden, longing with a physical ache for John, to be able to touch him, yet thinking that maybe she was just over reacting.

Despite the cold and the holiday season, she could still smell the odor of rubber in the air. How she hated that smell. She hoped that everything would be back to normal once she and John returned to Indiana. Or would it? The miles of space between them seemed to mirror the sudden emptiness in their relationship. Could it be over? She fervently wished she was just being silly by considering the unthinkable.

* * *

Within an hour after the tree came into the house, it was transformed into a wonderful specimen of holiday cheer. Frederick clipped and shaped it from top to bottom and drilled holes in the trunk to allow water in for freshness. He also bent branches to create a full and balanced tree, which stood anchored in a large milk pail.

Phoebe went upstairs to get an old, white sheet to drape around the pail as a tree skirt. The girls decorated the lower limbs, and Elsie the upper ones, with tinsel and bows. Phoebe made the star for the top of the tree from cardboard and covered it with tinfoil.

Evelyn sighed. "Ah-h, it looks beautiful."

"It does, doesn't it?" Phoebe cooed, making a few final adjustments by rearranging some of the bows and the paper chain.

"I can't wait to wrap presents," Evelyn said. "Finally I can get them out of hiding and decorate them. They'll look so pretty under the tree."

Lena smiled. "That sounds good. I'll do the same. It's the only thing the tree needs."

Elsie turned to her mother with tears in her eyes. "Mum, do you think strange things happen around the holidays?"

"No, luv." Phoebe put her arm around her daughter. "Come now, don't cry. Why would you say something like that? Is it about John?"

"I don't know. It just seems like bad things happen around the holidays when people least expect them."

"Even in the toughest of times, Christmas is a season of faith, wonder, and warmth. You'll see all that for yourself at the Christmas Eve service."

"I can see the magic of Christmas. There's just another side to it; a dark side. That's all I'm saying."

"*Who* doesn't like Christmas? Elsie, you're daft!" Lena said with a scowl.

"I didn't say I didn't like it. I just don't trust it, that's all." Elsie sighed and went to sit on the sofa, picking up a Vanity Fair magazine from the mahogany table beside her. "Look at this cover. It's a political illustration, depicting children from around the world decorating a Christmas tree with tools of war. What does that tell you?"

"I don't know when Vanity Fair turned so political," Phoebe said with disdain. "Who bought this magazine, anyway? Did you, Elsie?"

"Of course. I think I'm the only person in the house who's interested in politics. Besides, I needed something to read on the train."

"It cost thirty-five cents. That's a lot of money," Frederick remarked, looking from his handiwork at the Christmas tree to Elsie and back again. "Everyone here should be concerned with how much we're spending these days."

"Everybody's always worried about money. Always commenting on what things cost. The whole country is worried about money. That's another thing I love about John. He never complains about money. He's optimistic and generous."

"Elsie, that's disrespectful. If it weren't for the cost cutting measures your mother and I have taken," Frederick said, "everyone here, including *you*, would not have a roof over their heads."

"Is that why you love John, because he's not poor like James?" Evelyn asked.

"That's *not* why I love him. You wouldn't understand, Evelyn," Elsie retorted.

"Not everybody is rich like John," Lena said with sarcasm in her voice.

Phoebe smiled warmly at Elsie. "Luv, we need to cheer you up. I'm so glad you're here, even if it's just for a short visit. You'll feel inspired after tomorrow night's service. I guarantee it. Here, why don't you read the newspaper?" Phoebe said, handing her the morning edition.

She read the whole paper from cover to cover, but the news did nothing to cheer her up.

Chapter Sixteen

Elsie arranged a platter of holiday cookies for the kitchen table while her mother filled a carafe with hot chocolate to set beside it.

"Now, we'll only be gone a short while," Phoebe said. "The Goodyear luncheon is only an afternoon Christmas party. We'll be home for supper, which I've put in a slow oven; you needn't worry about it."

"Okay, Mum," Elsie said. "I'm spending some time with the girls today."

"Come dear, or we'll be late," Frederick said, steering his wife toward the door.

Elsie retired to Lena's bedroom where her younger sisters waited for her. Elsie sat down in front of the dresser, and put out all her makeup for them to see. She patted powder on her nose, rubbed rouge on her cheeks and applied a tinge of color to her lips. She combed her hair, lifting it from her neck and forward, close to her face. Then she placed a green satin bow on the left side and clipped it on. "Now it's your turn," she said to Lena.

Lena slowly applied the make-up, just as Elsie had done to her own face. She brushed her straight auburn hair back and picked up the other green bow, carefully placing it on the right side.

Elsie turned her toward the mirror and stooped down so close that their faces lined up in the reflection. "How do you like it?" she smiled, waiting for a reaction.

Lena beamed. "I look beautiful; like a movie-star."

"You do look lovely; all grown up. The bow is the perfect accessory."

"I *am* all grown up. I'm practically out of high school." Lena stared at Elsie, her eyes big and glowing. "Do you have a picture of your beau, John?"

"I do. I'll get it." She went into her bedroom to her suitcase, lifted it onto the bed, and opened it. "Come in here, Lena. I'm looking for it. It's a photograph of us at the Chicago World's Fair."

Evelyn sipped her hot chocolate as she wandered into Elsie's room after Lena. "I want to see it, too."

"Of course. First, let me find it. I know it's in here somewhere," she said, rummaging through the clothes in her suitcase. "I really should unpack, considering I'm going to be here for another week or so."

Elsie gently lifted a silver-framed photo from under her lingerie. She sighed, seeing how happy she looked with John. It was a picture of the two of them, standing in front of the Hawaiian Village, his arm around her shoulder. She smiled wistfully and handed it to Lena. "We had so much fun at the fair."

Lena stared at the image for a couple seconds and frowned. "Ugh. He's an ugly duckling," she said.

"He is not!" Elsie snapped. "What's the matter with you?"

"No, I was only kidding. He's handsome, just like Clark Gable," Lena cooed, falling back on the bed, her hands crisscrossed over the picture on her chest. "I want a boyfriend, too."

"You can't, stupid. You're too young," Evelyn said.

"No, I'm not. Are you crazy? I could be married at my age!"

Evelyn lunged over the bed, snatched the picture away from Lena, and stared at it in fascination. "He *is* handsome," she admitted. "Is he really your beau?"

Elsie bit her lower lip and nodded, feeling a twinge of anxiety flutter through her stomach.

"Cross your heart and hope to die?" Evelyn taunted.

"Don't be daft. I don't have to swear about love. I'm not a silly teenager. He gave me this—"

A knock at the downstairs door interrupted them.

"I'll get it. It must be Auntie Jane." Lena ran out of the bedroom, down the stairs, then opening the big wooden front door. On the other side of the storm door James Hunter smiled at her. "Oh, my word! James, is that you?" she exclaimed.

"It is, in the flesh. Merry Christmas, Lena. Is your big sister at home?"

"One minute, I'll get her. Just wait there." With a smirk, she rushed back up to the bedroom. "You have a gentleman caller, Elsie, and he's carrying flowers," she said, out of breath.

Elsie's eyes sparkled with anticipation. "Who is it?"

Lena gave a little high-pitched laugh, looking down the stairs. "You'll see. Geez Louise, will you be surprised!"

"You're a bloody tease! Never am I going to help you look beautiful and proper again." Nervously, Elsie ran a brush through her hair, quickly touched up her lipstick, and raced out. She opened the storm door, managing a wobbly smile at the sight of James. "Oh, James ... hello." She paused. "Merry Christmas. This is a surprise!" she said, trying to conceal her disappointment. "Won't you please come in?"

James crossed the threshold, smiling, and hugged her tightly. "I hope I'm not interrupting anything. I wanted to wish you a Merry Christmas. This is for you," he said, handing her a bouquet of Christmas roses and a small box of chocolate-covered cherries.

"Thank you," Elsie said. "Come on into the parlor."

Looking around in silence as though old memories had interrupted his ability to speak, he licked his dry lips. "May I sit down?"

"Of course," Elsie said. "Have a seat on the couch. I'll get these flowers into some water and I'll be back in a minute," she said, stepping into the kitchen. She returned with the steaming carafe of hot chocolate and the plate of holiday cookies.

"You look good," he remarked. His eyes moved from her face, down to her breasts, and lower, to her abdomen.

She looked down, uncomfortable with his scrutiny. Why must he look at her with sexual tension in his eyes? The best approach, she knew, was to ignore it. "Would you like to join me for hot chocolate and cookies?" she asked nervously.

"Thanks, I'll only stay a little while. My sister is picking me up at half-past two. The place looks good." He paused to look around again.

Elsie poured the hot chocolate and settled back into the sofa, leaving a comfortable space between them, then leaned forward to snatch a cookie. She looked at him with keen curiosity. He looked more like the man she had married; his hair was shiny, combed up and back in careful waves.

"I hope we can mend our marriage," he said. "Lately, I've missed you so much."

"That's strange. Why lately? You've been gone for years. What about all those years of absence? Didn't you miss me then?"

"I put you out of my mind," he said, seemingly with great remorse. "Not completely, but I pushed you way into the back."

She wanted to give him a piece of her mind, right then and there. But thankfully, her sisters chose that moment to walk into the room.

"We're getting bored. We don't have anything to do and it's Christmas Eve," Lena said, giving her hair a sassy toss.

Together, her sisters stood and gaped at James.

Elsie narrowed her eyes. "Girls, *what* do you say?"

"Happy holidays, James," Lena muttered with a chuckle.

"Merry Christmas," Evelyn piped up. "Where have you been, anyway?"

"Around, here and there." James coughed and cleared his throat, his eyes glancing from one to the other. "Lena, you've really grown up to be quite a lovely young lady. Your hair looks really pretty. And Evelyn, you're pretty, too. How old are you now?"

"I'm fourteen," Evelyn mumbled. "May I *please* have a chocolate cherry?"

"Why can't you just have a cookie?" Elsie prompted.

"I'm sick of cookies. I had a dozen yesterday."

From her place beside him, Elsie gave a quiet groan. "They're a gift from James. I haven't even opened them, but if you promise to behave and return to Lena's room, I'll give you both one."

They nodded and each stuck out a palm.

Elsie hurriedly opened the box and placed one chocolate in Evelyn's hand, and another in Lena's. Evelyn giggled and whispered to her sister as she turned to leave the parlor. "I wonder if she's going to tell him her secret? She has so many beaus."

Lena put her hands over her mouth and hurried up the stairs with Evelyn following.

Elsie rolled her eyes." I nearly forgot how much fun it is having two younger sisters."

"How was your trip home?" James said, his tone sounding more upbeat than when he arrived.

"Swell. The train ride was perfect. What about you?"

"I didn't take the train," he said, laughing. "I caught a ride with an Irish fellow who was traveling this way. It took us the better part of two days. You know, those dirt roads and how you can get stuck in the mud and melted snow. He shifted into neutral and coasted downhill every chance he had in order to save gasoline." James picked up a cookie and shoved it into his mouth. He grinned. "I have something important to ask you," he said, reaching for her hand.

"What is it?" she said, cautiously.

"Will you be my date New Year's Eve? My sister is buying the tickets for me down at City Hall," he said, still holding her hand. "They're having a jitterbug dance and I'd love for you to be my partner again." He put his right arm around her and moved closer. He was laying the conversation wide open for her to say something, to admit how she felt.

She had believed herself in love with James, but all that belonged to another life. The girl who gleefully danced with him no longer existed. Still for some reason, she couldn't bear to turn him down. "You're buying the tickets before I said yes I'll go?"

"Wishful thinking, I suppose."

"Yes, sure I'll go on one condition," she muttered.

"What's that?"

"That you promise not to leave me on the dance floor while you go for cigarettes."

He laughed. "Elsie, remember, if our relationship is going to work, we have to begin from this moment on. I'm not making excuses, but I met hundreds of men who left their wives."

"I know you weren't the only one." She brushed away a wisp of hair, her face flushed from thinking about bearing her secret. "James," Elsie started, and then hesitated. Something held her back. How could she profess her love for another man in front of him? "James, I'm confused about—"

"I know," he interrupted. "I confused you by leaving the way I did, and surprising the heck out of you in Rensselaer. But I've been doing a lot of thinking and I want you back. I want *us* back." He stared at her a long moment, emotions running across his face. "I'm not running around anymore, I'm staying right here."

Elsie thought it possible that the only reason he now wanted her was because of the hardships he'd endured on the road. He was tired, alone, and needed a home. His affections might not have anything to do with loving her at all. She remained silent, revealing none of her true thoughts. She remembered what John had said: '*I don't trust the guy.*'

James sighed, shook his head, and reached for his wallet. "Here," he said. "I've got, let's see, twenty-eight dollars. I had thirty and some change but I had to pay for the tickets to the dance and buy your Christmas presents. I want you to have all of it." He started to put the money in her hand. It's just a start, but I'm willing to work hard and—"

She pushed his hand away. His words confirmed her belief that he didn't understand her. "I don't want your money," she interrupted. "I want something else," she said, sinking into the sofa with a long breath.

He smiled, but his expression was touched with sadness. He put the money back into his wallet. "You really do want children, don't you?" His eyes seemed to devour her and she felt as if she were suffocating.

"I want children, yes, but that's not the point. Please don't bring things up that are irrelevant. I don't feel close to you any longer."

"I know, but I could change that." He touched her cheek, and bent forward to kiss her.

"Please," she said, pushing him away. "Please, don't do that. You can't just walk into my life after over three years of absence and expect things to be the same." The determination in her voice removed any hint of interest.

"I can work hard and we could buy a place of our own. I know I could do it. We could start over and everything would be better. I promise you that," James patiently persisted. "I want a son. I've been giving it a lot of thought."

There was a sudden intensity to his voice, revealing an inherent need. "I want children with you. I'm not giving up, Elsie. You loved me once, and you can love me again. Don't take offense, but you're going to be thirty. Don't you want a baby before it's too late?"

New beginnings emerged before her; motherly impulses rose up inside. It took a few moments before she realized that what she felt was a shred of hope. Hope for the possibility that she could have a child of her own. But the reality was she had fallen in love with a man who wasn't her husband. She took a breath and finally spoke. "We agreed that I would help you get a job at Goodyear, and I'm happy to do just that. I really shouldn't have even done that. I don't owe you anything. But now, you want to have a baby with me. That's going just a bit fast, James."

"I understand. I'll wait." His eyes held the sharpness of both passion and sorrow in a single glance. "It should have been different. We should have clung to each other through our difficult times."

He lowered his gaze from her to stare at the open box of chocolates. It took a long moment before he was able to speak. "I know I took you for granted. But I'm willing to do whatever it takes to make our marriage work."

Watching him beg, and get so emotional in front of her, made her want to disappear into the woodwork; if she could be anywhere else .... Uncertainty diminished the resolved for independence from him, which she'd so long held throughout the many happy months with John. In James's presence, pulled into the drama of his pleading, she suddenly did not know how to act, what to do, or what to say. His behavior was unexpected, and it stunned her to silence. Was he going to cry?

When the awkward moment became unbearable, James said, "Have you had a chance to talk to your father about job openings at the plant?"

"No, I'm afraid not," she said, feeling his hot stare covering her like a cloak. "I did speak with my mother, who is very concerned about your welfare. I think she's going to talk to my father. But I have to be honest and frank, James," she said, finally taking control of the situation with renewed surety. "Christmas Eve is not the appropriate time to say this, but I think we should get a divorce."

"What are you talking about? Divorce it too expensive! That's ridiculous. Give me a chance—a month or so—I know you'll change your mind. You're still upset with me and probably worried I won't be able to make enough money to support you. You need more time. I'll go now and let you think about everything." He rose to his feet with a seeming insecurity. "My sister is probably waiting outside? She said she'd pick me up. I'd better not make her wait."

"Does she want to come in?" Elsie asked.

"No thanks, not today. She needs to get home; she's going to a party tonight."

Elsie followed him to the front door. "Thank you for the thoughtful Christmas presents, and do wish your sister a Merry Christmas for me."

"I will. Do I get a Christmas Eve kiss?"

She kissed him lightly on the mouth. "Have a wonderful night and I'll see you New Year's Eve. Oh, wait one moment." She walked back to the kitchen and then returned to the front door. She handed him a small, folded piece of paper with her phone number written on it. "I wasn't sure you'd remember the number here after all this time."

"You're right." He opened it up and grinned. "That kiss wasn't much, but I guess it's a start. Let's not quarrel, or talk about divorce, okay? I'll be sure to telephone. You'll know where I am from now on. Merry Christmas, and I'll see you New Year's Eve."

Later that night, Elsie and her family attended midnight mass, sitting in a pew toward the back of the church. The church was full of people, but none of them she recognized. She kept glancing around, searching for a familiar face and feeling a little lonely, despite her family's presence. She was a muddle of guilt and confusion. Why wasn't she more forceful with James and tell him about the man in her life? The man she truly loved.

The tawny stone walls extended high above them to meet the church's stained-glass windows, which depicted the life of Jesus. The pianist played the traditional songs of Christmas with a joyous fervor. The choir stood and sang *O Come, All Ye Faithful* and *Silent Night*. Once the choir was seated, the minister stood at the pulpit and spoke. He read the Christmas story, and the children acted out the Nativity scene. Mary wore a halo made of cardboard and tinfoil; Joseph knelt beside her. Walking into the manger scene, the Three Wise Men dragged their robes across the floor. None of it made Elsie feel any better, contrary to her mother's promise.

Next, Elsie and the rest of the congregation stood and sang their hearts out to *Away in a Manger*. After the song, the minister's voice droned on in inspiring tones, words Elsie did not bother to listen to. At the end of the service, the minister asked the congregation to accompany him in a special Christmas prayer.

As Elsie folded her hands and bent her head to join in, she felt a little nudge against her arm. She looked up to meet her mother's eyes. "I'm praying for you," she mouthed.

Elsie grinned and silently bowed her head. *Please, God, I need your presence to guide me, to show me the path my feet should be walking. Forgive me, for wanting to divorce James. Bless my union and my love for John McDonald. I pray to be with him forever. He is the love of my life. Amen.*

Chapter Seventeen

S ince returning home to Akron, Elsie had awakened just about every morning to see Evelyn standing by the bed, staring, eagerly waiting for her to rise. Evelyn was the one member of the family, it seemed to Elsie, who was entirely fascinated with her love affair with John. She never seemed to tire of the romantic stories.

"Are you awake?" Evelyn whispered, stretching out on the end of the bed.

Elsie refrained from moving or speaking, in hopes that Evelyn would lose patience with the wait and disappear. After a few minutes, Elsie opened her eyes in search of the clock at her bedside, realizing that Evelyn was still lounging at the end of the bed and watching her. There was no escaping now. "What time is it anyway?" she asked, stifling a yawn.

"Nearly eight o'clock. It's dreadful out there," Evelyn said, pointing to the rain-spattered window. "It's a heavy downpour. I thought we could stay indoors and play Monopoly today. Plus, you promised to tell me all about the night when you first kissed John McDonald."

An old memory of John flared up, and Elsie was thrust into another day of longing. It had been nearly two weeks since she'd heard from him, and she was becoming increasingly anxious.

Evelyn peered at her, waiting for a response.

"I'm not up to telling you a story right now. I don't know what I want to do today. I should be heading back to Indiana."

"If you can't tell me about your boy stuff, would you play Monopoly before you leave? Please?" Evelyn begged.

"I just woke up, Evelyn."

"Pretty please with sugar on top? I'll let you be the banker."

"You're beginning to get on my nerves. Shouldn't you be in school?"

"Are you daft? It's Saturday."

Saturday … January fifth, nineteen hundred and thirty-five. John had already interviewed for that new job two days ago. Why hadn't he called with any news? She glanced back at Evelyn. "What's Mum doing?" she said at last, stretching her arms, swinging her legs out from under the covers, and placing her bare feet on the small rug next to the bed.

"Fixing breakfast, I think."

Elsie stumbled out of bed and into the bathroom, where she splashed her face and neck with cold water. "Give me half an hour. I'm going to bathe," she yelled, poking her head out the door and wiping a trickle of water from her face.

"Okay. I'll wait here," Evelyn called back.

After a relaxing soak in the tub, she walked out into the bedroom wrapped in a bath towel and found that Evelyn had disappeared. Hastily, she rummaged through an old chest of drawers in the room and found a pair of tattered brown pants. She picked out a faded yellow sweater, figuring that since she was probably going to remain indoors today, the old clothes would do just fine.

Downstairs in the kitchen, steam rose from three pots on the stove. Phoebe was stirring one of them with a large, wooden spoon as Elsie sat down at the table. Normally, the fragrant smelling delights would have aroused her appetite. But not today. "Good morning, luv. Oatmeal?" her mother said cheerfully.

"All right, just half a bowl."

"Are you trying to be like Katharine Hepburn?" her mother said, staring at her trousers.

"No, not really. It's pouring. What does it matter what I wear?"

"I like to look ladylike, regardless of the weather." Phoebe put several heaping tablespoons of oatmeal into a bowl and handed it to her. "What are you going to do today?"

Elsie poured a little milk on the oatmeal and smiled. "Evelyn wants to play Monopoly, but I should be going to the station to buy a ticket to Rensselaer."

"Oh, don't talk about that just yet. It's a splendid day for Monopoly. It's raining too hard to go to the station today. I'm going to venture next door to your Auntie Jane's to pore over her Butterick and Simplicity pattern books until I find a suitable style for a new Sunday dress."

Elsie nodded, agreeably. She spooned a couple of bites of oatmeal into her mouth and said, "Give Auntie Jane my love and tell her I'll be over for a visit before I leave." She looked up, listening to the rain pound the roof. "Oh, Mum, it sounds like it's raining cats and dogs."

"Yes, it reminds me of Maidstone, though I don't fear the heavy rainstorms. As President Roosevelt has said, you have nothing to fear, but fear itself." She smiled. "I always try to remember that."

"Well, I'm going outside to check for myself, but first I'll get a cup of tea." Elsie stood and went over to the teapot. Cautiously, she poured herself a cup, slipped on her coat, and took the tea outside to the back porch.

Instead of the morning's weather improving, it had taken a turn for the worse, with a foul, cold wind blowing the rain sideways, causing her to turn up the collar on her coat. She looked out to the backyard. This wasn't just the drippy kind of rain, but the bucketing-down kind that sent people scattering like marbles, trying to find shelter under anything they could. She imagined if she were back in Rensselaer, she and John would remain indoors, curled up on a sheepskin rug in front of the fireplace, sipping hot chocolate. They would chat for awhile, listening to Amos and Andy, or another show, and end up kissing and making love. Oh, how she missed him.

Quickly, she chased the daydream from her head. He had only called her a couple times since she'd been home, which had done nothing to allay her fears about the distance between them, or the fact that he may be slipping away from her. After all, he, unlike most people had the money to make long distance telephone calls. He could have called her more often. She took a deep breath to regain control of her emotions; she knew it was important to not let negative thoughts get the better of her.

The wind and rain swirled around the verandah. Perhaps, she thought with sudden abandon, she should give John a call this very moment and express her concerns.

She turned herself around with a take-charge attitude, walked back into the house, and into the parlor. The day was still early in Buffalo; maybe he was at home with his father and brother. She picked up the receiver, but in a moment, realized that no sane girl would call a man she hadn't heard from in almost two weeks, especially in her parents' home. She should play a little hard to get. He should call her. So, even though she desperately wanted to talk to John, she wasn't going to make the first move with her mother and father in the next room. Besides, she didn't even know the number to the community apartment telephone; she'd have to first call the information operator.

Her father's voice, calling from the kitchen, interrupted her thoughts. "Oh, Elsie. Could you come here, please?"

"I'll be right there," she said, abruptly replacing the receiver. She went back to the kitchen and stood for a moment in the doorway, watching the rain splash the windows. "Yes, Daddy?"

"I have some jolly good news." He grinned, tapping the seat of the chair beside him. "Sit down."

She smiled and sat down at the table where he was eating breakfast.

Phoebe poured her husband a cup of coffee and turned to face Elsie. "Can I tempt you with a cup, luv?"

"No, Mum. I'm drinking tea. Thanks."

Frederick stared into his coffee cup, then looked up into his daughter's eyes. "I found a temporary job for James in blimp manufacturing. It should last at least six months."

"Oh, that's wonderful." She sipped her tea and then nodded approvingly. "He'll be so happy to hear that. Thank you."

Frederick picked up a knife to butter his toast. "That's not the end of it. I found a job for you, too, in the insurance department. It's not teaching children, but it pays a decent wage and you can start next week." He threw her a somber look. "You belong here in Akron with your family, and if James is willing to take care of you … well," he looked down to avoid her gaze, "you belong with him."

Elsie shook her head, appalled. "I don't belong with him! James hasn't been much of a husband! How can you say I belong with him? He left me to fend for myself for more than three years." She could feel the hot sting of tears in her eyes. "And he never did come back to me. He didn't care to. If I hadn't found him in the hobo camp—" She paused for impact. "God knows what part of the country he'd be in by now. I'd probably never see him again. Ever! Besides, the marriage is over! It's been over for years! For God sakes, what did Mum tell you?"

"For one thing, she told me this John chap is younger than you and that he has never been married. He's not serious about you. He's just having fun. I should know; I was a young man once."

"You're not young anymore. You don't know! You don't know anything about my affairs!"

"You have a right to be angry," her father said sympathetically.

She put her hand across her mouth in an attempt to hide her feelings.

"I'm going to ignore how you're speaking to me. I know you're very upset, but I'm going to tell it to you straight. Elsie, you have to consider your moral responsibility. James is back now, and what I'm hearing is that he's trying to be honorable. That's why I'm sticking my neck out to help him. The bugger had better not embarrass me. He'd better do a damn good job."

Frederick wolfed down the rest of his breakfast and handed his dirty plate to his wife. "For Christ's sake! I've been an excellent employee at Goodyear for over twenty years now. I've found jobs for two people. Two people! When thousands are out of work."

Phoebe took her husband's plate and bent down to kiss him on the cheek.

Elsie hesitated, wanting to protest again, but she saw her mother shake her head, so she held her tongue. She raised her eyebrows at her father and stood up from the table, disturbed that he was a great deal more caught up in James's state of affairs than receptive to her own feelings. She breathed in deeply and decided to change her attitude. "I understand what you're saying, and I appreciate all you've done for James, but as far as I'm concerned, I'm delighted to be living and working in Indiana. It's my business and my life. I know Goodyear Tire is a wonderful place to work, but I'm not at all interested in a job there," she said, hoping to end the discussion.

"You *should* be interested!" Frederick snapped. "Jobs are difficult to find. Mostly impossible! Don't forget we're in mighty hard times. You don't want to end up selling walnuts door-to-door do you? Why, I don't know anyone who would turn down a good paying job. Nobody! You think about my proposition very carefully," he said, drumming the kitchen table with his fingers. "You have about two or three days to decide before I have to give the supervisor an answer. You're lucky this is the weekend. It'll give you a little time to come to your senses." His eyes narrowed. "This is a new year. It could be a new start for you."

Phoebe brought more coffee at that point, which gave the discussion a welcome break.

Frederick managed a faint smile for his wife as he accepted a refill.

Elsie sighed with a certain dread that only compounded her sadness. "I'll give it some thought," she muttered, beginning to wipe down the table in silence.

Her father gave her a skeptical look and scratched his head. "Another thing: didn't your mother tell me you were laid off from your teaching job? How are you going to support yourself?" He shook his head, disgusted. "I don't understand what there is to think about."

She felt a hot flash of embarrassment. "I *was* laid off, but I'm confident I can find something else. Besides, I'm managing just fine. I want to return to Rensselaer. Maybe if all else fails, I can work for Robert. And if that doesn't work out I have another job at Woolworth's. I'm only here on holiday," she said, slowly emphasizing each word. "I'm not a child. I can make my own decisions." Her voice rose. "For God's sake, I'll be thirty years old in a couple of months."

Phoebe ran her fingers through her hair as she looked at the expression on her daughter's face. "You *will* be thirty. That's significant. It's about time you started a family. I just hope, for your sake, it's not too late." There was no easy way for Phoebe to say what she was really thinking. She took a deep breath and just came out with it. "How can you be happy with a man who doesn't want to marry you?"

"He never said he didn't want to marry me. He said he's waiting for me to get a divorce. That's completely different!"

"Well," her mother continued, "you should have never gotten involved with him. And now you don't even have a real job. I'm not counting Woolworth's. Robert can't offer you anything; you don't know a thing about automobiles, or even bicycles, for that matter. Elsie, you spend all your time torn between fancying John McDonald, and trying to sort out your feelings for James. You can't have it both ways. You're going to end up losing. You'll end up alone and unemployed. You've already lost plenty."

Elsie cringed. "I'm in love; so is John. And you don't care a whit about *my feelings*!" There was nothing she hated more than unsolicited advice from her mother, especially when what she said rang true.

Her mother had a negative analysis of her current situation, but a possibly realistic one. Although, what really upset her, she knew, was the way the balance of her life had changed. She had been so happy teaching and living with John. Now her whole life, her happiness, was being threatened. She wished she had never run into James at the hobo camp, and for that matter, ever married him in the first place. And maybe she should have never gone home for Christmas. Now the die was cast.

Frederick glanced at the clock. "I have to get to work." He turned to face Elsie, determination in his eyes. "Listen to your mother. Think about what I said. There are people standing in line waiting to get jobs at Goodyear. Day after day, I pass these people on my way into the plant. They're hoping someone will open the door and announce that two or three jobs are available. The lucky ones at the front rush inside, and hundreds of others, heads down and shoulders bent, start the slow walk home again." There was an impatience and irritation in his voice.

He somberly picked up his jacket to leave when the telephone rang in the parlor, so he went to answer it. "Hello. Good morning,

Jane. No. Emergency storm warnings? No, our radio has been off this morning ... no reception. Yes? I'll make sure she gets there without drowning. We're leaving now." Frederick hung up and glanced at Phoebe, who had followed him into the room. "Your sister's concerned about the weather. Let me give you a lift. I'll pull as close as I can to her front door."

Phoebe smiled and removed her apron. She opened the hall closet to put on her raincoat. "Elsie, why don't you ring James and tell him the good news?"

Elsie leaned against the armoire in the parlor. "He's coming over tomorrow," she said in a clipped voice, still upset with the talk about working and living in Akron. "I'd rather tell him in person."

"Suit yourself. But I think he'd want to know as soon as possible," Phoebe said.

Frederick grabbed his umbrella, which hung on the coat rack. "Cheerio, and try to look on the sunny side of the street. And don't allow your sisters to get in too much trouble, now."

Great, Elsie thought glumly. *I'm back to babysitting.*

"Come now, Goodyear is a wonderful place to work," Frederick said. "On Saturdays you see how late I'm going in, and then they close early." His mouth pursed sourly. "Think long and hard, young lady. This is a golden opportunity."

Her parents both walked toward the front door, Elsie trailing.

Her mother stopped on the other side of the screen where Elsie stood in the open doorway. "Your father is just trying to help," she whispered. "You should feel grateful that he can do this for you." Phoebe frowned. "I pray you're not angry with me. I'm in a sticky wicket here. I've held my tongue for days," she said, opening up the screen door and laying a kind hand to her daughter's cheek. She then pulled her coat tighter to keep out the bitter wind.

"I know. I'm not angry. Disappointed maybe, but not angry." Elsie quickly said goodbye to her parents before either of them became drenched with the heavy rain blowing into the porch. She watched them leave, then hurried inside to catch the heat from the fireplace.

She swallowed, feeling sick to her stomach. Why had she ever come back to Akron? Everyday, the nightmare grew worse.

The rain was still rattling the roof as if a full parade were stomping over the house. Lena and Evelyn strolled into the parlor, Evelyn carrying the Monopoly box. "Let's play! We have all day. It takes a long time to play this game," Evelyn said. "It's raining so hard; you can't possibly want to go out to the train station."

"I'm really not in the mood right now to play a game." Elsie yawned, feeling drained from the heat of the fireplace and the horrible conversation she'd just had.

"Oh, come on. You don't have anything else to do. Monopoly is all the rage," Lena chimed in.

"It's the best Christmas present ever," Evelyn said.

Elsie came to a sudden decision. "You two can play. I'm going to write Robert a letter."

"It's better with three people," Lena whined.

"We'll let you be in charge of the houses and the money," Evelyn said encouragingly.

"No, thanks. Maybe some other time," Elsie said, climbing the stairs to the bedroom.

She turned on a tasseled green lamp for light and sat in the chair at the writing bureau, which was neatly stacked with a pile of blue notepaper and envelopes. All the feelings that had built up over the last few days were realized in a huge burst of emotion, swirling around in her head like the needle on a scratched phonograph record, jumping back again and again to what her mother had said about John's seeming disinterest in her: *'He doesn't want to marry you; he's only using you.'*

Time had a knack of chipping away all love, and his silence disturbed her. What was he doing? Where was he? Who was he with? Why hadn't he called?

She wiped a teardrop from the blue stationery before it could smear the ink.

Dear Robert,

I just had an awful conversation with my parents. It seems like no one cares about my happiness, not even my mum, in whom I'm so deeply disappointed.

I ask you, as my good friend, for advice—what should I do about my current situation? I'm torn between my love for John and the approval of my family and society. It nags me in the still of the night when I ask myself: why doesn't he want to marry me? Is it because technically I'm still married to James or is it something else? I'm not even sure that if I were available, would he propose? I wonder why John and I came together in life; if not to be married, then what? I know all too well that if I lose him now it will be the tragedy of my life. I can feel his interest fading. He should have called by now!

After finishing the letter, she wanted to keep busy; maybe do a bit of housework. In fact, she remembered thinking that her parents' bedroom could do with a good hoovering. She walked into their room and first switched on the smaller radio that her parents kept for private use, fine tuning it to WJAY, thinking that sounds of other voices might cheer her up. For awhile, she sat on her parents' bed, listening to the music, but it was fading in and out with the terrible weather outside. After awhile, she went to the closet with a lethargy she'd never experienced, and pulled out the vacuum.

She carefully pushed the machine over the carpet, and even kneeled to see under the bed, making sure the carpet there was cleaned, as well. After hoovering, she shut off the vacuum with the sole of her black and white oxford. The drone fell silent, allowing strains of last year's hit, *June in January*, to fill the room. The hard rain had stopped, and she could hear the music clearly; reminding her of so many happy memories of John.

Shaking her head in exasperation, she thought that in just a matter of hours she would take the train back to Rensselaer, and her life would hopefully go back to normal. Unemployment would be much better than loneliness.

Chapter Eighteen

John placed a kettle of hot water with several rags in it on the ground in front of the Ford, and folded back the motor cover. He hoped the trick would work. It was already Sunday, January sixth, and he needed to get back to Indiana with Elsie. One at a time, he pulled the wet rags from the kettle and let them drip before he leaned over the motor and strategically placed them on the manifold. He quickly opened the driver's door, climbed behind the wheel, and turned the key in the ignition. The motor roared to life, first with a bit of clunking, but as she warmed up, she began to purr like a top. He jumped out, removed the rags, and eagerly closed the hood.

Now that the car was running, he dashed back to the small, two-bedroom apartment to leave a note for his father and brother who were still sleeping. Having said their goodbyes the previous night; he now could get an early start. He left the paper tucked under a ceramic ashtray on the coffee table, picked up his suitcase, a tire patch kit and pump, a sack of apples and oranges for snacks, and rushed back out to his car.

He stored a few tools under the back seat along with the repair kit. In addition, he'd made sure to refill the gallon jug of water behind him on the floor, just in case the radiator boiled dry. On the passenger seat, he tossed a notepad, a road guidebook, detailing the route from Buffalo to Akron, his hat, and the sack of fruit. He threw his suitcase onto the back seat and climbed into the front.

He had dressed in his new feed sack shirt, sure to surprise Elsie, and over that a woolen shirt to keep warm. He wasn't altogether certain that the flannel slacks over long underwear he'd selected would provide for a very dapper entrance at the Obee door, but he wasn't taking any chances with the cold, winter weather. To top off his warm clothing, he'd thrown on his beige, doubled-breasted sports coat, and hoped for the best. Surely Elsie's parents would appreciate his practicality and timeliness on Elsie's behalf. He'd parted his hair on the side with water, which now replaced the pomade he had been using to achieve the suave look of film star, Charles Farrell. All architectural firms, especially those in the East, required their employees to be well-groomed. He hoped he would fit the bill, and that Elsie would approve.

Grasping the wheel, he glanced at his watch. Ten past six. He picked up the small notepad to calculate the distance: two hundred eight miles, traveling at thirty to forty-five miles per hour would put him in Akron before noon, if he didn't hit severe weather. At least that was the estimate. The temperature: twenty-seven degrees, was moderate for the first week of January.

Boy, was Elsie going to be surprised.

He released the hand brake and the automobile jumped ahead, chugging down the highway, heading east on Box Avenue, parallel to Lake Erie. The lake was frozen in a thick layer of ice, and he was glad for the blanket he always carried in the back seat. Before long, he would need to throw it across his lap.

Drives like this often put him into a philosophical frame of mind. In only three days, he would celebrate his twenty-fifth birthday. In retrospect, he felt his life was going well. Better than most fellows' lives. Under New York's La Guardia administration, he had been offered a job, working on a new concept of mass-produced homes, built in one area, all with the same floor plan. It should prove to be an interesting position, although he'd have to relocate back to New York.

He hoped Elsie would find New York fascinating, though would she actually want to live in Buffalo? As for himself, he had mixed feelings about the prospect of life in Buffalo. It would be a great career move, with more advancement opportunities and cultural exploration for the two of them. Aesthetically, he never cared for the industrial look of the city, especially lakeside, though he did find redeeming qualities in much of the urban architectural structures about town.

One of his favorites was the thirteen-story, steel framed Guaranty Building designed by the architectural partners, Sullivan and Dankmar. In addition, the architect he greatly admired, Frank Lloyd Wright, had designed several buildings in the city, including the Darwin Martin House, and the Davidson House. In his estimation, these dwellings were fine examples of Wright's philosophy of organic architecture, designed to adapt to specific environments, materials, and conditions. Buffalo also placed him close to his family. All-in-all, he felt certain he was making the right move, as long as Elsie agreed.

Traveling on the outskirts of town, he passed Buffalo's Hoovervilles—shantytowns named after President Hoover, built in the shadow of luxury. Just a few blocks away, the wealthy lived in elegant mansions lining the street, commonly known as Millionaire's Row.

He bumped along a rock-filled road that paralleled the railroad tracks. To his right he noticed how quiet the Curtiss-Wright Airplane factory was on a Sunday morning. He recalled driving past the plant as a child with his father, and hearing the loud irritating sounds of the screeching, rumbling, and banging machinery. It seemed that an airplane made almost as much noise being built, as it did in one of those steep descent dives.

He hit a smooth patch of roadway and picked up speed, however not long afterward, the road changed to a winding trail as the flatland disappeared and the terrain became hilly. He had to put the car into low gear and hope for the best on the steepest hills.

As the car wandered down a slowly descending hill, his thoughts turned to Elsie. Would she be happy when he appeared unexpectedly on her parents' doorstep? She should, as she loved surprises. He'd been reluctant to telephone the family home again and disturb anyone, or take Elsie away from them, since she was only staying such a short time. He did try once more to phone, but the line was busy so he decided to surprise her in person instead. Again, John wondered if she would welcome the notion of moving to New York. He sure hoped so. There would probably be more job opportunities for her there.

The trusty Ford coupe started huffing and puffing. He eased up on the accelerator, praying the car wouldn't die. How could he push it to go any farther with a hill rising up ahead? Thankfully, as the car chugged around the next bend, the road dropped down into a valley, and it was there that John spied a filling station, just before the road began the steep incline.

He pulled in and had the gas, oil, water, and tires checked. The mechanic also cleaned the plugs, and re-gapped and replaced them. John pulled out his gold money clip and handed the mechanic six dollars.

With gas receipts in hand, he did further calculations in his notebook. Presently, on his excursion, he was getting twenty-four miles to a gallon of gas. Pleased with the results, he considered returning to Cliff Road, which ran along the edge of vast Chautauqua Lake, thus skirting the unpleasant rows of company houses in the industrial city outside Portland.

Three hours. He ambled west on Cliff Road as his mind toyed with the number of hours he had been on the road. Traveling along the edge of the lake, his attention was caught by a small wooden marker on the side of the road. *'Chautauqua Institution 20 miles.'* He remembered Theodore Roosevelt describing the Institution as "typical of America at its best," and wanted to see for himself what made this nonprofit, seven-hundred-fifty acre educational center so famous.

Half an hour later, he came to a signpost: *'Chautauqua Institution.'* An arrow pointed straight ahead. He drove carefully past the line of parked vehicles, and found a spot against the curb. John tried to roll down his window, but couldn't. It was jammed, as usual, and he would ordinarily bang it with his fist before the glass would reluctantly slide halfway down. Since it was so cold outside, he couldn't imagine just sitting with the frosty air coming in through the window, so he stepped out of the car for a stretch, and to walk.

After judging the scope of the property for a few peaceful moments, he set out to get a better view of the buildings. The setting was park-like, with rustic cottages and Victorian gingerbread-trimmed buildings gracing the lawns and providing a restful atmosphere.

He strolled the grounds, trying to ignore the cold, eating the last apple. He stretched, and settled himself comfortably for the long drive ahead. He missed Elsie and could not wait to see her again.

Soon after crossing into Pennsylvania, he became conscious of the wind. Cold, buffeting winds blew, cutting under the windshield and around the edges of the ratty side windows, mercilessly burning his nose and cheeks. He sighed, relieved that he would be able to avoid Pittsburgh with its streets that ran up and down, and in circles. Not one road he'd ever driven there went in a straight line for more than a couple blocks; the city was built on a triangular plot of ground. Bridges had been built everywhere in order to cross three rivers at various points.

John looked down at the speedometer: forty-five miles per hour.

He pushed on into Erie, Pennsylvania. Erie had always been one of his preferred places to vacation and wind down, with its restaurants, shops, and incredible stretch of untouched lakefront. At an intersection, he sat waiting impatiently for traffic to move, his thoughts wandering, and found that he was looking at a long line of children. The boys and girls stood at the Salvation Army doors, holding containers. A sign above the door proclaimed: '*Milk Available Today—Children Only.*'

When the big truck ahead of him with cattle moved, he sped off, saddened by the sight of the children. The scene had made him think of families and homes, and his thoughts once again returned to his own home. Soon he and Elsie would be back there together, packing and looking forward to life in New York. He was anxious to be there, anywhere with her, as long as they were together.

His car slipped too far over on the shoulder in loose gravel mixed with ice chips, and he fishtailed from one side of the road to the other. He gently applied the brake and simultaneously turned the wheel to the right, putting the car back on the road. He'd better be more careful, he thought, or he'd never see Elsie again.

Driving out of Pennsylvania into Ohio, he went up rocky mountain trails with logs cut into the roads to get traction going up, forded creeks, and went through barren fruit orchards. The thermometer on the radiator gage started to rise after he reached the parkway. He looked for a safe place to pull off the road, and before long, the radiator boiled over and he had to stop.

While waiting for the engine to cool, he leaned against the car and pulled out Elsie's street address: *489 Champlain Street, Akron, Ohio.* The cold breeze that blew caused him to look up and contemplate the weather ahead. A winter storm still threatened, the inky clouds looming ominously on the horizon.

Again he looked at his watch: quarter past eleven. In another hour, at his current speed, he should be on Champlain Street, the road that led to Elsie. He poured the water from the jug into the radiator and quickly returned to the road. He added speed as the bumpy road left the densely populated area behind and changed from a narrow, two-lane street to a new, two-lane paved highway. The engine willingly responded to his command for speed, and he was now doing fifty miles per hour. Akron lay just twenty miles east.

Traffic moved slowly in downtown Akron. He rolled down the window, without any trouble this time, and took a deep breath. Even on Sunday, he could smell the odor of burnt rubber in the air from the Goodyear Tire factory. Elsie had been right about that. He quickly rolled up the window.

In an emotional moment, he conjured up Elsie's vibrant image—so full of life that it filled him with euphoria, remembering that she was the most fascinating woman he had ever known. He appreciated her sharp and clever mind, her quickness of wit, and her sensitivity. Hopefully, he was doing the right thing by showing up unexpectedly. He drove anxiously down South Arlington Street toward the south side of town. The cold wind continued to blow.

An old Model T in front of him rattled and backfired along Champlain Street, sounding as if it could die any minute. Champlain was a long, brick-lined street with cookie-cutter houses on both sides. A combination of dirty snow and mud lined the streets. At thirty-five minutes past twelve, he stopped across the street of house number four eighty-nine and switched off the engine. He stared at his reflection in the rearview mirror, his eyes tired, weary from the long drive.

He cursed the wet snow that seeped into his shoes the instant he stepped out of his car. He quickly found the dry sidewalk and stood there, taking in his surroundings and listening. The street was almost entirely deserted, with the exception of several parked cars along both sides of it.

As he reached the covered front porch, he took a deep breath and knocked. Above the doorway was a cross-stitched sign, gold-on-green that simply said, *'Peace on Earth.'*

Within seconds, Frederick opened the door. He looked at John pointedly as though he didn't understand exactly why he was there. "Are you selling walnuts?" Frederick said, smirking. "A fellow came by yesterday morning, selling 'em for ten cents a peck."

John laughed. "No, sir. I'm not selling a thing. Allow me to introduce myself." He extended his hand confidently. "I'm John McDonald, a good friend of your daughter, Elsie. Pleased to make your acquaintance," he said, giving Frederick his most charming smile.

"I've heard about you." Frederick shook his hand. A tight-lipped smile fractured his rigid expression. "I'm her father. What can I do for you?"

"I've been on the road about seven hours now. I came from Buffalo, New York to give Elsie a ride back to Rensselaer, Indiana. Is she in?" His eyes were sore and burning, but through the crack in the door he could make out a worn ottoman to the left of the fireplace. The room was hardly luxurious, but it seemed especially inviting in his exhausted state. He held back a smile when he noticed the "Women Must Vote" sign hung on the wall.

Frederick murmured a quick, "No, I'm afraid not. She's out," he said, adding hastily, "Don't know when she'll be back."

John shivered from the cold, aware of the man's stern, expressionless response. He thought it unusual that he wasn't extended an invitation to wait inside. "Well, would it be all right if I waited for her inside the house?" He gave Frederick a weak, tired smile. "I'm exhausted. It's been an awfully long drive."

Frederick shook his head. "I'm sorry, I couldn't do that. It wouldn't be proper. I have a sticky wicket situation here. You see, old chap, she's with her *husband*." He paused, giving John a penetrating stare, waiting for his words to sink in.

John's eyes widened to the shocking news.

Frederick continued. "Elsie has finally come to her senses and she's gone back with James, where she belongs. And, to tell you the truth, I believe she rather fancies Akron."

John knew that had to be an outright lie. Elsie hated Akron. What else was he lying about?

With a somber expression, Frederick added, "I'm going to be frank with you: James and Elsie have both found good jobs here in town. Here is where they can make the money. It's a bloody shame that you've come so far out of your way. You'd best be heading back to Indiana straightaway before you get yourself in trouble. I'll give you a few words of advice: next time you're out for romance, fancy yourself a gal who's unattached. You seem to be a nice enough chap." He looked up at the black and gray clouds. "Looks like it may snow any minute. Rensselaer, Indiana is a long drive from here, especially in this weather."

Though the man's expression was outwardly cool and detached, almost hostile, John could see the pride in his eyes. "With all due respect sir, Elsie and I had plans to go back to Rensselaer. She lives there now. She's just here on a visit. Did you forget that her husband, James, had abandoned her, and was gallivanting all over the country?"

Frederick raised a brow. "Everybody makes mistakes. James, like everyone else, found himself in hard times, but all that's changed. He's committed to my daughter now." He paused. "As far as I'm concerned, your intentions are less than honorable."

John nodded, "I see." He decided to make a quick retreat before Frederick had a chance to question his intentions further, such as where he intended to take his daughter. "Sorry to have disturbed you." He looked up, taking a moment to focus on Frederick's face. "I'll be on my way then." He shivered from the cold as he glanced up at the gray, cloud-laden sky. "I think you're right about the weather."

Nervously, he ran his fingers through his hair. "Will you please tell Elsie I stopped by?"

Frederick forced a smile and nodded. "I will do that. Good day," he said, turning, backing inside, and closing the door behind him.

The ground had just been swept from beneath his feet, leaving him stunned and in shock. He drifted back to his car, wondering what happened to his well-meaning plan. He should have called and let her know he was coming. Never did this husband scenario cross his mind. And he wondered about Elsie's father. He thought that maybe his unfriendly manner was an outward demonstration of fatherly instincts, combined with a cool British reserve. He didn't want to misinterpret his behavior as impolite, hostile, or even that his revelations were true or not.

He had to talk to Elsie.

Snow began to fall. Light sprinkles of small flakes hit his face and started falling harder as he stepped into his car. It was the dry kind of snow that fell for a long time and piled up, hour after hour.

Worried and discouraged, he leaned back in the seat and thought that he had come too far to leave without a fight. Maybe he'd take a drive through town to look for her, and while he was there, stop to get a bite to eat.

No, he quickly changed his mind—the drive could end up as pointless activity. A headache started to hammer behind his eyes. He had to speak with Elsie in person. He decided to stay put rather than ride around Akron, aimlessly. Maybe she would return shortly.

He sat for a long time without moving, his brain whirling as he replayed Frederick's words over and over in his head. How did he know what kind of a husband James would make from here on out? Why did he say his intentions were less than honorable? John blew hot breath into his hands, stomped his feet, and reached to the back seat for the blanket. He saw the time on his watch as he spread out the blanket over his legs. He had been waiting almost an hour.

Continuing heavy snowfall made visibility through the windshield almost impossible. He wondered what the temperature was, or how on earth he was going to get back to Rensselaer in the few remaining hours of daylight.

He leaned back in the driver's seat, closed his eyes, and tried to remember his last moments with Elsie at the train station. But as if he were chasing a dream, the scene grew vaguer the harder he went after it.

At last, two figures appeared, cast amid the early afternoon snowstorm. He cleared a patch of the driver's window so he could see better. He jolted upright in his seat. Damn it! It was Elsie, with a man who must be her husband, James. A sick feeling inside his stomach crawled up into his chest. He looked, and then quickly turned away. For some reason, he thought James would look different; more like a hobo. But this man was neatly dressed in overcoat and hat. John wanted to shout out, but remained silent. Should he turn around, go home, or walk up to them? He had the right. Time slowed. He sat perfectly still, staring through the driving snow at Elsie in disbelief, his eyes dark with sudden pain. Elsie's father was telling the truth; she was with her husband.

When James and Elsie reached the picket fence gate, James pulled her forward. She was in his arms, appearing to cling to him. With one hand he tucked her hair under her hat. They appeared to be getting along very nicely.

Dispirited, he observed her, thinking how stunning she looked in the dark purple coat she was wearing. He had never seen it before. It was a particular bluish-purple, like the wisteria growing in their garden in Rensselaer. He looked at her face in profile, and in the unforgiving winter light, saw a strange look of contentment. He was jealous; he could not help it as he witnessed the spontaneity of James's kiss to Elsie's flushed cheek.

He sank at once into troubled thoughts. His mind raced, seeking answers. He watched James give Elsie a quick hug, but was determined to make his move when he left.

When James is out of the picture, I'll go back to the house, knock on the door and talk to her myself. I'm sure there is a perfectly good explanation why the two of them are this friendly, especially after discussing divorce. What's he doing here, anyway? They must have made plans to meet up here when they were both back in Rensselaer.

Through the haze of falling snow, he anxiously watched James and Elsie walk to the porch, and approach the front door.

Abruptly, John rolled down the car window, banging at it to get it to move. A gust of snow blew in his face. "Elsie! Elsie! It's John," he yelled. "I'm here! Look across the street."

She seemed to turn in his direction. Had she heard him?

Just then, Frederick opened the door and whisked James and Elsie into the house.

John froze. He could have sworn she had heard him calling her. Was she ignoring him? Watching them nuzzle together was bad enough, now he was furious. *James was with her in the house.* He banged his fist on the steering wheel. *My brother was right! I should have never gotten involved with a married woman.*

He wasn't going to wait any longer! He was sick of waiting. Time to leave. Her father told him they had reconciled, and now he had witnessed them together with his own eyes. If she was going to end her marriage, she would not have allowed him into the house with her.

The fact that she was back together with her husband was devastating. Now it made sense why she wanted to return to Akron. He hung his head. A cautionary voice in his mind said, "This is enough. I won't put up with it." He knew in his heart, in his gut, that he should sever his connection to her once and for all. It was never going to be the same, even if she made an attempt to explain. It was time to return to Indiana and gather his belongings for the move back to Buffalo. There was no getting her back now. He was always good at moving on and now was the time.

He used up more driving time, sitting there along the curb, telling himself he was doing the right thing. Finally, he summoned all his strength to put the key into the ignition. He closed his eyes and sat for a moment longer, watching the snow gently fall on the car. Time to get moving.

He was going to miss her, he thought, as he pulled away from the curb. Whether on not he would miss her for a few days, a couple years or longer, he knew in his heart that his life would always be touched by her love. He longed for her infectious smile; what she represented to him, and how wonderful she had made him feel. But she had betrayed him. He blinked away the painful image, knowing he was starting a new life. *Anne sure was friendly at the Christmas party and she looked beautiful, too. Elsie isn't the only fish in the sea.*

More memories flooded his mind as he drove down Champlain Street, staring absently ahead as he turned toward downtown. The snow had stopped, and a low, puffy cloud hung over the horizon, giving the snow-covered landscape a nightmarish appearance. His recollections and memories of Elsie were the only things he had left on his lonely drive.

He remembered when he first met her on that warm, June afternoon in Rensselaer. She had worn a simple blue dress, but she had looked anything but simple. He remembered her voice, her vibrant energy, and the delicate scent of her hair as he touched it around her face. The back of his throat strung with tears.

He wanted to close his eyes against the pain of his loss. Immediately aware of the edge of the road under his right tires, he swung the car back into his lane. He had to put Elsie out of his mind and concentrate on the road.

Chapter Nineteen

E lsie woke, fitful and dreamless with blankets and comforter piled high around her. In the nightly confinement of her old bedroom, and in the presence of her parents' overbearing daily behavior, Elsie's childhood home had become her prison.

How long had she slept? What day was it?

Angry and depressed, she tossed aside the covers in the darkened room, threw on the clothes she'd worn the day before, and went out into the hall. Not knowing what time it was, she descended the stairs.

In the kitchen, the clock over the sink read twenty minutes after six. Was that AM or PM? Then she realized, with some embarrassment, that with everyone still sleeping upstairs, it must be morning, yet it was still too early for the girls to grace her presence in search of breakfast. Small blessings; she was in no mood to play "mother."

Elsie went to the window and pressed her nose to it, just as she had done when she was a child. She felt violated by her own act; indeed, she was relegated to the station of childhood, here in her old home, the place she knew as belonging to her parents, not her own. Still, the feeling of repulsion was contrasted by one of wonder. The view revealed a freshly fallen snow, blanketing the yard in a fairy-tale land of magic; the driveway, lawn, fence posts, and hedges were mounted high with a puffy, white marshmallow coating.

The fine, long lasting snow continued to fall and pile up in the yard. There was a kind of crushing silence under the weight of a sudden, heavy snow. She could hear the roof creaking with it, it bearing down, all around her; she felt buried by it, unable to escape. In the right company it could be beautiful, romantic, and cozy. Snow meant fire in the fireplace, and friends stopping by to share stories and sip mugs of hot cocoa. Wondering which of John's old friends he might be spending time with, a twinge of jealousy fluttered in the seat of her stomach. It was the kind of jitters that she could not sit to contemplate; her hands wanted to throttle someone, anyone, she didn't know whom, nor did she have proof of any wrongdoing. Her legs wanted to go, do something, run to relieve her anxiety; she was now ready to put on her boots and *walk* to Rensselaer.

With her dander up, she was now fully aware it was Wednesday, January ninth; John's birthday. Four days past the time that she and John had agreed to meet back at home—her *Rensselaer* home.

Escaping to the parlor, Elsie went to the telephone, removed the receiver, and listened. A woman's whiney, sing-song voice was going on about some silly, irrelevant gossip. At six-thirty in the morning? She sighed with impatience, wondering how in the world a party line could be busy at that hour.

She hung up, returned to the kitchen, rooted through the icebox, and came up with half of a peanut butter-and-jelly sandwich. Maybe if she ate she would feel better. It tasted disgusting, so she took tiny bites out of it, realizing that most likely, nothing would taste good just now on a turbulent stomach. However, something was better than nothing, she reasoned.

She went back and picked up the phone again. This time the line was clear. She slowly pressed the buttons in the receiver cradle three times, and the operator answered.

"Yes, Operator," Elsie said, with the fair amount of nervousness that accompanied telephoning a man. "I would like to make a long distance call to Rensselaer, Indiana."

"Telephone number please."

"Sixty-five, thirty-one."

"I'm ringing, one moment please. It will take only a minute. Was the number sixty-five, thirty-one, miss?"

"Yes, that's right."

"I'll try again." There was a long pause. "I'm sorry, that number has been disconnected."

"It can't be. There must be a mistake. You see, that's *my* telephone number in Indiana."

"I'm sorry. Let me try again." Another minute passed before the operator returned to the line. "No, I'm sorry, sixty-five, thirty-one has been disconnected."

Elsie's mind raced. *Disconnected? Where was John? Was he celebrating his birthday without her? Did he get the job and disconnect the phone already?*

The operator interrupted her frantic thoughts. "Is there another number you would like me to try?"

"Yes, there is. One-two-five-four. I know that number is working."

"One-two-five-four. It's ringing," the operator said cheerfully.

"Hello?"

"Robert! Thank goodness!"

"Thank you, Operator," Robert said. "I'll take the call."

Elsie heard a click and she knew they were alone on the line.

"Elsie … I was just about to phone you. I just woke up."

"Where's John? Do you know? His number has been disconnected! We were both supposed to return home by the sixth. He was going to call me with his plans first, and—"

"Whoa, slow down."

"Do you know something?"

"Well, yes … and, well … no."

"Good God. Tell me something—anything!"

"I don't know what's going on, exactly. I woke up a few minutes ago, opened the front door and there was this box on the porch. It's from John with your things inside. There's a note attached, saying— do you want me to read it?"

"Robert! Just read it!"

"Okay, okay. *'Robert, I thought there was something special between Elsie and me. I guess I was wrong—'*"

"Oh, no! That's not true! He's wrong! I *do* love him. You have to tell him, Robert."

"Do you want to hear this, or not?"

Elsie pulled herself together momentarily. "Go on. I'm sorry."

"*'When I went to surprise her and take her back to Rensselaer, she surprised me with her husband, James.'*"

"Oh-h, I'm going to be sick! James and I were out in front of the house last Sunday. It was snowing and I thought I heard someone call out my name. Robert! He *saw* me with James! Now he's furious, and probably jealous, too. We have to get in touch with him. Immediately!"

"Hold on, Elsie. Do you want me to finish reading?"

"I don't think I can bear it, but I have to know. Go on."

"*'Sorry, I have to leave so abruptly but something came up in New York. In the box you'll find Elsie's belongings. Could you give them to her? I'd like to take the dog with me, but I'm not sure where I'll be living. I'll be in touch. Take care; you've been a good friend. John.'* That was really nice of him to say that I was a good friend."

"This isn't about you," Elsie said irritably. "I'm sorry, but I have an emergency here and I need help! This is about me, and it's terrible! He said he would be in touch, but he didn't say when. Robert, you have to help me find him."

"Find him? How can we do that? We don't have any address for him, or even for his father. How about a phone number?"

"His father doesn't have his own telephone. He uses a common one, outside his door in the hall of the apartment building."

"That's great. I don't know how we're going to find him. Buffalo's a big city. Maybe we should just wait for him to contact one of us. He said he'll be in touch."

"Maybe you're right, but I can't stand idly by." Her mind raced in a million directions. "I'm not even sure he's in Buffalo. His appointment was in a town nearby—Amherst, I think. Did the note say that he'd gone up to my parents' door?"

"No, but he must have. Don't you think?"

"Unless ... he arrived at the house the same time as James and me. No. Not even *I* could have luck that bad. I'll ask my father. He was home all alone Sunday."

"If I hear anything, or think of a plan, I'll let you know. Don't panic. He loves you. It will work out."

"I have a bad feeling about this. *'Take care; you've been a good friend'* has a ring of finality to it."

"Don't get yourself in a tizzy. Calm down. Relax."

"I can't relax. He said I surprised him with James. That means he thinks we're together again. James and I—can you imagine?"

"When I hear from him, I'll tell him to call you. I'll tell him there's been a big misunderstanding."

"And a *big mistake* on my part by coming back here. I knew I shouldn't have come. I knew all along something bad was going to happen."

"It's too late now. But we can fix this problem."

"I hope so. Do you think we can? I better go. My father will be furious over this call. Bye, Robert."

"Bye, Elsie, and don't worry."

Not wanting to return to bed, she paced around the parlor until she thought she would go mad. Finally, in a fit of frustration, she switched on the radio to try and relax, making sure the volume was way down so as not to wake the family. She didn't care if her father disapproved of anyone listening to the radio all alone; she wasn't using that much electricity. At any rate, it did nothing to relieve her nerves.

After listening to *Dom McNeil's Breakfast Club* with still no relief, and still overwhelmed by all that had taken place, she put her head in her hands and groaned. She thought that maybe she'd feel better if she wrote about her confusion and frustration, so she went up to her bedroom and slid the diary out from under her bed. She opened it and began to write.

January ninth, nineteen thirty-five; the start of a new year, John's birthday, and I feel miserable. What happened to John and me? What made him leave Rensselaer and move back to New York without first talking to me? Even if he did see me with James, he knows that he doesn't mean anything to me. How could he jump to conclusions without giving me a chance to explain? I feel hurt and betrayed. His rejection is hard to take. I'm sad and despondent. I miss him! Help me, God! I'm so scared I'm going to be left here in Akron to live with my parents. I want to be with John! I don't want to spend the rest of my life working at a boring insurance job. I have to act before it's too late. Maybe Robert and I can drive to Buffalo and find his father's apartment. I know that's a long shot, but what choice do I have?

Perhaps I'm rushing to conclusions. Perhaps he'll get in touch with Robert in a few days. Maybe he'll phone here and I can talk to him.

Swallowing hard against the growing lump in her throat, she eased the bedroom door open to see if anyone in the family had awakened. The house was still, so she sat back on the bed and closed her diary. "Why?" she whispered. "Oh, dear God, why?" She was trying hard not to imagine what John was doing. She was trying to get used to not having him around, but it wasn't easy. Exhausted by emotion, she fell back to sleep.

* * *

Deep in thought, Frederick stood in the breezeway to his garage, sheltered from the slowly falling snow. As he contemplated his daughter's life with John McDonald, he went into the garage and began to pace. He stopped for a moment at his work bench where he had toiled to fix screen doors, build book cases and desks; he'd even made repairs to the family automobile. He had cut shingles by hand and made repair parts for the house, right there on that bench. He'd built roller skates, wooden dolls, and many other toys for the girls. He had worked hard at Goodyear, enabling him to provide well for his family, he was sure. But now it seemed that large parts of his efforts were falling apart. Falling—yes, that was it.

Elsie was falling into a deep hole, a pit of irresponsibility and immorality, and he loved her too much to let that happen. If left unchecked, her life path would be forever marked by this unacceptable behavior and lead to a ruinous life. He was not surprised; she had exhibited these fragments of opposition early in childhood. He and Phoebe had done everything to raise her right, so what had happened? Where had they gone wrong? Women voting and having boyfriends while married: where would it end?

Though he highly disapproved of the relationship his daughter was involved in, he was also more than a bit uncomfortable with the fact that he had not informed her about John's visit. He knew in his heart he should tell her. With a fair amount of apprehension, he walked into the kitchen to face her.

Elsie sat at the table, skimming through the latest women's magazine when her father walked in. She looked up as he approached. "Hi, Dad," she said, tensely averting her eyes from his brooding gaze.

"Elsie," Frederick began as he pulled out a chair and sat down. "Today's the day I need to let them know if you want that job." He looked at her with anticipation, though he could see that her expression was anxious and strained. "I hope you've given it considerable thought."

"I *have* thought about it, and I'm really torn." She paused, looking down. "I don't understand why I haven't heard from John. Which brings up a question: did John come by the house last Sunday?"

"A fellow did stop by. I believe he said his name was John."

"Why didn't you tell me? You *knew* I've been waiting to hear from him and you said *nothing* to anyone? Not even Mum?"

"To tell you the truth, I forgot all about it. He was only here a few minutes."

She brought her hand down hard on the table top. "How can you say that? I don't believe this! How can you be so cavalier about the whole thing? It's as if John doesn't exist and my feelings mean nothing around here?" Her voice cracked with emotion and she felt the hot sting of tears forming behind her eyes. "He came a long, *long* way to pick me up."

Frederick watched as his daughter abruptly jumped up and slammed her chair into the table with a bang. Her red-rimmed eyes were large and round and filled with venom.

"Now you've hurt me more than you will ever know!" Elsie screamed at her father. "I will never forget how you abandoned my feelings! For God's sake, Dad. What did you tell him? Were you rude?"

It was then, he realized, that for his own sake, he would say as little about John's visit, or their discussions at the front door as he could get away with. "I said you were out. That's all. Out."

"What did he say?"

"Is Elsie in? I said, no. She's out."

"What else?"

"He said he needed to get back to Rensselaer so he had better get going."

"He wouldn't have been that casual! My life is ruined! He saw me with James, and now I'm sure he's really upset."

He had to protect his daughter's interests. If she never spoke to John McDonald again, or knew nothing more about him, the better off she'd be. "He saw you with your *husband*. What kind of a fellow chases married women?"

Elsie snuffled her nose, and looked at her father through red-eyed pools of misery. "I love him! Did he say he would phone me? It was snowing Sunday. For crying out loud! He came all the way here in the snow to take me back to Rensselaer. Did you tell him I was with James?"

"I mentioned it, yes. It was the truth. Did you want me to fib?"

"Yes! You should have lied, for God's sake, or said nothing. Or invited him in. Now he thinks I'm happy with James. He either saw us together or took your word for it. *How could you?*" The pain of betrayal balled in the pit of her stomach. She had been hurt, betrayed, and abandoned by the very people she loved. She put her head down on the kitchen table and sobbed uncontrollably in front of her father.

Frederick changed his stern tone to a more pleasant one. "We have a telephone. He has our number. I pay the telephone bill so people can communicate with us more easily. Plenty of people I know don't even have a telephone." He hated to see her cry and softened. "He was always free to telephone you here."

"Thanks," she said between sobs. "Thank you for ruining my life."

"Look, sweetie," he said, his heart breaking with thoughts of her welfare. "It's not ruined. Let's talk about what's best for you now. Today. You don't have anything going for you in Rensselaer. No job, no family, no nothing. Well, there is Robert, of course, but you can't lean on him your whole life.

"Here in Akron," Frederick continued, "you have family, and if you give me the go ahead—a good paying job. People would *kill* for a chance to work at Goodyear. Think about it. Your life will be set. From the insurance department you could move up, be promoted. With both you and James working … you could buy yourself a house. Have a baby. You wouldn't have to worry. Don't you want that?"

She shook her head, the blood draining from her face. His attitude was judgmental, but she didn't think he intended to hurt her. "No, actually I don't want that." She glanced at her father, who looked like he was about to burst with frustration. She reached up with one trembling hand to wipe the tears from her cheeks.

To break the tension, and because her stomach was twisted in a sick knot, she stood to pour herself a cup of tea. "Would you like one, Dad?" she asked, thinking that her own father had stabbed her in the heart. Did he really think his actions would make her happy?

"No thanks. Your mother will be serving lunch soon," he said, sniffing. "Something smells good."

He continued with what he felt was his fatherly duty to give her a bit of sound advice. "You've been careless, or might I say, you've made some errors in judgment. But you're not a bad girl. If you make the right choices from here on out, you can correct your mistakes." His voice rose. "Forget about that John McDonald. He's not good for you."

How would he know? He only met him for a minute. The nerve, Elsie thought as she bit her lower lip to keep from shouting at him.

Phoebe came into the kitchen.

"Lunch almost ready?" Frederick smiled at his wife. "I'm starved."

"Oh, I'm not interrupting anything am I?" she asked, looking from one to the other.

"Not at all, dear. Elsie's just about to tell me if she wants the job at Goodyear," he said, fixing his eyes on his daughter. "You know, people look months for a job and come up with nothing. Some of your lady friends' husbands are looking right now, aren't they?"

Phoebe nodded, giving him a thin smile, though she could see he wasn't looking at her; he was looking at Elsie.

Elsie drew a long breath, marshaled her thoughts, and looked directly into her father's eyes. "I suppose when all is said and done I don't have much of a choice, especially now without John," she said in defeat.

"Then it's settled. I'll let them know straightaway."

She took two sips of tea and looked at him again, setting her cup down where it clattered in its saucer. "If a teaching job miraculously shows up, I'll have to quit. Or if I receive promising news from John, I'll have to go. In that case, I'll be moving to New York. You understand that, don't you?" She simmered, struggling against the urge to spring up and stomp out.

"Sure." Frederick nodded, instantly relieved. As he left the kitchen, he turned to his wife. "Lunch will be ready soon?" he asked again.

"In a few minutes, dear."

When Elsie was alone with her mother, she felt compelled to air her true feelings. "Mum, why don't you stick up for me? I need someone on my side. Daddy didn't even tell me that John stopped by! The love of my life comes here to the house to get me and take me back home and he doesn't even have the decency to let me know!" Her resentment for her parents was growing, and as a religious person, she knew that was dangerous.

"I know. He's sorry about it. He was just trying to protect you."

"I don't think he's sorry at all. Do you know how much trouble it will be to find John now? Does Dad think I should dismiss him and be happy instead?"

"Elsie, luv … I know you're upset, but—"

"Upset? You have no idea how *upset* I am! Don't you care at all?" She leaped up, so mad that her feet hardly touched the floor. Suspended in the electric sparks of torture she lunged for the sink, picked up a dirty glass and dashed it into the porcelain basin where it splintered to pieces. "There! Do you get it, now? Do you get it?" she screamed.

"Elsie! Get a hold of yourself! Look at what you've done," Phoebe said, alarmed by her daughter's potential for such ferocity.

Elsie felt like a wild animal, ready to pounce and shred, her eyes hot and bulging with the sting of her flushed face. "Look at what *you've* done to *me*, Mum. Just look. You and Daddy, both. Look. Just look. You and ..." she bubbled. Her arms abruptly hung limp at her sides, her shoulders slumped in defeat. Tears dripped off her chin and she swiped at them angrily.

"Sh-h," Phoebe said, reaching out and pulling her daughter to her chest. "Sh-h, now, luv. Sh-h." She smoothed her hair, holding her for a full minute, rocking and cooing before releasing her. "Come, luv," she said, guiding her by the shoulders to the table. "Come, sit down."

Elsie sat and stared without seeing, all of her venom spent, leaving her feeling haggard and lifeless, slumped over the table. Her hair was matted about her face, stuck to all the streams of tears on her cheeks.

Phoebe went to the kitchen cabinet for a rag to wipe up the mess in the sink. The porcelain would be chipped; about that she was sure. She would try to keep the ugly marks hidden from Frederick for a few days, she thought as she worked to scoop out the glass into a waiting trash bin and shaking the rag to make sure it was free of splinters.

"Elsie, luv," Phoebe began when she was finished cleaning up. "Things happen in life for a reason. Mistakes can rob a lifetime of happiness from a person. It looks like it's best for you to stay here," she said, heading for the stove to stir the stew. "Come now. Fix your face and hair and put on a smile. Be a good soldier."

Elsie bit her lip, just as she had done when facing her father. It seemed to Elsie that her mother was stirring the stew a bit too vigorously, but held her tongue out of respect. After all, she didn't reach this age all by herself.

"Maybe now is not the right time to go anywhere," her mother continued. "You should be happy about your new job, right here in Akron. So many people are out of work. You need money to live on, you know."

"I know. I know. I should feel grateful, but I don't. I know how Daddy is about long distance telephone calls, but I've already called

Robert to see if he knows what's going on. Hopefully, he'll help me find John."

"Elsie! You phoned Robert? Your father will be very upset about that."

"I have a little money left from my last paycheck. I'll pay him back."

"Why waste your time on that John fellow? He's not worth that much, is he?"

"Mum! You mean he's not worth a telephone call?"

"If a girl needs to call a boy, no, he's not worth it. It isn't right. I'm sure he knows that. Maybe he's come to his senses about the two of you."

"Mum!"

"I'm sorry, that's how I feel. He's not my cup of tea."

A few moments of awkward silence passed. "Are you going to have any lunch?" Phoebe opened the oven, produced a steaming loaf of bread, and placed it on a cooling rack. Brushing butter on its top, she was reminded of all the small things she did to care for the family. Elsie, she thought, should be grateful for her parents' help and consideration. She stirred the pot of stew again and began dishing out the meal. "Chicken stew is one of your favorites. Have some. It will make you feel better."

Elsie hesitated, then nodded. "All right, but just a little."

Phoebe turned to call through the kitchen doorway. "Frederick! Girls! Lunch is ready!"

Elsie sat at the opposite end of the table from her father, not saying a word. He muttered something to himself as he went to the icebox, pulled out the butter, and returned to the table. Phoebe handed him a slice of hot bread. "Thanks," he said, taking a sip of ginger ale.

Elsie's sisters sashayed into the kitchen. "What's going on?" Lena asked.

"Nothing," Elsie responded.

"What do you mean, *nothing*," Lena said. "Everyone looks like they've been yelling."

"Yeah, I heard yelling." Evelyn said.

"No one's yelling," Frederick said. "I have some good news for Elsie; she can start work at Goodyear tomorrow."

Both girls stared at their sister.

Elsie toyed with her stew.

"You don't look happy about it," Evelyn said.

Elsie didn't like where the conversation was headed, so she put her spoon down and stared back at her. "I am … and I'm not." It was all she could say at the moment.

"What kind of answer is that?" Phoebe asked.

"Where's John?" Lena asked. "What happened to him, anyway?"

Elsie gave her sister a look that came from inside a thunderstorm. "That's just the trouble—I don't know, Lena. And you can stop asking me about him."

Frederick changed the subject to cover his feeling of guilt. "What are you going to go today, luv?" he asked his wife, shoveling another heaping spoonful of stew into his mouth.

"Some laundry and then I plan to finish that sweater I've been knitting for you. This one is similar to the one I made you for your Christmas present, but in a different color."

"What color would that be?"

"Blue, a soft blue. You'll look so handsome in it. Your blond hair really compliments blue."

Frederick nodded and smiled supportively.

"You should wear more sweaters, Daddy. You won't look so old-fashioned," Evelyn said.

"That's not very nice," Elsie said, glad for the chance to reprimand her sister.

"It's a fine thing for you girls that I *am* old-fashioned enough to take care of this whole family," Frederick chimed in. "Goodyear is a jolly good place to work, Elsie. You've made a smart decision indeed."

She nodded and sighed in resignation. "I know it's a smart decision, but it's not what my heart wants," she said, swallowing her frustration.

"You're sure you want me to tell them you're ready to start? I've been thinking … I don't want you to accept the job and then take off the minute you hear from that John chap. Think of how that will make me look." He hesitated. "No more talk about John McDonald?"

"She's always talking about him," Lena said.

Elsie shook her head, took a final sip of ginger ale, and stood up. "No, no more about him to you, Dad." She took her dishes to the sink and cleaned up her side of the table. Then she excused herself and went straight to her old bedroom.

She looked into the small mirror on the wall, picked up her brush, and began to brush out her hair. Filled alternately with restless energy and anger, she abandoned the brush and paced the room, upset with John for letting her down.

How could he just forget about me? Doesn't he miss me? Why doesn't he call and let me explain. I pray he gets in touch with Robert.

It seemed to be all gone: the teaching job, love, laughter, and the man she needed so much. Her body ached for the touch of him. She felt that fate had been cruel to her, showing her a glimpse of what life could be like, how wonderful love felt, and then snatching it away the minute she began to believe it could last.

She could faintly hear the bell of the trolley car in the distance, and was reminded of the afternoon at the train station when she and James had agreed to return to Akron. The decision had been one big, bloody mistake. Soon, lethargy set in so completely that she lay on her bed, for hours staring into space.

Chapter Twenty

It was a pretty room with little pink roses climbing the wallpaper, and white curtains with tiny white dots on them. Elsie was learning to be comfortable in her old room again, and even though she loved the feminine charm of it, she still hated being alone. Sometimes she didn't fall asleep until close to two o'clock in the morning, and by a quarter after six, she'd be wide-awake again.

Even now, two months later, she would sometimes wake with a wet pillowcase from her tears in the night. She could see John so clearly through the details of her nightly dreams. There were times when she reached for him in her sleep, only to be disappointed when she opened her eyes. Sometimes she turned in bed, seeking the warmth of his body, only to collect an armful of empty sheets.

Though her heart fought against the idea that life with John had ended, she had to deal with the loss. She prayed every day that Robert would tell her that he'd received a letter or a telephone call from him. But each day was the same, with no word at all. It wasn't like John to say he'd be in touch then never follow through, simply ignoring his promise. With each passing day, she was filled with the certain conclusion that he had seen her with James on that snowy Sunday afternoon in January.

This was another morning like so many others: she was tired, she was depressed, and most of all, she missed him more than she thought possible. She quickly dressed for work, then dashed out the door. A cool breeze ruffled her hair and she pushed a wayward strand from her eyes. She had better hurry or she would be late.

She walked the length of the Goodyear grounds, churning out recollections of times spent with John, and thinking if only she'd seen him, or hadn't stood with James in front of the house on that day. Or maybe she shouldn't have invited James into the parlor for tea and cookies. Rushing along the winding path that meandered through the Goodyear gardens, her head was filled with the truth, and her heart was filled with despair. If only she could communicate with John. The misunderstanding ate at her day and night.

Ahead, she could see the office she worked in, adjacent to the insurance building, its windows dreary from the morning haze. She glanced up at the clock tower and saw she had only four minutes left if she were to be on time.

She hurried into the office and sat down to the piles of papers left at her desk from the day before. Though the two piles were neatly stacked to the side of the desk, Elsie never really knew how her boss felt about unfinished work at the end of the day. He was an odd duck; he never communicated very well. It left her feeling separate from the workplace and her co-workers.

Catching her breath, she looked out the window, thinking. Over the last week or so she'd been emotionally and physically drained, feeling increasingly spent. She knew it was wrong to ignore her family, but she also found it impossible to make new friends at work with the usual small talk. None of that meant a thing to her. Meeting people was a chore, and that chore required the energy to smile and feel pleasant. The only feeling left in her was perhaps a whole lot of regret that she had ever come back to Akron. Why had she bothered to help James secure employment, anyway? She was convinced he wouldn't have done the same for her.

Since she'd been back, they were living separately and barely even spoke to each other. Even though they were both at Goodyear everyday, they kept different hours and worked in different buildings. James had even agreed to a divorce, once he was convinced she was no longer interested in him—no matter what he did, or how he tried to please her.

In the end, Elsie thought he hadn't changed very much. He still wanted a gal who would bear his children, be a gifted homemaker, devoted and obedient. The one stipulation James had concerning the divorce was that Elsie must pay for it, since it was her idea. But it wasn't worth the money now since John was not in the picture, waiting for her freedom. She sighed, feeling all torn up inside.

Why hadn't John contacted her? It seemed he had rejected her without hearing her side of the story. The last time she spoke with him on the telephone, there hadn't seemed to be anything wrong. Yes, he saw her with James, but she could explain all that. Did he secure employment in New York and then move without any consideration for her?

Her supervisor interrupted her woeful daydream as he pulled a chair to the side of her desk and sat down. "How are you doing today, Elsie?"

"Very well. Thank you for asking."

"Can you type?" he asked coolly.

"My typing is a little rusty," she confessed, "but I can brush up."

His beady stare pierced her forced smile. It was a moment lodged into an ice wall between them. *Great, this is a great place to work. This guy is really getting under my skin. I wonder how much more of this I can take.*

"In that case, I'll ask one of the other secretaries."

"Do you have any filing you'd like done?" Not that she'd actually *like* to do it. But it was a paycheck.

"Well, yes, as a matter of fact I do. Just that pile," he said, pointing to a basket on the table behind her labeled *'File.'*

"I'll get to it right away." She quickly stood and took the papers from the bin. When she opened the drawer to sort through the files, she noticed that her hands were trembling. She was shaken by her boss's cold, watchful demeanor, never having outgrown feeling intimidated when confronted by an authority figure. Was that why she had not been more forceful in trying to locate John?

Even though she had only been at the insurance department for two months, she was already beginning to feel restless. Her only comfort, her only real source of optimism these last couple of months, was that she thought John must still love her. Some part of her heart felt certain he would come back for her. And when he did, she'd stick to him forever.

* * *

The spring rains had been coming down steadily for three days, and it was drizzling again today. Elsie heaved a sigh of relief that the work day had ended. She pushed open the front door of the house, stepped inside, and tossed her pocketbook into the chair next to the telephone.

"Elsie is that you?" Evelyn called.

"Yes, I'm home."

"You have a letter from Robert," she said, bouncing into the parlor from the kitchen and waving an envelope.

The weather had been miserable lately, reflecting the gloom Elsie felt inside, so she hoped the letter brought good news. She sat in the telephone chair with it, and Evelyn immediately went behind to look over her shoulder.

"Evelyn!" Elsie gave her sister a scowl that said *'go away.'*

"Oh, okay! You're so grumpy lately. Gee whiz!" Evelyn said, walking off.

The envelope fluttered with the tremble of Elsie's hands. She shifted uneasily against the soft cushions of the chair, put down the letter, laced her fingers together on her lap, and prayed for good news. She drew a long breath before she tore open the envelope.

29 March 1935

Dear Elsie,

I hope this letter finds you in good health. I've been worried about you. When we last spoke you sounded so down in the dumps.

I'm glad you were able to get a job working with your father at Goodyear Tire. There are still many people unemployed here.

I miss not having you and John close by. It was swell having you minutes away.

I didn't know whether I should have phoned or written to you about the recent news here. John's former employer stopped in to buy some gasoline so I asked him about John's whereabouts. He didn't have his forwarding address and said that the only thing he knew was that John was offered a job with the government. I don't know how we'll ever get in touch with him. It's been almost three months now and I haven't heard a word.

"Jo-ohn!" Hearing some news about him, but not the kind of news she wanted, was simply unbearable.

Phoebe rushed into the parlor, wiping her hands on her apron. "What? What is it?"

"It's nothing. Please leave me alone!"

Her mother backed up into the kitchen nearly as fast as she had come in.

Lena ran down the stairs. "What?"

"Nothing," Elsie groaned. "Just get out of here!"

"How come no one tells *me* anything? I'm old enough to know."

"You're still in high school," Evelyn said from the kitchen doorway.

"You should talk? You're the baby of the family. Baby! Baby! Golly," Lena said, stomping back up the stairs.

"Girls, leave Elsie alone right now," Phoebe said.

"All right, already." Evelyn slumped back into the kitchen with her mother.

Elsie returned to the letter.

I'll be arriving in Akron next month for your birthday. I'll be coming alone. Brenda wanted me to say hello to you, happy birthday, and that she thinks about you often. Millie says ruff, ruff. Take care of yourself, and give my regards to the family.

Love,

Robert

P.S. I'll bring the box filled with your belongings.

She stood, the letter dropping to the carpet. She began to pace the parlor, her mind spinning in confusion. She replayed that fateful Sunday over and over in her head. How on earth could she have been out with James when John came to pick her up? Why didn't she respond when she thought she heard her name called? She wanted to explain that she was with James only to discuss divorce, and to tell him about his new job at Goodyear. She was nice to him only because he was in such a good mood when he heard the news. He was thrilled to be able to work in blimp manufacturing. There was nothing more to it on that Sunday—only mild conversation.

In addition, she wanted to apologize to John for her father's rudeness at the door; that she was sorry for his refusal to invite him into the house. Her father had apparently treated John with cold indifference and she wanted to try and make amends for his ill behavior.

Now it was too late; she was never going to get the chance to defend herself. How was she ever going to find him? She didn't have the money to hire a private detective to go looking, and that's what she needed.

A knot of nerves twisted in the pit of her stomach. How could this happen to her? She thought she had gotten on so well with John. They had never had an actual argument; instead they had what she called "differences of opinion" once in awhile. John seemed as though he was always cheerful and happy to be with her. She felt physically sick with the realization that John had no intention of contacting Robert. The longer she let her mind spin out of the unhappy revelations, the more it all made sense.

John lived with her and loved her but never mentioned marriage, or ever pushed her to get a divorce. He could have offered to help her take legal action, but didn't. Like a bolt of lightning, she realized that he never loved her enough, or was never serious enough to help her make their relationship permanent. He could live without her? If he were miserable and lonely, she would have heard from him.

Now she must brace up to the fact that it was over. Reliving every detail, thinking about, missing, analyzing, or dreaming about John McDonald would not do any good. She must not heartlessly delay the death throes of a once great passion, now withered.

She forced herself to go outside and walk to further clear her head. With each step the words drummed in her head like a broken record: *It's over. It's over. I'll never see him again.* She hoped the thoughts that ravaged in her mind would somehow dissipate like a black cloud in a summertime breeze. But no matter how hard she tried, she could not ignore the emptiness that crept into her heart. She had lost the love of her life because of a terrible misunderstanding, and now he was living in another state. If he were in Indiana she might have luck finding him, but *New York?* She had only been there as a child. She really didn't know anything about the place. It seemed as formidable and far away as a foreign country.

It had stopped sprinkling as she randomly strolled down Brown Street, and then into downtown Akron until she found herself in front of a small, outdoor café.

This part of town had always been one of her favorite spots, but now it was dark and dreary. She smelled rubber in the air, even though the late afternoon was chilly, with evening coming on. She passed the café and crossed the street, where she found a spot to rest on a park bench beneath a row of elm trees. In front of her, several children had gathered at a small pond to feed the pigeons. Next to the pond, a group of boys were having a good time, tossing a football into the air and slipping around on the wet grass. It seemed that John had wanted kids of his own. Watching the charming play of the young children made her sadness all the more unbearable.

She tried to put John out of her mind, but before long a young couple sat on the park bench next to her. The man was good looking, dressed in a long-sleeved yellow shirt and dark trousers. The woman's blond hair was short and fluffy, and wore an apple-print spring dress with a cardigan to match. They spoke in hushed tones and laughed a bit, then the woman's eyes caught Elsie's, and she smiled. Elsie forced a smile in return. The man gently took the woman's hand and kissed it.

Elsie's heart sank, feeling she would never have that kind of experience again—a love so sweet, so passionate. She'd never spend her days sitting on park benches, sharing affectionate glances with the man she loved. She pressed her palm to her chest, trying to stop the pain in her heart.

The couple finally stood and wandered down to the pond. Emotion lumped in her throat, and tears began trailing down her face. She didn't try and stop them. She wanted to feel the pain of losing John, and the frustration of never knowing what the future might have held.

She cried until the tears wouldn't come anymore, and until the pain was a dull ache somewhere near her heart. Her memories of John were the only things she had left of the two of them. There would be no time together now to make new ones.

Drawing a ragged breath, she pulled a handkerchief from her pocketbook, wiped her eyes, and stood to smooth her dress. On the long walk home she pulled her sweater tightly around her ribs, and watched the mocking delight of the new spring leaves on the trees, fluttering in the chilly breeze. It seemed that nothing was affected by the misery in her heart. Life would go on with her painful memories and without John.

She *could* get over this loss. She *could* put her life back together and forget him. For whether she loved him or not, she really had no other choice but to move forward, as John had already done. The chance to continue her relationship with John McDonald had been mercilessly taken from her. The love of her life was gone. It surely looked like forever.

Chapter Twenty-one

The party came as a surprise to Elsie. Even Mrs. Pratt from across the street had been invited, arriving with a big jug of root beer. And all of them—Phoebe, Evelyn, Lena, Auntie Jane, Elsie's cousins Edith, Edna and Edna's young daughter, Rose, Robert, and Mrs. Pratt were gathered around the kitchen table, finishing the birthday lunch Phoebe had prepared. A tablecloth, with the word "Congratulations" embroidered on it, covered the kitchen table and looked as good as new, in Elsie's opinion, with birthday dishes carefully placed over the old, brown stains. However, even with the celebratory revelry, she wasn't much in the mood for a party without John in attendance.

Phoebe took the cake from the pantry where she had been hiding it all morning, placed it on the table and struck a match, lighting the three candles in the middle of it.

Evelyn stood, placed the heels of her hands at the edge of the table, and rocked back and forth, eyeing the cake with obvious appetite. "There's one candle for every ten years," she informed Elsie.

"Must you remind me?" Elsie asked. "When you're thirty, I'll remind you of that fact, too."

"Will you?" Evelyn asked, her eyes glittering with the hope of her big sister's promise. "But you'll be really old by then."

The adults around the table all smiled at one another and winked.

Evelyn's smile faded. "What?"

"Don't worry about it," Elsie said. "I'll give you the first piece of cake, okay?"

"Okay!" Evelyn said brightly. "After all, I helped Mom make it."

"Oh, Evelyn," Lena groaned. "Elsie gets the first piece. It's her birthday."

It was a fancy looking cake with vanilla frosting, chocolate cake underneath, and "Happy Birthday" written in curly chocolate icing on top. A sudden breeze blew in through the open window, almost making the tiny flames extinguish.

"Okay, everyone," Phoebe said, clearing her throat. *"Happy Birthday to you … "* she sang. Everyone joined in, finishing with, *"Happy birthday, dear Elsie, happy birthday to you,"* in a somewhat off-key rendition of the old standard.

Elsie, slightly red cheeked, made a silent wish for John to return, and blew out the candles. She felt sad, even though she was flattered that Mrs. Pratt and her family had taken such thoughtful care to remember her birthday.

After the cake had been eaten, everyone sat around the parlor and chatted, all but Rose who was tired and ready for a nap.

Edna excused herself and went upstairs to put Rose down.

Phoebe opened the closet where she had hidden four wrapped presents the day before, and took them out, carefully balancing them in one armful. "Why don't you open Robert's first?" Phoebe said, handing Elsie a box.

"I didn't miss anything, did I?" Edna asked, hurrying down the stairs.

"Elsie is opening Robert's gift first because he came all the way from Indiana to be here today," Lena responded.

Elsie carefully removed the pink ribbon from the box, lifted its lid, and gasped in the moment of discovery, "Oh, my—perfume." She unscrewed the cap and sniffed. "Mm-m, it smells wonderful— like roses. I love it."

"Whew, I'm relieved. I wasn't sure what fragrance to get," Robert said, chuckling, "so I asked the sales clerk to help me out. But you know, there's a more important gift than smelling like roses.

I remember way back when you were about fourteen, you not only gave yourself a gift, but helped give one to every woman; a grand gift that will last forever—the right to vote."

"I don't really want to talk about that. It was so long ago."

"But I'm really proud of you. Aren't you glad you marched?"

She knew that Robert was only trying to be supportive, helping to make her feel better about losing John. "Of course, I am. Now we're politically equal to men." Elsie smiled at her aunt.

"I was so proud of you that day, dear. You kept right on marching when the hecklers hurled insults at us."

"What did they say, Auntie Jane?" Lena asked. "Tell me again."

"Well, let's see, dear. They shouted, *'Stay at home where you belong. Women are unpatriotic.'* And things like that. One young boy even threw a rotten apple and hit me."

"I yelled, *'Dimwit!'* Remember?" Elsie laughed.

"Yes, yes I do." And you bravely carried that sign: *'I wish my Mum could vote.'*

"I'm surprised someone didn't hit *that* with something foul," Elsie remarked. "And the day after the march, the newspaper called women in the picket line unwomanly and undesirable. It didn't bother me, though, and you weren't the least bit disturbed by the rotten apple or the bad press, either. Things weren't fair. We were proud to support a woman's right to equality at the voting booths."

Jane smiled. "I would do the same thing today, if it were needed."

"Would you?" Phoebe challenged her sister. The corners of her mouth drooped in motherly consternation as she turned to speak to her daughter. "The Constitution says all *men* were created equal. It doesn't say *'men and women.'*"

"That's just something you learned so that you could become a citizen, Mum." Elsie said in exasperation. "*'Men'* just means all people."

"You didn't reflect my views, Elsie, and I didn't agree with that woman, Susan B. Anthony, either. I did not want women to have the right to vote. It's not ladylike."

"Elsie reflects *my* views, Mum," Lena said.

"I'd go along with her views, too," Robert put in.

"You always stick up for Elsie," Evelyn whined.

"No, it just means that women are allowed to vote and hold office, that's all." Robert looked from one to the other around the parlor. "What does everyone else think?"

Edna looked at her mother. "It's an old, beat-up issue now, but I'd have to agree with my mum. Everyone should be equal."

"It seemed like everything was all right the way it was, with just the men voting," Edith offered. "What was so wrong with it, you know? Men are here to protect us, and do the right thing in our favor."

Mrs. Pratt nodded enthusiastically. "You're right, Edith," she said, pursing her lips. "And I agree with Phoebe, too: voting is not ladylike. This generation is so different from ours. Just incorrigible."

Elsie looked down at the gift in her hands, deciding to quit the conversation. Her thoughts returned to John, wondering what he was doing on her birthday. Did he think of her?

Phoebe sighed in agreement. "Everyone says that it seems like all the women just want to be men."

"But you're from the olden days, Mom," Evelyn said.

Lena gave a snort in her sister's direction. "Evelyn, you're *so* rude. Anyway, I thought Elsie was opening presents."

"Let's make this a happy occasion, shall we?" Auntie Jane interjected, trying to sweep aside the negative sentiments. "It's Elsie's birthday, after all."

Elsie put on a smile to hide her sadness and merely nodded, slipping the blue bow from the package. She carefully removed the wrappings, and was pleasantly surprised as she pulled a garment from the box. "Oh, Mum. You shouldn't have." It was a champagne-colored, pure silk crepe dress, the fabric cut on the cross grain to provide a fitted bodice and waist, with the skirt flaring at the hem.

"You admired it on a mannequin in the window at Gimbles when we were shopping one day."

"You remembered, Mum. Thank you." Elsie stood, held the dress to her, and turned this way and that to demonstrate the visual effect for the others. "It's so fancy. Now I'll need a place to wear it."

"It's lovely," Mrs. Pratt said, nodding. "Lovely indeed."

"That's no feed sack." Evelyn pouted. "It cost one dollar and fifty-eight cents. I was with Mom when she bought it."

"Come on now, Evelyn." Phoebe scolded.

Elsie glanced at Evelyn who was sitting with her hands pressed to her face at the coffee table and pouting, as envious as any child might be who never owned a factory-made dress.

Lena exchanged a glance with Elsie. "Say, Evelyn," Lena said. "Summer is on its way. Why don't I help you with lemonade stands on the weekends out on the curb? I'll bet you'll have the money for your own dress from Gimbles in no time."

Evelyn sat up and sighed. "Oh-kay."

"Here, open ours next, Elsie." Edna said.

Elsie put the package down on the table and tore away at the paper. She raised the lid. "Oh, my—how lovely." The box held a crisp white sailor blouse, a lavender hand-embroidered sweater, and a big yellow bow for her hair. She read the birthday card that went with the gift. *'Happy Thirtieth Birthday. Love, the Coopers, and Edna & Frank.'*

"The blouse and the bow are from us," Edith said.

"Thank you all. Auntie Jane, Edith, Edna, and make sure to tell Frank I said thank you. I'm not too old to wear a bow in my hair, am I?"

"Don't be silly. You still look like a schoolgirl," Mrs. Pratt said.

"Thanks. That's swell of you to say so." Elsie smiled.

"Why are you opening up our present last?" Evelyn said abruptly.

Elsie thought quickly in her response in order to appease her sister. "I'm saving the best for last. Here, give it to me," Elsie said, taking the small package from her hands. The gift was wrapped in newspaper and tied with a white ribbon. She read the attached card aloud. *'To our big sister, Elsie. Happy thirtieth birthday. Love, Lena, and Evelyn.'* Elsie laid back the last fold of paper and there, inside, lay a red-cloth diary.

"Thank you so much. I needed a new diary," Elsie said.

"Do you have any secrets to put in there?" Evelyn asked, blushing.

Elsie grinned. "I'll never tell." It was much nicer than her old one, and had more room to write down her thoughts. Her mother and father might be tempted to peek in it, if it were left out in the open. And Evelyn and Lena would surely snoop to find it, then read every last word if they could get their hands on it. She knew she would have to hide this diary.

"She's probably going to write about John McDonald," Lena said.

"I have another present from my father," Elsie quickly announced, ignoring the last comment from Lena. "It isn't wrapped. He's treating me to an afternoon at the beauty parlor, and an evening at the picture show."

"How much?" Lena asked.

"What?" Elsie responded, hugely embarrassed.

"I just want to know. What does all that cost? How much did Dad give you?"

Elsie looked to her mother for any clues as to a response, then eyed her sister again, responding reluctantly, "Five—five dollars." She paused a moment deciding if she should air her true thoughts, then went ahead. "You know, you're just as rude as your sister."

Both Lena and Evelyn frowned.

"Five dollars, wow!" Lena said.

"Well, gee, that's a lot of money." Evelyn said, pushing away from the table and causing her glass of root beer to spill. "Oops, sorry," she said, giving a small, insincere smile.

"I'll get it," Phoebe said, running into the kitchen to grab a wash cloth from the sink. She quickly cleaned up the mess. "You have to be more careful, luv."

"That's a fine gift, Elsie," Edna said. "You must be having a wonderful birthday."

Elsie thought that it wasn't so wonderful without John, but said nothing except, "Yes. Yes I really am. Thirty doesn't seem so bad after all," she fibbed.

"Look at me," Mrs. Pratt said. "I'm still here, all fifty-six years of me."

Elsie smiled. "Yes, and you're doing just fine, I'd say." What she didn't say was that she didn't want to be like Mrs. Pratt, or anyone else in the room.

Evelyn nodded to her mother then turned to Elsie. "What's it like to kiss a boy, Elsie?"

Edna, Edith, Mrs. Pratt, and Auntie Jane giggled and cleared their throats, looking nervously at one another.

Robert wore a huge relaxed smile, waiting for Elsie to explain this one.

Phoebe waggled her eyebrows at Evelyn and put her finger to her lips for silence.

Elsie sighed with a musical lilt to her escaping breath and smiled coyly. "You'll find out soon enough, little sister."

"Will you put the kissing stuff in your diary so I can read about it when I turn eighteen?"

"Maybe, and maybe not. A diary is supposed to be kept private, you know." A pang for John struck Elsie as she reflected on turning thirty and her future without a love of her own, especially John. She couldn't believe she was that age. Most of the time, she did not feel that old, yet she didn't feel like a teenager either.

Rose's echoing cries upstairs interrupted the awkward silence. Edna stood and dashed up the stairs to attend to her.

"Well," Mrs. Pratt said. "I think it's time I headed for home. It was a lovely party, Phoebe. I'm so glad you invited me. Happy birthday again, Elsie."

Elsie stood, relieved that she now had an excuse to end the party early.

"I'm so glad you could come," Elsie and her mother said in unison.

"Oh, and Phoebe," Mrs. Pratt said from the doorway, "I'd like to get that cake recipe from you, if you don't mind. It was just delicious."

Elsie forced a smile, thinking how boring it would be to trade cake recipes among *her* married neighbors, if and when she *did* get married. "Thank you, Mrs. Pratt, and thank you *all* so much for coming," she said, looking around the parlor. "I had a wonderful time. And thank you so much for your gifts."

Thinking about what she might do for the remainder of the day, she fetched Edith's coat and brought it to her. She steered her into the kitchen, which was more private, while the others collected their belongings in the parlor to go home. "Edith, do you want to go to the picture show?"

"Today?"

"Yes, today. It's my birthday, after all."

"I can't. I have to get ready for tonight … wash and roll my hair."

Elsie shrugged. "Going out with Ray?"

"Of course. He's tops! I just love him, you know?"

"Yes, I *do* know."

Edith laid a hand on Elsie's arm. "Say, I just wanted you to know how sorry I am about what happened with John. Anytime you want to talk, just come on over. Maybe Ray knows someone you'd want to meet. We could double-date, and you could wear that beautiful new dress. What do you think?"

Elsie sighed with a little shake of her head. "I don't know. I don't think so."

"I understand how you must feel. No two men are alike, but it would be a start, anyway. We need to get you out of the house. What do you say?"

Elsie nodded slowly at first, then cheerfully replied, "Sure. Just let me know."

Edna came back to the parlor with Rose just as Edith and Elsie were heading for the front door. "Could you hold her while I get her some milk?" she said, handing Rose to Edith. The fully-awake toddler did not want to be held by anyone but her mother. She began to squirm and slipped out of Edith's arms, her feet scrambling to the ground. She ran to her mother and pulled on her tie belt.

"Mommy, Mommy," Rose cried.

Edna lifted the child, held her against her shoulder and sat on the sofa, full of pride and love with Rose in her arms.

The toddler quieted down and began to look around with curiosity, kicking her legs, and clutching at Edna's shoulder. "Down," Rose said.

"Just think," Edith said. "Elsie and I could be mothers someday, and have daughters just like Rose."

Auntie Jane beamed. "Wouldn't that be wonderful?"

An awkward silence hung in the room that made Elsie shuffle her feet and turn to Edna. "What about you? Do you want to go to the pictures with me? I suppose you have to take care of Rose?"

"No. Actually, I'm tagging along with Edith and her date. Why don't you take Robert?"

Phoebe was busy tidying up the parlor. She looked at Elsie, then Robert. "Yes, that's a very good idea. Why don't the two of you run along to the talkies?"

"Mom," Lena said. "They're called *pictures* now."

"Very well, then: *picture show.* Robert, why don't you go with Elsie?"

"Great. I'd love to," he said, jumping up from the telephone chair. "I don't have a date tonight, since I'm out of town without Brenda."

"Okay; suits me," Elsie said.

Robert took his coat from the rack next to the front door. "If we go now, we can probably catch the last feature. But I definitely don't want to see *It Happened One Night* again."

Auntie Jane, Edna, and Edith filed out the door with smiles and happy birthday goodbyes.

"Bye," Elsie called after them. "Thank you!"

She returned her attention to Robert. "It's my birthday: I get to choose. Besides," she said, laughing, "I'm paying your way. Beggars *can't* be choosers."

"Why not? I'm doing you a favor. No one else wanted to go, and don't forget—I'll get sick if I see that Clark Gable again!"

"Robert, that's why I didn't invite you *first*. I know you hate Clark Gable. I can't believe it. He's one of us—from Ohio."

"Don't be silly. He's Hollywood all the way. Just because he spent a few years in Akron. ...

"We went to the same college."

"I forgot about that. Okay, point well taken."

"Oh, we have such different tastes in movies," Elsie said with a wistful sigh. "It means a lot to me if you don't complain about seeing *It Happened One Night*. That is, if it's still playing."

"Say, you two. You'd better get going or you'll miss the show," Phoebe said.

"Can I go?" Evelyn asked.

"No," Elsie said. "I'll take you one day after Robert leaves."

"Me, too?" Lena asked.

"Yes, yes. We'll all go, and spend the rest of my *five dollars*." Elsie gave Evelyn and Lena a scowl.

"Go, while you still can," Phoebe said, collecting them without preamble and ushering them into the doorway.

Robert continued with his overview of the movie situation as he opened the door for Elsie. "You're gaga over Clark Gable the same way you were over Rudolph Valentino," Robert said with playful sarcasm. "All right. All right." He threw his hands into the air. "I know. It's your birthday and I want it to be special for you. Besides Gable is like an alumni of yours. Let's go, and you get to call the shots."

Elsie smiled at her mother. "Thanks, Mum, for everything." She stepped back inside, grabbed her sweater from the coat rack, and closed the door behind her, Robert in tow.

The day's weather had been perfect. The late afternoon sun slanted through the maple leaves, dappling the ground with dancing spots of golden light.

Elsie snaked her arm through her cousin's as they walked to his car. "How long are you staying in town?"

Robert shook his head. "Just until Tuesday. I wanted to be here for your birthday and to make sure you were all right. You sounded so down in the dumps with that depressing letter. But you seem okay now."

"I'm not okay. I can't eat and I'm having trouble sleeping. I'm feeling sad all the time. I miss him so much. It's terrible to miss someone this much. It's unbearable, and I just feel helpless to do anything about it."

"As a friend I miss him, too. But you just have to forget him. That's all. You just have to."

She stopped abruptly, making Robert jerk to a stop. "Do you think he loved me?"

"Elsie, he did, but things happen," he said, disengaging his arm from hers and walking ahead on the sidewalk.

"What do you mean? Is there something you're not telling me?"

"No, there's nothing," he said over his shoulder.

She hurried to catch up to him, pulling him around to face her. "You're sure?"

"I know exactly what you know. Sometimes things happen we have no control over. And sometimes they happen for a good reason that we know nothing about yet. That's all I meant."

"I should have never come back here," Elsie said, her voice high-pitched. "It was a big mistake; the biggest mistake of my life."

"You did the best you could," he said patiently. "Is James out of the picture?"

"Of course. He was practically out of the picture when we were married. There's nothing between us, and there never will be. I don't even see him around anymore. I've only seen him once at Goodyear, and then we just waved."

Robert stopped outside his car and turned to face Elsie. "Too bad. Are you filing for divorce?"

"I haven't yet. I don't have the money, and now I'm not really motivated."

"When you get the money you should do it. No sense in prolonging the inevitable."

She nodded in agreement. "You're probably right."

"That's the stuff. How can you find anyone else, otherwise?" Robert piloted her around to the passenger side of the car, unlocked the door, and held it open for her.

"Why thank you, sir," she said, trying to sound grateful for his gallantry.

He went back around the car, climbed into the driver's seat and glanced at her. "Have you checked what's playing? I'm sure they must have changed the picture by now."

"I'm not sure, but I do know I could see *It Happened One Night* a hundred times. Gable is such a smoldering romantic star. I love his movies."

Robert backed the car out of its space. "If a Gable movie is playing again, I'll see it just for you and I won't even complain. I'll suffer through it one more time. It's a special day, and you're a special cousin. I remember how you were so consumed with Valentino."

"I just love him, too. You know I sat through *The Sheik* five times and saw *The Son of the Sheik* just three weeks before he died."

"He's been dead ... for what, nine years now?"

"I guess so. It seems like only yesterday. Nineteen twenty-six was nothing but heartache for me. In August, Valentino died unexpectedly from a perforated ulcer, and Ruth Helen died that year, too."

"I loved Ruth Helen. She loved to play all the time, even after she became so sick. She was a smart little girl. Didn't she start talking early?"

"At two," Elsie said sadly. After a few moments of silence, she changed the subject. "How's my puppy doing? I miss her, too."

"She's fine. Remember? She's with her mother, Clementine. Don't worry about the dog."

"Maybe with this new job I can save enough money to move back to Rensselaer. I hate working with insurance; it's so dull, even though the money is good. I'll have to check into that special teaching opportunity with the New Deal programs of Ohio." She smiled at him. "Oh, by the way, I just love the perfume you gave me. Did I tell you that?"

He cocked his head and stared at her. "Sure, you told me. I'm glad you like it. You know, I'd love to have you back in Rensselaer, but I'm afraid it won't be the same for you."

"I know. But I'm optimistic. Maybe John will come to his senses and show up there when his job with the government is finished. Do you think that's possible?" Elsie said, hope rising in her chest.

"Anything is possible, but I wouldn't count on it."

"If it was true love, we'll be together again. If he is still in love with me, I'm convinced he'll be miserable without me. You can't be happy with someone else when you're in love already. I should know. Do you think he's thinking of me today?"

"Maybe," Robert said. "I don't know. Let's cheer you up and make this a happy birthday. Maybe you can meet someone else." He slowed down as they approached a dirt road, trying to avoid the water-filled potholes from last night's rain. "You're life is not over. You still look young and pretty. You don't look thirty."

"Please don't remind me, or tell anyone my age, for that matter."

"I won't." Robert promised, pulling in front of the picture theater.

"Look. There's Amy Sue," Elsie said, pointing to a girl walking toward the theater.

"Isn't that your old school chum who fainted years ago when you saw *The Sheik?*"

"That's the one, and now she's back for Gable. Lots of girls fainted with Valentino, remember?"

"I'm trying to forget. Oh, no!" he said, opening the automobile door and looking up at the marquis on the building. "My rotten luck—it's still playing. But thank God it's a double feature."

Elsie beamed, bouncing out of the car. "Oh, my gosh. They've held it over for another week. Akron does love its own."

Chapter Twenty-two

Elsie pushed the cozy duvet out of the way, leaned over her pillow and squinted at the clock beside her bed. The time was 7:10 AM; still early enough to get ready and make it to work on time, although *this* morning she barely had the strength to get out of bed. Her thoughts drifted back to last night's dream about John, still so fresh in her memory.

She wondered if he tossed and turned at night with images of *her* plaguing his sleep. Probably not, she thought. She moaned softly and pulled the sheet up over her chin.

There was a soft rap at the bedroom door. "Who is it?" Elsie called.

"It's your mum, luv."

Elsie brushed her fingers through her hair to smooth it. "Come in."

The heavy wooden door creaked as Phoebe gently pushed it open. "How are you doing this morning?"

"I'm fine." She sat propped up on beige lace pillows. She glanced at her mother and turned toward the window. Warm summer sunlight streamed in, though billowy clouds were forming and beginning to cloud the sky; the makings of a thunderstorm by afternoon. She yawned and quickly picked up a handkerchief on her bed stand, putting it to her mouth.

With a solemn look, Phoebe placed her palm on her daughter's forehead. "Why, your face feels damp."

Elsie managed a smile, averting her mother's gaze. "It was so humid last night. This humidity makes it hard to get up every morning. And I just dread sitting in that office at Goodyear every day… " she trailed off. "I really want to find another place to work."

"I know. That's fine, dear."

"I want to go back to teaching." Her voice faint, she repeated, "I loved teaching. I need some joy in my life. It's been such a hot, steamy summer. Every time I go outside I feel like I'm suffocating."

"I'm worried. You don't look well; you look thin." She stared at her daughter with concern. "I'll get you something to eat, be back straightaway with a hearty breakfast. How about eggs, hot oatmeal, and fresh biscuits? Making me hungry just thinking about it. You'll feel much better after you've eaten." Phoebe smiled warmly.

"I'm not feeling up to a big breakfast," Elsie whispered. "Just a glass of iced tea will do, thank you, Mum."

Phoebe left the room and Elsie closed her eyes in anguish. The emotional and physical pain she was feeling had become unbearable. It had been over two years since she last saw John. The pain had dulled, but it refused to completely go away. She prayed every night that her circumstances would change. Just the thought of him brought an acute sense of sorrow. After she dreamt about him she was sad, waking up to realize that there was nothing more to it than ghostly images. The pain welled in her chest, choking off her breath.

Even now, with the benefit of time, she missed him desperately. Each month since they had parted, she tried to remember everything they had done together, replaying the good times over and over, and forgetting nothing of what they had said.

This morning she reran the first day they had met. He had been sitting in Robert's front-porch rocker, drinking a beer, casually talking to him. Then she walked out to the porch and made her appearance. She remembered the expression on his face, indicating that he was glad to meet her. He had looked at her like no man ever had. That look was one she would always remember; it had meant something deep, meaningful, and lasting—it had to.

She sighed, trying to adjust her thoughts to a rational angle. Again, she thought that perhaps he had never really loved her enough to hear her side of the story. Those sentiments came into her thoughts often. She would probably never know for sure. Even if he did love her some, it wasn't enough to cause him to seek her out, to press her for a divorce.

For one brief moment in time her life had been good, with everything it had to offer: the love of a great man, happiness, good health, and a satisfying job.

She shook her head, trying to avoid spending any more time daydreaming. It was time to get out of bed. She struggled to her feet unsteadily, then glanced in the mirror and saw a pale woman with puffy eyes and unruly hair staring back. She looked like a young thirty-two, but fragile. She turned away from the vulnerable woman in the glass and slowly walked to the bathroom, one hand on the dresser, and a hand to the door frame to steady herself.

When she returned to the bedroom, a glass of iced tea and a scone were waiting for her on the nightstand. She picked up the glass and pressed it to her lips. The cold liquid felt good sliding down her throat. Though fighting to resist the trail of her thoughts, she was lured once again by the memory of John, his scent, that particular essence of his masculinity. In recalling, she drank the tea as memories, as though swallowing her dreams of John; something merely remembered, yet still alive. The sensation of her lips touching his, and all doubt, all fear melting away with the gentle contact, still left her weak in the knees after all these months.

Lena poked her head into the room. She was dressed in a green crepe skirt and white cotton, short-sleeved shirt. "I'm sorry you're still feeling so sad," she said, gazing at Elsie. "But since you're going to work today, you probably won't need your bathing suit." She headed into the room toward the closet. "May I please borrow it?"

"Lena! Whoa! I didn't say you could borrow it."

Immediately, Lena stepped back and stood in the doorway. "Geez Louise, you're still so cranky. May I please borrow the bathing suit … please? It's hanging there," she said, pointing into the open closet.

"Sure, I suppose so." Elsie smiled faintly. "Just make sure you wash it afterwards really well. Chemicals ruin a suit."

"We're going to the lake, but okay, I'll do that … and thanks," Lena said, smiling.

"Well, girls I'll be off to work," Frederick said, peeking into the bedroom. "And Elsie, please try and eat something substantial. Bye, girls."

"Bye, Daddy." They said in unison.

Elsie leaned forward in bed and whispered, "Do you have a minute?"

"Sure," Lena said, stepping closer

"Tell me about your new beau."

"Okay. Well, he's tall with brown hair and a touch of blond on the sides and on the top. He's treating me to a soda this afternoon, and then we're going swimming with the usual crowd. You met them, remember?"

"Oh yes, I think so, but which one was your beau?"

"William Mangus. Everyone calls him Billy."

"Oh yes, that's right. The one with the devilish smile and dimples?"

"Uh-huh. Anyway, I wanted to wear a real nice swimsuit. Thanks ever so much," she said, going into the closet for the suit. Her eyes widened as she turned around. "Oh, and Elsie, I almost forgot: he's got a super crooner's voice, too."

"I'm happy for you, and I hope you have better luck with love than I did," Elsie said, her voice fading.

"You shouldn't say that. You make it sound like your love life is finished for good. You'll have good luck again."

Lena stared at the perfume on Elsie's dresser. "Would you mind terribly if I tried a little?" She removed the crystal stopper from the bottle and sniffed at it.

Elsie nodded, and then watched as Lena dabbed a bit of scent along the underside of her wrist and sniffed again, slowly closing her eyes and inhaling. "Mm-m that smells divine."

"It's John's favorite fragrance," Elsie said.

Lena frowned and sat at the end of the bed. "Who cares about what he likes? Stop feeling so sorry for yourself. Forget about that John McDonald; he's making you sick. It's been such a long time since you've even seen him. I can't believe you're still talking about him."

A beat of silence followed her remark.

Elsie smiled sadly. "I still think of him. I can't help it. Does that sound pitiful?" She shrugged dispiritedly. "I thought I could handle it. I guess I was mistaken."

"Why would you spend your precious time fancying a man you never see?"

"Promise me you won't laugh if I tell you something?"

Lena crossed her fingers. "I promise."

"I believe strongly that someday he'll come back for me. He'll knock one day at the front door, and we'll all be surprised, especially Daddy."

"I won't laugh, but you are daft!"

"No." Elsie shook her head. "I really believe John still loves me. He'll be back—I feel it."

"I don't think there's any chance of that. He's long gone; probably married by now. Elsie, you're a smart cookie. It's dumb to think you'll see him again." Her eyes widened with her next proclamation. "If I were you, I'd get myself out of bed, put a smile on my face, and find someone better. Take that teardrop pendent off, too. The summer is here; you should be happy."

"Hm-m, maybe you're right," Elsie said without much conviction.

Lena stood. "Thanks again for the suit. It'll look swell. Billy will love the way I look in it."

Elsie wagged a finger at her. "You be careful, young lady."

A giggle escaped Lena's lips, and she hastily excused herself, closing the bedroom door behind her.

Elsie's body felt limp with the heat of the sweltering morning, then after a bit she no longer felt anything. Her life, once so full of dreams, was now dead to her. Quickly she stopped herself from thinking the same old morbid, negative thoughts, and turned her mind to something more positive. Bike riding, going to the picture show, and enjoying the rest of the summer—those were the things she ought to think about.

She picked a book from the bookcase to read at lunchtime, and glanced out her window. She was getting dressed when Evelyn knocked loudly on her door.

"Come in," Elsie yelled.

"Elsie, come quick! Amelia Earhart is missing!"

"Oh, no!" Elsie quickly buttoned her blouse and ran down the stairs after Evelyn. In the parlor, Phoebe was turning up the volume on the radio.

". . . On July second, Earhart and Noonan took off from Lae in Papua, New Guinea. Their intended destination in the heavily loaded Lockheed Electra 10E was Howland Island. They reported their last position near the Nukumanu Island, about eight hundred miles into the flight. The United States Coast Guard cutter, Itasca, was on station at Howland, assigned to communicate with them and to guide the Electra to the island, once they approached the vicinity. Yesterday, July sixth, four days after Earhart's last verified radio transmission, the captain of the battleship, Colorado, received orders from the Commandant, Fourteenth Naval District, to take over all naval and coast guard units to coordinate search efforts. At this time, all search efforts have failed. Amelia Earhart is officially missing. I repeat: Amelia Earhart is officially missing. We will bring you more on this riveting story throughout the day.'

"Oh, no! This is terrible news," Elsie said, sliding heavily into the chair next to the radio. "She can't be missing. She's only thirty-nine years old. I know because she's one of my heroes."

"Yes, luv," Phoebe said. "It's a real shame. They're doing everything in their power to find her."

"She's kind of a tomboy, but I like her gap-toothed smile," Evelyn said.

Elsie was dumbfounded. "What? You like the way she looks? Is that all you can say about her? I like the fact that she was the first woman to fly solo across the Atlantic Ocean. That's a real accomplishment."

"That *is* great, I suppose. She's not married, though, is she?" Evelyn looked at her mother.

"Who cares?" Elsie snapped.

"I care," Evelyn shot back. "Just because you're not getting married."

"What does that mean? I was married once. So what?"

"You don't care if she's married or not because *you're* not married, that's all. I'm going to be married forever, and have children, too."

"Good for you, Evelyn. But I'll have to correct you. Technically, I *am* married. And, Amelia Earhart *is* married." Elsie responded. "She married George Putnam in nineteen thirty-one, but referred to her marriage as a 'partnership' with 'dual control.' She kept her own name rather than being called Mrs. Putnam."

"Mom, is that the right thing to do; to keep your own name when you get married?" Evelyn asked.

"Not as far as I'm concerned, but I don't fly fancy airplanes and dine with movie stars."

Elsie was astonished. "How can you think like that, Mum? Amelia Earhart is a noted American aviation pioneer and author. She set so many records, wrote best-selling books, and formed the *Ninety-Nines*, an organization for female pilots. She has strong values. A couple of years ago when the Bendix Trophy Race banned women, she openly refused to fly Mary Pickford to Cleveland to open the races. Even Eleanor Roosevelt was inspired by her! After flying with Earhart, the First Lady actually obtained a student permit—"

"Elsie, enough! It's getting late. You should be off to work. You don't want to be late."

"I guess." Elsie quickly picked up her book and pocketbook before opening the front door. "It's going to be another hot day. Boy, the rubber smells even worse in this heat. Mum, keep the radio on all day for any news." Elsie waved goodbye and shut the door behind her. *I wish I could fly an airplane. That would be so exciting. I sure hope Amelia Earhart is okay.*

Chapter Twenty-three

John McDonald carefully tucked the conference itinerary into his business satchel, more than pleased with his recent promotion, and with it, the opportunity to present his firm's services to the ever growing list of developers in Ohio and other Midwest states. The morning train would leave in an hour, so he quickly tossed a few last-minute items into his overnight bag, took one last look around the house and left, locking the door behind him.

The newer homes and streets where he lived in Buffalo were laid out in a grid pattern, so he zigzagged his new Packard Coupe Roadster west and then north from Box Avenue, then with a few more lefts and rights, over to the train station on Curtiss. The building of Buffalo Central Terminal, to the tune of fourteen million dollars, had been quite an accomplishment for the city about a decade ago with its sleek, contemporary lines, and high-domed, main lobby. John greatly admired the grand scale of the project with its accommodation of over two hundred trains.

He parked his car and hurried to the station, which was busy with holiday travelers. Men and women talked and laughed in small groups as they waited for various trains out on the platforms, their chatter accompanied by puffs of frosty steam, and shuffles and stamps of their feet to keep warm. Children huddled in a corner near the front doors, selling baskets of bent willow for twenty cents, each held together with red ribbon and finished with a big, cheery bow tied to the side.

Inside the lobby, other patrons lined up four and five deep, waiting to purchase tickets at open windows against one wall. With the heavy ticket lines, John was glad he'd arrived early. It would be a long ride to Cleveland, and he wanted the most comfortable seat he could find.

Once on board, John managed to find an open seat next to the window. He removed his hat and placed it, and the rest of his belongings, on the overhead steel rack, then sank into the seat to settle down comfortably for the long ride ahead.

It had been an exciting week and, learning that he'd been assigned to attend the architectural conference in Cleveland, made it an especially interesting one. He was pleasantly surprised when he checked the train schedule and found that his route would include a two-hour stopover in Akron. Should he use the time to visit Elsie and surprise her? The last time he did, the visit had proved disastrous.

Maybe this time would be different.

Now, three years later, he still couldn't get her completely out of his thoughts.

Had her marriage been successful? She could be living in a home of her own with a husband and a child, or she might be divorced and living at the Obee home. He supposed, in either case, it wouldn't hurt to stop by just to say hello. Still, he wasn't sure what he ought to do. He sighed in a heavy whirl of indecision: should he see Elsie in Akron, or not? What purpose would it serve if he did?

I must finish my presentation for the conference tomorrow.

Corralling his thoughts, he pulled his notebook and fountain pen from his satchel and continued with the high points of his speech, but thoughts of Elsie kept interrupting him.

As a diversion to clear his mind he stood, stretched, went to the back of the car to get the Buffalo News from the rack, and returned to his seat.

The news wasn't all that interesting, except that the New York Giants had won the NFL championship yesterday. It was an impressive sports story with all the lowdown: *'December 11, 1938: New York Giants 23, Green Bay Packers 17.'* He'd been rooting for New York, and it had been one hell of a game. He was happy as a clam about the final score, and gave the sports section a smile of approval as he folded it and opened another section.

A labor group was crying foul about the recent minimum wage set at forty cents an hour. The group had wanted forty-five cents an hour for a forty-four-hour work week. John thought that was ridiculous. Forty-five cents was an outrageous sum for unskilled labor.

Day after day, the news from Europe was the same. The front page referred to Germany's Hitler and Mussolini of Italy, meeting to confer on combined agendas. Hitler had strong-armed his way into picking up a lot of political allies against Britain and France, and military experts on both sides of the Atlantic were worried about it. He was a real sap, John thought, not to mention a dangerous leader.

The rocking back-and-forth motion of the train ultimately made him drowsy and he began to nod off, but the rumble of wheels under him slowed, and the train came to a scheduled stop, bringing him fully awake. He glanced at his watch. Half-past twelve. It would be another three hours before he reached Akron.

He twisted in his seat when the train was underway again, trying to get comfortable, but the movement did nothing to ease his troubled stomach, which was beginning to feel a lot like the Giants and Packers slamming into one another. Soon he realized that the pain felt more like pangs of guilt as the train crossed into Pennsylvania and plowed ahead toward the Ohio state line, and Akron beyond.

Perhaps he'd jumped to conclusions that fateful winter day in front of the Obee home. Thinking that Elsie was happy without him, he had walked away from the love of his life, leaving her to sort things out with her husband. To abandon her was the hardest thing he had ever done, when all he really wanted was to return to Rensselaer, then move on to New York and to the happy days and nights of their usual life together. Driving away that day seemed the right choice to make under the circumstances, but now, with the passage of time, he thought that perhaps he'd made the wrong decision. Maybe he should have waited for James to leave the house, and then made his move.

A train attendant interrupted his brooding over the past.

"Ticket, sir?"

John reached into his shirt pocket. "Here you are," he said, smiling and handing him the ticket. "What time do we arrive in Akron?"

The attendant picked up his pocket watch, which hung at the end of a sparking gold chain. "Should arrive at about half-past three," he said, tapping the face of the watch.

John ran his fingers through his hair and nodded. "Yes, I thought so. Thank you."

He leaned against the window and watched the scenery fly past, reminding him of the failed trip he'd made to pick up Elsie and take her back to Rensselaer. He pictured her so easily, so clearly, especially the time he'd given her that promise ring; how ecstatic she'd been. He had promised his heart to her, and she had promised hers to him. Had she kept the ring? Did she think of him? It was quite unlike him to dwell in the past, but before long he realized he was hoping for … for what?

If he were completely honest with himself, it seemed that since he and Elsie had gone their separate ways, his life was progressing quite nicely. He was happy living in Buffalo, and loved his job. Maybe he should leave well enough alone. If he called at the family home, what if her father answered the door again? Should he take the chance? Maybe she was furious with him for not contacting her, or maybe she was doing just fine with James.

Conflicting emotions warred in the depths of his chest. He could certainly understand that couples looked forward to their futures together, but it was hard for him to reconcile why anyone would want to dig up a past relationship. Why would *he* want to revisit *his* past? In the end, he felt he owed it to Elsie to see her, and more importantly, he owed it to himself—he missed her.

The train pulled into the Akron depot five minutes early. John exited the car with his belongings and spotted a man on the platform, holding a sign that read, *'Need a ride? 50 cents to anywhere in the city of Akron. A buck if snowing.'*

"Excuse me," John said, approaching the tall, lanky fellow who appeared to be down on his luck. "Can you take me to Champlain Street?"

"Sure can."

"I'll need you to wait. I'm not sure how long I'll be."

"No problem, mister." The man took a step forward and stuck out his hand. "I'm Jack Pyle."

John shook his hand and smiled. "John McDonald. Pleased to meet you."

"I can take you anywhere," Pyle said. "That's if you have the cash to pay. Do you?" he added with a chuckle.

"I do." John pulled out his gold money clip with a few bills in it, and let it flash green before Pyle's eyes. *Cabs sure are expensive these days.* "This should do it. Where's your car?"

"At the curb, just outside the depot." Pyle picked up John's suitcase and quickly headed out the door. "It's not snowing yet, so it'll be fifty cents an hour. Driving, waiting—it doesn't matter."

John followed.

Pyle stopped in front of a shiny, black Packard parked in front of the station. "Here she is."

John whistled. "She's a beaut of a ride. It took me ages before I could afford one. You must have a great business going on."

"Naw," Pyle replied. "I ain't got squat. I just got lucky. My father-in-law loaned it to me. Get in. What's the number on Champlain Street?"

"Four eighty-nine." John said, slipping into the back seat.

Pyle turned the key in the ignition and sped away from the curb.

John felt nervous and excited, all at once. "Say, I don't have a gift with me. Let me ask you, Jack: I think I should pick up something to give my lady friend, don't you? You see, I'm going to visit an old flame." He watched for the cabbie's response in the rear view mirror.

Pyle's lips curved into a knowing smile. "Sure. Broads like flowers and candy. You can't show up empty-handed."

John nodded. "You're right. Where can I get some flowers?"

"Beats me. Flowers are out of season … unless you want poinsettias or holly? Let me turn here. I know where you can get some poinsettias in a girly little container."

Pyle turned down one street, then another, reminding John of the last time he'd driven through Akron alone on that snowy Sunday in January, 1935.

Pyle stopped the car abruptly in front of a small market with poinsettias lined up in the shop window. "I'll get them for you. I know the owner."

John did not have long to wait. He returned in three short minutes with a beautiful arrangement; the pot covered in green tin foil.

"You owe me two bucks," Pyle announced.

"Thanks, they're nice. "John exhaled a long, patient sigh, handing him a two-dollar bill. For that kind of money he ought to get some free advice, too. "Say, have you ever known a gal you couldn't get out of your mind?"

"Sure, buddy. My wife. But that was fifteen years ago. Now I can't wait to get out of the house," he said, laughing as he pounded the steering wheel.

"Yeah, you're a real hoot, Jack." John didn't think it was all *that* funny. He hoped he would never arrive at such a dismal situation with the girl of *his* dreams. He could live with Elsie for fifteen years, no two ways about it, and he'd be happy, to boot. At least he felt pretty sure about that, now that his career seemed solid.

Pyle screeched away from the curb and they were in front of Elsie's house on Champlain Street within minutes.

From the back seat, John placed his hand on Pyle's shoulder before getting out of the car. "Just wait for me here."

"I have all day. It's fifty cents an hour."

"I know. Thank you."

John took a deep breath and walked up to the front porch. He was flooded with bad memories. At least it wasn't snowing this time. He mentally crossed his fingers that Elsie's father was at work. The same sign, *'Peace on Earth,'* hung above the front door, just like he remembered it three long years ago. Suddenly, he felt like a little boy who wanted to run away without ever confronting his past mistakes.

He blew out the tension in a rush of breath, putting the flowers down on the ground, and shaking his wrists to release the nerves that had gathered in his stomach like a tangle of dark and threatening clouds. Strains of Christmas music swirled inside the house, loud enough to filter through the door and bring holiday cheer outside to the porch.

Someone is home. I hope it's not her father.

He took another deep breath, picked up the flowers, and knocked.

A young, pretty girl with auburn hair pulled back into a twist at the nape of her neck opened the door and smiled. "Yes, may I help you?"

"Are you Elsie's sister?"

"Yes, I am," she said cautiously. "I'm Lena. Who are you?"

He remembered the name, Lena, and felt a surge of excited anticipation, as if the sisters were tied in family communion; one household entity, with Elsie suddenly tripping down the stairs to stand beside her sister, or appearing from around the corner, looking as beautiful and radiant as ever.

"Maybe your sister spoke of me." He took off his hat and gave his greeting with a nod. "I'm John McDonald. Is Elsie in by any chance?"

He watched her eyes carefully assessing his demeanor and appearance. He hoped he would pass the scrutiny test. And if Elsie were in, he'd have a lot of explaining to do. Or maybe Elsie would explain to *him* that she and James were happily married. He wasn't sure what to expect.

Lena's smile faded, and that seemed a bad sign. Why hadn't she called out for Elsie? Nevertheless, she replied pleasantly enough. "Well, I'll be darned! Please come in, won't you?"

John could not understand the contradictions in her manner, unless it had to do with James. He stepped into the parlor, glad this time for the invitation in contrast to his *last* visit. The room was nicely decorated for the holidays; casual and comfortable in a way he imagined Elsie's family home might be. A large Christmas tree, trimmed in tinsel and red popcorn garland, stood at the bay window. There was an array of photographs sitting on a narrow wood table against one wall, showing the Obee girls at various ages. He paused when he spotted a picture framed in silver. It was a photograph of Elsie and him at the Chicago World's fair. *That seems like a good sign.*

Lena gestured for him to sit down on the sofa. "Let me take your hat and coat. I'll just hang them here," she said, going to the hall coat rack.

Returning to the parlor, Lena lifted the lid on an old cabinet Victrola, turned down the volume, and let it continue playing a Bing Crosby record.

"You know, John," she said, sitting down in a chair next to the telephone, "this is unbelievable! It's such a lovely surprise to finally meet you. Elsie waited for you to come back … every day."

"She did?"

"You bet. Every day! I can't believe you're here. I didn't even recognize you."

"Well, it *has* been more than three years since that photo of us was taken," he said, nodding toward the table with the pictures. "Is there a place for these? I thought Elsie might like them." He began to stand with the poinsettias, looking around the room for a place to set them down.

"Here, I'll take those," Lena said, relieving him of the awkward moment by placing the flowers next to the telephone. "They're very lovely, and in the Christmas spirit, too."

"Is Elsie *here*?" he asked, becoming more confused and feeling very much out of place by the moment. "Does she still live here? Maybe she's with James?"

Lena seemed uncertain as to what to say, glancing alternately from the tense expression on his face to the fidgeting hands in her lap, and back again. "Well—no. She's not," she said finally. "About a year ago … Mom was the only one home…."

* * *

Phoebe sat at the kitchen table, the new icebox hum accompanying her as she sorted through photographs of the family's cherished memories. On the table was a pile of colored construction paper, the photos, ink pens, a pair of sharp scissors, and a bowl of wheat paste. Dishes in the sink sat from the night before, along with those from the morning and afternoon meals. She sighed, putting off once more the effort to tidy up the kitchen until after finishing the Christmas cards. If she hurried, she could mail the cards, clean up, and have enough time to start supper. She looked up at the clock: twenty-five minutes past four.

She reexamined the photos and methodically pasted the scenic ones onto the red construction paper she had cut into greeting card sizes. She was happy and feeling proud that Frederick had taken and developed the pictures himself, using the basement as a dark room.

A darn fine job, too, she thought. Carefully, she folded each card with its photo outside, and reopened it to print a spirited Christmas greeting inside, along the fold:

'Hard times can't stop our family from wishing you a very Merry Christmas, 1937. The Obees: Frederick, Phoebe, Elsie, Lena, and Evelyn.'

It was peaceful outside; a calming silence in the air with a thin blanket of snow covering the ground. She thought of the Christmas card that had arrived in the morning's mail for Elsie in a green envelope, and went to the desk in the parlor to pick it up. Looking at the handwriting, she could tell that a child had sent it.

This should cheer her up, Phoebe thought. Elsie had been through so much pain this past year. No matter how difficult her life became as she deteriorated with the horrible "white plague," she remained positive. She was appreciative of the doctors, nurses, and staff who took such good care of her during her stay at the Ohio State Sanatorium. Her tuberculosis treatments had consisted of good food, rest, fresh air, and weekly pneumothoraxes, followed by fluoroscopies.

To receive a pneumothorax, Elsie would lie on her side and the doctor would insert a needle through her rib cage into the pleura, or membrane of skin surrounding her lung. Then, he and the nurse would force air through the needle into the lung cavity with a manometer, which also allowed them to control the air pressure. This procedure also collapsed the infected lung, prohibiting it from expansion, which gave it a healing rest. Afterward, they used a fluoroscope to check the tissue of the diseased lung and to see if it was healing. The nurse would stand on one side of a radiation screen, and the doctor would sit on the other side in order to study the action of her lungs as she breathed. Phoebe was so relieved those treatments had ended.

Wearing her face mask, she started up the stairs, feeling heavy all of a sudden. Halfway up, she realized she should have taken Elsie a cup of hot tea—that it would be good for her hoarse throat—but she continued on, wanting to show her the child's card first. The bedroom door was closed. She knocked softly. "Elsie," she said. "Elsie, it's Mum."

Silence.

Phoebe quietly pushed open the heavy door. The room smelled of musk and the stale, sour odor of illness. Dr. Lewis's nurse had come to the house earlier to administer a "hot shot" to Elsie, which Phoebe learned was a concoction of iron salt, sodium chloride, calcium gas, iodine, and other scary sounding ingredients.

The radio hissed with unchecked, uninterrupted static. She walked into the room and turned it off.

Elsie lay with her face pressed against the pillow. Phoebe moved in closer and shook her shoulder lightly. "Luv," she said. "I have a Christmas card for you from one of your students back in Indiana." She brushed Elsie's mussed hair away from her face, and knew with one touch that the end had come. Her forehead was still warm, and she looked like she was sleeping peacefully.

"Elsie, Elsie," she repeated, shaking her lightly. But she lay lifeless in the bed. She lay a hand over Elsie's heart, and put an ear to her mouth. She was not breathing. Phoebe stood back. "You've gone to be with the Lord. You fought so hard," she whispered, falling into the chair at Elsie's bedside.

She stood slowly, walked down the hall to the top of the stairs, and gradually descended to the telephone, not knowing if her feet touched the steps or not. She was drenched in a cold sweat with tears streaming down her face. Her hand shook as she picked up the telephone receiver, and signaled for the operator.

"Operator, could you please send an ambulance. This is Mrs. Frederick Obee. My daughter is dead. Inform the medics that she died from pulmonary tuberculosis," she said with grim purpose, the breath stolen from her lungs, her pulse pounding in her head. "And tell Dr. Lewis to come as well. Four eighty-nine Champlain Street." She hung up.

Her suffering has ended. Her suffering is over.

The words pounded her temples like a drumbeat. She left the front door open for the doctor and ambulance medics, and walked at a snail's pace back up the stairs to Elsie. She perched on the edge of the bed and held her by the shoulders, trying to comfort her one last time. "Elsie, you are the best daughter a mother could ever ask for. I'll miss you for the rest of my life, luv."

Phoebe sank to the edge of the bed, grasping at the sheets covering her beloved Elsie, her daughter, her own flesh and blood. She began to sob quietly, and when she started she could not stop. "Oh, my baby! You finally let go," she wept.

Phoebe went into the bathroom and wiped her face with a towel to calm herself, and to dry her tears. She went back to the bed and looked at Elsie again, but there was nothing, no life. She slowly walked back and forth between the bed and the bathroom in a mindless fog, with no idea what to do next. She cried and shook with grief, but also with relief that Elsie's suffering had ended. Now she paced back and forth, and around and around in circles, her own life draining hot and cold all at once from her limbs, leaving a hole in her chest that could only be filled with Elsie's return to life. But that would never be. She ended up, once again, in the bathroom.

"Dear God, thank you, her pain has ended," she murmured into the bathroom mirror. Over the weekend, she finally stopped praying for a healing. Now was the time to let Elsie go, but a mother's heart found it hard to accept the reality.

Phoebe returned to the bedroom. Elsie's life stretched out before her, all around in the room. The photo of Elsie and John McDonald stood on her dresser, taken at the entrance of the Hawaiian restaurant at the Chicago World's Fair. How joyful she looked. Phoebe realized that it must have been the happiest time of her life.

Through her mask she bent to press a trembling kiss on her daughter's forehead, buried her face in her hair, held her close, and bawled like a baby. Phoebe prayed for Elsie to be well and to come alive in her arms. She willed it. She willed it, again and again. But her daughter lay lifeless, her smile and spirit missing from the warm, limp body of flesh in her arms.

She heard a commotion downstairs. The medics and Dr. Lewis had arrived. "Up here," Phoebe called from Elsie's doorway. She walked down the hall to stand at the top of the stairs. "I'm up here."

Back in Elsie's room with the three men in tow, Phoebe's eye caught sight of the green envelope that had fallen to the bare floor. She stuffed it into her apron pocket.

"Please, Mrs. Obee," Dr. Lewis said through his face mask. "I think you'll be more comfortable downstairs."

"Yes, of course," she said, not wanting to watch the final medical necessities that might be performed on her daughter. She could not watch. She stumbled down the steps. It was silent in the darkened room as she descended into the parlor, filling it with her hot and cold, quiet desperation.

A moment later, Dr. Lewis slowly advanced down the stairs, and she watched him as if each foot dropped in slow motion, his shoes echoing on each step like the click of a metronome cueing the terminus of a beautiful sonata: the end. He stared at Phoebe, reluctant to speak, it seemed. She knew what he meant to say, before he said it.

"I know it's over," she said. "Her pain is *over*," she repeated more forcefully, shaking her head.

"That it is. It appears that she's been gone for more than an hour," he said.

She looked at the doctor and then stared at the hands clenched together at the front of her apron, a fistful of prayerful fingers, seemingly separate from her own body. Her words came out in a small, tearful whisper. "Please give me a few minutes. I want to call Frederick at work. He'll come home straightaway to say his final goodbye."

"I'm sorry, Mrs. Obee. They'll have to take her body now."

The two masked medics came down the stairs, carrying Elsie's body, which was covered head to toe with a white sheet, and placed it on the gurney they had previously wheeled in. Dr. Lewis signaled to them to roll it quickly out the front door.

He turned to Phoebe and spoke through his mask. "I'm very sorry, Mrs. Obee. I know she had the best care possible at the sanatorium. And I'm sure you attended to her splendidly. If there's anything more I can do for you—"

Phoebe shook her head.

He paused a moment, then seeming to accept her silence, turned for the front door. "Goodbye, Mrs. Obee. I'll be in my office if you need me."

Phoebe managed only a small nod and followed him. "Thank you, Doctor." She closed the door behind him and turned back into the parlor, feeling lost and vacant inside.

A single candle, set on an old credenza against the wall, threw a dim, flickering light onto the telephone, casting it in a ghostly halo, beckoning her forth. Phoebe could not comprehend the idea that she must call her husband and say out loud, "Our daughter is gone."

She walked stiffly toward it, sank into the telephone chair, and took out her handkerchief, reluctant to pick up the phone. Elsie had drifted away while she sat at the kitchen table, printing Christmas cards. The nurse had informed her in the morning that her daughter probably wouldn't make it to the new year. But amazingly, earlier in the day, Elsie had been sitting up in bed and writing in her journal. And she had stopped spitting up blood.

Three children dead. Her faith was being tested. It was only her faith that made death endurable, helping her to believe that death was merely a door leading to a new life with God.

She picked up the telephone, and this time dialed Frederick's work number. When he answered, her words tumbled out all at once. "Come home. You must come home now. Elsie has passed." She hung up before he could answer, and before any further words became lodged in her throat.

The "white plague" had ravaged her daughter just like it had ravaged human beings since the time of the ancient Egyptians. Phoebe had read everything available to educate herself about the disease. But the knowledge she had gleaned had done nothing to save her daughter's life.

Many conflicting emotions grew and swirled and filled her head, convincing her that Elsie's death was a blessing and welcomed, yet at the same time it was the bitter end. Before her demise, even though gravely ill, she *was* still there. Now her daughter was gone and yet still somehow alive, there in the room, her breath and smile still so near. Thoughts and feelings collided in contradiction with each other until she could not think anymore. It went against every motherly instinct to have to say goodbye.

Elsie's door slammed upstairs, the sound muffled by distance. And Phoebe wondered, while she waited for Frederick, if it were true what they say; that a soul flies free of its body on a swift, chill wind, leaving no survivors in doubt, that their beloved has gone to live in the shower of God's bliss— in the arms of the angels. The doors and windows were all closed, but Elsie was gone, taken from life, perhaps signaled by the closing of the door to her room. Phoebe sat there thinking about Elsie in the afterlife of God's kingdom until she was numb, leaving the well of her soul empty, with no tears left to cry.

She thought of Elsie as a child, and reached immediately into her apron pocket for the green envelope. She took it out. The printing looked vaguely familiar, much like Elsie's own hand at about the same age. She tore it open.

Dear Miss Wilkins,

Here's wishing you a Merry Christmas and a Happy New Year, 1938. I wanted you to know that I won the spelling contest at school. I received a white ribbon from school and five dollars from my parents. You taught me to love words. My mom said you moved away from Indiana. I'm happy you're happy to be back home. You were my favorite teacher.

Love,

Mary-Jean Lorraine Marks

Tears flowed down her face anew, thinking of Elsie back home in heaven with God. She remembered when they'd first arrived in America. Elsie had been a bright six-year-old, full of promise, with a zest for life. She had never imagined that her vibrant little girl could leave this world at the tender age of thirty-two.

Phoebe now had one duty left in these remaining minutes: she dumbly prayed for Elsie by rote, waiting for Frederick to arrive, her face and blouse wet with her previous tears as she stared into the cold space of the parlor, the pale light of that single traitorous candle, throwing insipid licks of Christmas merriment upon the wall.

* * *

"She died a year ago, almost to the day," Lena said. "It was December sixth, nineteen thirty-seven. She really suffered so much at the sanatorium. When they told us there was nothing else they could do, my father hired an ambulance to bring her home so she could die with her family near."

John rubbed his temple, unbelieving, trying to make sense of the story. A sharp rolling pain twisted his stomach as though he were being knifed by a silent, unappeasable foe. He felt helpless and stranded by his own silence of three years. The ache built into his head and began to throb behind his eyes, making them sting. "I'm so sorry. God, I'm sorry. I didn't know."

The news hit him hard, like a blow to the head, stealing his breath and bringing him near to tears. He took out his handkerchief and wiped the ill feeling from his face. "I really loved her. It's my fault. I left her. That's why she got sick!"

"Let me get you something." Lena went to the kitchen and returned with a cold glass of water.

"Thank you. I'm sorry for being so emotional." He took a couple sips. "I'm just so shocked!"

"You're not the only one. I'm still in shock myself. The house feels so empty without her here."

"How did she contract tuberculosis?"

"Nobody knows. But she wasn't eating properly."

"Wasn't there anything else that could have been done for her?"

"All the TB treatments were tried. And we've all blamed ourselves this entire year for not finding something else that worked. We all feel we could have done more for her. We kept telling her, before she got sick, to eat more nutritiously and get out of the house—get some air. She would say she would but…."

"Anyway, after she contracted the disease it seemed there was nothing we could do. She just kept getting worse and worse, even after the first treatment. Then the TB was found in both lungs. Advanced cases cannot be cured. But thankfully, the rest of us weren't infected. That would have been more of a nightmare. My mom was the only one allowed in the room, and she always wore a surgical mask."

"I'm still shocked. Tuberculosis is such an appalling disease!"

"It is. It's terrible."

"When did she get sick?"

"She was not feeling well at all in August of thirty-seven. But she was skinny and not feeling well way before then."

"She got sick because of me."

"*You* didn't cause her to get tuberculosis."

An awkward silence fell between them.

Lena looked at him and smiled. "I'm so thrilled you stopped by."

"Thank you. I would have stopped by a lot sooner, but I thought that all this time she was probably happy with James. And here I was, trying to wash her out of my memory and not hate James for turning my life upside down. How wrong can a dimwitted sap be?"

"It's okay. It seems now that your breakup was a giant mistake, and no one's fault."

Another silence fell between them. It seemed to John that they both might be thinking the same thing: Frederick Obee.

"I'm sorry about my father. I really am."

"It doesn't matter now, I guess."

"My father is very conservative. I think he was just trying to be protective of Elsie and her marriage on that day you came to the door. But the sad truth is, he could never accept how little James meant to her. She didn't want to save her marriage. She wanted you. It's too bad you didn't know. She didn't know how to find you."

John hung his head and stared at his feet, commanding his heart to hold together in front of Elsie's sister, willing the sting behind his eyes to stop. "The more I think about the great times we had together, the more terrible I feel. I wish we had stayed together. Maybe she'd still be alive today if we had. I would have taken care of her, and she wouldn't have been susceptible to that disease in the first place."

"We've all blamed ourselves this past year. We all feel we could have done more for her," Lena reasserted.

John nodded in silence.

"She wanted to tell you that she was sorry for our father's rude behavior. She was only with James to help him celebrate his new job. She always loved you and was very distressed about the breakup until the day she died. She never got over losing you. I feel I have an obligation to speak for her now. She really loved you with all her heart."

John could see that Lena's eyes were turning red, ready to well up with tears and spill down her cheeks. "We all miss her so much," she managed to choke out.

John took another sip of water. "So, she never did patch things up with James?"

"No, never. She never had any intention of setting up housekeeping with him. You were the only man for her; she always said so." Lena gave him a small smile. "By the way, what are you doing here in Akron?"

"I'm on my way to a conference and decided to stop in and see—" The name caught in his throat.

"To see, Elsie," she finished for him. "I'm glad you did."

He felt Lena's eyes on him as he studied the room once more, thinking of Elsie filling its spaces, laughing on the telephone, skipping down the stairs into the parlor, or coming through the front door and yelling, *'Hello? Anyone home?'* as she did at his house in Rensselaer. She couldn't be dead. The word was so contrary to the Elsie he knew; she was life.

Lena had followed his scrutiny of the room, and back to the space between them. "There are some things of Elsie's I'd like you to have," she said, climbing the stairs.

Moments later, she returned and handed him a small, bulky envelope.

He turned it over in his hands. It was slightly heavy and made a small sliding and chinking sound. He was surprised that the back flap looked unremarkable and new, as though it had never been opened; it was sealed without any sign of prying fingers or curious eyes. The front, as he flipped it back over again, was printed in a neat, even hand: *'To John.'* He could guess as to its contents, but instinct told him that mentioning it would only bring on another grapple with his emotions.

"I'm amazed," he said, shifting uneasily on the sofa, not quite knowing how to express what he felt without sounding secretive or rude. Or was he just confused, which only added to the heap of freefalling pangs of guilt and helplessness tumbling around just under his breastbone. If only his crushed heart could escape into the explanation of a nightmare that would soon evaporate and leave him sweating in a heap of last night's bed sheets. "I'm amazed," he repeated. "I had no idea she still thought of me. I mean, how could she … this isn't her handwriting, is it?" He wasn't really sure what he'd just said. Nothing made sense. If only he had an ounce more patience with her. If only he had helped her to get a divorce.

Lena laughed a bit. It seemed she was trying to make him feel at ease. "I put everything in an envelope for you, and well … I did what I thought she'd want me to do. Elsie always told me that you'd come back for her. Inside, I included the last page from her journal. I thought you'd be interested in reading it. She wrote everyday, even when she wasn't feeling up to it."

"Thank you for this," he said, looking again at the envelope in his hands. "But I just can't believe it. I thought the worst in coming here might be to find that she was happily married to James. But gone? She was so young and healthy and beautiful. I would have married her, I would have. But James was here and—" A growing lump in his throat again cut off the words tumbling through his mind. "I'm speechless. I don't know what else to say. I'm just speechless."

"It's all right. I know how you feel. Our family is still having a hard time with it."

"I'll read this later," he said, tucking the envelope inside his coat pocket. "Where *is* the rest of your family?"

"Well, Mom is next door at my aunt's house, Dad's at work, and my sister, Evelyn, is at the soda shop with her boyfriend."

"Oh yes, I remember your sister's name. We shopped for Christmas presents in the Rennselaer book shop for you girls. Listen, don't tell your father I stopped in, okay?"

"I won't." Lena laughed. "Where are my manners? He won't be home for awhile. Can I get you anything else to drink besides water? Coffee or tea? I have a fruitcake in the kitchen."

"No, thank you. I should be going. I have a taxi waiting for me outside, and I have a train to catch. I'm only here on a stopover. May I ask where Elsie's buried? I'd like to visit her, if you don't mind."

"East Akron Cemetery. After you go through the wrought iron gates, walk up the hill to the right, pass two angel statues, and look for a large, brown headstone on flat land. It has our last name, Obee, on it. Elsie's buried there."

There was an awkward beat of silence as Lena stared at him. "I just hate saying those words," she said in explanation.

John stood. "I wouldn't want to say them, either. And I hate hearing them."

Lena nodded and stood to show him out. "Thanks for stopping by. I'm sorry it was under such unfortunate circumstances. Please, take the poinsettias with you, for Elsie."

"I'll put them on her grave," he said, giving her a quick hug. "Bye, now."

"Bye," she said, returning the hug.

He turned and watched as she waved to him from the porch.

Pyle was slumped against the driver's windowpane when John tapped it. "Wake up, Jack. I need a ride."

Pyle looked startled. "Where to?"

"East Akron Cemetery."

"You're going to visit the dame in a cemetery?"

"She's buried there," he said, feeling agreement with Lena's reluctance to say the words.

"Aw, geez. Hey, I'm sorry."

Ten minutes later, Pyle turned sharply through the gate of the cemetery, opposite the Goodyear Tire & Rubber clock tower. John glanced at the sign: *'East Akron Cemetery, Established 1853.'* "Guess, this must be the place," he said solemnly.

Pyle pulled his automobile over to the side of the walking path and stopped. He turned to John. "Sorry again about your loss."

John nodded and handed him a dollar bill. "This should do it, for now. Wait for me here." He stepped out of the Packard with the flower pot.

"Sure. I'll wait right here. Take your time."

John didn't know where he was going, only that the grounds had a quiet peacefulness that seemed to counter his sadness and smother his feelings for the time being. The peaceful dignity of the dead, he thought. A cold breeze fluttered the American flags that the VFW had placed on soldiers' graves to honor them the month before on Veteran's Day.

John looked at the poinsettias and remembered the last time he had given flowers to Elsie. It had been the day she agreed to moved in with him. They had gone out for supper to celebrate, talking for hours on that wonderful evening in September. Later, when they returned home, they'd made passionate love. She seemed to be life itself to him, back then. He wanted so badly just to talk with her once more, to touch her and to say again how he felt, to thank her for teaching him how to love. But that option had been callously taken from him. He still couldn't believe she was dead. Maybe they hadn't spoken for three years, but he always believed he had plenty of time to make up for that absence.

He continued walking, past the pair of angels. He could smell the rubber Elsie always complained about. The air was cold. His breath came out in small, frosty clouds. Patches of snow, six inches deep, lay in small mounds around grave stones and next to burial plots. The rows of solemn headstones were getting longer in the older section of the graveyard, with two or more generations of families lying at rest. They were like cuts in the dirt, marking the passage of time.

He stopped briefly in front of the chapel, thinking vaguely of entering the house of worship; maybe seeing if a prayer might clear up the large and uncomfortable, unfilled space around his heart. He decided that because of his schedule, he had no time for such prayers and salvation on this day, and continued on with an even pace.

He walked past more graves, mentally calculating how old the people were when they had died. Lily Roberts was only three when she passed on. Two cherubs sat atop her tombstone, as if to protect the child from harm. Left of the tombstone was a small Christmas tree covered in tiny, red bulbs, standing on the dead, brown grass.

The emptiness John felt clung to him as he continued to search for Elsie's grave. The oldest grave sites appeared to be randomly placed near trees, and up and down the gentle slopes. A mound of freshly turned, brown earth sharply contrasted the winter-brown grasses. He now noticed that the surroundings matched what Lena had described. He knew he was getting close. Lena told him to look for a big, brown monument with the family name engraved across it. The tombstone would be on flat ground.

He took several more steps, then spotted Elsie's final resting-place. There sat the large headstone that had the name, Obee, on it. A hand-made marker leaned up against a small tree. It read: '*Elsie Obee, daughter, Apr. 23, 1905 – Dec. 6, 1937.*'

I'm a year and a week too late.

Stepping forward, he bent down and placed the Christmas flowers next to the tombstone. He put a hand to his chest. His whole body shook with the cold. He began to weep, almost doubling up, his body racked with sobs.

After a few moments the tears stopped, and he felt a presence. Nerves prickled the skin of his arms. He felt something stir in the cold air around him, but was not sure if Elsie's spirit was there trying to contact him, or he was just struggling to cope. He sensed she knew he was there. He could almost feel her essence and hear her laughter. In a moment he knew would last the rest of his life, he felt a coming together, a spilling of his life into hers. A flowing warmth washed his body, and he felt the weight of his grief lighten. Now, almost instantly, he was at peace.

He removed the blank card that hung from the flowers and began to write.

To my beloved Elsie,

You'll always be in my heart. I came back to see you, my darling. My life has changed for having known you—for loving you. Until we meet again,

Love Always,

J. M.

A custodian sweeping leaves from the graves waved to John. "I'm not rushing you, but we're closing the park in about forty minutes."

John swallowed to relieve the dryness in his throat, and tried to speak casually. "Thanks. I'll be out by then."

It was dark when John arrived back at the Akron train depot. A three-quarter moon on the wane rode high in the chilled, early evening sky. Its bright glow dimmed the sparkle of the blanketing stars. He felt confident that there must have been a reason for Elsie's death, even though he had no idea what it was.

Stomping the snow off his shoes, he went in through the set of double wooden doors and into the warmth of the station. He reminded himself that life was for the living. Even though he felt like a changed person, he nevertheless looked forward to returning home, with Elsie's memory tucked safely in his heart.

Aboard the train and settled in his seat, he pulled out the envelope from his coat pocket and opened it. The contents were as he had guessed. Lena had returned the ruby ring; his promise of love for Elsie, and the Christmas locket he had given to her that fateful afternoon on the train platform. He pushed them around in the palm of his hand, turning them over and remembering all the love and laughter they had shared. Then he pulled from the envelope the small sheet of paper with Elsie's precious words on it.

December 6,

I know my time is near. I can feel the final bits of my life draining from my body, but I'm not afraid. I feel a kind of peace. When the pain of my illness becomes unbearable I take myself back to the time I was with John, and the pain diminishes. When I think of it, I realize my life wasn't perfect, and that I experienced heartache, but I also experienced joy and a deep love. I'm taking that love with me. I have no regrets.

The story behind the story....

Hypnosis Sessions and Research

Mike lies peacefully on the couch. His eyes are closed and he is in a responsive hypnotic state, ready to accept past life suggestions. I am ready to begin facilitating an experience to take him back to another time and place.

"Can you go back to a time when we were together, in another time and another place, where you lived before?"

I am careful not to influence him by asking leading questions or by making specific suggestions about what he might experience.

The first images that appear to him are those of a man and a woman working together to paint a fence.

"Tell me where you are and what is happening."

Mike says he is in the country, in his backyard, having a good time painting, and that he is with a woman he cares about, but he doesn't know if they are married. He can feel the man's emotions of joy and happiness. Based on the strong, happy feelings of this experience, Mike knows that he enjoys being with this woman and loves spending time with her. The man and woman appear to be in their twenties. Mike thinks he is in the United States, and because of the landscape, believes it to be the Midwest.

"Are you a laborer?"

"No."

"Are you poor?"

"No."

Later in the session he says that he has a good job as an apprentice architect. I ask if he knows where he is specifically, and what his name is, her name, and what the year is.

"John David McDonald," he murmurs.

Mike senses the year to be 1934 or 1935.

As a hypnotherapist, I found this astounding. Everyone I had ever known who had experienced regression went much further back in time. But Mike was talking about a mere few decades ago, here in the United States.

He said the girl's name was Erin or Elsie Watkins, and that they were in Indiana.

After about twenty-five minutes of questioning, I counted him up, by counting backward from five to one. The first words out of his mouth were, "This is wild! I can tell you the name of the town I was in … Rensselaer … Rensselaer, Indiana." Neither of us had ever heard the name, Rensselaer.

I searched my road atlas and looked it up, fingering down the index of cities. I found Rensselaer in Indiana. With this discovery, Mike became unnerved and his demeanor changed. He paced my living room, uttering profanities. He hadn't known what to expect from a past life regression session and this was far more than he had bargained for. I tried to reassure him and calm him down. I told him I thought the details of the session were exciting, therapeutic, and asked him to regard the adventure as positive.

"I believe I was this guy … John," Mike blurted out. "I can feel strong emotions. Everything looks clear . . . like in a movie."

He was able to retrieve information and memories that were originally not available to him consciously, but the experience scared him. "I can't do this! It's too freaky," he ranted.

I gently urged Mike to continue working with me to find out if we were soul mates and if we were indeed the two people he had visualized.

Before we met, he hadn't given reincarnation much, if any, thought. But after some intimate conversations and coaxing, he acquiesced and consented to proceed with the hypnosis sessions. As with most anyone, he wanted to please early on in the relationship and this was a perfect way for him to do just that.

In all honesty, I had been a little skeptical about the accuracy of detail he would be able to grasp during this very *first* hypnosis session. I thought maybe he had heard of Rensselaer and had been somehow exposed to the small town. After all, he was born and raised in Ohio, which is adjacent to Indiana. The names John David McDonald and Erin/Elsie Watkins had possibly just popped into his head at random.

At the second session, without informing Mike ahead of time, I decided to quiz him about the layout and streets of Rensselaer. I suggested while he was under hypnosis that he travel downtown and name the streets he observed. He called out Main Street—a thoroughfare running through the town—Elm, Maple, Riverview, and Oak streets. He also recalled three female-named streets: Grace, Sarah, and Susan. He said Susan was split east and west by railroad tracks and ran into Main Street. He also was able to remember the streets Cullen, Varis, Washington, Jefferson, Van Rensselaer, and North Wabash. In addition, he knew his address in Rensselaer— Rural Route 2, Box 69. He said the postman could not deliver mail to the house. Consequently, he had to drive downtown to pick it up at the post office, located across the street from the public square.

As we further discussed what he had experienced during the regression, he told me he had driven his green Ford coupe around the city to find the names of the streets and to get other information. He said the driving experience was clear, comparable to reliving old memories. To further test him, I gave him a multiple-choice quiz. I read off the names of three streets (two I made up, one was an actual street in Rensselaer) and had him pick out the correct one in Rensselaer. His responses proved accurate all four times I tried this.

Next, when he was out of hypnosis, he drew a map of the town, positioning all the downtown stores, a couple roadways, a town square, the railroad, the water tower, and the Iroquois River. With assured confidence he handed the map to me.

It was eerie to scroll through MapQuest and verify the streets he had observed in Rensselaer during the thirties. Out of the fifteen streets he specified under hypnosis we found eleven in Rensselaer and one outside the city limits—North Wabash. Mike insisted that Main Street ran through town, but it didn't appear on MapQuest.

The next day, I called the Jasper County Public Library in Rensselaer and asked the librarian, Emily, if she could please research Main Street. I also mentioned a few other details Mike had drawn on the map, including the water tower, the town square, and a river near the center of town. In addition, I asked if she might be able to research the male and female names in Mike's recollection.

A few days later, Emily confirmed the location of the water tower, the town square, the Iroquois River, and Main Street. She went on to explain that sometime in the forties, Main Street was changed to Route 231, and therefore, did not appear on any current map. She could not, however, find any information on Elsie/Erin Watkins, and nothing on a John McDonald. Admittedly, some of the street names were common, but to distinctly recall Susan Street, which was split east and west, was impressive. Plus, he knew it ran into Main Street.

In the third session, Mike clarified some personal details that led to more significant information, verifiable through research. We found that John and Erin/Elsie had lived together for approximately three months in 1934. He first met her at his friend Robert's house, whom he believed to be Erin/Elsie's cousin. Robert lived on Riverview Street in Rensselaer. We learned that John worked in town as an apprentice architect for Herb Willis, and that he occasionally enjoyed meeting the local mortician, Will Baucher, for lunch. In addition, Mike thought that later in life, John served in the military as an Army sergeant.

Regressing back even farther, Mike recalled that John spent his early childhood in Massachusetts. His family lived in a small house or apartment in the poor section of town near Boston Harbor. He recalled he had one younger brother, Arthur. Mike thought John McDonald was intelligent, good in math, and that he had an easy and cheerful personality.

Poring over my notes, I felt the first three hypnosis sessions had been exciting and productive, including the find of two semi-solid names—John David McDonald and Erin/Elsie Watkins. Under hypnosis, Mike mentioned that John's surname was frequently spelled both ways. McDonald and MacDonald. Next, I needed specific dates in order to begin a serious search.

The following session uncovered grim details. Mike felt strongly that Erin/Elsie died very young, perhaps in her early thirties. He said that her death was from what he believed to be cancer around or before 1942. He thought she was buried in St. John's Cemetery, adjacent to an airport. Orchard Place popped into his recollection.

I researched cemeteries and narrowed down the search. I came up with St. John's & Rest Haven next to O'Hare Airport in Chicago, since O'Hare was formerly known as Orchard Park Airport. This was important information that I would investigate at a later date.

Mike said in another session that he visualized John standing in a snow-laden cemetery next to her grave. He could see Christmas decorations around the burial grounds and the surrounding streets. During this session, he was emotionally distressed when reliving her death and visiting the cemetery. Also, he shivered while he was "under" and complained bitterly of the cold. After waking, he drew a picture of the tombstone with two flowers carved on opposite ends of the stone and a ribbon hanging from each.

It saddened Mike to experience these cemetery sessions, and he felt depressed when he woke up. I actually needed to hypnotize him to snap him out of the depression after one of the sessions.

When I asked about John's and Erin/Elsie's birthdays, he gave the years 1910 and 1905. He thought John was born in June. But he was unsure which birth year belonged to whom.

At this point, I was having misgivings that these two people had actually existed. I referred to the online Social Security death index for John McDonald and more than 800 matches popped up. I then narrowed the search for Indiana only, which reduced the number to eight prospects, but not one matched our John McDonald. Also, nothing on Erin/Elsie Watkins came up on any of the name research sites I explored. Of course, in those days record keeping was nowhere as accurate as today. I was in a quandary as to how to go about proving or disproving conclusively the existence of John McDonald and Erin/Elsie Watkins. Frustration was beginning to take its toll.

I called the Jasper County Library in Rensselaer a third time. Emily verified that West Susan Street had an elementary school on it where Elsie taught school for a brief time and was split exactly the way Mike sketched it. But she couldn't find any data on Herb Willis, the architect, or Will Baucher, the mortician.

I was desperate for additional help. Mike and I discussed it and we agreed that we had to go back to hypnosis to find the answers.

Hypnotherapy studies confirm that the subconscious is a problem solver and is a servomechanism which can steer its way to a goal. We certainly had a goal: to find written documentation on John McDonald and Erin/Elsie Watkins.

Remembering a technique that might prove helpful in our search, I became once again optimistic. The technique involved utilizing an "inner guide" to uncover information. Working with inner guides is a method that gives form and voice to the unconscious mind or inner wisdom of the subject. This method helps the subject retrieve information that is already recorded in the subconscious, and in turn, give voice to the information.

Under hypnosis Mike became deeply relaxed while walking down the beach. (In hypnosis, a hypothetical, visual beach is suggested by the facilitator and used as a peaceful place wherein the subject becomes open to subconscious input.) I asked him to slowly look around ... someone may be nearby and waiting for him. He said a shadowy figure that appeared to be female was standing at the end of the beach path. I asked him to telepathically ask if she was his inner guide, and if so, find out her name and tell her he had the friendliest of intentions. The guide was delighted to make this kind of contact and said telepathically that she would help. She did not give a name. At this time I did not press Mike to have her answer simple yet important questions, but instead to just concentrate on trying to establish a continuing dialogue.

I directed Mike to set up a time to meet again, and to ask her where he could find documentation on John David McDonald. Although this session proved to be exhilarating, Mike was extremely anxious about making the second contact with his inner guide.

At the appointed time, however, contact was made and the results obtained this time, using the inner guide technique, were simply amazing!

While under hypnosis, Mike recited a set of numbers that he telepathically acquired from his guide. I wrote them down as he spoke, thinking they were probably John's death record number. But when Mike awoke he told me the numbers were John McDonald's Social Security number. It was truly astonishing, yet admittedly I was instantly skeptical. How could he do that? I couldn't believe it! His inner wisdom was able to accurately retrieve his Social Security number from another life. Some people haven't even memorized their own Social Security number in this lifetime. I needed to see if there was any shred of truth in this new information.

Immediately, I rushed to my computer to check the nine numbers. To my amazement, a *John McDonald,* DOA in 1946 in New York City, appeared on the screen. There it was in black and white; proof that John McDonald had lived and died. The information we needed had been stored in the recesses of Mike's subconscious all along. Facts that were disclosed in this death index supported what he had said earlier: that John McDonald died in November of 1946. Although he wasn't accurate about John's birthday date in June, (John's birthday: January 9, 1910) Mike *did* mention 1910 as one of the birth years and both months in question do begin with 'J.'

I was now ready to send away for the original Social Security application, which would hopefully provide more details on John McDonald's life.

Next, I turned my attention to Erin/Elsie to find confirmation of her existence in the haystacks of city, state, and federal data.

Our next revelation came in the following session. The inner guide informed Mike where to look for Erin/Elsie. He was directed to search in the Ellis Island "big book," as the guide called it, for Elsie and Phoebe Wilkins in 1911, clarifying the woman's name— Elsie *Wilkins* not Erin or Elsie Watkins. We found Elsie and her mother, Phoebe, on the Ellis Island Web site. The manifest for the ship *Campania* listed them as second-class passengers, sailing from Liverpool, England, to the port of New York in 1911. The discovery of these details was extremely exciting for us, as it further corroborated the accuracy of our sessions and the concept of reincarnation. This was one well-informed guide!

In the months that followed, I frequented several local libraries, visited the Latter Day Saints Genealogy Room, and spent many hours surfing every genealogy site on the Web. I even contacted a private detective I knew and asked her to try to find facts concerning John and Elsie. The only information the detective came up with was information I had previously discovered myself.

Next, I researched the Jasper County Records Office for a marriage license for John and Elsie, but came up with nothing. After a year of tiring investigation, I found out through the Social Security Administration that John McDonald was married at the time of his death. Due to the Privacy Act, the clerk at the Social Security office would not divulge the spouse's name. Mike said not to worry; John's wife at the time of his death was definitely not Elsie.

Mike was fairly certain that Elsie died in Chicago and was convinced that she had died young. Trusting him, I called the cemetery office and hunted down the names of the people buried in St. John's Cemetery in Cook County, Illinois, where he believed she was buried. Elsie's remains were not there. By checking online I found out that the St. John's cemetery grounds were in disarray and surrounded by controversy. And, it was primarily a German cemetery. It brought into question as to why a woman of English birth would be buried there.

I now had proof that these people existed, but finding anything further became an exhausting task. I thought I had depleted all means of finding additional information on my own. I desperately needed assistance and Mike suggested that he hire a student at Purdue University in Indiana to do research for us. It ended up that the student did not come up with any useful information.

Next, I sent for death records from Cook County and the results also came up empty—there were no reports on Elsie Wilkins. I then checked the Chicago death index from 1918-1949 and there wasn't any Elsie McDonald listed. It occurred to me that maybe they never married, so I tried her maiden name, Wilkins. She was, after all, liberated for her time and might have kept her own name. But again, nothing.

Mike was somewhat convinced that Elsie did not have a Social Security number during her lifetime. To double check, I reviewed all the Social Security name possibilities in the event that he was mistaken. There were no matches for an Elsie Wilkins born in 1905 in any of the Social Security indices. So I decided to go in person to my local Federal Building to check.

After a long wait, my name was called and I nervously approached the clerk. Despite the strict privacy laws, the employee reluctantly told me that there had been a number issued to an Elsie Wilkins, but the status was reported as inactive. There hadn't been any activity on the account. She never collected any Social Security benefits. Could that be because she never lived to be old enough to collect? The clerk would not divulge any further information such as the actual social security number for Elsie, or even disclose if she was deceased.

How could I find a woman's legacy, who, according to our research, did not bear any children nor had any descendants who might have done genealogy work on her? She had allegedly been dead for seventy years and in our opinion, lived in another lifetime. Without a Social Security number I had no way of tracking her down, no way of shedding light on her life and death—if she was indeed dead.

Once I had received John's Social Security information, I was then able to send for his birth certificate. Upon its arrival, I learned the names of his parents—Blanche Kendall and John A. McDonald. I also discovered his middle name was Arthur, not David. During hypnosis, Mike came up with the name, Arthur, as John's brother's name. Regardless, I was still amazed that Mike knew that the name Arthur was significant to John McDonald's life.

Now that I had uncovered information from John's birth records, I became curious about how he died. Mike and I discussed the possibility of him re-experiencing John's death. Experiencing anyone's own death under hypnosis can be an enormous undertaking, and emotionally disturbing. Because of this, I decided I would use a more detached hypnosis technique, a white light method, wherein Mike would be removed emotionally, as if seeing a stranger's death.

Witnessing his death as John McDonald, Mike felt would have been too traumatic. He had already felt strong negative and sad emotions regarding Elsie's short life, and didn't want any other disturbing emotions to deal with. Mike was emphatic about not bringing any more negative energy into the present. In Mike's view, death was negative.

Knowing the details of John McDonald's death would have to wait.

At our next official session, I had Mike perform the eye test, which consists of looking into someone's eyes while under hypnosis to see if you recognize that person. Mike gazed into Elsie's eyes and said my eyes and her eyes were the same. In addition, he mentioned that our speech patterns were identical and our temperaments similar.

By this time, I was consumed with curiosity and wondered if I was Elsie in this other life. I knew an experienced hypnotist, and called to make an appointment for a regression session for myself. From past experience, I knew I was not visual under hypnosis and could not respond to imagery suggestions. Most of the time, the subconscious mind works from imagery, but my subconscious can't see such things as the lush green countryside, for instance, or other visual details. My way of processing information is by auditory means. My personal backup system is kinesthetic, which refers to the sense of emotional and tactile senses.

Before we began, I explained my learning process, and strengths and weaknesses to the hypnotist. I told her the reasons I was interested in a past life regression induction, and emphasized how important it was to me to have a productive session. Accordingly, she said she would attempt to facilitate my visual sense. If I could see only blackness, she would utilize other senses to go back in time.

After giving it her best shot, the regression unfortunately ended unproductively. I did not see anything but streams of yellow and purple. I *did* sense I was Elsie, but her existence was so embedded in my subconscious by then, I doubted myself. I already knew too much about her, so I felt I could not be objective in any possible observations. I feared I would make things up and report them as truth. But I wasn't going to give up after only one attempt. I made an appointment with another hypnotist about a month later, but at that session there were still no visual images or progress. A third hypnotist didn't prove to be the charm, either. She could not even hypnotize me.

Again I returned to the Federal Building, this time to check the census records for the Obee family. I knew the name Obee from the *Campania's* manifest, as Mr. Obee had paid for Phoebe's and Elsie's tickets. I found in 1929, Elsie was married to a James Hunter. Oh, no! *She was married but not to John McDonald.* That didn't sound good. Both John and Elsie were married, but to other people.

In the 1930 census, James Hunter, age thirty, is listed as living at 489 Champlain Street with Elsie and her parents. But in the city directory for 1931, Mrs. Elsie Hunter is living at 489 Champlain Street with her parents; there is no mention of James. To my amazement, I found out from a volunteer of RAOGK (Random Acts of Genealogical Kindness) that by 1937, she was using the name Elsie Wilkins again, and still living with the Obees. She does not appear after 1937.

It was at this stage of our adventure that Mike began complaining about the sessions. He was no longer able to contact his inner guide. He said the visuals were becoming blurry and he thought it seemed as though he was scrambling the facts, resulting in inaccurate data. He began losing his patience as well as his confidence, and was protesting the hypnosis sessions. Finally, he admitted that he no longer wanted to continue. Hypnosis is useless with a reluctant subject.

All in all, we had about eight useful sessions. We agreed to stop hypnosis, and I put my energy back into research.

It took more than two years to uncover the documentation at the end of this book. There was one point in our quest where again it looked as though we did not have a story. It was the day I received a letter from Social Security, stating they did not have any record of Elsie Wilkins's death. *Oh, no. Could this woman still be alive? Ninety-seven, but living!*

If Social Security didn't know whether she was dead or not, who did?

Several months later, I used the same volunteer genealogist in Akron to help further research Elsie. She had already found Phoebe Obee's obituary in the January 1960 *Akron Beacon Journal.* The obituary stated that Phoebe left behind two daughters: Mrs. Lena Mangus and Mrs. Evelyn Grant. There was no mention of a daughter named Elsie. It was further proof to me that Elsie Wilkins was deceased. If she had been living wouldn't she be mentioned in her mother's obituary? There would be something like *preceded in death by her daughter, Elsie.* But that information was not in Phoebe's obituary. And Frederick Obee's obituary, found in a 1950 issue of the *Akron Beacon Journal*, also listed only two surviving daughters: more proof Elsie was deceased. However, a genealogy clerk told me that she had heard of children being omitted from parental obits for various reasons, such as estrangement. So it was possible she was still alive at the time of her parents' deaths.

My fears were put to rest a few weeks later when I at last found Elsie Wilkins Obee listed in the Ohio Death Certificate Index. Mike was right. She died young, at age thirty-two. I was surprised to find she was listed as Elsie Wilkins Obee in the death records with no mention at all of her husband, James Hunter. On the death certificate under Personal and Statistical Particulars was handwritten the word *single.* Not widowed or divorced: further indication that her marriage to James was brief, dissolved or possibly annulled at some point.

About Elsie's family tragedies: When Mike woke from one of the sessions he said that Elsie had a brother who died very young. He was sure the boy passed away before he could walk or talk, estimating that he lived less than a year. Mike was positive that if we found Elsie's grave, her baby brother's name would be inscribed on the tombstone. Mike thought the infant died from influenza. He wasn't sure of the baby's name, but said it was a common first name. Verification of Elsie's baby brother proved difficult, and it took months to finally get the information we needed. The same genealogist from Ohio helped us document baby George's birth and death.

Our research also found that Elsie had a sister, Ruth Helen, who died in 1926. She was only three and a half years old.

I found from death records that John McDonald had died from carbon monoxide poisoning on November 1, 1946—nine years after Elsie Wilkins's death. It was not determined if the death was an accident or a suicide. John's body was shipped from Northern California back to Buffalo, New York, for burial at Forest Lawn Mortuary. He was thirty-six years old.

I asked Mike what was the happiest day of John McDonald's life. He said it was when he took Elsie to the Chicago World's Fair. He remembered that they strolled along the promenade and were awestruck by the wonderful sights. He said John and Elsie had a wonderful time, and John thought the fairgrounds were magnificent.

Most of my research confirmed Mike's visions of John McDonald and Elsie Wilkins. The timeline and statistical facts fit and we were both born after the two of them had died. What was most interesting to me was the fact that Elsie lived as a married woman for less than two years, and chose to live the balance of her life as a single woman. In the 1930s it was highly unusual for a woman to have such a brief marriage.

Hypnosis is not an exact science and the lives in question were not observed as though watching a motion picture. Despite the successful regression sessions and my comprehensive investigative efforts, gaps remain. I've tried to fill in the blanks of the story by adding a bit of my own imagination, and I've retained the factual portions as documentation.

Afterword

As a final review of facts before submitting this book for print, I reexamined my notes for any information that may have been overlooked in my quest to uncover and verify details in the lives of John McDonald and Elsie Wilkins.

For example, one particular road that Mike mentioned during a hypnosis session was Susan Street, which I investigated further. I called the Jasper County Public Library in Rensselaer and spoke with Emily, who remembered me and my story from 2001, when I had called and asked her other research questions. During the conversation, she offered to send me an old map of the city of Rensselaer.

When the map arrived, I verified Mike's in-session pronouncement that several schools were located on Susan Street. In addition, I confirmed that the post office was across the street from the public square.

Another interesting piece of information that the story did not pick up, but which Mike revealed in one of our sessions, pertained to Bethlehem Steel. Its corporate offices were located in Bethlehem, Pennsylvania, and in the 1930s, Bethlehem Steel had grown into the second largest steel producing company in the United States. Per Mike's account, John McDonald owned shares of stock in Bethlehem Steel. Coincidentally, Pennsylvania is the state in which John had applied for an additional Social Security card, which seemed to corroborate Mike's detail about John's activity in Pennsylvania.

When asked about his youth, again under hypnosis, Mike recalled living in a somewhat dreary city near the harbor in a small house or apartment. He could not recall the name of the town in which he lived; only that it snowed, and there were several tenement buildings in the neighborhood. One vivid childhood memory for Mike was when John was about seven or eight years old. It was his duty to keep the furnace burning in the middle of the night, taking turns with his brother, fetching coal and firewood to heat the house in the dead of winter. He also recalled seeing his mother constantly cooking in the kitchen, boiling water on the stove. It was later revealed that John McDonald lived in Somerville, Massachusetts near Boston Harbor.

In one hypnosis session, Mike saw himself at about ten years old, selling newspapers. If he didn't sell all the papers in a given day, he would go through the tenement building, knocking on all the apartment doors to sell the rest of them. Mike remembered a very nice older woman who gave him a cookie rather than a penny for a newspaper, and later, the exact candies he would buy with the pennies the other customers had given him.

Another childhood incident was revealed during hypnosis that I only touched upon briefly in the story: Mike saw himself sitting on a hill with the neighborhood boys, watching construction workers, then later that day swimming with his friends in the river. Apparently, as Mike recalled, John almost drowned. Trauma from this incident would often disrupt John's sleep as a child, and he would wake up screaming that he couldn't breathe. His mother would go into his room and comfort him. During the session, Mike had difficulty breathing and I began to see some similarity, perhaps even a respiratory pattern between John's near drowning, his ultimate death by carbon monoxide poisoning, and Mike's inability to swim or to take an interest in lake, pool, or ocean swimming.

Elsie died in Ohio, and Mike was born in Ohio. Mike is left-handed and Elsie was left-handed. These four details, given in relation to each other, I also found fascinating and perhaps relevant to both the stories of John and Elsie, and of Mike and I. John McDonald had spent the end of his life in California and died there, where Mike and I both now reside. I was also able to confirm from the death certificate, that John was in the Army at the time of his death, a veteran of World War II, just as Mike had mentioned under hypnosis.

The volunteer genealogist from RAOGK sent me a photograph of Elsie's tombstone and there are two flowers on the grave marker with ribbons hanging down from each, just like Mike had said.

This book was not written as an attempt to prove the similarities between John and Mike or even the similarities between the two couples involved, but only that Mike's past life was real and should be shared.

Overall, this experience has been a richly rewarding adventure. I found it fascinating that when I assessed data given by Mike during the past life regressions, I was able to substantiate the information against known facts. Undoubtedly, Mike recalled detailed information about which he could not have conceivably known from his own life experiences. When he was immersed in the town of Rensselaer, Indiana, under hypnosis, he displayed emotions as if the events were happening to him in the present. The pull was strong and familiar. He had a feeling of attraction, a tugging of the heartstrings—one that he could not explain. It defied simple logic. He reawakened inner resources, opening up and expanding his awareness. He experienced only fragments of John McDonald's life, but what he did see was clear, and the memories strong with emotions.

Mike's memories of John McDonald were just as emotion-filled in the present as if he were living in the past. For him, the past and the present were interwoven, blending the energies of both eras. Mike told me several times that he felt he truly *was* John McDonald.

For me, the process of finding and retrieving information from Mike's inner guide was the single most incredible part of his entire past life regression experience. Without the guide I could not have moved forward to prove the existence of either John or Elsie, who would have otherwise become undocumented "guesses" on Mike's part. If that had happened we would not have had a story at all. Of course I had heard of the inner guide technique, but to have it provide valuable, specific information so quickly and to such a degree of accuracy was simply astounding.

As I wrote the story of Elsie Wilkins and John McDonald, I reflected on how Mike's past life experience has affected our personal relationship. We both feel we are closer because of this previous connection, and that there is a deeper purpose to our relationship.

Unlike many people who undertake past life regressions in order to eliminate phobias or unexplained fears, Mike did not share this purpose. He had no psychological traumas that could be eliminated permanently by the remembrance of an event from the past. His purpose in this exercise was to remember enough details to answer whether or not we had known each other before this life. His own subconscious was the best barometer for finding what was pertinent to this question. More often than not, whenever I hypnotized Mike, he went back to his life as John McDonald, where he lived a pleasant life with Elsie Wilkins in Rensselaer, Indiana.

Was it possible that Mike and I shared time in a previous life? After long and methodical discussions, coupled with amazing concrete and verifiable facts, we finally came to accept and believe that our paths *did* cross in a previous life journey.

I found through research that present emotions or experiences will bring forth past life memories in which the same emotions or events were experienced. Mike's recall as John McDonald occurred when his present relationship reawakened a similar past-life experience. When Mike met me in this life, on a spiritual level his soul remembered me and the events he'd experienced during our time together in the 1930s. Because the past relationship was short-lived in 1934, I believe we have been given the chance in the present to enhance the karma by balancing it and continuing the journey. Our emotional bond continues and is enhanced in the present. I feel closeness with Mike, and it feels like we've picked up the relationship where we left off in a previous life, almost as though no time has been lost between us. As in life and as in relationships, we have our differences but in the end we try and work things out.

During our research, we found that Mike had made a few mistakes when retrieving some bits of his past life data, but this is not a process from which an airtight case for reincarnation can be extracted. Regression doesn't work that way. In fact, if forced to provide only factual details, the whole process would likely be compromised. The stream of subconscious discovery must be left free to explore. It can be rationalized that anyone's memory can dim when trying to recall past events, especially those from a past life. In any case, most of the data that Mike retrieved proved factual.

Now, years after the regression sessions, Mike's memories of John McDonald have faded from his consciousness considerably. In fact, he remembers very little. Perhaps it is better this way. Dwelling on the past could complicate his present life. The spiral of life is upward and reincarnation carries us forward, not backward. Mike learned about the past, but does not live in it.

At the beginning of our sessions, looking at Mike, I saw someone from another era looking back. Now that phenomenon has also faded.

My purpose in writing this book was not to convince the reader of reincarnation, but to simply share my story. In the end, I've come to the realization that death is merely nature's way of recreating the same life anew, with similar props and life patterns on a new stage.

I believe there is no such thing as death, only a transition to another place and time, and I firmly believe we will return to Earth numerous times.

Lifetimes Ago was especially written for all who believe that we are spiritual beings engaged in earthly, physical experiences; that we're on the road to manifesting our individual destinies; that we have lived before, and that these memories lie deep within our subconscious.

Documents

REGISTRATION DISTRICT Maidstone

1905 BIRTH in the Sub-district of Maidstone in the County of Kent.

No.	When and where born	Name, if any	Sex	Name and surname of father	Name, surname and maiden surname of mother	Occupation of father	Signature, description and residence of informant	When registered	Signature of registrar	Name entered after registration
208	Twenty third April 1905 116 Wheeler Street	Elsie	girl	Thomas Edward Wilkins	Phœbe Wilkins formerly Garrison	Carman Journeyman	P Wilkins Mother 116 Wheeler Street Maidstone	Twenty fourth May 1905	J Anscombe Registrar	

CERTIFIED to be a true copy of an entry in the certified copy of a Register of Births in the District above mentioned.

Given at the GENERAL REGISTER OFFICE, under the Seal of the said Office, the ....15th........ day of ....April.... 2002

BXBZ 493922

Elsie Wilkins's birth certificate

▶ **Passenger**   ▶ Original Ship   ▶ Ship   ▶ View   ▶ Create an   ▶ Back to
    Record   Manifest   Annotations   Annotation   Search
                                                                    Results

PASSENGER RECORD   RECENTLY UPDATED FEATURE!

Here is the record for the passenger. Click the links above to see more information about this pa

First Name:	*Elsie*
Last Name:	*Wilkins*
Ethnicity:	*English*
Last Place of Residence:	*Maidstone, Kent, England*
Date of Arrival:	*Apr 22, 1911*
Age at Arrival: *6y* Gender: *F* Marital Status: *S*	
Ship of Travel:	*Campania*
Port of Departure:	*Liverpool*
Manifest Line Number:	*0025*

Elsie's passenger record *The Campania*

Marriage certificate of Elsie Wilkins and James Hunter

Elsie Wilkins Obee's death certificate

Photograph courtesy of Judy Anne Davis

CITY OF SOMERVILLE
MASSACHUSETTS
OFFICE OF CITY CLERK

Copy of the record of the City of Somerville, in the County of Middlesex and Commonwealth of Massachusetts, relating to Births.

Number 24   Date of Birth   January 9, 1910

Name   John Arthur McDonald, Jr.

Sex Male   Place of Birth   Somerville, MA

Father   John A. McDonald

Mother (Maiden Name)   Blanche G. Kendall

Residence of Parents   32 Derby Street, Somerville, MA

Occupation of Father   Teamster

Occupation of Mother   ===========

Birthplace of Father   Boston, MA

Birthplace of Mother   Hindsdale, NY

Informant   Mother

Date of Record   March 10, 1910

I, JOHN J. LONG CITY CLERK OF THE SAID CITY OF SOMERVILLE, DO HEREBY CERTIFY THAT THE ABOVE IS A TRUE EXTRACT FROM THE RECORDS OF BIRTH, OF SAID CITY, WHICH RECORDS ARE IN THE CUSTODY OF THE CITY CLERK.

John J Long

CITY CLERK

COMMONWEALTH OF MASSACHUSETTS

Somerville   April 17, 2002
MIDDLESEX

John McDonald's birth certificate

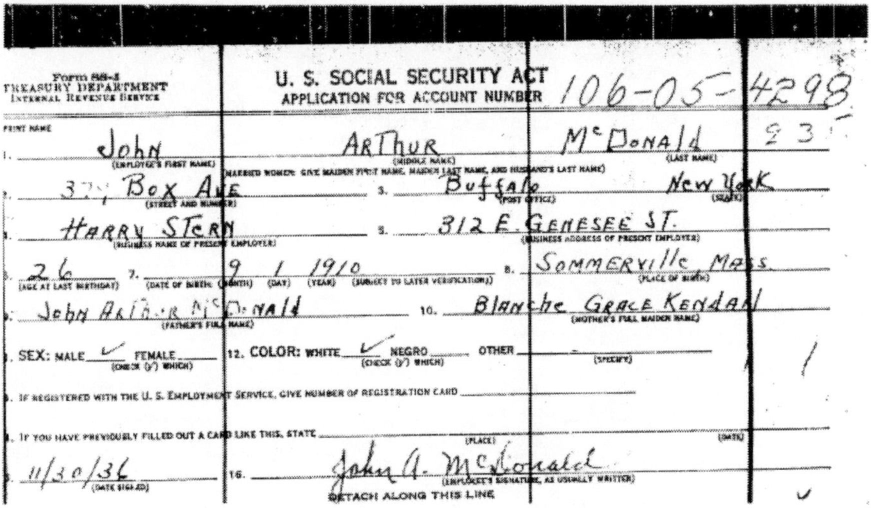
Form SS-5
TREASURY DEPARTMENT
INTERNAL REVENUE SERVICE

U. S. SOCIAL SECURITY ACT
APPLICATION FOR ACCOUNT NUMBER 106-05-4298

PRINT NAME
1. John (EMPLOYEE'S FIRST NAME) Arthur (MIDDLE NAME) McDonald (LAST NAME) 23
(MARRIED WOMEN: GIVE MAIDEN FIRST NAME, MAIDEN LAST NAME, AND HUSBAND'S LAST NAME)
2. 3?? Box Ave (STREET AND NUMBER) 3. Buffalo (POST OFFICE) New York (STATE)
4. Harry Stern (BUSINESS NAME OF PRESENT EMPLOYER) 5. 312 E. Genesee St. (BUSINESS ADDRESS OF PRESENT EMPLOYER)
6. 26 (AGE AT LAST BIRTHDAY) 7. 9 1 1910 (DATE OF BIRTH: (MONTH) (DAY) (YEAR) (SUBJECT TO LATER VERIFICATION)) 8. Sommerville, Mass. (PLACE OF BIRTH)
9. John Arthur McDonald (FATHER'S FULL NAME) 10. Blanche Grace Kendall (MOTHER'S FULL MAIDEN NAME)
11. SEX: MALE ✓ FEMALE (CHECK (✓) WHICH) 12. COLOR: WHITE ✓ NEGRO OTHER (CHECK (✓) WHICH) (SPECIFY)
13. IF REGISTERED WITH THE U. S. EMPLOYMENT SERVICE, GIVE NUMBER OF REGISTRATION CARD
14. IF YOU HAVE PREVIOUSLY FILLED OUT A CARD LIKE THIS, STATE (PLACE) (DATE)
15. 11/30/36 (DATE SIGNED) 16. John A. McDonald (EMPLOYEE'S SIGNATURE, AS USUALLY WRITTEN)
DETACH ALONG THIS LINE

John McDonald's Social Security application

John McDonald's death certificate

Baby George Obee's death certificate

STATE OF OHIO
DEPARTMENT OF HEALTH
DIVISION OF VITAL STATISTICS
CERTIFICATE OF DEATH

1 PLACE OF DEATH
County Summit
Registration District No. 1224
File No. 64418
Township
or Village
Primary Registration District No. 8493 Registered No. 2039
or City of Akron, O. No. _____ St., _____ Ward
(If death occured in a hospital or institution, give its NAME instead of street and number)

2 FULL NAME Ruth Helen Obee
Did Deceased Serve in U. S. Navy or Army _____
(a) Residence. No. 1177 Brown St., _____ Ward.
(Usual place of abode)
Length of residence in city or town where death occurred ____ yrs. ____ mos. ____ ds. How long in U. S. if of foreign birth ____ yrs. ____ mos. ____ ds.
(If nonresident give city or town and State)

PERSONAL AND STATISTICAL PARTICULARS

3 SEX F 4 COLOR OR RACE wh 5 Single, Married, Widowed or Divorced (write the word) Single

5a If married, widowed or divorced HUSBAND of (or) WIFE of _____

6 DATE OF BIRTH (month, day, year) Mar. 25, 1923

7 AGE Years 3 Months 6 Days 22 If LESS than 1 day ____ hrs. or ____ min.

8 OCCUPATION OF DECEASED
(a) Trade, profession, or particular kind of work Infant
(b) General nature of industry, business, or establishment in which employed (or employer)
(c) Name of employer

9 BIRTHPLACE (city or town) Ohio
(State or country)

PARENTS
10 NAME OF FATHER Frederick Obee
11 BIRTHPLACE OF FATHER (city or town) England
(State or country)
12 MAIDEN NAME OF MOTHER Phoebe Harrison
13 BIRTHPLACE OF MOTHER (city or town) England
(State or country)

14 Informant Fredrick S. Obee
(Address) 1177 Brown St.

15 Filed 10-19-1926 Registrar

MEDICAL CERTIFICATE OF DEATH

16 DATE OF DEATH (month, day and year) Oct-17 1926

17 I HEREBY CERTIFY, That I attended deceased from Oct 11 1926 to Oct 17 1926
that I last saw h ed alive on Oct 17 1926
and that death occurred, on the date stated above, at 5 P. m.
The CAUSE OF DEATH* was as follows:
Broncho pneumonia
Primary cause
(duration) ____ yrs. ____ mos. 6 ds.
CONTRIBUTORY
(SECONDARY)
(duration) ____ yrs. ____ mos. ____ ds.

18 Where was disease contracted if not at place of death?
Did an operation precede death? No Date of _____
Was there an autopsy? No
What test confirmed diagnosis? Clinical
(Signed) L. A. Freeman M. D.
Oct 19, 1926 (Address) 500 Second Nat'l Bldg.
*State the Disease Causing Death, or in deaths from violent Causes, state (1) Means and Nature of Injury, and (2) whether Accidental, Suicidal, or Homicidal. (See reverse side for additional space.)

19 PLACE OF BURIAL, CREMATION, OR REMOVAL
E Akron DATE OF BURIAL 10/20 1926

20 UNDERTAKER. License No. 805-A ADDRESS
Sweeney Bros Akron, O

Ruth Helen Obee's death certificate

- 308 -

SOCIAL SECURITY

Refer to:
S9H: OW7765

September 24, 2003

██████████

Ladera Ranch, CA 92694

Dear Susan Schecter:

You requested information about the death of Elsie Wilkins. There is no information available to us that indicate that Elsie Wilkins is deceased.

Thank you for your payment to cover the cost of searching our records.

Sincerely,

Willie J. Polk

Willie J. Polk
Freedom of Information Officer